An infectiously candid and thoroughly absorbing journey of self-discovery laced with wit and warmth from the incurable humanist and extraordinary observer of life's splendid uncertainties.

Swapan Mullick
Writer, critic and former Director, Satyajit Ray Film & Television Institute, Kolkata

On the Seashore

SAIBAL GUPTA

PARTRIDGE
A Penguin Random House Company

To order additional copies of this book, contact
Partridge India
000 800 10062 62
www.partridgepublishing.com/india
orders.india@partridgepublishing.com

On the Seashore

Part 1

. . . what impressed death was that she seemed to hear in those fifty-eight seconds of music a rhythmical and melodic transposition of every and any human life, be it run-of-the-mill or extraordinary, because of its tragic brevity, its desperate intensity, and also because of that final chord, like an ellipsis left hanging in the air, something yet to be said.

—José Saramago, *Death at Intervals*

CONTENTS

Death

I died last night. To be precise in the twilight of dawn, when time stops, when the earth seems to slow down, the best time to get off. I was told that this was also the time I got in, the best time to get in. People say it is the time of the Brahman, the Lord of the universe, the primal cause—causation—manifestation. I remember these things but even now do not know what they mean. I can see that death does not increase wisdom. I am not even sure that I am out of the body or having an out of the body experience. Everything is a blur, in shades; colours not yet come for the sun is not up. The seven colours of the sunray by permutation and combination form the colours of our emotion. I have no emotions now, so probably no colour. I was told that I shall go out like the tiny white core of the *munja* grass and the weed would die. Having no body I have no idea whether I am tiny or big. In fact even the question is irrelevant. The weed, my body, is lying as it always lay or I assumed it would lie, living or dead I cannot say. I thought of reentering just for fun and see what happens—entering and leaving, entering and leaving. But I did not want, not interested any more. I keep on saying 'I' but cannot even see myself. I heard a bird sing and looked out to see the little bird that flew in every dawn to the tree beside my window and sang and it was there like a blur on the dry twig of high summer, flapping its wings. Strange that I cannot see myself, see no colors but I see and hear the bird, at least I think I do. Perplexed I decide that what I call the 'I' has a mind. I heard so much about soul, about *atman* and all that and find none of that. But the 'I' definitely has a mind that can remember that my name was Ranajit and that mind has the shapeless colourless emotionless impressions of the life it has just left. Will that last? I do not know but with that thought

3

the mind automatically started to explore what was left behind, like the rewind and replay of a video without sequence, as it has lost the perception of earthly time.

People say that a drowning man can see his whole life in the few moments of death. As I remembered this oft repeated statement I smiled. I realize that this is the experience of death in any way you die given the time and the sensitivity. One's entire life is but a few moments when transferred to a different time scale, just a few moments in an eternity, not the entire eternity but a limited eternity that an earthling can grasp, or else the whole thing will have no meaning for him. Seema once made me read the conversation between Einstein and Rabindranath Thakur, our poet laureate. Einstein at that time was quite disturbed over the apparent anarchy in the Quantum world and the question whether there is a 'Reality' independent of human senses. Rabindranath's reply is immortal, 'There is the reality of paper, infinitely different from the reality of literature. For the kind of mind possessed by the moth which eats that paper, literature is absolutely non-existent, yet for Man's mind literature has a greater value of truth than the paper itself'. So it is natural that I shall not see the entire Eternity but only the part I can sense. Transferred even to this scale, my life experiences become a folded pamphlet that you can open and glance through in a few moments. The long earthly life has but a few notable things, the rest just mundane repetitions that is not even recorded. We are in love with this life and make it big with expectations. Take that last thing out and it collapses like wet paper to a few columns in a pamphlet. And I can tell you that the loss of expectations is such a relief! There lies peace. So, more in curiosity than out of desire, I look through my pamphlet that really looked ludicrous.

I was born in an educated middle class family in Bengal, a province of India. Why was I born there out of innumerable places on our earth? The question itself is absurd because if I am asked right now whether and where and when I want to be born again I shall not be able to answer. There is no expectation, only a great void. Are there other earths I can choose from? There is no answer. Just because I have come out of the human body does not make me any wiser. The only wisdom I get is by looking into my pamphlet and realizing how ridiculously small and irrelevant were my dreams, my concerns, the things I fretted about, hated or liked. That is the sum total of knowledge I have acquired by living as a human being for three score years.

My father had a comfortable middle class income though holding a high job because of his intense honesty and supporting poor relatives, a house and a family of three, since I had no siblings. Children having no sibling often become introvert and think a lot more than they express. It was so in my case too. I am rather amused to find that some of the questions I am asking now had occurred to me even then, although with much less clarity. As a child I was middling, not brilliant, not stupid, not telling truth all the time, not lying all the time unless absolutely necessary. I passed through school getting comfortable marks, comfortable enough to get into college.

Then three unexpected things happened in my life in succession as I was graduating after four years—the first line in my pamphlet. First came my graduation with first class honours in economics, then my father died of a sudden heart attack and lastly I became aware of Seema—all equally unexpected. I was good in my studies but never expected to get first class and not just first class, I was the first! My father was a quiet man not given to excitements and in sound health. He was feeling a little out of sorts for a few days, with indigestion, tired and slightly out of breath until he collapsed one day sitting at home after dinner. In those days we did not know that this was how a heart attack could strike. And lastly there was Seema. We did not meet in the modern sense of the term. I knew her, meeting occasionally in family circles socially. A little sprig of a girl, quiet and intelligent, nice to talk to, good in her studies and very well read with a passion for physics and philosophy, in her final years at school. She was nice to talk to; she would talk me out of my shell.

My world collapsed with my father's death. From middle class we became lower middle class. It took a lot of effort on my part to help my mother going. Our only resources were my father's meagre savings and the small family pension for mother. We rented out the ground floor of our small two storey house and lived in the two rooms above. Mother forced me to continue studies and I enrolled for the Masters in

Economics and took a night course in business administration. There were no MBA courses those days and it was not fashionable to study business. I thought of offering private tuition to school children in my spare time but mother would not have it. She wanted me to concentrate on studies. I do not know how she ran the house and the kitchen.

That is when I saw Seema for the first time in our house talking and gossiping with mother in the kitchen and actually making her laugh! She had passed school with very high marks winning the general merit scholarship, and got admitted to Presidency College, the grandest college those days. She came with sweets and cakes to give mother the news. After that she came off and on, always carrying some delicacies. Mother objected only once, as far as I know, and tears rolled down her cheeks. To this day I remember her answer 'isn't a mother always a mother whoever the child is?' and mother had no answer. Those were different days, people had not yet become cynical and suspicious and it was perfectly natural. I never met her at my house but we used to meet around the university and Presidency College, usually in the gap between my university classes and my night college, not regularly but often. We would sit somewhere and she would bring out her Tiffin box and we would share. I used to object in the beginning but then surrendered. This was our entire romantic story. The friendship and sharing was so deep that nothing else came up. I do not remember ever having held hand, not deliberately.

I finished study and kept looking for a job, difficult in those days. Somehow I found a job in a business house as a trainee intern though that was not the term used in those days, on a small salary, more like a stipend, on the recommendation of a teacher. I had to work hard till odd hours and whatever spare time I had I spent with mother. Her health was failing but there was no obvious disease. I took her to doctors who gave medicines but she continued to be weak and did not like to take her medicines. Seema would visit her whenever she could but we seldom met. She had graduated with first class Honours in Physics and was doing Masters. For Masters she had to do a thesis or dissertation and was busy with her studies. The day her graduation results were out mother invited her and cooked a delicious dinner. We sat side by side to eat as she served. She refused to sit herself and with a loving gaze kept looking at us. I never forgot the deep affection with which she watched us eat with a smile hovering on her lips and Seema never raising her head from the plate. When we went to wash hands I grabbed her hand. She stood still and then looked up at me, blushed purple and snatched her hand away and ran to where mother was. When I found them she was sitting beside mother looking down and contemplating her fingernails and mother was affectionately patting her beautiful head and the mad rush of black hair falling to her waist. She wanted to do her hair but she shook head in silence. As I came she got up, touched mother's feet, bade her goodbye, gave me a quick glance and ran to her car waiting downstairs, not allowing me time to see her off. But that glance I still carry in my memory. After that we met seldom and when we did, that endless chatter of our younger days was over.

Mother was becoming weaker every day, she seemed to be dissipating. My work position was improving and I was given a permanent staff appointment with a steady salary. One day mother raised the question of marriage and asked me. I said: 'marry whom'? Mother suppressed her smile: 'why, marry Seema'. I said, 'Are you mad? She comes from a rich family. Can I give her that comfort?' She said, 'That does not matter. I have this last wish of seeing you together before I die.' I told her to forget it and she was not going to die only if she would eat properly. She did not protest but she did die. She died peacefully in her sleep. I felt shipwrecked and paralysed. Disaster had hit me so many times when coming up in life that I felt I had no strength to rebuild my hopes. Seema came and took control. We had a few relatives but not many. They came and helped but Seema was in control. There were whispers though everybody in our family knew Seema by now. She could not care less. When all the rites were finished and people had left she faced me and asked, 'Now, what are you going to do?' I looked at her dumbly and she said firmly 'Marry me'. I said, 'What, how?' She replied, 'What do you mean by how? You are a man you do not know how to marry?' I said lamely, 'Who will get us married?' She blazed: 'We shall get us married. Get out of your stupor and come with me. A man must know how to recover and you are such a man. Come with me.' Eventually she took me to a Marriage Registrar's office, made me sign papers. She even had my birth certificate, mother must have given her. Then she took me to her house and declared to her parents everything she had done. To my surprise they were overjoyed.

I knew they liked me and loved me. I was the only stupid one in this drama. I broke down and started crying that I deprived mother of this joy out of my weakness. They understood and took me to the room already kept ready for me, and Seema sat beside me until I fell asleep after we had our first tentative inexpert kiss and hug.

We signed our vows in front of a large photograph of my mother and I could not look at her I could hold back my tears only thanks to the firm pressure of Seema's hand. We also had a Vedic marriage and a gala reception thrown by my in-laws where all my relatives were invited. Then at Seema's insistence we came back to our small house, which now was only mine and had been repainted and redecorated in the meantime by my newly wed wife. We spent our honeymoon preparing for Seema's Masters examination that she passed with distinction but not as high as she could have done. Gradually our life fell in to a routine. Seema rejoined the university to do her Ph.D. and I continued to rise in my profession. My company also started growing and the headquarters was shifted to Bombay as political controversy engulfed Calcutta and we had to move to Bombay. People started calling me an economic genius that always made me laugh. The only negative thing was that Seema could not continue her Ph.D. as children started coming and my job and position meant that we traveled a lot, happy in each other's company. But Seema was always the driving force, the decision maker of the family.

This story took only a few moments to pass through my mind as it has done many times through my illness. The sorrow that stabbed my heart continuously like a lance through my ordeal was that I shall not be able to do anything to console her through her grief as she had done to mine. I had rerun our story so many times through the terminal phase of my illness that even now it runs through my mind like an opera staged many times. I took a long time to die or I should say I died many times before I actually died. I died of cancer. It was so unjust, so unfair! Here I was in prime health with a good job, a loving wife, and two nicely growing kids living in a large company apartment; with a car to move around and enjoy the social graces; looking forward to retirement and life in peace. I look around and think and feel satisfied lying in bed with my wife. I had got it all organized, everything under control. And as always, disaster struck me when I was at the peak. I do not care about my life, my career, my ambitions but only that I am not able to console my beloved wife as she had done in my deepest grief.

I feel a twinge of pain near my shoulder one day, must have bumped against something, and rub a little balm and forget it. It is a busy life. But the pain does not go. After a week or may be more I feel some swelling in the area and tell my wife. She says, 'Why don't you go see the doctor?' I say, 'I am so busy these days, will find some time next week.' I go to see my doctor, he sends me to another and he sends me for some tests, looks at the reports and sends me to another doctor. I feel irritated, my organized life is getting disturbed, and work is suffering.

I go to the last doctor and he looks glumly at whatever I have to show, my body, my reports and all that; with the anxious wife by my side; taking an inordinately long time tapping his fingers on the table. I impatiently think these doctors are so dumb. If he was in my job and took so much time to make a decision he would be fired. At last he says 'You have to take some treatment.'

I smile, confirmed in my evaluation of him, and say, 'That is what we are here for.'

He clears his throat with a funny croaking cough and says, 'It could be a long one.'

Impatiently controlling my voice to what can be termed a suppressed shout, I ask, 'What for? What have I got?'

He hesitates, takes a deep breath and mutters 'ummm, ah, what you have and all these tests point to something like some sort of a cancer', then adds quickly 'but it can be treated with strong possibility of cure.'

Now it was my turn to stare at him. He was obviously telling a lie and saving his license at the same time. I was in a rage and thoroughly helpless inside, and looked at my wife. She was a total wreck staring at the doctor with white bland expressionless face. That is when I died the first time.

I transfer my gaze at the doctor and ask softly 'why?'

He asks in return 'why what?'

'Why do I have a cancer?'

'I don't know. There are theories, there are possible inducing agents, but we do not know exactly, almost impossible to tell in an individual. We only have statistics. But do not lose hope, some patients are cured.'

I keep looking at him and wonder how this man survives doing this every day. Does he die every time he faces a patient and utters these words? There must be some safety valve somewhere. When he goes home does he just press the 'delete' key? I wish I could press a 'delete' key somewhere.

I ask him 'so what is it that has happened inside me? I feel perfectly healthy and have no trouble apart from this little pain. What is it that has gone wrong inside? Can you describe it in some easy language?'

He warms up to this question and says 'basically what has happened is that some of your body cells that were old and should have died and been eliminated refused to die, the controlling mechanism became faulty, and they kept on growing and multiplying and preventing the normal cells to grow. From birth as we go through life billions and billions of cells die and are replaced by new young cells. Why this mechanism fails we do not know, not at the final point.'

In spite of the emptiness inside me, I felt amused and mad and told him, 'you mean that just because some of my cells, 'my cells' refuse to die I have to die! But I not only cannot refuse to die, I do not have an inkling of the rebellion going on inside me! Can those cells think, do they have a mind, do they realize that by their rebellion they kill the body they live in and ultimately will kill themselves? Our workers and factory managers are more intelligent than whoever has made this body, God, nature, evolution or you,' shouting at the end.

At this point my wife broke out of her stupor, pulled me out of my chair, apologized to the doctor, supported me to my car and drove me back home while I cringed and clung to her like a child shivering with fear and my tears drenching her dress. She kept consoling me like a mother. That was the second time I died.

As we neared our house she whispered, 'We are going home and the children will be waiting. For their sake you have to pull up yourself. Think of the trauma to their innocent minds. We have to spare them that trauma as long as we can so that the realization dawns gradually,'

I pulled myself up and dried my face. She rearranged her dress and we strenuously put up an appearance of normality. She did it by bringing up an incident from our early conjugal life when we turned up at a friend's house with her dress not prim and proper and a faint smear of her vermillion on my cheek and she accosted me with, 'It was your doing,' and I retorted, 'No yours'. She brought up the story just as we would alight from the car and we were laughing when the front door opened and the children rushed out led by Rupa. She was an expert at creating such moments that would lighten serious situations and this one was the gravest. I was supposed to grab and hug Rupa as always but I cringed as if I had an infectious disease. She managed that also by stepping forward and catching her and then led me straight to our bedroom telling Rupa that we should change since we were coming from a clinic and pulled me into the bedroom smiling at her and closed the door. The last glimpse I had of her face told me that she was perplexed. It is difficult to fool the female sex of whatever age. The little lady was distressed.

Inside the closed bedroom I lost all control, fell flat on the bed and kept hitting the pillow with my fist. I got up and moved around in rage shouting at I did not know what. I picked up a flower vase and tried to throw, it was saved by Seema. She was crying too, tears streaming down her cheeks amid sobs and cries of distress. I do not know whether it was audible through closed doors. But at the same time she chased me around the room taking off my jacket and tie and shirt and then pushed me into the bathroom, saying, 'Take a shower and control yourself.' That terse command gave me a little bit of sense. I looked at my distorted face in the mirror and was shocked. Standing under the shower my tears mingled with the water and I stood as long as it would take to stop. I could hear Seema in the room. She was not opening the bedroom door, not taking any chances, and I could hear her pathetic crying with her face close to the bathroom door. That made me quiet and I came out when I was sure. Seema had changed in the meantime and she was dazzling with extra colour on her face. She looked at me and asked, 'Are you ok, dear?' I nodded. She helped me dress and then we went out to face our children. I whispered, 'When was the last time you dressed me' and she gave me a pinch. We were ready to face the world.

After that I died many times as treatment after treatment failed and at each failure and each recurrence I would die. Seema was always there to take me through those periods. Her usual happy buoyant personality was changing to serenity and she actually looked more beautiful. Her easy adaptation to a different life was remarkable. She was reading a lot and reading to me. I was not always living in fear of death, nobody can and in between when I was feeling better we would go to the cinema and occasionally dine out and meet close friends. Whenever I felt better I would go to office, employers were kind, and mine was mainly office work on strategic thinking that could also be done from home. We came closer than we had been for many years and I rediscovered her.

The last days arrived when there was no further treatment to try. My body refused to take any further therapy. There was nothing to do, no further option to look forward to except wait for death. It became unbearable. I was going mad inside but trying hard not to make everyone's life miserable. Seema understood my effort and on occasions would squeeze my arm and say, 'I am so proud of you,' looking up to me with those lustrous eyes. Our son Asim, his name kept matching with his mother, was in hostel and came home only to see his mother. Rupa left hostel and commuted to college and helped her mother as much as she could.

Seema was remarkably calm. I would beg her to give me sleeping pills so that I could die peacefully. One day she said, 'You have no physical pain. I understand your mental agony but you have the power and personality to handle that.'

I only said, 'I cannot any more.'

She said, 'Of course you can. Do you want us or your friends to go to jail for helping you to commit suicide? Shall I read you something from a book?'

I said, 'Religious books? You know I am a born atheist. I cannot stand them. And coming to your comment why are they not legalizing voluntary death, the stupid fools?'

She said, 'Show them what a man you are.'

I was calmer, 'What book you were referring to?'

'A science book you have not read.'

'Oh, yes, I forget that you have done a science masters. I have really spoiled your life.'

'You have done nothing. We do not spoil other people's lives, we can only spoil ours.'

'OK, I shall listen if you can make it easy enough for me.'

She raised a book, 'This is 'Order out of Chaos' by Ilya Prigogine who won the Nobel Prize in chemistry in 1977.'

I say, 'Wow, there goes, it is way beyond me.'

She says, 'Yes, it is difficult reading. I shall only tell you what I have understood as the main message of the book, without going through how that is made through intricate discussions on science, mathematics and philosophy. Like it?'

'Go ahead. Let us give it a try.'

'In our universe or probably in any universe entropy will always rise. That means the universe with us in it is continually moving towards disorganization, the chaos. The vase will break to pieces when it falls and it will fall some day given the eternity. When it is intact you look at it and admire or place it from one shelf to another—deterministic course. But when it is in the chaotic stage of breakage it can take several paths—you can glue the pieces together and repair the vase, you can brush off the pieces to the garbage can, you can order and get an exact replica—which means that in the chaotic stage there are many options and possibilities but the fate of the vase cannot be determined in the sense that it depends on many variables. Are you with me'?

'So far I get the general idea, yes, with some difficulty. What you are saying cannot be that simple. But go ahead and let me see where it leads.'

'Prigogine says and proves with a lot of scientific data that this inevitable journey towards chaos is not a linear one, not a ticket without stops. Since the universe is uniform in any direction we look, this holds true not only for the big universe but also for the small areas in time and space that we observe, including us the human society. He has given many examples in the book but the easiest one to me is the flux in the population of a tribal society, how it becomes chaotic with increase in numbers, then reorganizes itself in some way or other, and switches back to peaceful organized life when things become predictable. Our knowledge of things is influenced by this—crudely speaking, the chaotic state is in the realm of philosophy and the predictable determinate state is that of science. I say crudely because science is also learning to deal with chaotic state and the two knowledge areas in the human brain are coming closer. This may be evolution as it is today.'

She stops for breath. I keep looking at her. She is so beautiful, especially when she is animated as she is now. Did she read all this just for me or had she been thinking about all this for a long time? I thought the latter was right, which revealed to me a side of her I was not aware of. How little we know about people, even those nearest to us. I kept on loving her with my eyes as I used to do before we were married and regrettably forgot.

She started again, 'The next part is my deduction,' and she smiled shyly. 'I have been thinking about these things for some time and it seemed to me that in principle it is applicable even to individual human life. Take for example your life. You passed through so many hardships and uncertainties in your youth when we were students. You fought through all that. Life was chaotic and uncertain but not without rewards, not really unhappy, because of the joy of action with many alternatives for the future. Then it got channeled to a course and you excelled and enjoyed and life took a definite predictable course. Look at our love life, passing through so many doubts, how we fought and quarreled and then I could not resist you any longer. You won me and we settled to a married life.' This time she laughed her very sweet laugh, held my hand and squeezed. I stared at her, how long was it since I noticed her shy laugh or enjoyed this closeness? I could not remember. We pass through life oblivious of the most precious things around us, running after what we think we do not have and do not even need! I felt a mild remorse but there is no replay button in life. Aloud I said, 'Wrong. I did not marry you, you married me, and I cannot say you won me because it seems you are losing. You should have married someone else.' I regretted the moment I uttered these words because she started crying. I could not bear it but there was nothing I could do but offer hollow words of consolation. I died inside once again.

We were immersed in our own thoughts. I remembered Sarit, not after years but after ages and was surprised that I would do so. Where was he? Is he still alive? He should be, unless of course he had a cancer like me or a heart attack. That is unlikely, for he is occasionally in the news. My reverie was broken by her tug at my hand, 'What are you thinking?' 'Nothing,' I said.

'You cannot think of nothing,' her eyes were deep black pools. 'I have come to the present, I have passed over all the intervening years, its tensions, happiness, problems, children growing up, difficulties with career and money, the boredom of a long but sadly not so long married life, I have come to you.' I stared speechless at her. Did I ever really know this woman?

She continued after a long pause, 'We are facing the last chaos in life, unlike all the others before for we have no idea what lies beyond. You have faced every difficulty, every chaos in life boldly. You have to ride this one too, I am with you and I know my lion-hearted husband can ride over this and stare death in the face and laugh. Your brain is intact, that is why you are suffering and that is why you are alive. If you were a vegetable you would not have suffered, you would have been dead even if your body was healthy. We are what our mind is. The body changes a billion times but we are alive as long as our mind is intact. So get up and face the last chaos, the last battle.'

I almost went into a trance under the impact of her speech and conviction. She brought the universe at my doorstep, a picture so huge and grand that nothing mattered, my death only a speck in the background of an eternity. I remembered that in my very young days I read Einstein's writings about religion. I cannot remember the details but he wrote he could not believe in a personal God who has made the world and rewards and punishes like a judge but he could believe in Spinoza's God. So I read about Spinoza. I am neither a philosopher nor a scientist, so I read only excerpts from his most important book 'Ethics Geometrically Demonstrated', an unbelievable creation in his time. Today's scientists would want to give it a quantum definition and fail because physics has not gone that far, but has gone very close. He said that everybody should see his or her self against the background of an eternity, not of his house, city or country, but as integral part of the universe. Then death loses its meaning, fear of death vanishes. Death kills the ego, the ego that keeps us separated from the universe, the ego that is a part of the body not of the mind, but a part of the mind too when we live in a body mind complex as we normally do in our life. My mind was calm. I looked at Seema. She was staring into space not seeing anything, sat in a trance by the force of what she said. It comes rarely in the life of a human being, it had come to us and we shared it.

A change came over me with a calmness that made me aware and responsible to my surroundings. I had a lot of things to do to organize my life and secure those of my family and I did not have a lot of time. I seemed to be planning for a long journey and the thought of death receded in the background. I resigned from my job and got whatever my dues were. I looked at my assets and investments and transferred them to appropriate places so that my wife and children faced no hardships and at everything I took my wife's advice. Our life became busy but I could see she was suffering. I asked my children to take a holiday for a week or two from whatever they were doing and come home and stay. The house was full but not glum as I kept all of them busy and we had family sessions of talking, joking and laughing, going out and enjoying now and then as if we were on holiday. We never discussed my disease and doctors, apart from close friends, who were not coming much anyway and they were surprised by our joviality but never mentioned anything. We shared anecdotes and memories of the past and laughed. I exchanged my car to buy a smaller one after long animated discussions with my son that brought us closer. I looked through my personal papers and memorabilia and destroyed or distributed them and kept some where they were so that the house still looked a home as it always has. It is funny how we store them, unnecessary objects as if our life lay in them and would continue to be needed. Life still wants to cling to them. Among some very old papers I found loose pages of a diary written irregularly with long gaps from my very young days till about the time of marriage—a few useless pages from a time when life was chaotic. I was going to destroy them and then hesitated for no obvious reason and just dropped them in the pile. With the newly acquired clairvoyance in a relaxed mind I seemed to see farther into the past and present. This is how I justified the vision of my death when I saw in a flash how and when I would die. Is it not curious? It is like Hamlet saying there are more things in heaven and earth and so on. In a friend's house I once heard a holy man say that those who lead a life of honesty and purity can sometimes foresee death—that is not so unusual or mystical. I presumed honest and pure meant consciously honest to one's own self and society and not by compulsion or circumstances. I do not know that I was that honest and pure but may be tolerably so. That is why the room is empty and I am enjoying my death alone. I had taken precaution in case I had seen it right. I did not want even Seema to stay and suffer and invented a ruse to make her sleep with her daughter. Soon people will know and there will be a crowd and crying and I shall be gone by then bidding my body farewell.

Love

A year has passed since Ranajit left me, left us. Rupa and Asim came for the short annual remembrance ceremony that was private for the three of us. Life has gone back to the same lonely existence. Time, they say, is a great healer. Time is lot more than that. Our ancient philosopher scientists said time is eternal, goes on and on. They said time is a relation between two events and since events would always keep happening in the universe, time would also go on to infinity. The Universe goes through cycles of creation and destruction and time progresses through it. They termed the cosmic time as *Mahakaal* and terrestrial time as *kaal*. We are born and die, laugh or cry through *kaal*, and *Mahakaal* is the witness thereof. The flow of time is the great divider that divides the universe to small areas of perception. It divides the flow of energy and its waves into packets of energy that assume shapes and images. That is how galaxies and stars and planets appear and we come into being with our science and technology comfortable in dealing with predictable events, like switching on an electric bulb. We find it difficult and almost impossible to go to the great beyond.

Modern science has discovered time—from terrestrial to cosmic the phenomenal discovery of the twentieth century. As late as 1988 Stephen Hawking wrote for us laymen (his scientific paper must have preceded by a few years) that the arrow of time reverses as the universe begins to contract after the phase of expansion. Even a great mind such as his must have conceived expansion and contraction by the usual human experience of both. In 1996 he wrote, and I cannot help reproducing it with an excusable giggle. He wrote, 'I wrote a paper claiming that the arrow of time would reverse when the universe contracted again . . . had made my greatest mistake, or at least mistake in physics: the universe would not return to a smooth state in the collapse. This would mean that the arrow of time would not reverse. It would continue pointing in the same direction as in the expansion.' There has been further development of knowledge in this field.

Science is still in its infancy and so it is not yet able or would care to come down to the ordinary level of human life and emotions and chooses to remain in its ivory tower. Is that right and desirable? The answer, as in many such questions on human knowledge, is both yes and no. The ivory tower needs to be there for the purity of knowledge and perception but there has to be communion at the ground level not only to have a scientific basis for ethics but also for its own growth. Our ancestors took recourse to imagery to convey experience. Was that correct and adequate? The answer is: everything is correct and adequate for some length of time and nothing can be eternal in the human world we live in. The imagery of our ancestors came to be derided as mysticism in the vocabulary of science once the connection was lost. Both I and Ranajit were admirers of Spinoza, and wondered how this poor man, rejected and excommunicated by the church, family and society like an untouchable, could live quite content in his small shop polishing lenses and could not care the least. He perceived much of this phenomenon in the seventeenth century in the largely desolate world of western philosophy from Plato to modern times with very few exceptions like Kant.

My thoughts flowed from my confusion over a letter, a few tattered handwritten papers that I held in my lap—letters from the dead. That is the only way I can describe them. Almost forty years old, they are not even letters but written soliloquies could be the best way to describe them. Ranajit wrote them over a small period of his life. It is not a diary because it is not written in regular sequence but with random entries, just a few of them. These were his innermost thoughts in that period of his life when he was going through a chaotic phase, afraid of things he could not control. The things were unimportant after some time and his writings stopped and I do not think he ever wrote anything later in his life. But the curious thing is that last piece written at a later time is an unsent letter written to me but not directly addressed to me. The contents are however pertinent to our lives and not known to anyone else. I wondered why he did not destroy these pages when he destroyed all his personal papers. Did he want me to read this? Why? What is the message from the dead? Once again I read what I have read so many times.

'Sorry for the delay in writing to you and in compensation this is going to be a long letter. I shall write you a story. It is not a great story, not even a unique one and the characters are so familiar that they need not be named, yet you may not know everything about them. Do we ever do?

'I happened to meet one of the characters in this foreign land after many years. You must still remember him for it is difficult to forget him, not because he is handsome or imposing in any way but there was a special something in him that one felt in his presence. He was not voluble, was good in studies but not with shining intelligence, he had a palpable intensity around him. A man of medium height, medium build, medium intelligence, not aggressive in manners, yet something special. This is as best as I can describe him and he was my friend. Coming from a higher middle class family of professionals with an easy life and strong ethical values and learning, he was a man wedded to science and thought and lived science. Like most young men of his days he grew up through emotional difficulties and some trauma that was common then in our society that he accepted and absorbed with nonchalance and a basic love for humanity that I could only attribute to a strong philosophical grounding. It is difficult to get very close to such a man and love him. I was probably his only close friend. He shared with me openly his ideas, his dreams, his passions that centered mostly on science. I was a patient listener though I was not inclined to carrying such a heavy baggage through life. I took life more easily, more casually; to be lived with joy with all the human amenities that could be procured without undue stress and of course love. Love was very important to me as I did not have enough to satisfy me but he seemed to be on a mission to find something in life. I like men with a mission but keep a little wary distance. I did not think he would be so expressive to anyone else as he was by nature reserved and did not talk much. I thought I was doing him a service lending him my ears.

Our lives separated after graduation and we went our different ways. I heard that after postgraduate qualification he had gone for research and was making a name. One day after may be three years of our last meeting he turned up after calling me on phone. That was typical of him. His problem was that he was in love and I was surprised that even for that problem he had to come to me. He went into an eloquent description of his beloved. She was not so fair, well educated girl from a middle class family was not obviously exceptional in any way but with an easy grace and charm that soothed and did not burn. He became poetic in his description. While traveling by train if you looked at the vast green farmlands you would suddenly find a cluster of trees shading a clear pond and a bunch of cottages, so ordinary that you may miss them easily, but if you look closely you would see a shaded beautiful place like a girl with peaceful eyes laughing at the mad rush of the world.

I asked him whether he had expressed his love and been reciprocated. He said he had expressed his love and her reaction was a shy restraint without discouraging him but just keeping her reserve. It only fuelled his love and he was sure that she loved him too. So I asked him what the problem was. He said the problem was that he had received a scholarship from a famous university overseas and a warm invitation to join the research team and he had to leave within a short time. He wanted to marry this girl and take her with him. The visa and other formalities were easy those days. He asked for my opinion and my help. I stared at him. I had never known him to be interested in women, he actually shied off from them, even from those that were interested in him and made advances. He was not unattractive with his scholarly reserve and obvious affluence, if not opulence. I was silent, still staring at him. His description was so vivid but impossible! Not able to decide what to say I advised him to ask the girl first.

See what an ordinary story it is, nothing to be ecstatic about. He turned up after about a week and was disheveled, looking mad and angry, something I had never seen in him. He kept talking in an unusually loud voice complaining that it was all a misunderstanding, she was one of those cheap flirts who loved to tease men and play with them without any commitment. I do not remember everything he said but he was very upset and I sat dumb. He stormed out of my room. I kept wondering whether I should do something or not but could not decide and felt very uneasy. I did not have to wait long as he came back after two days, this time unannounced. He looked calm and poised. He smiled shyly and apologized for the previous day and said he was a fool and had misunderstood the girl and said such bad things to me that hurt his sense of decency and I should forgive and forget. His eyes were actually shining with his faith. I asked him what she had said and he replied that he was a fool and did not know that she was already engaged and did not want to betray whoever the lucky guy was. I sat quiet unable to decide what to say. I did not even ask him the girl's name. He walked out of my room in peace.

You may be wondering why I am telling you this story. That is because after so many years I met him yesterday in this foreign land. It was in the newspapers that he was in this city, the deputy leader of a scientific expedition to Antarctica, one of the first. The picture of the Professor of Astrophysics was also there. We met accidentally in the hotel lobby. He called me and was very happy to see me. We got very little time together. He was bubbling with enthusiasm and the entire time he talked only about his work. He was a changed man, dynamic, lean, healthy, happy. As we bade farewell I asked about his family and he smiled and said he was not married, not yet, and then pressing my hand warmly he looked at me with knowing eyes and said 'no luck' and laughed again.

The unsent letter ended here. It had to be at least thirty years old for that was when he made his first trip abroad. There was no date on top unlike his other faded earlier scribbling, because that is what they were, apart from this letter. Why did he leave this one among his old papers? Obviously he wanted me to find this letter some day and read. Why? I am an old woman now and he is dead, why decide to leave this deliberately when he knew he was dying? I started to cry the moment I read it the first time and the pain was so intense that I could not stop crying for days. His death is such a loss, not just because he was my husband but the loss of such a large hearted magnanimous decent man is a loss to society as all his friends say. He went very high in his profession as an economist and economic strategist and planner. There was a rumour that he would soon be invited to join the Planning Commission and as advisor to the Prime Minister but it never showed on him, his happiness lay in his life and family. I was never in any doubt, not at that young age and never later, that I had chosen the right man and that he was God's gift to me and tried my utmost to love and help him in everything till the last day. I used to think that I must have some goodness in me to get this gift. Given a million options I shall choose him and love him every time and he would do the same, I know in my heart. There was never any discord, never any misunderstanding between us. Irritations will be there in family life with two growing up talented children but they vanished the moment he took me in his arms. Those strong golfer's arms are not around me now. He was almost professional in golf too that he took up late in life and as usual gave it his best shot. We travelled round the world. Why leave this letter for me now, and my tears would not stop. I shall pass my days only in his memory.

I knew Sarit as a friend and a senior colleague. I was doing my Ph.D. after Masters. He was talented and had done his Ph.D. in a short time and was engaged in research and looking for opening abroad. He used to help me occasionally. His advances increased over time and used to embarrass me but he was a gentleman and I did not worry, just kept the distance. I had no idea that Ranajit and Sarit were friends at one time. I met Ranajit through family connections and instantly fell in love that he did not notice for a long time. Actually we were never engaged formally since in our society that happens only when families settle a marriage. Still struggling with our careers we had not told our families yet. I never told him about Sarit because there was no reason to discuss a colleague. He never told me that he knew Sarit even if he knew that he was a colleague of mine which I doubt. He was not that kind of man. We were in blue heaven meeting whenever opportunity came and oblivious of the society around and hiding from it most of the time. I told Sarit that I was engaged out of kindness, and because I was already mentally engaged. I knew he would take that word at face value and not ask for details, he was so innocent! I saw his despair and felt sorry and should have told him the very first day he proposed, but

I was confused and did not know what to do. I told him at the very first opportunity after that day and was so relieved when he took it sportingly. I knew that his first wife would always be science and he would not miss me. I respected him for that and knew he would go far. That was the end of this fiasco and I forgot Sarit.

But why my beloved never told me the contents of this letter and never mentioned it once even jokingly during our whole life together? Only he knew the whole story but it was not an important story as it is not unusual to get advances from other men and my husband was not of the teasing kind. Then why reveal the story now when he is dead and the story was dead a long time back! Can't he see that this hurts me so much? Didn't he think that it would? I cannot even ask him and feel his arms around me and then everything would have vanished in laughter.

I tried to think calmly. In his last days he was more worried about me than his impending death. He had arranged most of the material things around me so that I would not suffer. But what about my loneliness, he could not help that. I had not built a career for myself though I could have. I did not complete my Ph.D. The shock of Sarit's advances actually threw me into Ranajit's arms and I was so happy there! We got married soon after. He asked me now and then to pick up the threads and continue. But it is not easy once you go off line. My line was mainly theoretical but nothing can be totally theoretical. Even for theoretical work one needs the environment, interaction of people and thoughts. I subscribed to Nature when engaged in research and that continued. I would correspond sometimes with authors of papers, sometimes getting replies and reprints. They became fewer with time. I am almost an old woman now. I resent that. No woman gets old in her fifties nowadays. I am still fairly good looking and that I saw in my husband's eyes and enjoyed thoroughly. It is just that I allowed myself to get wasted. I have got rusted but may not be beyond repair. Intellectually I am alive otherwise. It is just a question of shifting priorities. It is difficult but gettable. Mathematics is a thing that is not easily erased from a brain once used to it. I may not be able to do a groundbreaking thought experiment or *gedanken* like Schrödinger or Heisenberg but I can keep myself amused and busy with little things. But the last thing I need in life is fresh male company. I just cannot be troubled. The memory of the man I loved so much will remain fresh till I become senile.

Did my beloved husband suggest a lifeline, a mild suggestion, not as a male companion but a direction? That would be very much like him. He never asked or ordered, he always suggested, whether at home or at office. That was his style and that is why people liked him. He was an artist; he would draw a big picture of a possibility with great care and put it before others. Sometimes those who would accept, later thought it their own, not to cheat but sincerely, and he did not even resent that. That was his secret of success, not conjured but natural. He was the greatest philosopher I know, a selfless philosopher and a friend, the only friend to me, a man to love. He was a friend to many others, people depended on him. I regret that I did not see all these in such great detail while we were together. I could have loved him so much more! We pass through life blindfold, unaware of the precious things around us and bogged down in the mundane. We do not realize that failing to give love to our heart's content is as painful as not getting it.

He put before me Sarit's name to suggest what I could have been and still can be, what would fulfill my life even in his absence, in his gentle way and gave me a link. Never would he think that I would run to Sarit and throw myself at him now that he is not there. He was not a crude man like that, he would never dream it. He also knew me very well, probably more than I knew myself. My heart was full with love and I started to cry again. How much tear has God kept for me? How much suffering would make me fit for him? Am I worthy of such great love? If he was alive he would smile and say, 'Yes you are and for even more.' I do not think I was this much in love even when we were just married.

I pushed all thoughts of the letter and its contents to the back of my mind and thought about my future. As long as I am alive I have a future and I must be ready to embrace it and make it. I am an educated person in perfect health and there must be a place in the future for me and I must find it. I am single and lonely but seen from another angle I carry no extra baggage and the tensions of young womanhood. The children are a delight. Rupa is studying at IIT for B.Tech in Physics. She loves to stay home when she has a day off.

Her favourite pastime at home is to cuddle up beside me. We pass
our time in all sorts of girlie talks about her friends, classmates, the
teachers as if they are all familiar to me. In long holidays some of
her girl friends come to the house. The children of today are so much
smarter and so much more free and intelligent than our times. They
are also better informed and it is a delight to talk to them. Sometimes
when they are by themselves I hear their whispers and giggles from
the next room and snatches of excited whispers tell me that they are
discussing boys, something we could not dream of. All of them think
Rupa's mum is super, M.Sc in physics and so pretty. Rupa is very
beautiful and if I even hint at that so that she is careful she would say
'I wish I were like you'. A single mother has to act a bit dumb but not
too dumb and I play the role expertly. This was a pleasure I could not
have enough of. She rarely talks of her father. His suffering and death
has made such a deep scar in her mind that she avoids that topic. I
bring it up sometimes to erase that scar slowly. I tell her of her dad's
qualities, how super he was, in a more adult fashion. She would ask,
'Two of you were very much in love, were you not?' And I would say,
'Yes, very much'. Then the inevitable question, 'How did you meet?'
And I parry and avoid the question but she would not let go and pull
my sari and say, 'Please ma please'. I would say, 'Not like you guys'
and she would keep jumping, 'How do you know, how do you know
what we do' and there would be a lot of jumping and chasing. She
is still a kid. A child always remains a kid, specially a girl child to
a mother, with an image of parent that is cruel to break. To this age
I cannot fathom how a western mother or some in our society start
another life without hurting the child. Hurting is not the same as
growing up, it confuses them, must be difficult for both.

Actually my intimacy with the children took a new turn from the
beginning of Ranajit's illness. He needed my constant support and
encouragement so that he would not break down. I was dying within
but had to keep a brave face with optimism as if whatever was
happening was not much to be scared about. Ranajit had a strong
mind and not easily affected by adversity but even he was refusing
therapy and I had to talk and tell him stories of successful treatment,
sometimes concocting stories and find hopeful data although I knew
his disease had already spread when it was diagnosed and it would be
a miracle if he came out of it. As for the children it was even more

difficult as they were confused and frightened. Surprisingly they had not even heard the name of the disease, none of their friends had told them of any such thing in their families, the first time such a thing broke in to their consciousness was with their father. So I had to force my mind away from fears and act normally, laugh and smile naturally, giving logical answers to their innumerable questions with an optimism that I did not feel myself. I had to stand like a pillar of strength for my family to embrace for support, a task that so long had been my husband's. It was so difficult to make the switch, feeling a hollow inside me all the time. Ranajit displayed a remarkable switch of personality as treatment progressed and he gradually grasped that it was not going to succeed. As the inevitability of the outcome dawned on him he became calm and aware of his family. I had read about such switch as happening in battlefields when death loomed inevitable but never imagined it could happen in the battlefield of life. Cancer is a disease like a battle, a campaign that slowly unfolds with the outcome seldom clear until much later, when subdued emotions come in to play as despair or exceptional courage, heroism and humanism. As a result we had some of the finest moments of family life. The children had never had enough of their father as he was always very busy, now he was mostly home when they came back from school or college. We planned outings, dinner evenings, film shows, theatre and the children were excited. When Ranajit could not cope they would hold him up. Rupa was the best in this, for her the disease did not even exist and we all joined in her mirth. She was hurt the worst with all sorts of behavioural anomalies to start with and she recovered and adjusted the best, ageing fast to a fine woman.

Asim's initial reaction was anger when he learnt what his father was suffering from. Ranajit took him into confidence the very first day we knew of the disease. I did not think it was a wise decision. Behind a stolid exterior he had a deep seated sense of insecurity that only a mother could tell. He was the first born and I had a difficult and prolonged labour and he came out somewhat asphyxiated. I read much later that such children may carry sub clinical damage to certain areas of the brain and can have minor but significant behavioural maladjustments. I do not know whether the prolonged birth had something to do with his sense of insecurity. He knew the name of his father's disease and scourged the internet to know whatever he could of the disease and it turned to anger at everything around him, against the whole world as if it were a conspiracy. He became silent and uncommunicative. I was at a loss over how to bring him to a level field and the only thing I could think of was to behave naturally and kindly, not to take notice of his angst but to engage him in ordinary soothing family chatter. I think it was Asim's attitude that made Ranajit conscious of the difficulties his near and dear ones were suffering. It was then that he started asking Asim whether he was free to accompany him when he was going to see the doctor or going for therapy. He would ask his opinion on everything concerning the house and the treatment till Asim started to act the adult role. I am so grateful that Asim settled down by the time Ranajit was far advanced and suffered in silence with us.

Asim is no longer a boy but a strapping young man in the final years of his computer and software course at the IIT and he thinks himself older than he actually is. He is my little guardian. So I behave as an old woman with him, listening patiently to his many advices on what and how much to eat, to be careful on the roads and all such things. On his insistence thankfully I have not become a vegetarian as a Hindu widow is supposed to be. It is said that one has to have a bit of acting talent to keep a happy household. A single mother has to be doubly wary with teenage children. Not that I did not enjoy doing it.

So the days passed. One relief was that I had no financial worries and still able to keep the car and a driver though I knew driving. But with children and the traffic as it is, a driver is much safer. Ranajit had arranged for everything with his managerial skill and foresight. I decided to keep the flat, purchased with advances from the company, at least as long as the children were studying. I rearranged my books and the journals. I had the material and started studying seriously from where I had left off. Socializing and gossip or taking part in various NGO activities was not up to my taste. I enjoyed reading, my interests ranged from physics and related sciences to philosophy and literature. My life continued in this mode for about two years until the kids passed out from IIT, first Asim and then Rupa. Asim got a good job and was sent to the USA where he changed job and got into silicone valley striking out by himself. Rupa having passed with high grades got a scholarship to study higher physics in an American university. I encouraged them to go away not to spoil their careers for my sake.

I was lonely again. I decided to relocate to Calcutta or Kolkata as it is now known. I know many people there and there were relatives. I contacted my old department where everything had changed but on my past records they would consider an association of some sort without salary. This suited me well. Ranajit had refurbished and redecorated our house after the tenants vacated and we used to stay there off and on when we went to Calcutta. So it was not completely desolate. I decided to sell our flat in Bombay, now that the children had finished their education and following their own lives. Fortunately Ranajit's office offered to buy it back, saving me a lot of hassle and at a good price too that added to my wealth. Everything seemed to have jelled towards Calcutta and I had already decided to shift there and continued calling the city I loved by its name Calcutta. The company took the trouble and expenses of home shifting as the last service to the man they respected. There was not much to shift anyway.

When I settled in my own house the past seemed to embrace me. Every nook and corner had a memory. The kitchen, though refurbished now, held the memory of my late mother-in-law, a loving mother to me and her affection surrounded me, so poised, so mild and sweet and wise. In front of the now modern bathroom there still stood the old wash basin where Ranajit first held my hand. The small flowering trees planted by mother and then by me had been kept alive by the old gardener Ranajit employed. He now lived in a downstairs room with his old wife. They had no children. She cooked for me and we shared the food as I never cared much for exotic food. I was at peace.

Actually it is not too bad to live alone as a senior citizen if you are healthy and you have interests to pursue, with a mind still keen and intent and you have no financial worries nor are you rich. From outside others may think you are lonely but you feel rich inside. I thought what the ancients termed as Vanaprastha was this or close to it, to embrace in the last phase of life, a life of contemplation. The renunciation part was what came naturally, never forced and rarely total.

Life

I did not want to leave Mum and come to the USA but she almost forced me. Father's death was such a shock to me and I did not want mother to live alone with that loss. He was dying slowly right in front of our eyes and I could not stand it. I wanted to scream in bed at night and could not check it once and she came running. After that I used to bite the pillows to check the screams and she noticed the marks but said nothing. I was father's little darling daughter. When he came back from work the first thing he would do was to shout 'Rupa' from the doorstep. I would not miss his homecoming if I could help it. I would run towards the door and leap at him and embrace him and he would say 'slow, slow, you are a big gal now,' mimicking what I would call myself when I was small. If I could see his car before he came up I would go to the door and wait and as he came in give a whoop and pounce on him and he would feign a scare and embrace me, 'Oh my God, you frightened me.' That was when I was a little girl, not very little though. He could not bear to send us to hostel, me and my Dada, big brother Asim. He was not much older, just over two years, but he behaved as if he belonged to the elder generation. So I had names for him, Oldie and Buro, saying Dada only in front of outsiders and Mum. She did not like me teasing the big brother as he used to get easily upset. So I gave it up as we grew older just restricting myself to hiding his things and whenever he would not find his pen or his shoe he would call out 'Ma' and almost immediately Mum could call 'Rupa' and I would scurry and give him his thing and hide myself. Our childhood was very happy and most of the time we were great friends and we shared our little secrets from Mum and Dad.

Most of all we loved our vacations and travelling together. Those were real treats. Asim is and always was a serious boy intent on knowing and learning everything and asking father about everything and he had answer for everything. He was such a learned man! When we went to a historical place whether in India or a few times abroad, he would describe the history of the place and the nation or kingdom in great detail and make the place come alive. Similarly he would talk about the technological marvels and stories behind discoveries and inventions. Mum was equally brilliant and their conversations on present and past civilizations and societies and cultures were so erudite that we would listen with gaping mouths and only occasionally asking questions and they would be so happy if it was a good question and we would get a pat or a kiss. At other times I was a tomboy climbing every tree in sight, exploring on my own and rarely, very rarely getting into trouble. As I grew older I began to understand the depth of love and mutual respect that bound them together. It is funny how a female child develops those sensations much earlier than the male child and I would lecture to my big brother. Once, but only once Mum caught me in the act and laughed and pinched my cheek. She was such a knowing mother that she could see through us. We were never restricted except in an ethical boundary, there never was any restriction on what we could ask or talk about as long as it was rational and not mischievous, and that never happened. We learned very early in life almost instinctively how not to hurt others. I know now that children are the greatest detectives of their parents' life without even understanding the details. When you find an offspring loving and respecting their elders you can be sure that they led an honest and loving life.

This family life full of joy suddenly stopped one day that I can remember precisely, it was so sharp. It was the first time in my life Mum and Dad returned home both smiling that looked more like crying, father not whistling or calling my name, mother with a handkerchief in hand stealthily wiping her eyes as she entered. For the first time I hesitated asking if anything was the matter or follow them to their bedroom on my father's arms. Mum understood my bewilderment immediately and called me in, embraced me and said, 'Your Papa has got a slight illness and needs some rest that is why we are just a bit worried, it is nothing.' I looked at Dad with surprise and asked, 'You are sick? But you look the same, not a bit ill. What have you got, not the heart?' That was the only dreadful disease I had heard of till then. At this he laughed loudly and hugged me and tried to lift me as he would do when I was smaller and said 'ouch' and dropped me. I admonished him lifting a finger and said, 'You must not do that, Mum has told you many times. I am not a kid any more.' To this he roared with laughter and mother smiled and all seemed to be well. But not quite, for he was rubbing his shoulder and following my gaze he said, 'I have got slight pain here, not much, that is all.' Then he called me his little mother and kissed and cuddled me. Asim was at the door all this time. Father knew it would not be easy to fool him so he told him, 'Don't you have a test tomorrow? Go to your study I'll join you after I change.' Mother sent me on an errand to the kitchen. So the two of us were gone and the bedroom door remained shut for quite some time, rather unusual, and then they came out smiling and Dad went to Asim and I helped mother to arrange tea and noticed her eyes were red. We sat down to tea with usual merriment but mother spilled some tea that was rather unusual.

I am describing the day vividly because some images are never erased from a child's mind and we were not really babies. Asim became more silent and serious. He spent most of the time at home in front of his computer scouring the internet for every bit of information on father's disease. I could not do computers and nobody told me anything. I would beg of him, cajole him as I sort of divined what he was looking for all the time but he would not tell me. Nobody would tell me anything! And I could see and feel that father was looking like a man destroyed, so confused and depressed that he could not even see us, his beloved children and did not even talk to me! I used to have fits of anger and fight with Asim and so would he. His anger surpassed mine as I would fiddle with the computer in his absence which he would discover when he came back and get very angry. He even hit me once, something that had never happened before and since. Mother forced herself to come out of her sorrow and reverie and one day she sat us together and talked to us. Calmly and quietly she told us everything, sometimes choking on her words. The sessions continued for days and in between we could not go to school and feigned stomach aches or colds and mother would not protest or say anything. She was busy taking father to doctors or for therapy. He was admitted in a hospital for a few days and mother told us that he had gone for some investigations. She would go to hospital every day and stay as long as she could and ask us whether we would like to go too and then advised we had better not and we did not protest. She told me that since she was busy with father would I mind looking after the house and keep an eye on what is being cooked. She asked Asim to check the mails regularly and answer the phone and keep note. We were included in the team with responsibilities till we gradually calmed down. By and by we got the whole story from her in bearable installments. We learned that father's disease was already advanced when it was diagnosed and had already spread. I had no idea what that meant. She replied that it was beyond operation in answer to a question from Asim. To this day and probably as long as I live I shall not be able to fathom how she could suppress her sorrow and despair and talk so easily and plainly to us. I shall never be able to fathom the depth of her character! The only outward sign of torment was the occasional choking of her voice.

Gradually we started going to school and college as she impressed on us that nothing would please father more than to know that his children were studying and doing well. That will even give him relief is what she said and I remember it to this day. She did the same to father as he was getting weak and thin and actually withdrawing himself from everything, even us. I heard her talking cheerfully to father in the bedroom as long as he was awake and coaxing him to come out and sit at the dinner table. At the table she was her usual charming self without overdoing anything. One day father could not eat what was served and he said he had no appetite and mother promptly got up and pushed away her plate and said there was something wrong and she could not also eat and took father inside telling us to finish eating whatever we could and winked at us. We finished our dinner silently. One day father suddenly vomited on his plate and she jumped up exclaiming, 'I told the doctor not to give that medicine, it never suited you;' and she named some medicine that meant nothing to us and she took father to the bedroom and settled him down and came back to clean, all in one go, with a calm face. Then she went to the bathroom and I crept to the door and heard her crying helplessly and at the same time trying to suppress it. It was so pathetic! I tiptoed out and did not tell Asim. At night I was lying in bed unable to sleep. Mother came into the room silently later in the night, and came to my bed as she always did, and I sat up and she said, 'Oh, you are not sleeping let me rearrange your cover.' I hugged her waist and hid my face in her body and whispered, 'Mum you can cry whenever you want to, we would not mind;' and she broke down hiding her face in my lap and after a glance at the door to see it was closed, cried her heart out as long as she could, as I have done so many times with her. Only now she was the daughter and I was the mother and I kept on stroking her head and passing my fingers through her beautiful hair as she used to do with mine. That night, I think, I graduated to womanhood.

After the first cycle of therapy, though I did not know what that meant, it was probably radiotherapy as I remember from conversations at the time, father showed some improvement. He was able to take food better and though he was still thin he was able to move better and the pallor of his face cleared. Our sessions at dinner started getting livelier and father would smile and laugh and mother was all busy looking after her family. One morning as we were getting ready after breakfast mother was taking a lot of time with father in the bedroom, and then she came out with father behind her all dressed up in his best suit hanging a bit loose on him. Mother told us triumphantly that father was going to office and we shouted in joy and did a dance around them. Mother said, 'You people get dropped and then send back the car and I shall drop father at office.' We got out fast so that father was not delayed and shouted at mother we shall come back by ourselves. Mother ran after us saying, 'No, no, Asim has late classes, he can come back by himself but Rupa, you must come back in the car. I shall send the driver in time.' When my classes were over I came out to find the car waiting and asked the driver when father would need the car. He said that father was home by lunchtime and mother sat in the car the entire time he was in office, only once going to the nearby mall from where she came out soon. Poor mother probably needed to go to the bathroom, I thought, and silent tears streamed down my cheeks. This hide and seek went on for days and weeks. Mother warned us that we must be cheerful at home, no talk of disease, do our chores normally and keep the home happy. We did likewise but I could see mother was getting tired and she was fast losing her normal gorgeous appearance. Occasionally we would stare at each other longer than usual and she would know that I knew and I knew that she knew. Another of the hide and seek games we played. After a few weeks father announced one day that he did not need to go to office and would work from home on the computer and people would come from office with papers when needed. I was glad for mother. I had a suspicion that father's office found out that his wife was spending most of the day sitting out in the car and sent him home. Anyway it was good for all of us except that both Asim and I started bunking classes and returned home on false pretexts. The parents must have understood but did not say anything. We were good students after all. We forced them to go to bed after lunch so that we could have evenings together. If father was feeling well we would go to see a film together or have a light dinner at a suitable restaurant. Our family was relaxing a bit with new optimism.

But alas this interlude did not last long, only a few months, a little over eight months may be. The time passed very fast and we were relaxing. Then father started having new distressing symptoms. Again visits to the hospital, fresh testing, and they said he has a recurrence and has to be started on chemotherapy. This time father broke down and the façade could not be maintained nor was there any necessity as all of us realized what was in store but we never talked about it. He had a helpless look about him, broken in both body and mind. He was a tall man. He lost a lot of weight and now looked gaunt with a stoop and the hearty smile that reverberated around the house was gone. Our home looked like a cemetery. Mother spent long hours cloistered with him. We had no idea what they talked about but father seemed to pull himself slowly out of despair. There must have been some magic in mother's words. We learnt of that much later after father was gone.

This is what kills patients and their families in this dreadful disease. One time you are high in optimism and the next you are in a deep hopeless abyss. It comes in waves relentlessly. The doctors probably know what to expect or what may happen but the families do not know. They are now elated and now depressed and the patient hopes and then finds it was a false hope! It kills a man, takes away all his dignity and makes him psychologically a wreck, a cabbage! We could not bear to look at father in that state. In our anger Asim and I discuss what do the doctors do when they have cancer? We lay people do not know what to expect in which cancer. They are all the same to us. But what about the doctors, they know what to expect or what not to expect in a particular disease, how do they cope with it? In his anger Asim rummaged through all literature, all internet sites for answer. There are stories and stories but rarely one finds a man behind those stories. There are brave doctors who knew and faced the finality with calmness doing their last bit for society or their institution. But why is it that the whole picture or the possibilities not explained to the patients who do not know the subject so that they can face it with dignity? In our anger we forgot that possibilities were probabilities not certainty. To prepare a patient for a possibility that may not happen would mean pushing him to unnecessary despair and worse. I could reason this way but not Asim. His anger would not abate and I could see it spreading. I was worried and told mother and she probably told father and whether because of this or not there came a change.

Under mother's psychotherapy father gradually stood up and faced everything with a shrug and a smile. I learnt much later how she revived him when I was able to understand and it was not magic but science and since then I simply worshipped her. Like the last man standing father would smilingly go for chemotherapy and come back probably tired and sick to the bone but still with that smile, refusing any supporting hand, and would somehow reach his bed and declare that he would be resting for some time and would be up for dinner. Within a day or two he would be up and about with his devil may care attitude and work through the day in his office at home shifting and signing papers, sending instructions on internet not only to his office but also to a host of people. I learned much later that he was not working for his office any more but preparing for his departure and organizing our life when he would be no more. After a short afternoon nap if he was feeling better we would go out for a drive and have ice cream by the seaside. Sometimes we would go to his club and he would talk and joke with friends in his best party manners, laughing at any concern expressed about his health in his usual manner. We were instructed to behave in a similar manner and enjoy fully whatever we were doing, always walk straight and look at people in the face. At home too we were enjoying most of the time, sitting around and talking about our holidays and who did what funny things and laughing about it. He made us laugh all the time telling us funny stories from his life and travels. Or we would play cards or scrabbles and there would be a lot of fun. Even Asim started to relax. The only person not relaxing was mother but she was trying her best. Sometimes she would sit in the office with father shifting papers, signing some, sorting out others and they would be discussing things seriously. This usually happened when we were out but sometimes when we were studying in our rooms. The strict instruction was not to neglect studies. Then one day he had what I thought was his last chemotherapy and he raised his hands and said with enthusiasm, 'This is the last one, then I am through'. He was working feverishly at home. One day he told me he had finished all pending work. Now he would have time and we shall only enjoy. I ran to Asim to give him the good news and he only stared at me. I asked him, 'What is wrong with you, can't you even smile?' In response he only showed his teeth in a sardonic grin and ruffled my hair, a rare affectionate gesture from him. I stuck out my tongue at him and then he smiled. It seems I was the only one in the house who did not know that chemotherapy had failed and there was nothing else to be done. He was a terminal case.

I shall never forget that morning when I was awakened by mother's loud crying and I thought of the night when she cried in my lap. Why is she crying now? I walked groggily and went where she was and found that father was dead. I do not remember what my immediate reaction was. I probably smiled, that is what dad always wanted me to do. I had a nice smile. Father was smiling too, a smile fixed on his still face. Was he smiling when he died? Last night mother came to lie down in my bed. This was not unusual before his illness, but had never occurred since he was ill. I was a bit surprised but not much. Children do not analyze all actions of their parents, at least not when they are half asleep. I was happy that she had come and cuddled against her and had a deep sleep. But why did father ask her to sleep with me? He must have asked or else she would not have come. Did he know he would die that night? How? Did he want to face death alone? I shall never know. I could not ask mother. She was crying continuously and never afterwards to bring back that devastating memory. But in my mind I felt that father wanted to face death alone as he had done in all family crises to protect us from trauma. He must have had some premonition. Much much later I would recount the day again and again and feel that he wanted to face death alone without fear and almost challenged it to come and take him with a smile on his face as the man he was. I felt very proud of him. Mother felt guilty for a time, but I suppose she also gradually realized that she could have done very little and felt proud of her husband. Even to the last moment he protected her. If this was deliberate he was such a great man, greater than we ever knew! I have carried two cabinet size photographs of my father and mother all my life wherever I went; not only because they were my parents, but because they were a great couple. Father shouldered every misfortune, every problem whether in family or profession without blaming or demanding or getting angry, and mother had been beside him since childhood supporting, caring and loving him as an intellectual partner and wife from the first to the last day. They met in chaos, married in chaos and separated in chaos never complaining.

And Mother

I was reading for the umpteenth time the piece I had written the day after I had cleared the Masters with high credits. My dissertation received a special prize that won me a scholarship to do my Ph.D. On graduation day I was proud and glad but there was no one to share my joy. I looked around at the proud parents everywhere, but there was none for me. Through the ceremony I sniffed continuously in my handkerchief and surreptitiously wiped my eyes once or twice. By the end of the day the handkerchief was all wet. As soon as the ceremony was over I ran to my room, threw myself on the bed and cried my heart out. By the time I had exhausted my tears there was a knock on the door and I rubbed my face, combed my hair, rearranged my dress, and then opened the door to find Bob standing at the door with a melancholy face. I grabbed his neck, hid my face in his best suit and started another bout of crying spoiling the suit, and then retracted, trying to repair the damage, but still crying. He grabbed me by the waist and brought me inside the room and sat me down looking at my face and lending me his handkerchief. As I was spoiling that one too, he said calmly, 'Cry as much as you can but it has to stop sometime.' He stroked my head, lifted my chin and cleared the hair that had fallen all over my face and looked at me calmly and touched my cheek with a tenderness that I have not known since I left home. That night sitting alone in my room I was ruminating my life, and my parents', going over my sensations since I was a child and the cultures and experiences through which I was travelling like a dinghy carried by a fast moving stream I do not know where. Western culture would consider such contemplation as mystical; life as a journey through many births towards God or *nirvana* was supposed to be an eastern idea. The western idea of life was based on what you aim and get, be decisive and conduct your life on what you want to do and go step by step where you decide to go, with God as your witness. In our long discussions Bob and I agreed that both play a part in our lives. To deny one for the other would not be an intelligent choice. Bob was knowledgeable on early Christian history and said that in the theological confusions of the early centuries, at some point of time through the four ecumenical councils from 325 CE at Nicea to 451 CE at Constantinople, the concept of transmigration of the soul and reincarnation were rejected by Christianity through voting. In modern times they are being reborn in Christian nations as New Age movements and Regression Psychoanalysis, which is bizarre. I said Hinduism of all sects and Buddhism believe in rebirth and it is integral to our social psyche. There are many proved cases of children remembering their past lives, but it is not considered an advantage, actually the opposite, and the sooner forgotten the better. The immortal soul or *Atman* going through rebirths may be nice to believe. But viewing the past life with the same father, mother, brother by regression psychoanalysis for some benefit in this life is too much to believe and smacks of commercial use of a philosophical concept. That night I wrote the history of my life so far, as this life had enough to teach me without going to my past lives. Accustomed to keeping notes on my studies and ideas arising in my mind, I started writing notes on my life lest I forget its details later.

I must introduce Bob here. Mr. Robert Lind immigrated to USA as an infant with his parents. His name was changed when he entered school to conform to the new society. His father carried the Dutch surname of van der Linde. Most immigrants have to do that to make it easier for tongue-tied Americans and an easy nickname helps to be in with the crowd. I have no such problem as my name Rupa Roy is both easy and could be from anywhere, now that Indian names are becoming fashionable in the west. That way Bengali Indians are lucky because most of us have names that can be pronounced easily unless parents have the funny inclination of drawing rare names from mythology that even Indians find difficult to pronounce. I have known folks who have had to amputate their names either at the head or tail. The funniest ones were the Europeans with tongue twisting names. Look at the Greeks, Pannayotis sliced to Pano or just Pan and to think of the impoverished royalty and aristocrats of Europe with all those titles! One day Bob and I made a list of the most audacious and possible amputations and had a lot of laugh. Bob's father was an engineer, a first generation immigrant who got an important job in an aircraft factory not far from town and used to commute from home.

When Bob was in the eighth grade his father died in a car crash, actually a pile-up in fall frost. Bob's mother was a school teacher back home but it took time to make a home in a new country and get certification as a primary school teacher. His mother somehow managed to keep the house and keep Bob in school and then send him to a respectable college after high school. Bob's academic brilliance was a help and as a research assistant doing Ph.D. he now had the job of assistant librarian on the evening shift at the college library. Things are better now but Bob has to help his mother. When we first met I was richer because of my scholarship. Now he is richer but he has responsibilities. And another thing he has in short supply and that is time. Our dates are mostly eating doughnuts together during a break under one of the trees in the campus and this is how we met, eating doughnuts day after day as afternoon snack in college cafeteria. Bob used to say that if ever anybody made a film on us it would be titled The Doughnut Affair. He has this great attribute of looking at life on the funny side in spite of being very serious in nature, and we laughed and laughed all the time. Ours is a deep friendship and nothing more. His European reserve and genteelness and my Indian reserve are complementary. I sometimes wonder whether he at all considers me a woman, that is a female vanity and I quickly brush it off. He once took me home to meet his mother and she is as mothers normally are all over the world. I thought that probably because I knew only one mother, mine. But generally the Indian view of the West, derived mainly from films, gives a distorted picture except to the discerning. Especially the western academic life is all hard work with virtually no free time even in weekends. The holidays are few and far between and taken up by chores that are not possible at other times. My free time is spent mostly by talking to mother, that is one luxury in which I happily indulge. International calls from USA are cheaper and I call and go on chatting without looking at the clock, asking for her opinion on everything including Bob, and her inevitable reply is 'Do what you

think best, I have full confidence in your judgment baby,' she still calls
me a baby. She also says she looks forward to meeting Bob some day.

Mother was confident about my judgment but I was not. There was
something missing in our relationship that I could not put a finger
on. We were no doubt very good friends but it stopped there. There
was a thin line between us and we were not in real love. We had long
interesting conversations but never a heart to heart talk or taking
chances with each other like touching and holding. We would kiss but
not furtively, more of a formal smooch or a peck on the cheek. He had
other female friends of course and I was not jealous, or may be just
a little bit, but his behaviour with them was more casual and playful.
With me it was more serious. I used to take that as mutual respect and
a serious relationship. I was not experienced in love, never having had
an affair before, and I could not discuss it with anybody. I took it as
an Indian girl would take it. Only if mother were here! I had no close
girl friend either. This sort of affair would be normal in India of those
days that I had left behind but I did not know what to expect here in
America. Other girls whispered and giggled among themselves as girls
do, but they would shut up and be polite when I joined. I remained a
foreigner even with my boy friend, not knowing what to expect in my
new country of residence.

We never even had a fight. How do you know you are in love if you do
not have a fight! Only once there was something if it could be called a
fight. He kissed a girl in my presence, the same smooch that I thought
was reserved for me. I left the place and did not turn up at our usual
place for three days. On the fourth day he accosted me or rather I made
myself visible for him to come running. That pleased me no end. He
asked, 'Are you very busy or are you making yourself scarce?'

I replied nonchalantly, 'Could be both.'

He asked, 'Why so?'

'Which one would you want to hear busy or I made myself scarce?'

'Let us have the second one first.'

'Well, I am still a foreigner here, so not familiar with the ways of people, not a great deal.'

'So what has that to do with being scarce?'

I fumbled and stammered, 'Thought I should mix with more people and get to know how they behave and what is friendship and what is love, what is the social norm'—and I had the urgent need to inspect my nails.

He screwed up his eyes and looked intently at me for a minute may be, and then laughed loudly, 'I get it now it is Mary, is it not?'

I was flustered, 'Who is Mary?'

He was still laughing, 'The girl I kissed the other day. I knew the moment you turned around and left. We have been together since kindergarten, more like a sister. She too noticed you leaving and said there goes your girlfriend. Can I make amends now?' And he grabbed me then and there and kissed so hard that I thought my lips would start bleeding and there was a hoorah all around.

I was ashamed for I knew I had been stupid, at least not intelligent enough. Angry with myself, I pushed him away and walked away fast. He chased me and asked what was the matter and I replied angrily, 'We Indians do not make a public demonstration of our love. I did not like my first lesson of love in the great America.' He did not stop walking with me, and chase to a more secluded spot to hold me and kiss me tenderly. I disengaged myself and walked back to my room without a word. He stood looking at me for some time and went back. I was not able to decide whether I was happy, not so happy or unhappy. But I could not leave Bob. He was my only friend and thought that time would give me the answer.

The only family member I could talk to was Asim but he was in the West Coast. We talked often on phone. Our first meeting was nearly six months after I arrived. I was received at New York by a close friend of my father and I stayed for a week in his house as auntie helped me to get over the jet lag and see places of interest. Then uncle reached me to my college on the appointed day. Asim came to meet me on a long weekend. I was eagerly waiting for him and talk to him about everything we have left behind. The first thing he asked for after entering my room was a beer as he was very thirsty. I had none, so I asked what about a fruit juice or a coke, and he said he would rather have cold water. Reminiscing our life in Bombay was the last thing in his agenda. He knew nothing about Calcutta. He still harboured resentment against his country of origin, peppered now by a false American aggressiveness. It was impossible to talk about our father. The deep scar of his illness and death was still raw. In his opinion, everything that was done to father was wrong. The doctors were ignorant idiots and rascals. He gave me points one after another where his treatment went horribly wrong. He resented that father did not come to America for treatment that he or his company could afford. I meekly quoted American death statistics that only increased his anger. 'How would you know that Father's disease was not that advanced, you were only a baby?' he shouted. So I meekly ask, 'What do you want to have for dinner, what shall I cook?' He laughed loudly and said, 'No cooking little sis, nobody cooks at home in America except in families. You are not a family and I am not a family. We shall go out, be my guest. I have done my home work and there are nice joints in this town. Let us go out and have dinner and dance. I bet you have not seen any of them.' I do not have a car so he called up a car hire. I said it would be expensive and he retorted, 'You are not to worry about that. You cannot survive in America if you count chickens all the time. It is a go get country. The more you spend the more you will earn, that is how this country works, reverse of what we learnt in poor India.'

So I kept mum and dressed as well as I could in western clothes. Asim looked at me with appreciation and said, 'Sis you are so good looking, a stunning beauty when you dress like this leaving your stupid Indian clothes. I can say there won't be another like you, you will be the craze of this evening.' He frightened me even before I stepped out. 'The joint' turned out to be a nicely decorated hall with a large dancing floor, a long bar with bar stools and some tables and chairs. Asim ordered too much food. The food was not bad but nothing special. Asim started boozing the moment he landed and it went on. I tried to caution him once but he got irritated. As we finished eating the dancing started and it was a good band. They played some old numbers and then went to jazz and then God knows what. Growing up in Bombay, dance was nothing new to me and as a matter of fact I was a good dancer in our girls' school. The floor was filling up with new people coming in, those that came only for dance and drink, and some of them looked doubtful characters. But then I had no experience of such places. I danced a couple of dances with Asim and then two modern, one foxtrot and one Charleston, not expertly but so so and it was fun. And then Asim vanished to the bar and I was left standing and the crowd went mad. I was grabbed from one corner of the floor to the other, not able to stop and go to my seat, I have not faced such grabbing ever in my life. I looked for Asim and he was at the bar gulping booze and not coming to my rescue. I then tore myself free, came to our table and broke a glass with loud bang and started for the exit door. I went to get my coat and a couple of fellows still following. Asim turned up groggy with the effusive apologies of a drunk. I was beginning to know America and maturing fast as a woman.

We reached my room and he fell flat on my only sofa, thankfully leaving me the bed. Next day he slept past midday. He had to catch an early evening flight. I cooked an authentic Bengali dinner as I sometimes did on holidays. I woke him up. He washed and became decent and then sat down for early dinner. He looked at the spread and sat down demurely. He ate, lustily appreciating each item and finished most. 'I did not know you cooked so well just like mother cooked' and tears welled up in his eyes that he failed to suppress with effort. I could not help crying and made no effort suppressing either the sound or the flow of tears. He got up, washed his hands and hugged me from behind, kissing me on the head and saying sorry repeatedly. I could only say through my crying 'Can't you get a cook like me for yourself,' I felt so dreadfully sorry for him. He sighed, caressed my head, and shoulder, and said, 'Sorry sis, I have gone too far, I don't have the luck.' I retorted angrily, 'No, you have not gone too far, you can always turn around with effort, you are your father's son, you have a good well paid job and you are in America where effort has its rewards, you must try or else I shall tell mother.' The last word worked like an electric shock. He straightened up and took up his bag and said, 'It is not easy, the reputation precedes you'. I jumped up, 'What reputation, that you are alcoholic? You have not gone to drugs, have you? No, OK, why don't you come to this town and keep in touch with me.' He took a deep breath like a drowning man, and said, 'ok sis, stay well, bye,' and walked out.

After that day I used to call him more frequently. The conversations were not long but he seemed to be cooling down. I had threatened him that I would tell mother and I did, not in all the gory details but enough. Mother started writing long letters to him as letters are more effective than phone calls and email messages. Letters stay as long time reminders unless thrown away, and even then. Mother used to say that with emails and phone calls we have forgotten the art of transmitting emotions. Letters are a form of literature and move minds. Mother wrote to friends and relations in the USA, sharing her concerns about both of us, trying to create a caring circle around us. I did not mind as I had nothing to hide, least of all Bob, as everybody liked him. My mother is great. Something happened in the last few days and I have started writing this piece at the weekend because of that.

A few days back my professor who guides my research sent me a note asking me to meet him at his office. I wondered why and went to meet him. When I entered he was sitting at his table with some journals before him. As I was sitting down he asked me to come to his side of the table. When I was beside him he took the latest number of Nature and pointed to a page that carried a letter to the editor. Published letters in the magazine are not full scientific articles but opinions or observations on some intricate scientific problems of the day. As I said they are not original papers but paperlets, if I can use the term, more in the nature of suggestions or insights backed by some facts or preliminary work, mathematical or otherwise. It is rare for Nature to publish letters, and not more than one, if at all, comes out in one number. The letter that he was pointing to was on physics. I thought that this was something related to my work and started reading. He told me, 'No, don't read now, you can do that later. Look at the bottom of the article for the writer's name'. And the name was Seema Roy!

I was speechless, looking once at my teacher and then at the journal incomprehensibly. He asked softly, 'Who is she, do you know her,' an impish smile playing on his lips. Incredulously I asked, 'My mother?' He was now even more mischievous, 'How would I know? Look at the name of the institution given below, the city. I thought you should know? Why ask me?' He still held that smile. Now I got it and with a shout, and jumping up and down, I kept on saying, 'My mother, my mother,' and tried to snatch the magazine from him. He said, 'Wait a minute, this copy is mine. If you want it won't you say please?' I said, 'Please please please' and he gave me the journal and I started running, and then stopped suddenly. He asked, 'What happened?' In a dazed voice I asked, 'Where shall I take it?' Now he was laughing loudly and said, 'I have another copy so you can take this one anywhere you like. But if you have not made up your mind where to go, would you mind sitting down in that chair instead of jumping and tell me about your mother?' I dropped into a chair with a thud and staring at him with wide eyes, I started telling him about my mother from her young days as a student till father's death, as rapidly as I could as if I shall forget it if I did not tell quickly. I do not know how much he could follow but with a few pointed questions he filled in the gaps, and then asked, 'Did you or do you know whether she is still working?' I said, 'Yes, she has been given an honorary position without salary or rank in view of her past academic record to do whatever she wants.' My professor was tapping his fingers on the table and with an affectionate smile, said 'Well you can tell her if she wants rank and salary she may get them here.' I moved my head side to side and said, 'She will not come here'. He asked, 'Why' and I answered, 'Because of father.' He asked, 'But is he not dead, you just said so?' I said, 'Yes, he is dead but she lives in his house in his memory.' He looked incredulous, 'Living in memory and doing theoretical physics! What sort of people are you?' I jumped up, 'Good sort, can I go?' He laughed again and waved me out.

I ran to the nearest telephone and called Asim. At the third dialing he answered and complained, 'I am working, what is the hurry.' I blabbered in excitement and he understood nothing. 'What are you talking about,' he asked. I slowly said, 'You have heard the name of Nature?' He was irritated, 'Yes, so what?' 'You get the latest number and open at the last page you shall find mother's article. Read that and stop drinking' and I slammed down the phone. He rang at night, 'Sis what a great thing it is! Did you know she was working on such things?' I said, 'No I did not know but I now know that while his son can become an alcoholic in the sorrow and anger of prematurely losing his father the mother whose loss is irreplaceable and whose sorrow is deepest can work on the most difficult problems of Physics.' For the first time he was not angry at complaining about his drinking and says, 'Come on, stop ragging so much, I have almost given up drinking. Instead say something sensible. Shall I hook up a conference with mum, the three of us, later tonight, when she gets up from bed?' I jumped up receiver in hand, 'Yes yes, let us do that. But do not give her a surprise, her heart is getting weaker. I shall call her first and then when she is ready I shall call you and you set up the conference. I am calling her right away, no not now, a little later. She may not have heard yet that her letter has been published. The journal reaches India late. So we, rather you shall be the first to give her the news and I shall tell her of the job offer here that I know she will promptly refuse. But still it is worth trying, at least as a visiting scientist for a few weeks. We shall have a gala time.'

We did as we planned. At first she could not understand and then she was happy. She said, 'I was told that it would come out but did not know in which number. The journal has not yet reached us. I shall see when I get it.' Then a bombshell fell on Asim, 'Have you now stopped drinking'? Asim muttered, 'Yes mum I am trying'. Then another for me, 'Have you and Bob decided on marriage yet?' My muted answer was, 'No mum, not yet.' Mother said, 'Ok, I shall ask the doctor whether I can go to the USA on a short stint, employment is out of question. He advises me against going because of my heart. I shall ask again.' I asked this time, 'What is wrong with your heart mum'? She answered, 'Nothing much, just old age. In any case both of you straighten up your lives so that I can die in peace and think about visiting me once together.' Click, that was that and connection was cut.

That was our mother. Children were more important than a paper in Nature. Not careless about health but not overcautious.

Backtracking

It is autumn now. The festival of Durgapuja is round the corner. The holiday mood has set in. I remember the excitement of my childhood. Everybody becomes a child in this season. Torn white clouds float down an emerald blue sky after the monsoon season is over. But now seasons have changed with climate changes and it is raining heavily beyond my window as I sit lazily on this Sunday. A Bengali, wherever he may be in the world, looks up at the sky this time of the year and comes home to his childhood even if for a moment. He thinks of the milk white fields of wild *kash* flower, a beauty you cannot grab, cannot bring home, cannot possess, can only enjoy from afar, for if you grab, the white fluff comes off and attaches to your hands and dress, and as a child you just laugh and run. You cannot uproot it and take it home for the fluff and petals will fall off by the time you reach. It is like life itself, enjoy it and it endures, try to grab it and it slips through the fingers. In a way it is the life of Bengal, a riverine terrain of soft alluvial soil, the rivers changing course breaking one side and rebuilding the other. Life and achievements go down in the river on one side and new ground comes up on the other to rebuild, to rejuvenate. Monuments man's arrogance creates are washed away; nothing remains for ever, for long. I dream the scene in Satyajit Ray's *Pather Panchali* where little Durga and Apu are running through the vast fields of *kash* flowers towards the railway track far beyond, with a train coming. In one master stroke life's drama is painted—running through an ephemeral dream towards the reality of modernity, but only the dream is real. I do not know anyone round the globe whose heart has not been touched by that scene. In a way it is as our life is. Man's civilizations arose beside the rivers and the seas and the undulating waves created the waves of their lives, it started in the jungles and the mountains, and he forever desires to climb and struggle through the weeds, whether in ancient jungles or in the modern jungles of concrete and steel. Somehow I think of Manhattan and Wall Street.

That wakes me up with a start from my reverie and the first thing I think of is my children in that country. They could be lonely. As I think of America I smile as I remember my undeserved, unsought, newfound fame that continues. Fame is like death, it changes life. I remember Jean Paul Sartre running away and hiding from the Nobel Prize. Thankfully in my case it is not so big but it is changing my life. I was glad to get a place at the Institute not because I would do something great. I loved to play with the mathematical figures as children love to play with toys as I used to love as a child that I still remember. Plus the environment, the muted excitement, the bright eyed enthusiastic youth who love me and call me grandma, I love it all. They are so young, so vibrant, so unconcerned about the world around, at least most of them are, that they take me to another world. The men and women are both intellectually aggressive, no meekness or inhibition even in women that was expected in our young days and we suffered.

One day a very famous professor came to visit us and delivered a lecture. That was not unusual. We have visitors regularly as we have some eminence in the world of science. The professor delivered a lecture on Quantum Reality, the problems at the boundary of micro and macrocosms. I love the subject and love to hear the lectures juggling with Quantum mechanics and such exotic things as Multiple Universe and String Theory. When the speakers get animated they look like children, rubbing hands in glee at some clever point and then hee-hawing when they are not sure what they are talking about. This lecture was particularly nice. At the end of the lecture the speaker invited questions and comments. A few hands were raised and to my utter surprise I found that my hand was also raised. It was totally involuntary. Amid all those young people and a few graying professors a sari clad white haired woman must have stood out like a lighthouse so that I was invited to speak first and not only that, I was called to the dais. He must have thought that I was the dean of some faculty or a visiting scientist like him. My legs trembled.

I must concede that at the end of the day I did not do so badly. It was not something earth—shaking, just plain common sense. When we try to wed Quantum Mechanics to Reality we tend to think that Reality is static. Crudely speaking, Reality is something we perceive with our five sense organs. We have another organ called mind. Here I am close to our very ancient philosophy of *Sankhya*. Mind is the perceptive organ of the senses and therefore influences our perception of Reality in a two way relationship—we may see what we imagine even if it is not there and we may not see what is there because the mind does not see; such experiences are not very rare. Our sense of Reality has changed through the evolutionary process over the centuries. From Descartes and Spinoza in the seventeenth century to the geometry of Lobachevsky, Bolyai and Riemann in the nineteenth and Einstein on Space and Relativity in the early twentieth century and then the knowledge of the Quantum world, there has been a sea change in the conception of Reality, even the ones we perceive with our senses, which is a two way relationship. Euclidean geometry and contemporary similar geometry in India, without going into the controversy which predates which, served humanity well, producing grand palaces, temples, churches and mosques and was the Reality. Similarly Newtonian mechanics is adequate to send man to the moon and send interplanetary rocket probes. But these Realities were changed by Einstein and later by Quantum Physicists and further new Realities would probably be needed for interstellar and intergalactic travel.

Feynman's work in quantum physics may indicate where the confusion occurs and clear some of the clouds. His most famous work is contained in his book QED, where he works out 'the strange theory of interaction of light and matter'. To emphasise the fundamental importance of this work I shall quote from another book. 'QED is so important because the interactions of electrons with one another and with electromagnetic radiation determine almost everything about the world around us. The world, and ourselves, are made of atoms, and atoms consist of a compact central nucleus surrounded by a cloud of electrons. The electrons are the visible 'face' of the atom, and interactions between atoms and molecules are really interactions between the electron clouds. The way electrons interact is by exchanging photons. An electron emits a photon, and 'recoils' in some way, or an electron absorbs a photon, and gets a 'kick'. Everything that happens when atoms interact can be explained in these terms. All of chemistry is explained by quantum physics, and specifically by QED, biological life depends upon the behaviour of complex molecules such as proteins and DNA, which is also chemistry and also depends, ultimately, on the quantum properties of electrons.' The quantum property of electrons also applies to light. Light does not really travel only in straight lines, but by every possible path through space from a source to an observer. It just happens that when one adds up the 'histories' they all cancel out except for the ones close to a straight line. This is what is known in quantum physics as 'path-integral' or 'summation of histories' approach and Feynman got the Nobel Prize for that. In Feynman's own words 'Light does not really travel only in a straight line, it 'smells' the neighbouring paths around it, and uses a small core of nearby space.' This statement made for ordinary people like us may create confusion as it implies volition or consciousness in the photon or electron.

But is this misconception totally wrong or is there an interface? Looking at the thing from another angle, to an observer like us who sees the light coming in a straight line, it is a Reality and others are Illusory, but to a quantum physicist photons swarming through all possible trajectories are a Reality and the straight line is only an Illusion. But both are true depending on how an individual mind looks at it. A boy studying in class five today will learn the first Reality and will learn the second one when he reaches the higher postgraduate level but fifty years from now he will probably start with the QED. So it is the mind that determines or comprehends the Reality and it is always relative to the previous one. Is it possible to go beyond the relative Realities to a supreme unalterable Reality? Does such a thing exist? Both physics and spirituality believe that it does exist and tries hard to find it. It is this faith that seems to be fundamental to the human mind and keeps mankind going and growing in mental capability; it is an act of faith.

Science is beginning to believe, though not universally, that for an understanding of ultimate Reality an understanding of the mind is essential. Spirituality knew it for a long time, but how it came to know that was not known? Mind is also not ultimate because its logic brings in a contrasting duality; a solution gives birth to a problem, which is only a step beyond. Spirituality found a place for the mind that is beyond logic; it may be that the mind vibrates and understands, in resonance to the surrounding world like a song and this faculty could be developed to vibrate in resonance to the universe. But if we go beyond the logic of the mind can something that is beyond be captured and analyzed by mind? If science ever reaches it, will it not be as incomprehensible to deductive logic as spirituality is? The physicist already says that all photon transfers over a large area of space or even the whole space are timeless, no past or future can be ascribed in the microcosmic world. Our eyes actually emit photons as part of an exchange with photons radiated from a source of light that may be as distant as the moon or Jupiter, but they do not show up in the everyday world because of the way the probabilities cancel out. But how do we know that the calculations of physics are right? We do that by verifying their predictions, the effects, and the reproducibility of the calculations by anyone who wishes to do so. The physicist exercises his mind beyond ordinary everyday experiences through the logic of mathematics and predicts effects that we then see and accept.

It is the same thing in spirituality—the effects prove the fundamental. And what is the mind? If eyes emit photons can the mind not emit energy that can interact with the vast strings of energy that vibrate through the universe? Electrons are actually known to move in and out of the human brain to the environment, for example, during induction and recovery from general anesthesia. That makes the whole universe one, including the human mind and, on our level, a conscious entity to us. In Reality who knows whether it is conscious or unconscious and what do the words 'conscious' and 'unconscious' mean? By what standards do we judge that? But as long as human beings remain, knowledge becomes a question of attainment, whether for the scientist or the spiritualist. As Vivekananda said a hundred years back, 'If you can simply get to that subtle vibration, you will see and feel that the whole universe is composed of subtle vibrations.' If this is mystical then many of the predictions and calculations of physics are mystical. The myth of yesterday is the Reality of today. If proof is necessary then the statement of Vivekananda delivered spontaneously in his Lahore lecture long before quantum physics and String theory were conceived is a proof and the knowledge existed even before that. Is it reproducible? Vivekananda has said yes. Is that statistically significant? Statistics would then have to handle infinite randomness. Quantum physics does not like infinity but studies a small area phenomenon to come to a generalization and predicts effects. If the predictions tally then the truth is accepted as general. This is a common interface of defining between science and mind or what may be called spirituality. But one must not transgress the logic of the other.

I stopped there already overextending my limited knowledge. The professor asked softly whether I have done any mathematical research on these lines and I shook my head in the negative. Then shyly I looked up and said, 'Just a little bit, nothing worth speaking about'. In his gentle kind voice he said, 'I shall be much obliged if you would be so kind as to let me know this little bit not worth speaking about in a letter,' and he extracted a card from his pocket and gave it to me. All the children, I call them children, broke out in applause and I had to spend money that day to entertain them with afternoon snacks. Little did I imagine that a month after I wrote, which took some time to write, I shall hear from Nature that my letter will be published shortly, recording the date of receipt of the manuscript.

Soon after the letter is published I get excited phone calls from my son and daughter. They are so excited that they can hardly speak coherently, words tumbling one over the other. And then there is the invitation to go to America and an invitation from their professor to join them, even have a job. I am so happy that my offspring are so proud of me. It is in some way good for them as it helps to make them balanced people responsible to the world and themselves. In my institute people look at me with a new heightened respect. All these are pleasing but not of much purport to me because I have no expectations. I am happy living as I am, in peace and quiet with my mind as company, without any need for extra accolades and least of all any change in my life. So I cool them down and remind them of their own responsibilities. I did the same as best as I could in my institute. But they gave me some extra space to work that I did not grudge. There was no question of funds as I did not need any and the financial health of the institute was precarious in any case.

Contacting

I do not remember exactly when it happened. It was probably months after all this hullabaloo. I was entering the institute one day when someone told me that I had a visitor who was waiting in the waiting room. I looked in. The room was empty apart from an old man sitting in one corner with his back turned towards the entrance. I walked towards him and standing in front of him asked whether he was looking for me and told my name. He looked up, an old creased face with scraggy half shaven beard as white as his hair and his right hand was shaking in obvious tremor. He just kept looking at me and I asked again 'My name is Seema Roy, were you looking for me?' A faint smile stretched his lips and he said 'yes' and in silence he only looked at me. Then in a flash I recognized; it was difficult after a gap of nearly fifty years. He tried to get up and was doddering, about to fall and I quickly grabbed his arms and steadied him and asked, not just in surprise but in shock, 'Are you Sarit?' After a pause he nodded his head in a somewhat funny movement with a smile on his lips, his hands trembling even as I gripped his elbows. I made him sit down in a comfortable position and pulled a chair and sat before him. Surprise, shock and bewilderment played in my mind and must have been obvious on my face as I asked, 'How did you find me?' He grabbed a book lying beside him and raised it to me and I saw it was that copy of Nature that had my letter. Tears came to my eyes that I suppressed and stammered as I asked, 'How are you, I mean what is the matter with you?' I remembered Ranajit's description of the robust young professor of astrophysics so many years back. He replied haltingly, 'I have Alzheimer's' and a spit formed at the angle of his mouth. I did not know whether Alzheimer patients can say what they are suffering from but quickly brushed off the thought because there are many variations of the disease. Instead an exclamation came out of my mouth, 'Why, I mean how, when? How could you find me? Why didn't you ring?' In reply he only raised the magazine. I understood he came to the address printed in the journal as he had no other clue. I asked again, 'Are you visiting Calcutta or live here?' To this he replied, 'I live' and tried to smile. I asked, 'Where do you live, at your old house?' He nodded in agreement. I told him, 'Let me take you home, do you have a transport,' and he shook his head looking down. I called my driver to bring the car to the front and helped him get up. I found a middle aged man outside the room as he came forward to help. I asked him who he was and he replied that he had worked for the family for many years and has been looking after the house and now he looked after Sarit.

I knew where his house was but had never entered it. It was not far. In the old distant days he sometimes gave me his car to drop me home after dropping him at his. It was a medium sized two storey house with a compound with signs of disuse written all over. The compound where there had been flower beds at one time was now unkempt with weeds covering most of the area. He got down from the car without help and looked back at me questioningly. I realized he was asking whether I would come in. I got down and accompanied him. We entered a drawing room which was dusty with old furniture most of which had seen better days, now in shambles. He took me to a room where obviously he lived and was comparatively clean with a bedstead and a couple of sofa with a table that had seen better days but usable. He went to a cupboard and took out a towel to wipe his mouth and carried it with him, and sat down. He pointed to the other sofa. I sat down and he asked, 'Tea,' and signaled to his attendant who went to make tea.

As we settled down I asked, 'How long have you been here?' He replied, 'One month.' I asked, 'Do you come here often?' He replied in the negative by shaking his head and said, 'Five years back.' I asked, 'Last time you came five years back? So why have you come now?' To this a smile broke out on his face, rather sweet smile like a child and he pointed at the magazine that I did not notice his man carrying from the car. In surprise I asked, 'Because of that article?' He was still smiling and nodded. In amazement I asked, 'You came to see me after reading that letter?' With that same smile he nodded and said, 'Congratulations.' He could not pronounce last part of the word clearly and wiped his mouth with the towel. He was conscious of his drool. 'What about your family in USA?' I asked. He said, 'No family,' still with that smile. I wondered whether the smile was part of the disease or deliberate. I got the answer as his man came with the tea and as he took the cup and sipped once, the smile was not there. As both of us had a sip and put the cups on the table, I asked, 'You never married?' The smile came back and he shook his head. 'Who looked after you there?' and this time the answer came, 'A nurse and I looked after myself'—without the smile. I realized that social service provided a nurse to come and look after whatever needed to be looked after and the rest he managed himself. She probably cooked and shopped for him or brought half cooked food and kept in the freezer. He was looking at me and said gravely, 'I am not gone far,' and I was ashamed. I asked, 'Who would look after the house and other things over here? You need a lot of looking after in this city, and this is not America.' He pointed in the direction of the man who had probably gone to kitchen and said, 'He has been a long time.' I asked, 'How long do you plan to stay?' His answer was prompt, 'Not going back,' and his face was serious. That day I left with a heavy heart.

I continued coming off and on. I used to carry some food or other things he might need. If I asked whether he needed anything the inevitable answer was in the negative. Most of the time I saw him sitting in a chair on the veranda and staring vacantly at nothing. At other times I would find him on the bed not asleep but just staring at the ceiling. Whenever he saw me there was a childish glee, not knowing what to do and the smile would return. I saw that he could manage personal hygiene and took care of his clothes but often they were clumsy with no order or care. His Man Friday took care of shopping, cooking and cleaning his room, and he was equally silent. One day as I came he took me to the bedroom and left me there, but I could not find Sarit. As I looked around he came out of the bathroom after a bath, and seeing me in the room he was so startled that the towel wrapped around his middle dropped and he frantically tried to put it on and fumbled and uttered a groan like an animal. I ran to him and with motherly care settled his clothes and sat him on the bed. He started crying like a child who had misbehaved. That broke my heart. I realized that with no human contact his disease will get worse very fast and he will become crippled with no help. I made up my mind.

Next time I came he was relaxed, sitting on the veranda, and I talked and talked to make him laugh as a mother does, telling stories to a child. Then I said that I live alone in my house with nobody to talk to and suffer in the loneliness. Would he mind if I request him to come and live with me? I have a spare bedroom with attached bath and a cook and a maid who will look after him when I am out. And then when I come back we shall talk and have fun and have dinner together or else go out for dinner in some nice restaurant. I shall love to have somebody home to come back to and talk. Would he agree? He looked gravely at me for some time and then suddenly broke out in smile and glee and said, 'Live together?' I blushed scarlet and felt hot behind the ears and to hide the embarrassment laughed loudly and protested, 'No no, not in that way not 'livetogether', just live pause, and then together. We are too old for the first one. OK?' I need not have worried; his lucid period had gone as fast as it had come. I asked again, 'Well, how about that, would you agree?' He asked, 'How about what?' He had already forgotten. 'How about living in my house instead of living alone in your house?' His answer was bland, 'All houses are same.' I replied, 'So, ok, you are going to live in my house. This Sunday I shall come, take your things and move you to my house. Whatever else you need we can collect later.' He was silent, busy staring at something.

As I was driving back that day I was thinking deeply. Life plays such funny tricks! We cannot even see what is on the other side of a wall but we think we shall pass our life as we plan and what is present will last forever. Ranajit's death was a blow that shattered our life and I have changed so much since then. I do not know whether I am the same person I was; I am not in many ways. If he happened to see me today he probably would not recognize me. My life will now flow in a different channel that I did not foresee. Is his life also flowing in a different channel if it does flow? After his death I once asked a very holy monk whether there is life after death and are we born again and if so why. He answered gravely, 'Where do we come from, where do we go and why do we come are questions that have no answer. Does anybody know the answers?' I was surprised as I thought he would speak of life after and rebirth, as he was a venerable old Hindu monk. But he was not accustomed to talk much and his gravity was such that it was not possible to repeat the questions. He was absorbed in himself. I interpreted it to mean that our only task was this life and to pass it with responsibility, purity and ethically, beyond that we have no way of knowing and should not worry. I also felt that there were perhaps deeper meanings and other ways of interpreting those words. Our realizations and experiences of life and the philosophy we form is our own and not always understood even by us in clear terms though it enriches us but is not transmittable. It is like realizing God, an experience that cannot be transmitted and will not be understood by others. I thought, did Ranajit know I shall meet Sarit one day when he left that letter for me? It is said that men become clairvoyant in the face of imminent death. But I ruled that out too.

I was in such deep thought that I almost woke up from a dream when I reached home. I was busy the next few days arranging the house. The other bedroom on the first floor was across a small hallway from my room that was used as a dining place with a small table and chairs. I thought that bedroom would be best for Sarit. I could keep an eye on him. He probably had difficulty negotiating stairs. I did not know how far he was gone and he could saunter out if he was on the ground floor. He could be helped down to the back garden by the gardener if he wanted. I remembered his one expression of 'live together' but discounted it. I could take care of myself. I thought of what other people, especially my children would think and whether I was doing the right thing but my conscience told me I was doing the right thing. I told the gardener and his wife that my distant cousin, a brother, was very sick and I am bringing him home as he had nobody to look after him. I gave a short description of his disease and what to expect. I knew that a payment from his account in USA reached a local bank every month as I asked him how he managed his expenses and the upkeep of the house. Probably his attendant had the authority to withdraw cash. That has to be looked into.

So my new life started. How many lives one has to pass through in one life? The answer is many; we pass through all of them in one

life without prior knowledge and we see it as a continuum and worry
about death! After initial adjustments it was not really bad. Sarit was a
quiet man immersed within himself most of the time. In the beginning
I did not go very close to him. Then I realized that mentally he was
like a child who could look after his personal hygiene and that was
all. He made no attempt to get intimate nor did he ever thank me.
The gardener and his wife looked after him well. Their attitude was
of tending to a good natured child with obvious affection. They had
no children of their own. The uneducated people acting on instinct are
more natural than we educated ones who tend to judge and are rigid.
I wondered how Sarit got the impetus to take the decision to come to
Calcutta after reading my article. It was not possible unless the feeling
was strong. Did he remember me that much after all these years?
Sometimes old memories persist but more recent ones are forgotten.
Was my memory that strong in his mind? I had no sense of guilt but
then I had something I could not define. There was another unexpected
thing. Among his belongings was a Stradivarius violin in its case. Did
he play the violin? I asked him once but he did not reply. One day I
took the violin out of its case and put it before him and asked him to
play. He looked at me without responding and then shifted his gaze out
of the window and sat silent.

A few days later I came back late from work. Since Sarit's arrival
I hardly went anywhere other than work. It was evening when I
reached home. As I reached the front door I heard the sound of violin
coming from the house. Without disturbing anybody I opened the
front door with my key and tiptoed upstairs from where the music
was coming. Sarit was playing in his room and the gardener couple
was seated in front on the floor, wiping tears from their eyes. Sarit
was in a trance, oblivious of his surrounding playing with passion.
I stood transfixed at the hallway door. The notes were tearing at my
heart. I know very little of this music but I could not suppress my
tears and ran to my room and put my face in the pillow and cried.
There was such pathos and its intensity made more profound by
occasional notes of laughter. Music lies deep in the brain and he is
bringing it out from there. The music stopped after some time but
it was reverberating in the house. I do not remember how long I lay
in bed. When the gardener's wife brought food and called me I got
up and went to Sarit. He sat still. I put the violin carefully back in

its case. I held his hand and bade him to come for dinner. He rose like an automaton and came to the table, picked at his food and went back to his room to lie down. He did not reply to a single question of mine. Next day I went for my usual short morning walk in the nearby park. My next door neighbour, an elderly gentleman, also used to walk but we had never talked. That day he addressed me with folded hands and asked me, 'Excuse me, who was playing violin in your house last night? He was playing pieces from Mozart's Requiem Mass. It was Mozart's last composition and he was convinced that he was writing his own funeral music. It was brilliant.' Without saying another word he went away shaking his head.

That day I could do no work. I looked up Wolfgang Amadeus Mozart in the encyclopedia and read about his life and music. I read about Alzheimer but found very little about music memory. I asked one colleague who was knowledgeable about western classical music and he raised his eyes when I mentioned Mozart and asked whether that was my next project and little else. I went to a music shop and listened and bought a couple of Mozart CDs. I returned home early and Sarit was asleep like a baby. I did not want to disturb him but I was disturbed myself. How little we know of a human life and even there we make our own picture and paste it on another. The man I brought to my house was an exceptional man. A famous scientist, an adventurer, a man of classical refinement, but everything has been blocked in his brain. A self contained and contented man, who did not need a family, did not need wealth, must have had admiring friends but now has nothing. Why did he have to come here for what, for an unfulfilled childhood love? That is impossible. He could have that love a hundred times where he spent his life. May be he was deeply hurt in some way and that made him a recluse and as his disease progressed the childhood is where he wanted to go back to, like his music. My name in Nature brought back his memory of childhood. I am not a lost love but a marker of his childhood that he remembered and came back to. His whole life is a blank page I know nothing about, yet in my house he found solace. What can I do apart from giving him a shelter? There is nothing else I can give that he can understand.

I thought of enriching his life as much as I could. I purchased a good music system for him and a collection of CDs of classical music, some modern, to see whether he liked it. He played some of them but was generally apathetic. One day I asked him with my new found knowledge, 'Why do you play only sad music, can't you play for example Eine Kleine Nacht Musik?' His face glowed with smile and he opened the violin and started playing the Waltz dance music that was considered vulgar in the Austro-Hungarian Empire. He started jumping to the rhythm sitting on bed as he was playing. I was so caught in the rhythm and his joy that I started swaying and clapping to the rhythm. And so went our duet I on the floor and he on the bed. Never did he come on the floor, I doubt if he could, nor did he want to touch me. It was so bizarre but we enjoyed thoroughly. So went our evenings not necessarily with music, I would talk mostly and he would respond in monosyllables or unintelligible sounds. Sometimes I would read to him that would make him tired and he would fall asleep. He never touched books as if he was allergic to them, apart from that particular copy of Nature. If a name had to be given to our relationship I suppose it had to be called 'love undefined,' for there was no desire or possessiveness, so not even a mother and child love. He did not miss me when I was not home, probably even forgot, but was happy when he saw me. In a nutshell he was the thing I missed in life and did not know until I had it.

Life went on like this and then a letter arrived from Asim that he was in between jobs and wanted to spend one or two months with me. He wrote he was a good boy now and free of the drinking habit and others. He changed after seeing how I withstood my sorrow and returned to productive life. That inspired him to change himself with a lot of effort and this new job he was going to was a prized one with a lot of responsibilities and he would not get another vacation for quite some time. He wanted to spend this time with me. I was very happy and alarmed at the same time, not knowing what his reaction to Sarit would be. I did not inform my children about Sarit as letters were not the ideal medium to break such unusual news. In spite of their love and respect for their mother, it is difficult to predict their reaction to a letter and to be honest I was a bit shy myself. I could send Sarit home but it would be too long a time and he might break down and get worse. It also hurt my pride to think that I want to hide him. I decided to take the chance and see how Asim would react to him. If he has really reformed and learned to accept the unexpected he would find Sarit harmless and I would know he has come of age and really reformed. I took the chance and prayed that everything went well for everybody. I made one change though. I shifted to the ground floor bedroom and rearranged my room for Asim.

Restructuring

I received the news from mother that Asim was going to spend some time with her at Calcutta with a mixed feeling of relief and worry. My last meeting with Asim, the second after I came to USA, was as shocking and traumatic as the first and it has aged me and taught me many things. This experience I hope will always remain with me and will never need to be revealed to anybody. I used to ring him up during the weekends, not every weekend but most. During the week he used to be busy and was irritated if called. The day I read mother's article in Nature was an exception. But there came a time not long back when I could not get him through one whole weekend even with repeated calls till late at night. I thought he had probably gone out for the weekend. But the same thing happened the following weekend and I got worried. Next I called during the week in a late evening when he was expected to be home. There was no reply but I kept calling at intervals. After the third or fourth call a voice answered, thick and groggy. It was not Asim. Still I asked, 'is that you Asim?' The thick voice answered 'wha, whadya saay?' Frightened I shout, 'Asim.' Recognition dawned and the voice said, 'Ow ya, Ass. Who are ya honey calling so late? Ya lonely? Com ova, no problem.' I asked, 'Who are you?' 'Me? Me mister Fish, Fish an Ass'—and he guffawed. Still persisting I command as harshly I could, 'Give the phone to him.' Fish replies, 'No way, he gone far.' I ask, 'Where?' He laughs hysterically, 'High, high, no gonna come down now.' Frightened I drop the phone.

My mind in turmoil, I kept thinking. After considering all alternatives I decide to pay him a visit all by myself. I cannot take anybody with me least of all Bob. But I do not dare to land in an unknown city in the evening. I book an early flight next Saturday morning and take a taxi to his address. I arm myself with a spray that Bob has given me to ward off anybody with a single hit on the face. The building is a medium apartment house in an old quarter for small families or people living singly. I give Asim's name to the single guard and tell him I am his sister. He looks quizzically at me and lets me pass. I hold the spray in my hand and press the bell. I see that a neighbour's door is ajar, some consolation! Asim's door is opened by a half naked weirdo with a splash of colours, half shaved head and piled up hair, the sort I have seen on roads but do not know what they are called, Bob has never told me. As much in fear as anger I shout as loudly as I could, 'Get out or I am calling police' holding up my spray and the phone. He was startled, still in the process of waking up, and backed into the room. I follow him and shout again that wakes up Asim in the stinking studio apartment. I spot the man's shirt and throw it out of the door and repeat my command and he gingerly goes out. I slam the door shut.

I look back at Asim not knowing how to start a conversation. It was he who spoke first, 'Why are you here?'

'To see how you are,' was my cautious reply.

'And what do you see?'

'What I see is not very nice. What have you done to yourself? You do not pick up the phone when I call, never ring me,' and I started sobbing.

He sinks back to bed and says nonchalantly, 'I live the way I like. I do not care about anybody's comment on how I live,' with a special emphasis on 'not'.

I was angry and sad at the same time and not finding the time suited for conversation I ask for his door keys. He asked why and I said I have to do some shopping and I found stores in the next block. As he looked around for the keys I spotted them on the only table in the room and picked them up. Then I asked him to go to the bathroom and have a shower while I come back with what I need. He was still too groggy to reply and I slip out. I remind him not to lock the door from inside. He only stared at me.

I came back with groceries, fresh linen and table cloth, room fresheners and flowers. I came back as quickly I could and he was still in the shower and I could hear the sound. Feeling relieved I drop the groceries in the kitchen piled with dirty utensils thrown here and there and come back to the room. I remove the dirty linen from the bed and others scattered around the room and make up the bed nicely. There was a dirty linen chest in a niche beside a tiny balcony and I drop them there. I opened the windows to air the room and clean up as much as possible. I spray the room freshener liberally. Then I spread a table cloth on the sole table removing everything from it to an almost empty bedside cabinet. Surprisingly there was not a single book in the room and Asim was an avid reader! I put the flowers in something that could be used as a vase and put it at the centre of the table. By the time I had gone this far Asim came out of the bathroom wearing a towel and halted. Not taking any notice of his surprise I looked sideways from what I was doing and said, 'There are fresh towels on the back of the chair. Drop the old ones in the bathroom. I shall wash them or throw them away on merit,' and smiled at him. He obeyed.

I entered the kitchen. The task here was heavier with a pile of dirty and crusted pans and pots, the oven splashed with all kinds of things. I quickly cleaned one and made fried eggs and bacon and hot coffee and a few rolls heated in the microwave. I placed them on the table and called out, 'Will you please come to the table? I am famished.' He obeyed gingerly and started eating, slow at first and then in a manner that showed he had been starving. Tears came to my eyes and I ran to the kitchen to replenish. I had some cheese and a jar of marmalade and some more rolls and bacon and coffee and they disappeared fast. When he seemed satisfied I pulled him, holding his hand and asked him to come to bed saying, 'It seems you need some more sleep. Sleeping after breakfast is the nicest thing for me,' and he obeyed. I put him on the cleaned and perfumed bed, drew the blanket on top, closed the windows and turned the air conditioner on. Without saying anything I entered the kitchen to bring some order there. When I looked in he was in deep sleep like a baby.

I put the kitchen in order. I had brought cleaning and scrubbing things and I restored the pans and pots as many as I could. Those that were beyond redemption I discarded and put in a corner. I cleaned out the refrigerator and the cupboards, nothing much to remove there. After restoring the kitchen to health I arranged the groceries I had brought and started to cook. I cooked general Bengali food and one special meat dish without much spice. After that I started with the apartment, the things I could not do in the morning. It was a decent sized studio apartment with good furniture and a lot could be done with it. In one corner there was a decent sofa cum bed and some settee that I brushed and rearranged. There was a combo bookshelf cum television with a few old books. The balcony had a good view and I removed some rubbish from there. By the time Asim woke up late in the afternoon the apartment was looking livable. We sat down for a late lunch. Asim liked the food and ate the major portion. I did the dishes and came back to the room to find him seated in a settee and I occupied the other and smiled.

He commented, 'The apartment is not too bad after all, looking nice. You had a lot to do.'

I said, 'Not a lot, just a little week end cleaning,' and remained silent, deciding to let him do most of the talking.

He demurely said, 'Needs a feminine touch.'

I said, 'Not necessarily. Bob keeps his much smaller room in good order.'

He asked, 'How is your boy friend? Are you in love, I mean real love?'

I knew what he meant and felt a bit warm behind the ears and said, 'I am not sure yet.'

He said, 'Be careful, no harm in waiting and remaining just friends.'

I got my opening and asked, 'How about you, any girlfriends, anyone close?'

He laughed, 'Plenty, which actually means none.'

I asked, 'Why not?'

He looked uncomfortable, 'You are returning my question.'

I said, 'No, we are discussing like brother and sister, not probing.'

He was silent for some time and then said, 'Our situations are different.'

'In what way are they different?'

'In many ways. First, you are in a university environment. Men and women are in the same age group with similar levels of culture and education. I am a working man in a business even if it is a knowledge business with people of different age groups, different backgrounds and different life experiences. Second, as a woman in your environment you are generally sought after by your own kind. As a man in my environment if I am sought after it could be of a different kind, different on both sides.'

'I do not understand in what way it is different.'

'Oh sis, it is difficult to talk about these things with a young sister I have grown up with as children.' Then after a long pause to think he said, 'But I shall try.' I waited.

After another long pause he seemed to surface from a dive, took a deep breath and in a rush blurted out, 'As a first generation foreigner with no background of wealth and family I am not a prize catch for the role of a husband or for a long relationship. I am a fly by night curiosity for one night stand or may be a couple, enough. With my background I would like to have some meaningful relationship, but every time I dream I suffer a crash. I have rolled through a lot of relationships of that kind with a sensation that I am only a performer giving sexual pleasure to a woman who did not mean to go any further and in the end meant nothing to me. Many working women want to live their life that way. Where is the satisfaction in that except as a performing ass? This sort of relationship is mutual masturbation that leaves me emotionally crippled. To desire somebody, to chase and cherish somebody and love her has died in me.' His eyes were moist.

I felt sad and wanted to give him a hug, but checked myself, not yet, not before he has purged himself. So I said quietly, 'Is that why you have gone for male bonding?'

He woke up as if from sleep with red eyes and asked, 'What male bonding?'

I added quietly, 'Fish, Fish and Ass?'

He was angry now, 'What are you talking about? Fish is a nice boy, a high school dropout and his parents are separated. He has nowhere to go. He is at least a companion, a nice one in fact, no demand, just looks after the house and no, not what you imagine. He is a school dropout with no parents and I am a highly educated outcast with parents separated too, so what is the difference? You were not the kind to take such a mean view of people you knew nothing about. Did I not have a circle of men friends in India? It was natural and nobody called us gay and we were not. Just because I love a woman does not mean I must have the desire to take her to bed. It is the same between men, and more so because it is not comfortable. It is true only in societies of cardboard cutout prototypes for easy fitting. Most civilizations in the world have gone through that stage and it was not necessarily healthy. You threw Fish out, he will not return.'

Suffering inside, I was in no mood to give up and added quietly, 'And what about the acrid smell I choked on as I entered? Those things usually are the first steps to male bonding.'

'God damn it that is hashish, the most innocuous narcotic mood elevator that is used by Indian hermits,' and he emitted a garish loud laughter that shook me, 'And can't I take it because I am not a sage? I have nothing, there ought to be something for me too.'

I got up, saying I was going to make some tea and went to the kitchen. When I returned with a pot of tea, cups and saucers and some small cakes and biscuits, he was pensive and did not look as angry. I poured the tea and gave him a cup and pushed the plate of snacks. He sipped tea silently and seemed to like and almost finished the snacks all by himself. I wondered again how hungry he was, almost a calorie deficiency. After tea I put the television on and surfed through the channels. There was nothing of interest. Asim had a magazine opened on his lap but not reading, his gaze fixed on a point in the wall.

It was getting dark. I asked Asim what should we do for food, we could go to a movie and then have dinner somewhere or stay in and I could cook something. He said we would go out and take it cool and easy. We saw a just released nice picture and ate in a quiet Greek restaurant. We were relaxed when we returned, and I took to the sofa amid protests from Asim and slept soundly.

Sunday morning was nice and clear and we woke late. I rushed out and bought fresh from oven croissant, jam, sausages, eggs and coffee, and had a hearty breakfast. After breakfast we were relaxed and were lolling on the sofa and bed. My flight was in late afternoon as I had to start work early and it was the same for Asim. Bob will pick me up from the airport. We decided to have a leisurely lunch outside and then he would reach me to the airport. As we were talking I suggested that he should visit mother and spend some time with her. She was alone. Asim said he was also pondering that. He had an offer of joining another business, a larger one in another city in a higher position, a real career jump. He could resign early from his present job and have a two month gap in between and visit mother. I said it was an excellent idea and he agreed and we were very happy. The dark shadow of the previous day was passing and we were friends again. I went out and bought more provisions to pack his larder. Then we went out for a delightful drive by the sea and ate at a seaside restaurant and he reached me to the airport. We were both emotional when we bade farewell and hugged tight patting backs. People around would have been surprised if they knew we were brother and sister and not a couple—different cultures.

A surprisingly long letter came from Asim after more than a couple of months that I have preserved not only for its surprising quality but also for its quantity, the only letter I have ever received from him.

He called me a couple of times before he left. I of course called him once every weekend as usual. I never heard Fish's voice and we never discussed him. Knowing Asim was soft hearted beneath his rough exterior I think he must have made some arrangements for him, at least I hoped he did. I felt sorry for him.

Writing

Dear sis,

You will be surprised to get this long letter from me. This is not my routine but I wanted to have a long chat with you. By nature I am not very expressive and a talking chat often goes in wrong channels and ends in argument. I admired mother and your penchant for soliloquy writing what is ordinarily called keeping a diary. But I know it would be more than a diary because you are not only keeping track of events but also your thoughts as you pass through events. You probably got it from mother that I never practiced. But I now realize that it is an excellent way to not only record events, analysis and emotions but you lay down part of your life on paper and they take on a life of their own and challenge you when you look at them again. You may think at a later date that whoever wrote it was stupid or immature or very wise and you realize that you have moved from there. We move continually through our lives for better or for worse from one premise to another and may forget where we started and where we are going. A self judgment is possible only when you keep a record as our slide through life is not a continuous conscious process but in reaction to many things that happen in our lives.

So I had to make a long return journey to where I started resenting my world and that affected my world view. The return journey was not easy. I had to mentally reach the spots that made me angry, afraid or hopeless and rewind myself to as I was and not only judge but also put down on paper so that I can be honest about them later and not cheat myself. It is a difficult task and took a long time to record in bits and pieces. But I stuck to the task until they gave a continuous rational picture. I am sending the result to you, I dare not show it to mother. As you know I am spending my time with mother at Calcutta in the gap between two jobs that I was fortunate to get. I have nothing to do except chat with mother, get my facts right and go back to that point of time and relive and write it down. In the process I am relaxing as knots are getting untied and I am not drinking and I am sleeping a lot in between writing and seeing Calcutta that I never had an opportunity to do. You know mother, she is probably aware of it all, but has never asked a question and never made a comment. She is just a very loving soothing balm. She cooks for me, spends some time at her Institute and the rest of the time she is home with her books and sometimes reminiscing our past lives but never too much.

The first thing she did after I reached home was to take me upstairs to one of the two bedrooms where an old man was sitting and introduced him by saying, 'This is your Sarit uncle, a friend of your father from our very young days. He is a bit sick now as you can see and since he has no living relative he is staying with me. He was a renowned person and still is, a famous professor of astrophysics in the university close by where you stay and worked for the space organization and related laboratories till his retirement, and Sarit, this is my son Asim, a software specialist working in USA.' She finished the entire introduction in one go without any pause as if whatever shock there was to give and whatever happens should be now and not left for the future. I could see that she was not very sure about me and I could not blame her. I looked closely at Sarit uncle and he was a grizzly old man suffering either from dementia or Alzheimer. What sort of a friend he was to our parents and how close that we never heard of him was not relevant, as mother had thought it fit to give him shelter was good enough for me. He was a Professor of Astrophysics in USA and suddenly it struck me and I exclaimed without thinking, 'Is he Professor Sarit Sarkar who was in the first or second expedition to Antarctica, probably both and whose pioneer work on Earth's magnetic field and electromagnetic radiations and a lot of work on sensors and other sensitive equipment in extreme conditions paved the way for the first space ventures?' My exclamation startled both of them. Mother stared at me and

Sarit uncle waddled out of bed and stood mute in front of me with an extended hand as if to shake my hand. I hugged him and said, 'Uncle, we never knew we had such a great uncle.' From his tremors and rapid breathing I could feel he was excited with emotion and I held him in front of me and asked, 'How could you become like this and people who know you are searching for you not knowing where you have gone.' He was crying and uttering words like a child I did not understand and mother took over. Calming him with soothing words as she used to do with us, she took him back to bed and made him lie down and sat beside him patting his shoulder and still talking till he was almost asleep. Then she got up putting a finger on her lips bidding me to be silent and we tiptoed out of the room. As I tried to speak again she silenced me with a raised hand and whispered, 'later, later' and took me to the next room.

'This is your room,' she said as we entered as if nothing had happened so far. I was familiar with her amazing power of recovery from unexpected situations. The atmosphere and smell of the room was clearly feminine. I bent down and put my head on her feet and stayed like that for a minute. Then I got up, put my hands on her shoulders, and looked at her and said, 'Mum, I am no longer as bad a boy as you knew me to be; I have grown'—and she started crying. I made her sit on a sofa, gave her a handkerchief, put my forehead against her shoulder and holding her let her cry, cry out all the fears, frustrations, separation and loneliness she had suffered over the years. How much she suffered, suffering for everybody, like Mother Earth! Once she had checked herself, she was still sniffing. I put my face over her back, caressing her back and unable to face her, spoke behind her back. 'Mum, I am your unworthy son, please do not make me more unworthy. This is your room and your room it always shall be. I shall sleep in the ground floor as your gatekeeper. If you are not there to keep an eye on Sarit uncle, he may do something silly like he ran away from America. Do you know what he is? Most of his work was classified or else he could have been nominated for Nobel Prize and get it. They are no longer classified but science has overtaken him in its progress as it does to all but he is on every textbook. Life has also overtaken him. Please look after him, he deserves that and I am proud of you. We do not know what his relationship was with you or father and we do not care do not want to know. I am your unworthy son. I have passed through a prolonged adolescence but it is over. I have grown and please forgive me.' I do not remember what else I said or that I said those things or only imagined I said, but she held my head at her bosom and kissed and caressed my head as when I was a child.

Sis, I tell you when people say that if you have done something good in your past life you get the reward sometimes in the next life, I do not disbelieve them altogether. I must have done something good in my past life to get a mother like this. I could add a sister like this too, but I am not surrendering to you that easily, you are after all the younger, got it? I am just teasing but I have not teased you for so long! What happened to me? The day father told me about his disease and explained how it would go and what the likely outcome was, I could not accept it. What arose in me was not concern but anger, a blind rage. This could not happen to me, I was thinking of me only. The anger in the beginning was against father as if he had betrayed me by deciding to die early; then it covered the whole world. In anger I left the country and came to USA and faced hostility as every immigrant does at the beginning. And I fought with the rage I brought with me. I was good at my work and that aggressive rage is what Americans appreciate and I progressed well. But it left my personal life in a shambles. I would not accept anything, question everything and trust nothing. I was boozing heavily to sleep at night, driving my car like a maniac, just managing to stay within the law but not always, I took flying lessons and passed, but fortunately did not have enough money to buy a plane. I had girlfriends galore, did not know how many hearts I broke, if any, may be none, I was that cynical, taking joy in torture and sorrow, using them like commodities. The more I injured others, I was injuring myself. You got to know some of that, didn't you? Your stinging rebukes, mother's words and achievement made me stall and think. Mum's letters were long but did not contain any advice or rebuke, just described her life, how the house was and what she did on a particular Sunday, actually made me a part of her life. Mum is the greatest transcontinental psychoanalyst in the world. She pushed her friends to get close to me and invite me and all that. I tell you they were the real sorry stuff, well most of them. And to make matters worse, some of them had grown up daughters eligible for marriage! I could give some of them run for money and maybe they would have enjoyed, but you know, mum was looming large, I did not dare. Ah well, a growling tomcat must leave some leftover for others. You realize of course, the language I am using is my language from those days, not of now. You won't recognize me now.

And there is Sarit uncle. Even what is left of him is magnificent. I would pass my day with him when mother went for work. I would keep chattering about science and its future and he would keep bobbing his head with that perpetual smile on his face. It is not an unintelligent passive smile but one of habitual love and encouragement as I gradually found. Actually not much entered his head. You know what is our favourite game during the day? It is the snakes and ladders. Every time he gets to a ladder or I am swallowed by a snake he would clap his hands and jump up and down on bed, laughing loudly. I buy children's toys for him and he would be so excited when a ball drops or a train runs. As for music he is a master depending on his mood. I gather mother first heard him playing Mozart's Requiem Mass. I requested him many times to play it but he would not. He preferred being a child not a grumpy old man. Then once I heard him in snatches when he thought he was alone in the house. It was magnificent. You know I love to play the guitar but I have not brought my guitar. So I went out and bought a new one and our musical evenings started. I would play a tune and look askance at him and he would play it on violin followed by the usual clapping and laughter. One day I asked mother to sing. When did you last hear mum sing? She still sings beautifully. When she sings Sarit uncle is mesmerized. For his benefit mum would sometimes sing classical tunes with long *tan* and he would follow on the violin. Thus go our life and thus I was healed. You should have been here. Mother's health is failing but she brushes it off as my old hang-up.

Oh yes, there is something else. There is this software specialist, quite qualified, you know, from IIT Kharagpur, working in an up and coming software firm in Sector V. You would not know what that is, it is in the Salt Lake area where the IT sector has been built and developing well. I met the CEO of that firm by accident and he invited me. I find this software specialist doing a project for some foreign client rather expertly and the boss left on some errand. I discussed the project with her; did I say this was a female? Well, now I have spilled the beans. By and by we talked about a lot of things, and she is quite knowledgeable. I asked her whether she ever considered locating abroad and she asked what for? I said there would be more money and chance to go up and that she could get a good husband. She was not interested in either. I asked whether she was married and she asked whether NRI culture was to ask unknown women personal questions. I was soundly rebuffed. Only thing I knew about her was that her name was Rati. I did another uninvited journey to that firm ostensibly to meet the CEO but did not have to meet him as Rati was not in her seat and her next seat colleague said it was her day off. I gave up and did not ask for her phone number. Just another stuck up female that is all, not a big deal. As fate would have it, I saw her when I went to buy the guitar. She was in there asking for her Sitar given for stringing. It was not ready and she was upset. She did not even look at me and was going out, but I could not help jump at her, my male ego working. I blocked her exit and asked, 'Hello do you recognize me?' She said, 'Sort of familiar but cannot place.' I said, 'I went with your boss to your firm'. She said, 'Oh now I can place, you are the man who asks every woman whether she is married?' I said, 'not every woman.' She said, 'That is better. What is the frequency, one in every three, five or seven or is it time gated, once every week or twice?' I said, 'Jokes apart, would you mind if I invite you for a cup of coffee next door?' She asked, 'Are you married?' I was taken aback, 'No'. Before I could react she shot another, 'How long?' I asked, 'What do you mean?' She said with pauses, 'It is simple, how long are you unmarried?' I was exasperated, 'I was never married.' She seemed to have solved a puzzle, 'Ah, I see, you are a live together man.' I was angry by now and said, 'I am only inviting you for a coffee not to go to bed.' She patted me on the arm and said, 'Don't be angry, truth is always disturbing. No uninitiated man asks a female whether she is married at the first encounter. Good bye,' and she left. I was in a rage but have learned to control it. As luck would have it, I found her standing at a bus stop in the middle of a terrible traffic jam as I was driving home. I took the risk of veering and stopping in front of her amid shouts and blaring horns and lowering the glass shouted, 'I do not do live together in a car but I can drop you,' Several heads turned in curiosity, and she to escape the curious onlookers, jumped into the back seat. I gnashed my teeth and asked, 'Where would you go ma'am, this taxi has no meter.' She was cool like a cucumber, 'Just drive on I shall tell you where to turn.' I could see in the mirror she was smiling. I gnashed my teeth again and drove on and her directions brought us to the same street as mother's house and soon we were before her house. I said angrily, 'No charge for the taxi as that one is my house,' and drove off and heard her exclamation, 'Seema mashi's house!' As I parked in front of my house, I saw in the mirror that she was standing on the footpath and looking in my direction. I got out of the car and entered home without looking back.

Next day mum asked me in the middle of doing something, 'Rati's mother was telling me that you have met her.' I said angrily, 'Met her? More like bitten by her, she is a viper.' Mum said, 'I know, she is very beautiful,' as if that was the point of discussion. Next day was Sunday and mother got busy making a grand breakfast and announced that to me and Sarit uncle who as usual applauded. We sat down to breakfast and it was grand Bengali breakfast. As we started eating there was some commotion in the stairs and in came a middle aged lady and behind her almost hidden Rati. I did not see her till she was at the table and this time I blushed much more than she did and food got stuck in my throat and I coughed. Mother expressed unusual concern and said, 'Take some water quickly, Asim, or you will choke,' and there was laughter, and that girl Rati hid her face in the pallu of her sari and must have been laughing. I tell you sis, I shall take revenge some day when she comes to US but for now I am hooked. She is really beautiful and so polished and soft. I mean not physically but in manners. We have been out a couple of times and she has not allowed me to get close. She says, 'Waiting makes it romantic,' May be it does, I don't know but I feel very happy. I have been to their house for dinner, a really long dinner and we talked and talked. She is very well read and very nice to talk to. I ask Sarit uncle, 'Should I marry that girl,' and he claps and bobs his head up and down. He is also happy.

Well, now do you believe that I am restructured? I am ending this letter here; already tired of writing. How are you doing and how is your Bobby; any news on the background; shall meet you when I get back. Love.

Your loving and grateful brother
Asim

PS: We have not decided yet but we are thinking of relocating to India whenever an opportunity presents, now that the IT industry in India is booming and many foreign companies are relocating to India.

Branching

How time passes! How many arrows of time are there? The psychological arrow, the cosmological arrow, the thermodynamic arrow, real time and imaginary time of the quantum world—how about personal time? Time seems to accelerate at some phases of life and decelerate at others—that is not physics that is psychology, not psychological arrow of time. So is that of no importance? In certain phases of life time moves fast for you and not so fast for someone you love. Would there not be a mini chaos, formation of a time gradient? Would there not be a shift in time relationship? Does generation gap occur due to this different perception of time? But then science is ignorant of human beings. Put a man who is nothing but a manifestation of mind, because man cannot be imagined without mind, somewhere in an equation, and science goes haywire and calculations go wrong. In a nutshell the gap between mother and us, Asim and I, were widening. There were conversations, exchange of 'how are you, take care' messages, but the emotional bond was loosening. We had a fast paced life but her time scale was slow and steady.

Asim and Rati took time to settle down what with all the paraphernalia of marriage between two countries in keeping with emotional issues and practical issues of visa, residence and job permits and getting a job. The last thing was the easiest as Rati was really good at her job with high credentials especially with her client in USA. She did not agree to work in Asim's company under him. All these things took time to sort out. They are happily settled now. Asim has transmuted from tomcat to highly domesticated cat and they are really in love.

They want to prolong their honeymoon as much as possible putting reproduction in the backburner. That is probably natural as they did not have a long enough prenuptial relationship. They would call mother from out of the way places, sometimes from the car phone and ask, 'How are you mum? We are in so and so place,' and mother would reply, 'I am fine, you take care,' and that was that.

With us things were a little different. Bob and I had to work hard to keep our positions and grants and to feel secure with enough left over. His mother was getting on in years and he had to make her secure. With all this going Bob suddenly realized that I was a female after all and in a silly careless rush to make up for lost time made me pregnant. It was more of an accident. Then all hurry started because I was too shy to face mother with a fully grown 'premature' child and sacrificing the child was out of question. We had to go through a hurried marriage and to invent all sorts of other reasons to make it look like a practical decision. Mother lamented that she could not be present during the ceremonies and we assured her that she will see all of it live on the net. I wanted both Church and Vedic marriage and so did she. Fortunately that is not difficult to arrange in America of today with priests, both 'part time and full time professionals from back home' being available, the latter costing a bit more. That was managed because one of our friends was having a family marriage in traditional style and they were rich. With a moderate incentive the priest could be made to accept a second assignment. The next problem was Bob—he did not want to chant Hindu mantras without knowing what they meant. I tried to assure him that I would not change to something else, say a vampire, with his chanting of mantra. He did not trust that. But lo and behold, English translation of Hindu marriage mantras were actually available and Dr Robert Lind did make a thorough study of them in his usual manner and was disappointed that these were the usual soothing words of welcoming the groom and exchange of hearts and pledges of love and responsibility for life with Sri Narayan and Agni as witness in place of Jesus Christ. I assured him I would not mind if he shouted abracadabra now and then. So we ran from the Church wedding in the morning to Vedic marriage at our new home in the evening, followed by the entourage. Asim looked very important as he gave away the bride twice with just one pinch from me that nobody saw. Rati looked smashing in her sari and she knew all the intricacies of the ceremony and I think she improvised a few of her own. And every bit of action was transmitted live to mum and Sarit uncle including the reverse one of their blessings. With two expert computer and software experts in the family transcontinental marriage seemed quite easy. Enough number of friends was available to make it a suitable mayhem and we did not rush anywhere for 'the honeymoon', home was the best and cheapest place and we had the bed decorated with flowers.

We had selected a house that we could afford for our conjugal living. It was a very busy time arranging the deposit and the mortgage. Then by the time we could decorate it enough to make it decently habitable our wedding day arrived. We managed to have a 'respectable' marriage with expert choice of dresses under the direction of Rati. I had not started bulging yet. And we had a hilarious post-marriage ceremony in our back garden with champagne and eats. Neighbours were nice as they were invited and came to see this curious wedding and nobody complained. Fire was lit in the fireplace without breaking any law and the Vedic rituals and mantras were perfect. It was extremely emotional for me, and Bob was equally affected. Brides in India cry even to these days when they are given away and have to move from their parents' house to their husband and in-laws'. I was not moving anywhere but I cried under cover of the fire and smoke during the fire ceremonies, remembering my father and mother and their absence. Bob and Rati were the two people who understood, and whereas Bob could do very little except looking at me with sympathetic eyes, Rati really acted as mother, holding me from behind and whispering in my ears. Bob's mother was there throughout the ceremonies and kissed me tenderly when it was over. Bob and I took advantage of the long weekend that followed to enjoy our honeymoon privately and then went back to work as we might need to take leave later.

I went to work with gusto to finish my part of the project before I take maternity leave. I attended antenatal clinics regularly during off time and a normal delivery was predicted by the clinician. I was in sound health, needed no psychic help and the baby was growing normally and it was a boy. I named him Ravi before he was born. Ravi means the Sun and I prayed that he would be the sunrise in our lives. Bob loved the name. I was so relaxed that when the labour pain started I was actually working at the university and it was near closing time.

I calmly finished whatever I was doing and checked the time that Bob will soon come off. There was no point alarming him because he will get too excited. When he came looking for me I told him quietly that I have to go to the hospital. His reaction was memorable, first his jaw dropped and he was paralysed, next he burst into extreme energy almost ready to hold the baby. I assured him it is not going to be that quick, arranged my work papers and handed them over to my colleagues with apology that I may not be available for some days but I have finished whatever I was doing. It was their turn to drop their jaws. I took leave from my superior and he wished me everything he could think of. I followed Bob to our car where a small package used to be kept in recent days with small things I might need and asked him not to rush. There was no need for either, because I was booked at a private clinic not far, where everything was taken care of. After I was settled the doctor examined me and assured Bob that there was nothing to worry about and he could go home and have a few hours' sleep. He would be informed in good time. I prevailed over him to go home and rest and he obeyed but I do not think he slept much. In early dawn Ravi came smoothly, neither overweight nor underweight, and what with an Indian mother, could be a slightly premature baby to likely gossipers and announced his entry to the world with a lusty cry.

I took the entire maternity leave after Ravi was born. This was probably the best period of enjoyment of my life. I would feed him, cuddle him and bathe him to my heart's content. I cooked for Bob and when he came home enjoyed the baby's company together. We had nothing but home food during this entire period. Ravi was a nice baby, intelligent and responsive, with a free expression of glee and laughter and very little crying. When the leave was over I requested an extension without pay and it was granted. So I enjoyed his constant company almost till toddler stage and all early vaccinations including some extra for a likely visit to India. The last thing did not happen as I had to rejoin work and it broke my heart every time I left him at the crèche. But that is probably essential to a baby's development. Gradually he became a very sociable child and loved both the home and friends in the crèche. We looked forward to the weekends when we enjoyed at home or drove out to scenic places around with parks and playing fields. He was introduced to his Grandma through web camera and would also spend time with Bob's mother. The day he pointed to mother at the screen and uttered 'Ganna' as a sort of victory cry was a memorable day and gave much pleasure to mum. Before we could count months and years he had passed through two birthdays with fanfare. From crèche he graduated to playschools. Every time I thought of visiting mother, I had to put it off for something or other. Every time I apologized to her, she would say, 'What's the hurry? I am fine and your prime concern is the baby. Do what is right for him.' I knew she was pining for us and as always she would put her own wish last in the order of priority. I sometimes cried for her silently at her emptiness since father died and she devoted herself to our development and well being. And she was also looking after Sarit uncle. She would look after anybody in distress, even animals. I have seen her rescue kittens from the gutter and look after them until they could be sent somewhere. This did not happen much where we lived in Bombay. But when I was very small I remember that sometimes our house was full of cats well looked after and well fed. I remember hearing father only once raising an objection, but cats continued in variable numbers. I still do not know what her compulsions were about Sarit uncle and how he was related to us, but one thing I know definitely that he needed mother's care and she would never hesitate if she thought she could provide it to anybody. Beyond that I have never learnt to question.

Breaking

The unforeseen had to happen one day and it happened. Mother had a heart attack. I got the news from the neighbours when she was moved to hospital. I was frantic. I kept asking what happened and how, which hospital she was in and who was the doctor and his phone number. They could not give any details. I asked to give me at least the name of the doctor and his mobile number. They said they would try and next day could give me those. I called up the doctor at a suitable hour, introduced myself and asked for details.

At first he kept on the usual platitudes that she was stable and had a massive heart attack and being looked after with all care. I was impatient and told him that here in USA heart attacks are immediately converted with intervention and damage to the heart is minimized. What happened to my mother? Was any of this done? Are there facilities in Calcutta now for such care? I want a detailed report. Now he was more alert. He said that such facilities existed in his hospital. But unfortunately mother reached hospital too late and no intervention measure could be taken. Then he asked if I was a doctor and I replied, 'No, I am not a doctor but we have many friends in the profession including heart specialists and I could ask them what should be done if he would kindly send us details of what happened to her as she has no one there to look after her.' In the end my voice broke and I started crying. His voice became kind and sympathetic. He said that in spite of possessing facilities for immediate resumption of circulation to heart in a heart attack only a few patients can be saved as most do not or cannot come in time before their heart muscle is damaged. This was due to lack of awareness, financial problems and lack of social infrastructure. In my mother's case the situation was different. She had a painless infarction and attributed the symptoms to indigestion and dyspepsia. She was brought to hospital when she started having breathlessness about three days after the attack; it was too late to do anything immediately. There is lack of awareness and knowledge in the medical profession in addition to that of the public. My mother has therefore been kept on intensive medical treatment. She is showing signs of improvement and has to be kept in hospital until more recovery and then assessed and investigated for possibility and need of intervention and revascularization. I pleaded with him that treatment must not suffer on account of money because there is no problem on that score. I also requested him to allow me to keep in touch on phone as frequently as possible. He agreed to respond on phone unless he was busy otherwise.

In the third week after admission, mother underwent a coronary bypass surgery. I was fretting and wanted to go but there was Ravi. I beseeched Asim but he was tied up and could not go. He asked me not to worry too much because we could do very little and had to depend on the doctors. Mother recovered from the operation but was very weak. The doctor said she already had a weak heart and how much improvement would come from the operation had to be watched but he expected that there will be some. After about another three weeks he informed me that there has been about twenty per cent improvement in cardiac function from what it was before operation and she needs to be discharged and closely 'cared' at home for gradual recovery. This time there was no option and I had to go as there was nobody at home to look after. I requested him to hold on for a few more days till I come. I discussed with Bob. He said I should take Ravi with me as he is a tough boy and would withstand change. We consulted the pediatrician and he advised a couple of vaccinations that were done. I felt sad to leave Bobby alone but he asked me to go ahead and if possible bring mother and Sarit uncle to USA. Ravi was a US citizen so there will be no problem with him. If mother becomes fit to travel he would arrange the rest of the things. Bob was due for a sabbatical shortly but not yet. If I am delayed he would try for an early sabbatical. So I left for Calcutta, a city I left in my childhood and did not know how it would be taking Ravi with me. He took the whole thing sportingly with a bit of excitement at the prospect of meeting grandmother but did not comprehend he would have to miss Papa until it was time to board. Then he broke into a bout of crying making me even sadder.

Rati's family was at the airport to receive us and we went straight to the hospital to meet mum. I could not check my tears nor could she. She was sitting in bed and I embraced her gently and she caressed my head. She was delighted to see Ravi but he was a bit scared by the hospital. I met the doctor and thanked him profusely for everything he had done and made an appointment the day after next when I would take discharge of my mother and all instructions from him in detail.

I reached home I remembered vaguely from my early school days and one visit with my parents after that. The house seemed smaller than I remembered. Apart from that it was quite in a shambles. The gardener was much older than what I imagined and his wife only a little better. I thanked my luck that at least they were alive. Then I went upstairs to meet Sarit uncle with some trepidation. What I saw horrified me. The room was as dirty and disheveled as it could be and in the middle of the bed there sat an old man with his head between his knees. As we entered he looked up with a vacant face and Ravi clutched my dress to hide. As he noticed Ravi a smile broke out on his face that frightened Ravi even more. I said I was Rupa and this was my son Ravi, spoke in Bengali first and then in English. He seemed to understand, nodded his head and then went back to his posture. I forgot my jet lag as there was so much to do to make the house livable. I knew mother always kept her house spick and span but for more than two months she had been sick and the gardener couple did what they could. I had to bring mother home in two days' time and look to Ravi's minimum comfort. That was enough work and could not be finished in two days. I rang up Bob to say that we have reached safely.

I brought mother home in an ambulance provided by the hospital. The car had not been in use for more than two months and the driver still enjoyed a long paid holiday and was earning extra by working elsewhere. The driver was an old loyal hand gone rusty. I threatened him with discharge and when he relented I asked him to rehabilitate the car nicely as fast as he could. I had time only to get mother's room ready on the upper floor across the little hall from Sarit uncle's room. I decided to live on the ground floor with Ravi. Mother wanted me to stay on the more airy upper floor but I said it would be more convenient if both of them were on the same floor. I had already worked out the strategy of making this house a nursing home and more livable, after all I was mother's daughter. First I renovated the kitchen by cleaning it thoroughly and buying a new gas oven and grill connecting the gas cylinder to that instead of the open stove and buying a water purifier and an assorted collection of kitchen utensils and a kitchen table to cook a variety of food for the baby and the two old people as hygienic as possible. I took charge of the kitchen myself helped by the gardener's wife and asked them to cook their own food. The gardener was entrusted to rejuvenate the garden to make it a happy place. The upstairs hall being used as a dining and sitting place was rearranged and the old refrigerator was exchanged for a modern one. An air conditioner was installed in the ground floor bedroom for Ravi, keeping a largish place for his playthings. I wanted to buy two for the upper rooms also but mother said they were not used to it and would like as it is with ceiling fans. The bathroom attachments were revamped in the ground floor with minor constructions and installation of a bathtub for Ravi and also on the upper floor as much as the users needed, with replacement of leaking taps and scrubbing of floors with addition of cleaners, disinfectants and deodorants. I purchased a washing machine and installed it in the spare wash room in the ground floor and taught the gardener's wife how to use it. She was younger than her husband and more enthusiastic. I purchased new curtains with muted bright happy colours for the whole house. I would have liked to repaint the house but that was not possible. Instead I visited an auction house and purchased a nice small sofa set with matching tables for the downstairs hall. I replaced all lights with nice cheap domes and modern incandescent bulbs. I found that in Calcutta everything was available if you were prepared to pay the price that did not amount to much if converted to dollar or pound but in rupee was not affordable by many. I felt sad that what was commonplace in western society though available here was beyond the reach of most and there were many who could afford but considered the modern things superfluous. Through mother's doctor I had contacted a nursing agency and appointed two dependable nurses, one for the day and the other for the night before mother came home, to nurse the two people upstairs—one cardiac and the other neurological. I beseeched the doctor to make occasional home visits when needed and have a cup of coffee and a snack in addition to being disturbed by me on phone now and then. He suggested one of his junior colleagues would make home visits and report to him. I also requested him to recommend a neurologist to look after Sarit uncle and he did.

It took about a fortnight to finish all this, rather fast by Calcutta standards. Workmen in the west want to finish a job as quickly as possible, here as slowly as possible but there is no difference in expertise and much cheaper here. That was another experience. But the main thing of rehabilitating mother was not easy and I was in her room most of the time helping the nurses. She was very weak. She could hardly get out of bed and go to the bathroom without help. The night nurse said that she would get up some nights and ask for extra pillows as she felt breathless. When reported to the doctor he advised keeping an oxygen cylinder at home. It helped but I was unhappy. I had nobody to share my unhappiness with. When Bob called I would relate my anxieties at length but what could he do? I sometimes forgot to ask how he was, how he was managing his food and how was his work going and when we disconnected I would repent that I did not talk about any of those. I depended on him to call as calling from here was expensive. The fund situation, though not alarming, was getting a bit serious. I was spending through my debit cards from my account in USA. Bob sent some money now and then. Mother had been living on savings and investments structured by father more than ten years back and the situation had changed through all these years. It still sufficed for day to day living but not the extras. Medicines were expensive and they were many with frequent changes. Ravi was getting restless being home all the time. I admitted him in a nice kid school nearby and he liked it. The teachers were young and understanding.

Another month passed and the house settled to a routine. I was offered the temporary position of a physics teacher in a rich private school nearby and I accepted it. I was told I could continue as long as I wished, a Ph.D. from USA was an asset after all. I was not busy the whole day and could come home in between. The driver was reliable and he reached Ravi to school and brought him back and I could call him when I wanted. I could see that my life was settling in a different track and I wondered for how long. Asim seldom called and my only connection was Bob and I whined and complained to him, sometimes crying. There did not seem to be much hope of taking mother to USA. She would not stand the journey. Two more months passed and mother improved slightly but still needed the oxygen now and then. Her tests showed improvements but not enough to travel to USA. She could slowly come down the stairs but needed help to go up, sometimes had to be carried. I took her out for a drive by the riverside or somewhere she wanted to go when it was cool. Once she sympathized with my predicament and separation from Bob and told me to return to USA as she was able to look after herself with all the help I had arranged, but I stopped her by saying I had left her once but cannot do that again. She wiped her eyes and never repeated. How strong mentally she still was!

My only link with the life I left behind was Bob and I waited eagerly for his call. They were coming less frequently now. I rebuked myself for not seeing the situation from his point of view. It is difficult for a man in the USA to live alone in an empty house and every time he calls I lament on the situation. That is not very enjoyable. In this whole drama we are the only people suffering apart from mum, but she would never express herself. I did not have that strength of mind. On the brighter side Ravi was well adjusted and liked his school. He was very popular, especially with the girls, according to her teacher and the cynosure of all eyes at birthday parties that were quite frequent. At least one of us was enjoying. He also loved his grandmother and would sit by her and keep talking about his school and friends. He would invite her to the next party as other kids' grandmas were present and I would hear lively discussion on what she should wear and how she should conduct herself. Mother really enjoyed the baby talk and it made me happy that she is getting some return after all for all her sufferings. I felt a bit fulfilled that way but would think of Bob and feel sad almost immediately. I never complained to Bob that his calls were becoming less frequent sometimes skipping weekends, and also stopped whining and complaining. I would ask about his research and what position he was expecting at the university and what was happening in my section and all that. I never once mentioned his promised sabbatical. I did not want to put him under pressure.

Many months passed and then one weekend he called rather late, knowing that I shall be awake. He said that the long labor weekend was coming and he was thinking of extending it over the week next and come to Calcutta. I was overjoyed, barely succeeding to keep my voice low and not wake up the whole house. I said, 'that would be wonderful darling, please do come, Ravi will be delighted.' He did not say anything, so I added, 'same with me,' still no reply, and I added, 'I promise I would not cry,' and felt silly. Next day I announced it to the family and mother was happy but there was something in her voice I could not catch. The day was very near and I thought I would not have enough time to be ready and planned so many things. Ravi was happy to hear that Dad was coming but not exuberant like me. The red letter day came and I was at the airport long before time and waited impatiently for his plane to land. At last I could see him coming and jumped and waved and as soon as he was out of the gate ran forward and embraced him and kept on kissing, forgetting that this was India. We came home and he went up to meet mother. I knew he had a deep respect for her. As they were talking I went to the kitchen to see that everything was all right. When I came to mother's room they were talking seriously. Mother told me, 'What a nice husband you have got. I am so happy to see all of you together, you, Robert and Ravi. What a nice family you are. My wish is fulfilled. I was telling Bob, can I call you Bob, to take you back to where you belong. I shall be able to manage myself.' I was beginning to protest but mother held up her hand and said, 'A woman's place is in her family with her husband and children, anything else is not quite normal. There are duties we cannot always fulfill, like I could not go to your wedding, could not keep your wish to visit your department. Among duties you must be able to decide which one is priority and not try all at the same time.' I was silent and so was Bob looking down at his fingers as was his habit when in deep thought. I broke the seriousness and exclaimed, 'Ok, we will discuss all that, but now it is supper time and the food will be cold. Mum, you also come to the table and we shall eat together'.

Bob was tired and went to sleep after eating and slept almost continuously next day to get out of his jet lag. Then I took him out to see Calcutta, all possible sights, one theatre and to see a film, a hit Bengali film with English subtitles. I took him to restaurants of various types of local cuisine as he loved to sample new food, some western places and joked about the Bengali western and the Indian Chinese. Ravi was with us whenever possible, and he liked these outings with father. Bob was sometimes animated, but often silent with occasional humorous comments, and I would laugh my heart out as he smiled. This to me was a rewind of our life together in America that I missed. His departure date came close and I was exasperated. That night Ravi was asleep when I came to bed and I embraced Bob to wake him, kissed him passionately on his lips, face and neck and untied his shirt, kissing and tickling him on his bare chest and gradually he responded with half his mind elsewhere. We made love. This term so much in use in western life always made me laugh. I used to say, this making thing is funny, it is like making pasta or making kebab, some things have to be mixed and stirred and lo and behold it comes. We used to laugh together and it was never as bad as this time. After the ritual ended, I lay silent for a time, and then impulsively, without thinking, turned towards him and asked, 'is there someone else Bobby?' He was silent, looking gravely at me. I repeated, 'Please tell me do not hide. Are you in love?' There was no answer. I took his hand and played with his fingers as I loved to do. One of the fingers was a little crooked and I always used to kiss that one, which I did. Then with a deep breath I said, 'Look, Bobby, please look at me, we were devoted friends. Our friendship was deep and long, so long that we were never really in maddening passionate love, at least you were not, but I was, and waited patiently when you will see the female in me. It was my earnestness to which you responded, it was not your own. Now if you have found real love I would understand. We have been separated so long, it is but natural that there will be others around you, because you are a nice man and I have no right to criticize. But please do let me know as a friend and if you want me to sign papers, do send them, but with friendship and a little bit of love if you can spare,' and I started crying that would not stop and I bit my pillow. It was a total monologue; he never interrupted or showed any reaction, looking on like a zombie. He was only stroking my head and hair lightly as if in mild regret or apology or something. Next day passed with the usual chores I followed mechanically. There was an eerie silence in the house, nobody talking very much, and the next day Bob left. I was in a daze. So many years of friendship, courtship, marriage, child and family life could end so fast! A line from T. S. Eliot kept repeating in my head 'This is how the world ends this is how the world ends not with a bang but a whimper'. Well, there was at least one half hearted bang, I sarcastically thought and felt myself polluted. I wondered whether he had produced another oops baby for the woman he was banging now and kept on flagellating myself. I could not conceal my external appearance of sorrow in spite of my pride, and people wondered and sympathized, but not mother, she became silent.

On The Seashore

It took me weeks to adjust to my new situation. Gradually I could reconcile to that and realized that I have to restructure my life to adjust. It is not easy to turn one's mind from such a severe and sudden loss and think positively, but as I said I was my mother's daughter. At least she was beside me. Her presence was a great source of strength though she never asked a single question and never offered a single word of advice. My first action in my comeback was to meet the principal of my school and submit an application for the permanent position of a physics teacher. She kept looking silently and as I was feeling uneasy asked me how long was that likely to be, and I said, could be quite long as mother was not recovering well. She kept looking at me and asked nothing more. Instead she said, 'I believe your son is going to a good preparatory school, how old is he?' I told her and she said, 'As you know we have a fairly good preparatory section and at his age he is eligible to come with the youngest. Would you consider transferring him to our school? I could make a special case and you shall be eligible for some benefits as a teacher.' Tears came to my eyes that I could not conceal. Through that blurred vision I could barely say, 'Yes, thanks.' In a thoroughly businesslike professional manner, without a glance to the handkerchief I was pressing to my eyes, she took out a form and scribbled on it while I finished working my handkerchief, and passed it to me to write my son's name at the top and sign at the bottom. I did that and then asked as an afterthought, 'Can the name be changed at a later date?' and she said in the same professional manner, 'Yes of course, with proper papers.'

As I came out I thought of God, a word that was never used in our family as an excuse or an entity to rely on though we were all believers in the way most or all physicists were from Einstein to Oppenheimer to the modern day physicists. But for our life we depended on our self and knowledge, intelligence and determination. But today I could not help thanking Him whoever and wherever He might be. I also realized that man's religiosity cannot be defined by the terms theist, atheist and agnostic. Chance plays such a huge role in our lives both favourably and unfavourably. What is chance to a non-believer may well be God to a believer with faith. The psychological and social impact of the latter cannot be ignored. But is that true? Supposing Jesus Christ said He was the Son of Chance, would that be understood and would the Mongols and Huns have understood the meaning of the English word 'chance' and would Attila have refrained from attacking Rome or more provoked? I smiled within at such wayward thoughts. There is no going away from God whether you like it or not.

I was still smiling when I came home to mother and she asked, 'How come you look so happy, what is the matter?' I told her what happened at school and she was incredulous, 'The prospect of a job at school was enough to compensate a broken marriage,' and the reality struck me and I became glum. She asked me to sit beside her and made space on the bed. As I sat with bowed head she put her hand on my head and for the first time in front of her I burst out crying and hid my face on her lap and she kept caressing me. After some time she asked, 'So what was it you were smiling about?' I lifted my head and told her what I thought about God and she burst out laughing and I was laughing and crying at the same time. She wiped my tears and said in deep affection, 'You are still that little girl laughing and crying at the same time,' and I embraced her tightly. A lot of cobwebs were lifted between the two of us.

Some days or weeks later, I do not remember exactly a thick envelope came from USA carrying papers for me and enclosed was a fat cheque in my name with a slip attached that said 'for Ravi'. I was thankful to Bob that in his decency he had kept certain areas blank, the most important of which was the custody of children. When I got some time I took the papers to a senior lawyer recommended by friends. Thankfully it was a lady especially knowledgeable in such things.

We took a few days to discuss things and what I wanted. We argued on the point of alimony and maintenance that I did not want and she objected, saying it had more implications apart from money. But I would not listen. I said one has to forget the past to build a future and I could not do that carrying a crutch all my life. She made no comment. On the custody of children, I said Ravi will be mine, and I asked whether I could change his name. She was quite surprised and asked, 'Why do you want to do that and what change'? I said I wanted to change it from Ravi Lind to Ravi Lind Roy. She mused and said, 'Such change could probably be done. Do you have his birth certificate?' I did and showed it to her and she saw that my maiden name was written on it. She mused for some time and said, 'Let me think about it and see books to find whether that can be done under Indian and American laws. Normally it can be done after divorce is granted but I am not sure it can be done before.' I said, 'Please see whether it can be done because I want his new surname to be written on the divorce application form, if necessary with an affidavit registered in India.' She looked at me for some time and said, 'You really are a very determined lady. I understand your sorrow but one has to be pragmatic in such things. Even if this is accepted it has to be entered in the US National Registry or his nationality will be in jeopardy with all its implications. I am sure you do not want that.' I said, 'He has a US passport and if the name change becomes official he can have a new passport from here.' She said, 'logically, yes, but one has to see the laws and practicality.' After some pause she said, 'Are you absolutely sure there is no possibility for reconciliation? Any man who can leave blanks like these in a divorce application is a kind man and in future may repent losing a sweet wife like you. You have to think also about inheritance, one cannot see that far in future. Your son can blame you some day.' I kept thinking. About reconciliation I had no doubt that if it happened it would be in spite of this change but about other things I was not sure, whether I had the right to mess with my son's future. I said, 'Can I not insert the proposed name change in the form and write to him whether he could see to it that the new name is inserted in the US National Registry?' At last she smiled affectionately, seemed to relax and said, 'This is an excellent idea. If you are going to write in any case, then write first, before filling the form. You can write on the internet and keep a hardcopy and see what he says in return. Let us sleep on that and you come back after discussing with your ex-husband.' Then she added knowingly with a smile, 'Divorces can also be friendly and that is the best way.' In the end the name change did not take place. I got to keep Ravi in my custody and Bob did not have to fork out an alimony he could ill afford and money kept coming in Ravi's child account without any agreement on quantum or frequency and thus the end of my marriage was settled.

I wanted to change Ravi's name because in ancient India children could carry a mother's name and identity. From Vedic times the story of Satyakama and Jabala in *Chandogya Upanishad* was well known as an honoured social example. Jabala was a freewheeling young woman who would be called a prostitute or hooker today but were usually known as *Naagarika* in those days, literally meaning 'daughter of the city' as they were an essential part of society. They contributed to much of our ancient heritage of art, music and dance and their figurines adorn the walls of old temples and some still live through local folklore. Her son Satyakama was a handsome erudite young man who desired to be a celibate sage and join a famous teacher of the day and live in his house. So he went to the famous sage and expressed his desire. Their conversation in Sanskrit went like this, 'To him he said 'To what lineage do you, good looking one, belong?" He said "Sir I do not know this as to what lineage I belong. I asked my mother. She replied to me, I got you in my youth when I was busy performing many duties and remained engaged in serving. Being as I was, I do not know this as to which lineage you belong. But my name is Jabala, and your name is Satyakama. Sir, such as I am, I am Satyakama Jabala." His truthfulness was accepted as his mark of nobility and Satyakama Jabala became one of the learned sages of his day.

In the Ramayana Sita could be deserted by Rama but her twin sons, Lav and Kush were born unknown to the father and had a normal social status and they defeated Rama in battle not knowing he was their father. These were not isolated stories as the tradition continued in Hindu India. With Muslim and Christian conquests and clash of cultures the traditions got a severe beating with generations of protectionist and ultra-conservative social mores in Hindu society, and much that was sublime got deranged. But even in modern historical times Laxmibai, the Rani of Jhansi, went to battle against the British with her infant son tied to the saddle behind her as she valiantly led her soldiers to attack the British Army and died in battle. The epithet 'single mother' was a derisive one in western culture until modern liberal times when by the sheer force of numbers they earned their rightful place but the stigma still continues. A mother is a mother who gives birth to the child regardless of whether it is a patriarchal or matriarchal society, and she should not need a qualifying adjective to describe her children for their rightful place in society. Today a woman can choose the man she wants to get a child from, without necessarily marrying him and in many cultures they do. With progress of science she does not even have to choose a man. In future society a woman would be more empowered and more emotionally balanced because she can bear a child that a man cannot. So I chose to be a woman instead of a title to define married, unmarried, widowed or single, and my son should be known by my name. All my university certificates bear my maiden name, so why not he? I have been lonely when Bob had to spend time with his mother and look after her. Even as a family we have stayed together in his mother's house. The periods were not as long but that was only geography. I did not think of divorce. He could have chosen the sabbatical and any institution in Calcutta would have been glad to have him. But then he was a man. That was what I resented and felt insulted. To discard someone who is on another shore is neither humane nor manly.

My life continued on this track quite nicely, I must concede, carrying no extra baggage. The only problem was Ravi's occasional questions but they became infrequent. He took to the school lustily as the school used English for medium of education and he was with his likes. Some time there would be a remark by somebody as it happens in Indian society since people do not respect privacy, but gradually he developed the reflex to handle them. He was a sturdy boy and not to be messed with, though he had his father's mild nature otherwise. I was so happy to see him grow. I went to my mother's institute a few times as she sent me on some errand. The people there were polite and courteous with me. The senior professors liked me and some of them asked me about my work in the USA and how the workplace was. I told them about the projects I have done and the one I was working on when I returned, the word I always used for my homecoming. They said there was nothing on those lines being done here, but if I found something

I liked or if I wanted to use the library I was welcome. One of them even assured me that I would not work for free like mother as funds were available nowadays. I did not agree to any of that because I really loved my work to teach school children. I loved their keen honest simple faces filled with curiosity and I loved to talk to them about great scientists and other countries that they gulped hungrily. I felt that if I could stimulate even one formative mind all my education and sorrows would be amply compensated. The children were much less rowdy and more receptive than children in the USA in the age groups I was teaching.

One whole year passed since my coming to Calcutta and rolled over to the second. Mother had improved further but not much. She would walk to Sarit uncle's room and the two would communicate in a way that I could not fathom but he looked happier now. I did something else that could be called naughty. Arranging mother's things and cupboards one day I came across a fat file tucked in a corner below all those saris. I opened it casually, finding old papers; some of them tattered, some in father's handwriting and some by mother. There was also an unbound notebook more like a school exercise book almost filled with mother's handwriting. I realized this was a diary, in fact all of it was, not written regularly but more of random entries, some were long and others not so. Decency prevailed over curiosity and I kept it in its place carefully. One day I mentioned it to mother swearing that I have not read its contents. She laughed and said, 'Why not? Yesterdays secrets are today's heritage. Does anybody mind if you read all those secrets of Rama and Karna and Kunti in the Ramayana and the Mahabharata? The papers you have unearthed are almost that, lost their privacy.' So I started reading them, not all of them at the same time as they needed to be arranged to make any sense. I saw that in my first scanning. So I took time to arrange them chronologically in sequence. It seemed like going through the Dead Sea Scrolls. The comparison is not right because there the characters are dead but here they are not all dead. There are historical characters that never die. Sometimes a story and its characters remain dead for centuries and millennia to be dug up and the characters come back to life as in Nag Hammadi Papers and the life of Mary Magdalene. In many respects she has actually become contemporary. The story I was unearthing was somewhat in this category though more modern.

I read through father's early memorabilia of his hardships and frustrations and how he faced them with courage and determination. The story of his grandfather's death and how it affected him came much later and were comparatively recent. He must have written these after he had himself developed cancer and probably close to his time of death. I think when he knew he had the disease he remembered the courage of his grandfather. What a grand man he was! He came alive for me. Did he have a premonition of death because the last writing actually describing his death was eerie! More tattered than these ones was his unsent letter to mother, must be in their early married life. It was left for mother to read after his death. I spotted Sarit uncle after reading through mother's writing! What a story, what love dripped through every word! How were those days when men and women could love so much? Have we forgotten love in our careerist fast modern life chasing mirages instead of the most important things that endure? Father could have gone much higher in life if he lived longer but there is no sign of loss or remorse neither in his writings nor in mother's. I compared that with my life and tears welled up. They lost so much in life but still it was full and I have lost so little yet I am empty. And then came mother's story of unhesitatingly accepting Sarit uncle without the least thought of what others will think, because he needed her and later she realized that she needed him too. But she took him initially because she could see that he would not survive without her and that was enough for her. These people knew what love was and did not need to 'make' it. I bow my head in great respect to all three of them and consider myself lucky to be born to their heritage. As I thought of this unusual love triangle through sleepless nights where only one side was complete and the other two did not connect, even irrelevant at least to our ordinary mind yet so sublime, I wondered what love really meant. What was that world and that culture where distance could not wither it instead made it stronger? I have read about it in Saratchandra Chattopadhyay's novels in childhood but always thought it was fictional and unreal and now it has taken such real form in my own family in contemporary time! It is so precious and is obtained through so much suffering but makes life worth living. For the first time after so many years I was feeling that calmness that I saw in my mother since childhood without even thinking about it as it was just a part of life. But now I am an inheritor to the perception of that depth that makes life worth living.

In spite of the love and admiration I felt for mother I could not help teasing her. We became great friends, able to look at our lives lightly as if on a stage playing our parts. It brought her out of her sorrow for me and her silence. The mother-daughter interaction was so frank, unhurried and intense that I shall remember to my dying days as one of the most memorable periods of my life. I would tease her 'when Sarit uncle first proposed you must have been moved and at least a little bit in love with him—confess it confess it confess it, no I shall not leave you until you confess'.

She laughed and laughed, pinched my cheek and patted and said 'you are being very naughty. Anybody expressing love makes you happy doesn't matter who, whatever sex and age of whatever relationship or unrelated, for example your nanny when you are a kid or even me telling you now will make you happy. Love does not have only one form as in your present day world.

I said, 'Ma, don't try to evade, it was a proposition,' and she immediately replied, 'yes, so it made me even more happy but I was not in love with him.'

'But he must have been there in some niche in your heart that you thought of in some idle moments,' I said.

'Have you people ever given me an idle moment?'

'But still, were you not happy when you saw him?'

'Happy? I was horrified. You must understand that in our more traditional generation purity was important, purity in love too, and that place was occupied by your father. Purity in our culture has always been the most important attribute for a woman and also a man, the only way to reach self realization. I suppose purity meant purity of emotion and purity of desire for as human beings we shall always have desire. Even a prostitute could be pure in ancient times, pure in her love for somebody while she could give her body for her livelihood or any other reason and it applies to men too. It is true for men too.'

I said parodying her, 'Hmmm, you are very modern too and I admire you and love you.'

She immediately said, 'See, you have made me happy,' and we burst out laughing.

There would be many such sessions and I would literally glean from her the beauty and honesty with absolute practicality of action through her long suffering life and her poise and balance. She was very knowledgeable on a wide variety of subjects as I had noticed even when I was young and she would not budge from truth even when discussing our lives, hers and mine, and would frankly talk about our points of weakness and strength. Asim said she was the greatest psychotherapist on earth and I could see why.

In this vein I remember another episode of our interaction. My divorce was hurting me. One day that subject came up and I complained to her it was not my fault or was it? She was silent for some time and then asked, 'Can you look at it objectively?'

I said, 'yes I want to, but can't.'

She said quietly, 'There was a maturity gradient between the two of you.'

I was taken aback, 'What, maturity gradient? Is that another one of your laws of physics?'

She sighed, 'I hope it was as accurate as a law of physics. You are a physicist yourself. Physics is an obstinately rational science. Those who follow it, even in those who are not great the psychological process of rationality becomes ingrained. If you study and ponder over the mindsets of those that became great you can sometimes see a connection between their psychological profile and their thought process and discoveries. It is more apparent in those whose complete lives are known and who are gone, like Poincare and Einstein but also some in modern times. A close example would be Roger Penrose.'

I asked, 'so what do you mean by maturity gradient?'

She said, 'You have yourself told me that you and Bob were great friends with a sincere and close friendship for a long time and you often wondered when he would notice you as a female. You matured sexually ahead of Bob and were passionate. His adulthood might have been delayed due to genetic or family conditions. It may be seen in young men with doting mothers. Your deep friendship was a matter of trust, deep trust is as valuable as love, sometimes more so, but is not really love. Love is a word used very loosely but real love is when it overrides all other emotions and practical problems of life. I can give many examples but . . .

I interjected, 'You don't have to, you and father is a practical enough example.'

She laughed, 'My, my, my little daughter is maturing fast! It does help to see when the example is close at hand, where giving becomes as satisfying as getting. It takes time.'

She was silent and I did not want to disturb her. I could feel what was going through her mind. Then she seemed to wake up and said, 'You have had a child but that did not mean much to him, just an accident. It is quite common that a woman becomes more satisfied after a child is born than the man. Actually his passion may increase and you see all those extramarital relations happening without either side wanting them. In your case there was even a physical separation, regrettably because of me.'

I almost shouted, 'No, no, don't ever mention it, not even think about it. You are not the guilty party, we are.'

She smiled, 'This is where objectivity and rational thought is necessary. You should be able to think rationally about life without casting aspersions or blames even in your mind, neither to yourself nor to others. It is the most difficult part of life without which you shall never get peace. This is almost practical spirituality.'

We were both silent. I did not know what she was thinking but to me what she said was enormous and stunning. I kept looking at her in admiration and awe.

She spoke after sometime, 'Even without physical separation your marriage would have gone through difficult times with irritations and conflicts and may be you would have ultimately reconciled because both of you are nice and kind people. It may even happen now, given the chance that we cannot foresee.'

This time I laughed. 'Chance or God, I have taught you that. Now you are down to earth, a dreaming mother. A moment back I was afraid that you will develop two wings and fly off. Now you are in my grasp as mother and I can love you for dreaming the impossible,' and I embraced her. We were back to being mother and daughter, laughing and crying in each others embrace.

Mother's health kept improving probably faster because of the relaxed environment in house with gaiety and laughter. Sarit uncle also looked better and easier to manage. I was thinking of a holiday somewhere as mother was rarely using oxygen and mother mooted the idea first. I discussed with doctor and he said a change by the seaside may be good for her but the oxygen and at least one nurse should accompany. I thought of Puri as a friend of mother had a house by the seaside that he used to let out as a guest house and was ready to book the upper floor for us for a fortnight. The journey was not strenuous on a night sleeper train reaching in early morning. So for the next school holiday I purchased train tickets in time to book a four berth coupe for both onward and return journey. We reached station early and in two wheel chairs carried mother and Sarit uncle to the compartment and laid them in the two lower berths. They slept comfortably all the way. The house at Puri was a small two storey house with a garden in front and on the upper floor four bedrooms and a balcony overlooking the sea with deck chairs and garden umbrella. There was a cook and other staff to look after everything.

Everybody was happy about the vista including Ravi and the two old people occupied the two deck chairs till the sun went up when we moved indoors. The days passed peacefully in the balmy weather and we enjoyed thoroughly. Ravi wanted to go down to the sea and every morning with sunrise I would take him to see the large breakers rolling down to the beach and wet our feet. I forbade him to go in the water although helpers were available. We came back when sun was up and spent the rest of the day inside with our books and playthings and as temperature dropped at night we would sit on the balcony enjoying the breeze and the open sea and the sky. The food was tasty and light. A week passed like this and one day mother wanted to visit the temple. I objected that it would be too strenuous for her as it was a steep long walk from the road. Our family priest or panda was coming everyday with Prasad and he kept encouraging mother that I objected to vehemently. Mother was becoming sentimental and told me one day, 'I will probably not come here again. Last time I came with your father shortly before his illness when you people were in hostel and stayed here for two days and we visited Lord Jagannath together and loved it so much.' I said, 'But the God did not do much good to you, did he, why do you want to take this risk?' She did not protest but remained morose and it made me sad. I talked to the priest in private and he could make arrangement to have mother carried inside for *darshan* and carry her back to the car at a less crowded hour. I said no going inside and told mother she could go if she did *pranam* from outside the gate. That is still a valid obeisance and she agreed. So we went keeping Ravi and uncle in the care of the nurse. But when we got out of the car there were two sturdy men who offered to carry her by locking their hands and they called her mother, the most venerated word in our language. That was not difficult as she was so thin and fragile. Obviously the priest had arranged this without telling me. There was no stopping mother. So we went and came back as quickly as possible after she worshipped the Lord and touched his pedestal as directed by the priest but it was still strenuous for her. She was so happy and satisfied that I thought I had probably done the right thing.

We went before the evening vespers. By the time we reached home it was already dark and mother wanted to sit on the balcony.

I objected and said, 'No you have done a lot today, and you must lie down in bed and rest and have some oxygen.'

She was frantic, 'No no not now. Look at the moon it is a full moon night and the clear blue sky and the sea, it is blue all over and not another light nearby. Put off the balcony light and see how gorgeous are the moon the sky and the ocean, the reason and causation of life on earth, it is not a night to lie inside with oxygen but a night to embrace this grand creation naked in body and mind. Let me recline in peace on this chair for some time and then I promise I shall go inside have oxygen and do whatever you want.'

I relented. I was also getting mesmerized by this grand vista. Not a cloud and the sky was a canvas painted light blue near the moon gradually to dark azure blue where it met the sea. The breakers were high and breaking on the beach with roar creating milk white surf spread over the beach and the undulating sea. It was indeed a sight for gods. I heard mother was muttering and sat close to her and put my recorder close to her mouth. Hers was a monologue.

'This creation is a great mystery that will never be fathomed by man. Think where it started. The young earth a fireball was hit by another fireball giving it a magnetic core of iron, an increased mass with just the right gravitational pull, altering its orbit to the narrow green zone around the sun with right temperature and probably also the spin. Has anybody done the exact mathematics how this was achieved, not to speak of why and when, not to my knowledge? The magnetic field produced a cosmic radiation shield around the earth. Gravitation captured an atmosphere created from chemical reactions in the boiling mass as it slowly cooled that further increased insulation and it captured the moon at the right distance; cooling also produced a solid crust. The moon is slowly running away but not in the life time of man on earth. Huge explosions combined hydrogen with oxygen to produce water and gravity kept it over the crust, not only in crypts and crevices. Earth's axis tilted to a precise angle with the orbit and seasons appeared. Moon played on the sea producing the tides, the high and low creating a rhythm. That rhythm produced a rhythm of life in the sea and life appeared gradually. But that was not enough, life had to develop and change so other rhythms were added, many rhythms and we do not know them all. The crust hardened and became thick and then huge continental masses moved and collided raising mountains and deepening seas, which were the nurseries of life. The rhythm of the sea would now inundate and now desiccate areas of land alternately spreading, destroying and creating life forms. The primitive organisms divided and metamorphosed along different lines. These were unicellular ones, those that utilized carbon dioxide and released oxygen and others that needed oxygen from the water and produced carbon dioxide. The former gradually migrated to land as they came out of the rolling seas and over time became static trees as they did not need to move since atmosphere was everywhere and their need of nitrogen was thrown to their feet by thunderbolts creating nitrates and they increased their output of oxygen in atmosphere. The oxygen users came out of the seas later at first hesitantly as oxygen content of atmosphere increased and then in greater numbers developing organs that could take oxygen from the atmosphere and nitrates from the trees. The great rhythm of a biological cycle was established.'

She paused for breath. Her respiration was a bit hurried. I was alarmed and asked her to stop. She brushed aside my hand and continued, 'No no even that was not enough. The earth was crowded but more rhythm was needed, some life had to be eliminated to make room for others. So huge changes were necessary in the major cycles of basic rhythm of environment and weather, the Chellos may be or the Master's baton? We do not know much detail of those except the ice ages and we think there have been eight ice ages but know no further detail. We know only of the last ice age that brought air breathing fast moving mammals that gave birth to babies instead of laying eggs and nursed the babies in their reproductive cycle. And last developed man, physically the weakest of the mammals and less adaptable to environment but an ability not with his body but with his mind to develop that adaptability and even influence the environment to some extent. And as he used his mind he was faced for the first time in evolution with the questions of 'why and how' of this creation. You can classify human evolution through anthropology of course but more poignantly by what answers they had for 'why and how' in each epoch. No final answer has come yet and nobody knows if ever, at least at this stage of evolution.'

My second attempt at stopping her failed and she continued. 'But do you not see that it is all a question of rhythm and cycles? The cosmos and galaxies are all rotating and so are the 'particles' that constitute them. You take any rotation and plot it on a plane in sequence, it becomes a stretched spring, waves joined together in a string that can coil and uncoil in different ways to different degrees and that is a rhythm. And they join together to fill the cosmos and its fields with the energy of the coil. The rhythm of the cosmos is violent and high energy and on the earth they seem to have been muted and slowed and less energetic, a pleasant one, loving and caring and not only to the living things even the mountains and the seas seem to love it that you see in their contours and movement, the living and the nonliving are one and the same. The cosmic rhythm has been translated to a gentler one in the small auditorium of earth. Again the questions of 'why and how' come forth, one sometimes predominating over the other but basically the same. This is the symphony of the universe and as a symphony it was created and in symphony it will dissolve. I am calling it a symphony because so many instruments are at play. Rhythm is music to us and music is rhythm and this cosmic rhythm as it is transformed in the small auditorium of earth can it produce what we call music; other animals even trees might be knowing it? If the cosmic energy of rhythm impinges on earth's atmosphere can it not produce sound waves? Rationally it should. It is said that ancient Rishis spending years in isolation in meditation could hear this music of the cosmos and it had a name and it was very soothing, calming the mind. I think I can hear that now filling me with peace. To tell you that I had to talk so much but now I am at peace and have nothing more to say,' and she stopped and I got alarmed.

I called the nurse and asked her to check the pulse, blood pressure and respiration and I used the cell phone to call the doctor. Fortunately I got him and he was free to talk. I described everything to him about the evening and said I was worried. He asked if there was any particular reason. I said her breathing was a bit hurried and she talked too much about things that got me worried. I gave the phone to the nurse and she described the parameters. Doctor talked to her for sometime and she listened attentively and then gave the phone to me. He told me that there is no change in her conditions except that she may be a bit tired. He said, 'I have told the nurse to give her the usual medicines and add a mild tranquilizer that you are carrying.' I said, 'She is tranquil.' He said, 'Still she needs a good night's sleep. Give her some light refreshment preferably liquid and keep the oxygen attached through the night. Ring me in the morning and report how she is.'

All that was done and I told the nurse to put Ravi to bed after feeding him and uncle and to stay with Ravi. I sat by mother. The night got deeper and in the silence there was only the distant rumble of the sea. I was dozing in the chair and woke up with a start as I felt mother's hand on mine. I looked at her and saw her smiling and caressing my hand. She said, 'It is late you go to bed I am all right.' I said I was not tired and preferred to sit by her and saw that her eyes were shining as if with a light of their own. She squeezed my hand and said, 'You are a big gal now,' as she used to say when I was small, 'Do not worry too much. Go to bed everything will be all right.' So I went to bed next door and woke up the nurse and asked her to pull a couch beside mother's bed and stay there. She was a nice girl and said she had slept enough and will be awake through the rest of the night; I need not worry. There was a connecting door between my room and mother's and I went there and lay beside Ravi. I woke up to see dawn breaking and the nurse shaking me and stifling her cry with her sari. I jumped up ran to mother and stood by her bedside and saw she was not breathing. She was dead but still smiling and her eyes were half open staring at something. I was paralyzed and just stood. The nurse came back after closing the connecting door and started crying loudly and shook me and asked me to close her eyes. I did that and broke down embracing her.

I do not remember how long I stayed like that, could have dozed with my head in her lap as a child when I was woken up by conversations across the hall. It was full daylight by now. I went across to Sarit uncle's room and found that Ravi was trying to describe something to him. At his age Ravi did not know what death was and was trying to describe all that happened with great gusto swinging his arms. Sarit uncle was enjoying the performance swinging with him slurping to control his drool that nevertheless was dropping and laughing. In exasperation Ravi started shouting because he knew this was serious, not a laughing matter. Then with utmost effort he gesticulated pursing his lips 'ganna dod' with dramatic movement of arms, he called mother Ganna, his own abbreviation. That penetrated uncle's mind and he looked up and saw me noticing me for the first time in that state. Suddenly the mist of his mind cleared and there was a remarkable change in his face. The static face mask changed to a grave expressive face. He stood up erect without help and looked at me. For a few moments I saw how handsome he was in his glorious youth when mother first saw him! Then he held my hand and walked slowly to mother's room without faltering a step. He stood looking at mother and then looked quietly at me. A single question came out of his mouth 'When?' I said, 'About two hours back.' He nodded and sat down on the floor and took mother's hand in his, the first time I saw him touch her. Then he put his forehead on her hand and sat still. I kept holding him from behind I do not know how long until Ravi came and gave him a push to wake him up and he rolled into my lap. He was dead. I did not cry this time; the shock of losing my two dearest people within hours paralysed me. I remained still like a statue with Sarit uncle on my lap holding his head passing fingers through his grey hair as if to console.

I do not recall much of what happened later. I was practically unconscious, not in body but in mind nothing registered. My connection with reality was Ravi and his incessant questions. How do you explain death to a child? In the end he became tired and silent. The nurse and the priest arranged everything through the day. My next memory was that pyres were lit for cremation, two pyres side by side on the beach, and I did the first rites. The cremation ground beside the sea was practically empty at night and I sat looking at the sea beyond the two flaming pyres consuming the two bodies. I was empty floating in space with no attachment apart from the little Ravi whom I brought along knowing he would remember this all his life. I could not help noticing the grandeur of the scene. The azure sea in bright moonlight kept rolling, breakers breaking on the shore throwing up incandescent white foam of surf beyond the flaming pyres with total unconcern. Mother spoke of the rhythm of the cosmos rhythm of the sea and presently it was playing the rhythm of death. I remembered the Requiem Mass played by Sarit uncle, the music he remembered in patches and loved to play. We are born out of the sea and the rhythm plays in our lives, now it rises and now it falls from the highs into the troughs.

The sea is unconcerned; it gives and takes away, takes away and gives but never the same not caring for what you think you want, different things to different people. The deep blue of the sea and sky lighted by moonlight dancing on the waves made Lord Sri Chaitanya jump to the sea in ecstasy of Krishna at this very place as the legend goes; love for its rolling majesty gave Ernest Hemingway the Nobel Prize; sitting by its shore on the rock at the southern tip of India Swami Vivekananda realized his self and his task; strolling by its shore Isaac Newton realized that he had only collected pebbles on the seashore while the great unknown lay beyond. These were the great ones but it gives something to lesser ones like me too. Does it distinguish between greater and lesser or you get what you are fit for? What has it in store for me? What do I desire; nothing at the moment. It gave mother sudden deep perception within her self and she knew she had fulfilled her stay on earth and it was time to go. It is strange that both father and mother knew when it was time to go. It is as if they connected to the great unknown in the last hours or days of life. Father connected may be one or two days earlier and wrote before he went though there is no way of knowing whether he went the same way he wrote. Is this what salvation is? Not everyone sees their death, it is rare. It is not for everyone. I remembered mother's last words to me, 'Everything will be all right,' and I believe everything will be all right for Ravi and me.

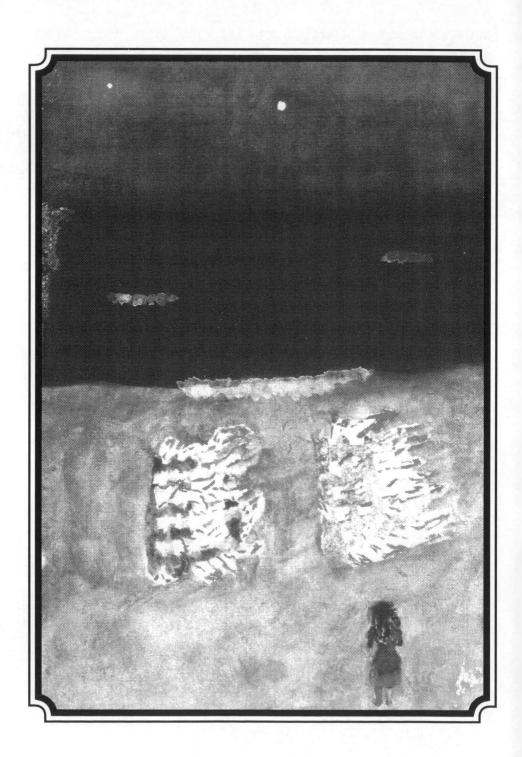

On The Seashore

Part 2

There is a tide in the affairs of men,
Which, taken at the flood, leads to fortune;
Omitted, all the voyage of their life
Is bound in shallows and in miseries.
On such a full sea we are now afloat,
And we must take the current when it serves,
Or lose the venture.

Shakespeare

'Julius Caesar'

CONTENTS

High Seas

Atin was hurrying down the College Street, after getting off from bus to reach his college. He had become a doctor a year back passing the MBBS examination. It is a common saying among seniors that it is difficult to get into a medical course, it is more difficult to pass the course and it is most difficult afterwards. This is a profession where graduation means nothing. It is only a stepping-stone. His friends who had gone to other professions graduated early and were already in jobs or in professional courses like MBA assured of good campus recruitment. Some continued studies holding jobs. He seems to have stepped out into an enveloping darkness. The student life was filled with fun and frolic, only hard task being to pass the examinations. Now there is no charted course. The books he read and memorized and the practical instructions on so many subjects that he had to remember to do well in the final examination have either no use or jumped out of the books and changed in real life. He has done well in the final, standing first in university and wanted to be a surgeon. But the road ahead is long and uncharted and the dream of a golden future seems to recede to darkness. He has completed his internship and is a registered doctor now. The student years seem a distant memory. The only link is Sohini, one year his junior, completing her final exams now, but already seems to belong to a different generation. He was a star student winning prizes, medals and scholarships every year enjoying free tuition, a system that still exist. He is a strong young man from years of physical excrcise and sports and a cynosure of all female eyes and enjoyed it until Sohini caught him. Today is her last exam of final MBBS.

He smiles as he remembers their first encounter. It was towards the end of his fourth year, one more year to go. Groups of fourth year and third year students were attached to each teacher for clinical teaching to learn how to examine patients and make a diagnosis and then chart the course of investigations and treatment. In surgical discipline a student was occasionally asked to assist at operation. Being a star student Atin was frequently called to assist and his poise, handiwork and concentration were appreciated, may be not in so many words but apparent in encouragements he received. That extra layer of glamour did not mean much but he was too young to know. It now seems such a distant past. Sohini was a junior member of the same group and she could not take her eyes off him. Atin noticed and felt pleased, but did not know how to handle. Youth took longer to mature those days. It was impossible not to notice Sohini. She was very sober and at the same time very pretty with a sweet voice, intelligent and serious in study as the girls usually were. But their interaction was limited to eye contacts, an occasional comment in discussions and much less frequent brushings and accidental hand contacts that remained memorable as they reminisced later and laughed for those were not all accidental. Then the day came when Sohini accosted him after the class and said, 'Can I ask you something?'

Atin was startled and croaked, 'What?'

'I find Pathology so difficult to understand, can you help me?'

Atin's heart gave a somersault, 'What, Pathology?' Sohini nodded and waited for answer. As was revealed later she was suffering from dry throat.

Atin gulped and asked again, 'Pathology? It is not such a difficult subject.'

Sohini would not be defeated so easily, 'Some parts are difficult. If you explain them to me I shall find it much easier to understand. I feel shy to ask a teacher every time.'

Atin had by this time controlled his palpitation and said, 'Yes, of course, it will help you to memorize if you understand them. But when do I teach you, where?'

Sohini was ready, 'You can come to my house, and it is not far. I don't mean everyday, say once or twice a week?'

Atin watched fascinated at her blush, 'I could but how about your elders?'

Her colour rose further and Atin learnt for the first time what a blush was, and how beautiful it could be, 'We are only four people in the house apart from the servants, my father, mother and a brother who is much younger to me. Nobody would mind.'

Atin took the plunge in spite of the tremor inside 'Yes I can go with you tomorrow after classes to see your house and then we shall see.'

Atin had by now reached the college offices and collected the forms for sitting in the postgraduate entrance examination. This was a farce he thought, that has been started to screen candidates who want to pursue postgraduate studies as if the marks or grades they score in their graduate studies were of no value. These examinations have brought the students from academia to political process. There is no guarantee that this screening is more honest and impartial. There is some merit in admission tests on a national basis, in a large country like India, but they were not yet in place. Undergraduate education suffers if two close tests at the same level are held in the same university. Was it good for society to discard the heritage of past values? How does a society survive by devaluing things once valued? Was not development by improving things to the demands of the present better than wholesale rejection of the past? A totally new and untried structure may not fit into the accustomed curriculum. Societies are better off with evolution than revolution unless in a catastrophic situation. He stood first in MBBS from Calcutta University in a thoroughly impartial examination. It was not easy to do well but he has nothing to show for it. The university is bankrupt and the endowment for a gold medal that he should have been awarded at the convocation has vanished. There is not even a mention in his certificate. He has to appear again at the same level to some other body and may even fail to qualify. There is no practical and no viva voce in this test. It is an examination with multiple choice questions and invisible examiners where there is no pass or fail, only the rank is important. The whole thing clumsily organized has no relevance to the curriculum and method of study over the five-year course. The people who set the questions just copy them from foreign source collected in a handbook. Many students do not study the textbooks or seriously involve in practical work during their entire student career as their only aim is to somehow pass the MBBS to be eligible for this test. They spend time to swallow wholesale the standard questions and answer from the handbooks, without any conceptual knowledge, and vomit it out at the examination. He smiled as he remembered that his only prize for standing first in MBBS was a kiss from Sohini, their first.

By now he reached the examination hall, and found the final gong has not sounded and Sohini has not come out. He sat down on a bench to wait for her. Actually his decision to appear for the entrance test led to arguments between them. Sohini does not want him to appear for this test. Her idea is to move abroad. She wants him to appear for tests to obtain registration and jobs in UK or USA. The fees for appearing in those tests are high, and even after qualifying one has to have money to travel and survive until a job is available and that is not easy. Atin is the younger of two brothers. Elder brother Amit was more brilliant than him, and went for engineering study in the newly developing field of computers and software. He was doing very well in college, but somehow got embroiled in the ultra left violent Naxalite movement of the time when he was in the final year and ruined his career. They were a middle class family, his father proudly holding a school teacher's job in what is now Bangladesh and suffered partition of India. They knew nobody with social or political influence. Amit could not come out of the political stigma as many did, with family influence and money. He was doing small time jobs with his knowledge of computer and electronics, earning enough for his personal expense, but unable to donate to the family coffers. Father had retired and his small pension was the only livelihood of the family. There was no way Atin could find the funds to go abroad and needed to earn for the family, whatever little a fresh graduate could. Sohini came from affluent family of a Punjabi businessman father and a Bengali mother. She offered to help. Both of them could stay with her relatives abroad until at least one of them found a job and could send money to his parents. She implored, and said he could pay her back in good time. Atin knew her offer was serious and practical, as she always was, but he was as proud as his elder brother and could not accept. He sighed as he saw Sohini come out and wondered whether he would ever be able to give up this woman he loved so much! She was his life. What fate had in store for him? Sohini believed fate was something one had to plan to achieve. Is pride more important than love? Would love survive if he gave up his pride? If he succeeded in the entrance examination he might get an attachment, and some job or a scholarship, and that would be a relief to his hard pressed family. What should he do?

Sohini saw him and increased her pace to sit down by his side and asked, 'Why are you looking so glum? You must be worried that I shall fail the exam, is that it?'

Atin smiled, this was typical of Sohini. She would make any situation light. It was so relaxing to be with her. He replied, 'As a matter of fact I was wishing just that. If you fail you shall appear a second time and if you fail again, a third time. Then you pass, and do one year of internship, and by that time I complete my postgraduate provided I get the admission this time, and then we decide what we do and where we go together.'

Sohini gave him a hard pinch, 'And I thought you were my friend! To please his lordship I have to fail twice,' and she moved her hand as if to swat a mosquito on his cheek which Atin knew so well was a ruse to touch him. This was as much as was allowed in public by the society of the time.

She bent forward and looked at his face, 'And do tell me why can't we be together now?' Her brownish dark eyes were two deep pools.

Atin jumped up and laughed saying, 'Enough is enough. Get up now. I did not know that exams make you horny. How did it go anyway?'

She got up feigning to tumble and clung to his arm. 'Actually they do and make me very hungry,' and she winked. 'Let us go have some food.'

Atin stiffened. This meant that she would foot the bill as he had no money. She realized immediately, and pulled his arm grabbing closely, 'Come on you male chauvinist pig, if you delay this any further I shall eat you live.'

Atin never had the strength to rebuff her and followed meekly asking, 'To get back to the beginning how did your exams go, I want to hear all of it till this last exam as I did not want to disturb you in the middle?'

She pouted, 'Your little disturbances give me energy but you deserted me. To save you from disappointment, it all went like a song. I am very pleased. I had to do well because if I fail it would be a discredit to my teacher, after all the fees I paid him, wouldn't it? But I am not going to stand first, so don't worry.'

She had moved forward and looked back with an impish smile. Atin jumped and gave her a slap on the back, 'You have given all the fees and what about me, what have I given?' She blew a kiss and said 'tonic' and ran forward beyond his reach.

They were seated in her car and Atin thought, 'Another one of the big places today that I would never have been able to enter, and not in foreseeable future' and he could not help feeling small. He knew it was foolish in a relationship but could not get out of it.

Sohini could read his mood without looking at him, sometimes even when they were not together, and would ring and ask, 'What are you worrying about now?' It was curious. Once he asked, 'How do you know what I am thinking, it is rather scary' and she laughed and said, 'Don't be scared, I would never ask who was the woman you were with.'

This time she turned around to face him and asked, 'What? What is it this time? Oh yes I know, you are thinking how you are going to repay all these food bills if you leave me.'

Atin smiled wanly, 'And a lot of other things.'

Sohini became serious, 'You do not owe me anything. We have loved each other and yes, made love, not by design but spontaneously. It binds you to no commitment. This is the second time we are having this dialogue and there will never be a repeat. You have no idea how much you are hurting me, and making me feel cheap for something we shared so lovingly,' and her eyes were moist.

Atin drew her close as much as was possible in a car with the driver sitting in front and took out his handkerchief to wipe her tears and said with deep emotion, 'Please please don't cry and forgive me for hurting you. I am a beast, don't make me more unworthy.'

He repented the moment the words came out of his mouth. Sohini tore herself away and accosted him with flaming eyes, 'Worthy worthy, that same word and I hate it. Why are you unworthy? Just because your father has less money than mine, just because you are riding my car instead of me in yours, you become unworthy? I know what it is it is your sense of guilt for having sex with me. Just imagine you are driving your own car, and have the money to pay for me, and you would be worthy? You want me to become a whore, and I am telling you that I love you so much that I would not mind becoming a whore, to satisfy your Bengali middle class morality. Your mind does not allow you to be happy, and that is a disease. Learn to take life as it comes' and tears trickled down her cheeks.

Atin sat paralyzed without a word, for it was best not to say anything, and sat holding her hand. She was tired after long examination schedule and she was right. They made love not by design. She needed help to prepare for her final exam, and he prepared for his own joint entrance exam, and studied together sometimes till late into the night, the curriculum being more or less the same. They had decided that he would not join as house surgeon during this period, as he would automatically become a trainee surgeon after he qualified, and they never doubted that. They came close spontaneously. Normally this would be the ideal, as they were two budding doctors intensely in love. What was not expected was his self doubt, whether he could honour the responsibility of that love. It was his fault, if it could be called a fault. His doubt came from the uncertainty and inequality of opportunity in a backward society. He could not take this relationship casually, as something that has happened, and might or might not last. That was not his cultural tradition.

There have always been divisive forces in Indian society at least as far back as herd memory went, especially so in marital affairs and even in love and sex. At one time it was religion and caste. Religion was still strong, but money had taken the place of caste in many parts of urban India, and was no less strong as money drove culture with that same intensity in money crazy Indian society, with a long history of deprivation and hunger. Take any Indian and dig deep, and in the turmoil of recent centuries there would be a rural or semi urban generation in the past, suffering deprivation and even hunger regardless of caste. One would have expected the caste barriers to dissolve, but that did not happen. Instead a craze for money security added a class barrier, in addition to caste. Atin analyzed his society, and felt sad about the severe shortcomings in the roadmap of development to a united democratic society, and felt the frustrations that many of lesser intellect would not be conscious of, but little did he imagine that one day this would come up to confront him in his own life. Fortunately the driver was programmed to reach the restaurant, and not having knowledge of English he did not waver, and they reached their destination without any further conversation, with Sohini still sniffling. Atin looked at her with affection and resolved that he was never going to fail or hurt her.

Reality strikes

After all those emotional storms and planning Atin did not score high enough rank to be eligible for entry to any of the surgical disciplines of General Surgery, Orthopedics, ophthalmology etc. Other super specialized branches of surgery came at the next higher level after passing the Master of Surgery or M.S. in General Surgery. He did not want to get in to anything else, his aim was General Surgery. He broke down. He realized that he had concentrated more on Sohini's studies than his own. She had done much better and passed with honours. In his case he had rusted somewhat, during internship and it was difficult to identify where deficiencies had crept in and to polish them. His teachers had warned him and asked him to concentrate but the diversion of Sohini distracted him as he dreamed more than her and worried more about the future. It is a curious thing that happens often in a filial relationship that the woman takes it in her stride without fantasizing much, once the bondage is made, whereas the man finds it difficult to take his mind off. Male sexuality is tense and even more so at the beginning, even achieving an erection is a matter of tension. This is probably the way the higher mammalian world functions. The female sense of practicality is of evolutionary importance for continuation of species. The lioness hunts ungrudgingly to feed her cubs and her master and he literally takes the lion's share, leading a lazy life and keeps his lionesses, the asset that he has won, keeping them happy with protection and sexual satisfaction without which she would look for a more worthy mate. If the lion had a higher mind he would worry about losing his asset but he is lazily happy until a competition appears. If we multiply this simplicity a thousand times to the complicated psyche and life of man today it would be obvious why Atin had failed and Sohini did so well.

He was in more trouble than one. He had no earning, and the little that he had saved was all gone. He had rejected the chance of a job as house surgeon in the institution to devote entirely to study, and he had to look for job elsewhere. He joined a private hospital, more a nursing home, as a resident medical officer. That solved his problem of board and lodge, and though the salary was small, he earned extra by assisting surgeons at operation both in the hospital and outside. He was a good assistant. This threw him to the world of private practice of which he had no knowledge. He noticed that most private surgical practice was of minor nature, a substantial part being taken by obstetrics and gynecology. As the only resident he had to participate in all specialties including medical problems and oversee the patient care when the specialist was not in. Mostly the lower income patients were the clienteles and the concept of intensive care had not entered in such places and was not required by law. He was scared from the day he joined that something would go wrong and often consulted friends, but he need not have worried too much. Wrong treatment did not attract any retribution if you 'managed' the situation well and the legal framework was very lax those days. Gradually he adjusted and being one of the better graduates and sometimes better than the consultants who admitted patients, he was able to help them. The hospital as a whole was happy with him.

But the world of competitive private practice at this level was so sordid and crude that it revolted him. Haggling with patient and relations for fees mostly happened before admission but its effects did not entirely end there. Any deviation from routine adding to the cost of treatment upset everybody, the patient, the hospital authorities, the doctors and quarrels broke out, sometimes muted but sometimes not. The patient was the cow and whatever could be milked was then split, to be shared by the surgeon, the anesthetist, the referring doctor's commission, the hospital administrator and sometimes a small portion for him. At first he cringed from accepting anything, and then he gave in because that was the system. The patient's relations were mostly suspicious of neglect or wrong treatment and he had to face them. Even simple procedures could become risky because of lack of infrastructure and rashness. Every one was in a hurry especially the anesthetist, as demand for his services were higher and he had to rush from one clinic to another. Sometimes they would leave a half recovered patient to his care and he used to be very scared. Sometimes relations would push money in his hand imploring him to take care. It was so demeaning but unavoidable. Nobody likes a man who is out of the system.

Unfortunate accidents leading to even death did happen and the expertise to hide it and gloss over took a long time to learn. The specialists were more adept in this than him, and that revolted him. Even those that were unavoidable by the very nature of the disease had to be given a different explanation, which would be acceptable to the relations. They would not accept a rational explanation. For some it would be waiver of the fees, for some would be the excuse that the patient had a bad heart and it failed even if he was young. Daily involvement with such unethical practice led to depression, and the extra undeclared money gave rise to drinking habits among doctors. Atin's personal life could not remain the same as before. There were no regular hours and concentrating for study to prepare for the next exam became difficult and so was meeting Sohini. She could not keep pace with his irregular and difficult hours and their meetings became less frequent and even then he could not relax. She would excitedly describe new things and new operations she had seen or learnt but that would leave him cold. He could not even describe his experiences and sorrows to her, she would not understand. She came to his room at the hospital a few times but the atmosphere was least conducive to love. He would be grumpy and she felt helpless.

One day she came in unannounced, it was before the days of mobile phones. His room was dark and he was sitting like a zombie in stupor. He did not even welcome her. She switched on the light and seeing as he was, lifted his face and asked softly what was wrong. Tears came to his eyes and started streaming down his cheeks. She was alarmed and asked anxiously, 'What is the matter? Your parents are all right?' He nodded but remained silent. She insisted, 'Tell me what it is. I have never seen you like this, please tell me' and slowly he told her.

'A girl came a few days back bleeding severely and in shock.' He was silent.

She prodded him, 'Bleeding from where?' He avoided her eyes.

'She was bleeding from vagina. She had an accidental unwanted pregnancy. She was a young girl, a college student. Avoiding any help out of shame, she went to an untrained midwife for abortion; her insides were severely mutilated and still hiding it from her parents she got infected and continued to bleed. She came with septic shock.'

Atin could not go on and Sohini started crying and thumped him, 'What happened then?'

'A surgeon was called and he operated, stitching injuries from below and somehow stopped the bleeding. I implored him to open the abdomen as there must be a perforation of the uterus and to stitch it or remove it to save her life. He called me a fool and said opening the abdomen in this state may cause death and if that happens it would be a police case. Who would explain to the parents? They would not believe, and who would foot the bills? Who will face the police enquiry if she died on the table and it became known? He told me to control the infection and then he would see. I did not leave her bedside for two days and nights. She died this morning,' and he completely broke down.

Sohini cried out as if she had been hit and shouted, 'Why didn't you operate, I know you could have done it.'

'I do not have the license, I am nobody. If death happened in my hands I would have gone to jail for manslaughter. Her parents were here, an old couple completely deranged from grief. She was their only child in late age. They did not believe she could be pregnant and kept telling she was not like that. They were not giving consent for operation and then relented as they had no money to go to a better place,' he looked wildly at Sohini, 'Just imagine if this was you!'

Sohini took control of the situation and pressed his head in her bosom and said, 'Don't be silly and hysterical. Why did she do it? She could not be that innocent.'

Atin almost shouted still crying, 'But she was! It happened in a friend's house, her only close friend and it was the friend's brother who she thought was very nice.'

Sohini was practical, 'She should have confided to a better person than you. Now you come away with me to my house and leave this ghastly room immediately.'

Atin said, 'Yes, I would do that. There are no more serious patients, the only one is dead. Let me call the hospital superintendent.' He called him on phone and said that he was leaving. All papers of the dead patient have been completed and left with the matron. He is leaving his room locked and will collect his things later. The letter of resignation is on his table and he is keeping a copy signed by the matron.

The cool breeze in the car was soothing. They sat silent. The car passed through the Park Street and Atin was staring at the festival lighting, the lighted shops, the glitzy restaurants and continuous stream of people strolling down the street and beggar boys in rags running zigzag through the crowds. At one corner there were gaudily dressed girls loitering and busily going in one direction and turning around. He knew these were prostitutes and their pimps are there in the crowd somewhere. Christmas was not far away and the lighting was a legacy of the British Raj. This city, that Rudyard Kipling found 'chance directed chance erected' and the British called the garden city east of Suez at one time, has gone through so much in this twentieth century. It has seen greatness in scholasticism, culture, arts and sciences with Nobel Prizes in Physics and Literature in the first decades of the twentieth century, the two sublime pillars of human intellect, new revolutions in religious universalism that is sweeping the world, the cradle of Indian Renaissance, the melting pot of the East and West, of social and political upheavals, has also gone through so much misery. It saw the rise of violent struggle for independence, as also the nonviolent one; it was brushed by the Second World War with possibly the greatest man-made famine in the world in 1943, carnage of communal frenzy, the city and state that contributed and suffered the most for independence partitioned at the birth of free India, with probably the largest migration of people in modern times amid murders, riots and destruction. Nobody in the world has cried for this city, because it has not died, it is vibrantly alive as it always has been, ignoring equally the praise and blame of the world, but almost brought down to knees with misery all around.

Atin had no idea what Sohini was thinking, until she suddenly said, 'Why do you want to stay in this miserable city with no development and only going backwards in all fields, even in its great heritage of human decency?' He realized she was still thinking about the girl and feeling sorry for her. This was so typical of her. She was so soft and tender inside, with a surface of practicality and hard headed decision maker. He smiled and squeezed her hand and said, 'But this is my city and you have no idea or may be some, how poor and miserable its people are behind the veneer of this glitter we see around us, and yet so soft and sensitive like you.' She pulled away her hand in mock anger and said, 'Instead of serenading me you should think how you are going to introduce me to your mother. I shall be in your house for the first time whereas you made my house your love nest. I am already having palpitation my lord' and they laughed. He assured her, 'You are not unknown and you will like each other but not tomorrow. I shall collect my things tomorrow and go home. I shall take you under better circumstances.'

Collapsing Waves

The happy situation of taking his beloved home to meet mother did not happen after all. As he entered with his bags and books his mother was alarmed, 'What happened, why are you back home?' He embraced her after touching her feet and said, 'I have left my job. The work was too heavy and I was not able to study. My entrance examination is close. I shall be home and study, till they are over. Do not worry. I have saved some money, and I shall not bother you much.'

Mother's eyes became moist, 'You think a son coming back home bothers a mother? The days have changed so much. We were never rich and all our resources have been spent in bringing up Amit and you. Yet we have spent a happy and peaceful life. Little things gave us so much pleasure that would probably seem silly to your generation. People are so unhappy these days. I see our neighbors, and they never seem to be happy. I sometimes wonder what do they really want what would make them happy'.

Atin was still embracing her and said, 'Now now do not go on, where is Dada'?

Mother extricated herself from his embrace and arranging things in the room said, 'You are asking about Amit? We have stopped asking and worrying a long time back. When he went to the engineering college and you were home we were so happy with our two bright sons, two gems, people used to say. I think their jealousy spoiled everything. We used to dream so much, that one son will be a big engineer and the other a big doctor and we shall be so happy in one large family, with daughter-in-laws and grandchildren. Your father used to say we have to build another floor. I don't know why Amit had to mix with those bad people'.

Atin embraced her again, 'They were not very bad people Ma. When are you going to give me a cup of tea,' he whined like a child.

Hearing all the commotion father came out from the next room calling out, 'Who has come, Amit or Atin?'

Mother said, 'It is Atin. He has left his job.'

Father stopped in his track in shock, 'Left his job? Why?'

Atin touched his feet and said, 'No, I have not left. I am on study leave'.

Father heaved a sigh of relief and turned towards his room. Atin kept looking at him. He has become senile so fast! He was a school teacher in a government school, very proud of his profession. He entered service after graduating with second class honours in English, the first one to do so from their village, lost in East Pakistan, now Bangladesh. He did his MA while teaching and then married mother. Atin can remember him reading Shakespeare to them when they were young. Getting a job was difficult in his days and that also a school teacher's job. People did not change jobs those days, started with a job and held on to it till retirement, and life was spent with small annual increments in salary. Losing or resigning a job was unheard of and a calamity. You stick to it and marry get a family and look after them and after retirement reap your benefit in the form of provident fund, a small pension and the comfort of established children. That was life and fulfillment. With that much expectation, they led their lives through freedom movements, World Wars, famines, communal riots and partition adjusting in their small niche, jealously guarding their family. Retirement brought emptiness, difficult to fill without the close support of the family. Those who did not have that grew senile fast as has his father. The assets he had to show for his struggling life are the two sons and a small two bedroom house in a fringe of the city, with a verandah in front and a kitchen, a bathroom and a small courtyard at the back that was mother's relaxation as a garden. Since independence life has changed so fast that he found difficult to keep pace. He does not understand his sons, grieving wildly for the elder one. Why did he throw away a bright future for what, he could not understand? He could not cope with the life getting rapidly complicated in the second half of twentieth century. Now he was at sea with television, media, and life in modern society and the communists and he was not familiar with any of those! The area where he built his house with open spaces all around was rapidly filled up with people coming as refugees after partition. They squatted on empty land occupying them forcibly and built houses! Their aggressive younger generation, many with unfinished education indulged in aggressive violent politics without respect for the older generation. He strongly disliked and hated them finding no remnant of his old memories of the land he has left behind and was alienated from the society around. Mother found it easier to cope with life, as probably the women usually do, her only sorrow was that his sons did not become as she dreamt they would be. That is why Atin did not bring Sohini without preparing them for the event. It would have shocked them to find a girl friend and they did not even know what that was. Atin's revelry was broken by mother's entry with tea and he smiled, at least she was still the same. He smiled at her and said, 'Ma, we are so lucky to have a mother like you.'

Mother wiped her face with the end of the sari and said, 'I shall make this room ready for you. There is no certainty when Amit will suddenly come, then you have to share.'

Atin laughed, 'As if we have not done that before. You don't have to do anything I shall arrange it all.'

Mother said, 'Only if one of you brought a wife, I shall not need to work so much at my age but that is my fate. Amit did not sit for the final examination and ran away God knows where, with all those boys. But I tell you those boys were nice. They would call me mother, but come in the darkness of night have their food and melt away in darkness.'

Atin laughed loudly this time, 'Ma, even if Dada and me had one wife each, we would never allow them to cook, it will be your cooking every time,' and thought he would mention it to Sohini to tease her. At least he made mother happy.

Lying on the bed at night he was reminiscing. Amit was caught when he was not home. Police came for Atin too, but he was not in the list. He was too young when all this broke out. As he dozed to sleep he remembered that Amit used to call him Bacchu, meaning Kid, indicating that he was only a child and that became his nickname. Amit was released from jail when he was in the third year in Medical College.

Atin's sleep was broken by sounds coming from the next room, his mother calling his name and crying at the same time. He rushed and found his father groaning, and mother sitting beside and asking him what was wrong, with no response. It did not take him long to realize that he had a heart attack and his pulse was feeble. He rushed out to find a transport and was fortunate to find a taxi, and woke up the driver who lived nearby. He took father to the nearest hospital. There was no choice, his condition was so poor. The hospital had a small intensive care unit, without much modern facilities. He woke up the duty doctor, and together they managed to hook up instruments to revive him and make him fit for transfer to a cardiac centre as electrocardiogram confirmed a heart attack. He was in poor shape and his heart was failing. A senior consultant was contacted and he rushed in. An external pacemaker was inserted to keep the heart going and medicines were started to dissolve the obstructing blood clot, if there be one. Little more than an hour had elapsed since he got the attack. But he was frail and in shock, and the heart could not be revived. By mid-morning all efforts failed and he passed away.

Atin was in deep sea. He did not know how to handle the situation, and where to turn for help. How can he face mother and break the news of father's death? What was his priority now? He has seen lots of death but does not know what does one do when it happens in the family? He collapsed in a chair in the intensive care unit covering his face.

The senior doctor saw and came to him. Placing hand on his shoulder he said softly, 'You are a doctor and you have seen deaths. Do not break down when it is your near and dear one. Who else are at home?'

He looked up with tears in his eyes, 'Only my mother. I do not know how to face her. We do not have any close relatives and none staying nearby. I have mostly lived in hostel and have no contacts. Father used to know some' and tears streamed down again.

The doctor said, 'So you shall have to handle it all alone. You have to face it and cannot afford to break down. All of us have to face it at some time or other. Let me drop you home. Where do you stay?'

Atin got dropped close to home not right in front. He walked around the streets trying to organize his mind. There was a group of young men at a street corner and he knew a few faces. The unemployment was so high that one would easily come by such people. One of them came forward and asked, 'Aren't you Atin? Why are you walking around like this? Is there any problem?' Atin gave them the news in short. They said, 'Do not worry, we are neighbours and what are neighbours for if not to help in such hours? Uncle is in which hospital? Have you been able to contact Amitda?' They knew Amit very well, quite a celebrity in the locality. Atin told them which hospital father was lying in and said, 'If you go to the hospital after couple of hours I shall be there by then and take delivery of the body.' One of them said, 'I shall inform Amitda.' Atin looked at him and he looked familiar but these were not times to disclose familiarity unnecessarily.

Atin left them and went home. Before entering house he went to a small hair cutting saloon in the locality and rubbed his face to wipe marks of tears, combed his hair, tucked in his shirt and made himself presentable. Then whistling a tune he went in. Mother was sitting in the outer room. She sprang forward and asked about father. Keeping his face straight he just said, 'Improving' and then he said, 'I am hungry, do you have any food?' Mother said, 'No, I am waiting for you. Brush your teeth and wash your face I am coming.' He made himself ready and as mother brought food he said, 'That is too much for me you also have some, let us share.' Mother said, 'I am not hungry you eat.' He ate some and then said, 'I have eaten enough, you eat something now. Last night you did not have much.' He went out to wash his mouth and when he came back he found mother standing with an expression he never saw before and she said quietly 'your father is no more, isn't that so?' and she broke down crying without sound. He hurried to her side holding her in an embrace and she howled in anguish. The sound of her crying brought some female neighbors, as the houses were very close and the news spread bringing more. There was nothing to say and Atin just sat by her holding her. Some of the men folk asked for relations to inform, but Atin did not know their phone numbers. Mother had to bring out an old worn out diary and they took down some phone numbers.

Atin came out of the house and found his new found friends of the morning have come with a small pick up truck. They said, 'Let us go and bring uncle back home when you are ready.' The friend who offered to inform Amit said, 'Amitda has been informed and he will be here by the time we bring uncle.'

So it was that Atin brought his father's body home after completing the formalities at the hospital. He did not have any money and promised to clear the bills after completing father's last rights. He was a doctor and the hospital knew the youth of the locality and they agreed. Still it was more than two hours before he could reach home. He found Amit as he entered and the burden was somewhat lifted from his shoulders. Now the entire manpower of the locality was at their disposal, and everything was Amit's duty as the elder son. He went with the crowd to the cremation ground and loitered around desolately as Amit and his friends made all arrangements. He had less duties as the younger son, and after completion came back home with the crowd.

When they returned mother was still lying silent in bed surrounded by a few ladies but not crying any more. Atin thought there must be a limit to the fluid that can be generated by the lachrymal glands, and immediately regretted for such irreverent thought. But he knew he could not help such oblique thought and it is not always unhelpful in medical career, though it sometimes made Sohini mad.

Amit sat beside mother holding her shoulder, and talking to her soothingly and after sometime actually made her smile. Amit had this capacity and she obviously loved him more, Atin thought with a pang of jealousy. He was the first born in a young family and mother cuddled and caressed him longer and then suffered with him in his predicaments. Atin was more of a recluse. He went out for fresh air. Strolling around he thought of calling Sohini, but that would be difficult. He cannot bring her home now, and would have to answer many questions regarding father's death. She was not foreign to Atin's periods of silence, and trusts him in spite of those. He loitered around aimlessly for some time walking through the familiar roads in the evening darkness. His thoughts were aimless as he was unable to focus his mind on anything. In just a few days his life has changed as all his plans have collapsed. With father's death his pension money would stop. Mother is supposed to get widow pension, but that would be nominal and the hassle to get that would probably take a long time, if ever. It is pathetic to think that with two qualified grownup sons that would be her predicament. But even that small money that was mother's right was necessary and he decided to visit the concerned offices. He pondered on how much his life has changed in a few months. His life was focused until he failed the postgraduate entrance examination, and then suddenly all moorings were gone. Only this last week has destroyed what remained. Here he was, a registered doctor who is licensed to treat patients and there is no dearth of them, but he is jobless and aimless. This is unacceptable. He had to grab life with both hands. He had the responsibility of looking after his mother, and there was the woman he loved and who loved him. He had to be firm and confident and hold on to his moorings and not let go in despair. He is a strong young man and must not collapse in misfortune and feel lonely.

He found a telephone booth on the roadside and walked in. He dialed Sohini's number hoping she would be home. She came on the line and asked why he did not call her. Her voice was urgent and excited. Before he could reply she said, 'I was waiting for your call all evening yesterday but you never called. I met Professor Ghosh yesterday, the Professor of Surgery and told him what happened in the nursing home and that you have left it. He said you have done the right thing and told me that he is looking for an assistant to assist him in his practice and he would be glad if you join him. You know he has a large practice and it would be almost full time with enough time for you to study. He wanted you to come and meet him today but you never called. You call him right now he would still be in his chamber. You know how much he loves you. You have this habit of neglecting people who love you' her voice broke at the end.

He then told her what happened after he left her and how his day has been so far and she started crying. His sorrow returned with her crying; it was embarrassing in the public booth and he said he was hanging up and would talk later.

Now came her command, 'Where are you at the moment' and he told her. She mentioned the nearest point at a local cinema hall and said, 'You just wait there, I am coming.' He protested, 'Not now, not at this time of night. You do not know this area,' but she would not listen. So he mentioned another point further on, a tea stall beside a college campus where they had been once and asked her to start after fifteen minutes and she said, 'Ok, I understand. I shall start after half an hour.' She knew that he would be walking the distance as he had no money in his pocket. That was Sohini.

He could not pay the phone booth but promised to pay next day and started walking at a trot to their meeting point where there will not be much light at this time but it is trouble free generally. He could easily run the distance in twenty minutes but Sohini being what she was, would not let him run and postponed their meeting by three quarters of an hour.

Brisk walk at night brought the energy back and Atin started feeling more relaxed and determined. Depression seemed to vanish at the prospect of meeting Sohini. He thought of that as he increased his pace, what wonderful animal we human beings are in our body mind complex and we are unaware of most of our attributes, at least not conscious of it. A targeted action breaks our depression, the vision of a helping hand brings back the energy and the future does not seem so bleak after all.

He reached the place with time to spare. The tea stall was open with very few customers. He sat at a table with a view of the road and ordered a cup of tea. If Sohini does not turn up he would not be able to pay for the tea, but that did not bother him. All his self doubt has vanished and he felt confident. The cup was not finished when Sohini's car turned the corner and came in view.

Sohini came to the shop carrying a number of bags and bundles. She was still panting and Atin remarked, 'I have almost run and you have come in a car and still panting.'

Sohini gave an angry look and said, 'You would have panted like me if you did shopping at my pace, in fact you always pant when you enter a shop' and deposited the bags on the table. Then she picked up a biggish plastic bag and said, 'This here contains one kilogram of *atap* rice and one kilo of ghee; this one is one kilo of potato; here are two packets of Maggie noodles; this is a card from Professor Ghosh so that you stay in touch; and this lastly' and she picked up a black cardboard box 'is a new innovation in your life, a mobile phone all charged and ready to use for you to remain in touch with the world so that you do not feel darkness all around. Don't get upset, I did not buy it, given to me as a gift and I am passing on to you for you are more difficult to get than me and you will need it for your practice with doctor Ghosh.' As he was about to remonstrate she held up her hand and said, 'Don't, not here. You can return when you don't need any more.'

Atin looked fascinated and spellbound, not at the merchandise but at her. She was still breathing heavily with sweat on her lips and red eyes ready to rain tears. She wiped her face with the end of her sari, he had scarcely seen her in sari and she looked beautiful. He was speechless and kept staring unable to speak. She retorted in mock anger, 'What are you staring at, these are things that are normally brought to a house of bereavement by friends and even foes' and he saw she was close to tears. He silently extended his hand like a beggar. She again said sharply, 'What do you want' and he replied 'Just one rupee to pay for the tea and get out of the shop.' She smiled for the first time and they paid for the tea and got out with the bundles.

They got out of the shop and made for the car and taking advantage of the driver's distance from the car and darkness Atin kissed her on the cheek and she pushed him away and said, 'Give the driver the direction to your house and show me from a distance and then get off with your luggage. I shall not enter your house this way. But I shall come back tomorrow properly with more things needed and they would be from my mother. This is just emergency ration.' He asked what he should tell mother. She replied in the same tone this time in English, 'Tell your mother that you are in bad company of a woman and she has given these things with her regards and pranams' and now she could start crying in silence covering her face.

Atin entered home awkwardly carrying the bags to find Amit sitting alone. He asked, 'Where is mother?' Amit said nonchalantly, 'She is inside resting. But why did you not bring the girl in?' Atin was surprised, 'How did you know?' Amit laughed, 'Bacchu, you shall always remain a bacchu? You left house tormented and went to the phone booth and then went running to the college tea shop and came back in a car and I would not know that? Our party may have gone out of action but our lookouts are still there—bondage of brotherhood. You have been seeing this girl for years and you have not brought her to mother yet. She is a nice girl and you are an idiot. When she comes tomorrow introduce her to mother and do not behave as if you have stolen these things.'

Atin gaped at him, 'How do you know she will come, what are you, a spy or gangster or a terrorist? Everyone knows you have left that life behind.'

Amit guffawed loudly, 'What have I left behind? I am neither a spy nor a gangster nor a terrorist. I have never killed anyone. If I had would I be out of jail and free to move? Even after being a doctor you are still reading comic stories of spies and gangsters? I was one of the backroom boys, a planner, a technocrat of sorts,' and he smiled at his bewilderment.

Atin asked 'So what do you do? I only hear stories, you have never told your younger brother anything. I know nothing about you' he was almost in tears.

Amit said, 'By and by, all in good time. But you have no reason to be ashamed of me like you are with that nice girl. Welcome her nicely and proudly when she comes tomorrow.'

Atin asked, 'How do you know she is coming?'

Amit knocked on his head and yawned, 'Deductive logic and you have just confirmed; I am going to sleep. If you are hungry there is some soaked rice and yoghurt over there. And if you decide to boil some Maggie call me, I love the stuff. Do not disturb mother.'

Atin ate the rice and yoghurt and prepared Maggie while wondering about his brother. He was very hungry not having eaten the whole day and he called Amit and the brothers lustily finished both packets of Maggie.

Sohini came late in the morning next day, with a big basket full of provisions carried by the driver. There was more rice with generous supply of many kinds of vegetables, fruits and sweets. She touched mother's feet and said, 'You have two sons and now you have a daughter' and mother smiled and touched her chin and kissed the fingers as mothers do the usual affectionate blessing. Atin introduced her to brother and he whispered loudly to Atin, 'Do not blush more than her, it doesn't look manly' making him angry and Sohini burst out laughing.

Mother asked her to stay for lunch; she agreed and immediately got busy in the kitchen with mother, ignoring her protests. Atin wondered whether she has ever cooked anything in her whole life.

Amit dragged him out of the house and taking a few paces lighted a cigarette and looked at him squinting his eyes, 'Now Bacchu, you are screwed, what are you going to do? You cannot run away from her as you have been trying to do, mother and I will be on her side.' Atin started to protest and he held up his hand 'You are a greenhorn penniless doctor and she, also a doctor but a rich man's daughter, difficult, eh?'

Atin looked on helplessly. Amit laughed 'You are in more trouble than me man and we do not run away from trouble, we face it. That is how we grow up, sharing pain and pleasure. So now you have to plan for both of you and not just yours. Think about it.'

Atin stammered, 'I do not know what to think. I tried to dissuade her from coming.'

Amit could not stop laughing, 'Never even think of trying that. She is more dynamic than you are, she will be your energy. Prizes come rarely in life and when they come you have to learn to grab and not be scared that you cannot handle it. Work it out Bacchu.'

Atin had somewhat recovered and replied, 'May be you as the big brother should give me some courage and energy instead of taunting me. I do not even know you. Come out and tell me about your life so that I get some courage and show me some ways and means.'

Amit said, 'You are right, we have a lot to talk about and we shall have time now.'

They sat down for lunch, mother forcing Sohini to sit down with the brothers while she served and kept looking at the trio with loving eyes but could not help her tears. Sohini got up and made her sit down beside her and kept holding her hand. The food was tasty and at every point she gave the credits to Sohini while she kept protesting and blushing throughout. Only once she looked up at Amit and said, 'Dada I have heard so much about you'; Amit raised eyebrows and said, 'Really?' She said hesitantly, 'If you have no objections I want to hear more' and Amit replied, 'Then you shall'. Lunch ended and Sohini left after touching mother's feet.

Amit

The following days there was nothing to do until the *Shradh* ceremony, the worship for the last rites. Normally this is a very busy time as relations and friends have to be invited for the ceremony followed by a joint meal to break the austerities. For this family the tasks were much less, as they had only one relation to invite in case they agreed to come. Other people to be invited were few immediate neighbours and the local boys who helped in cremation and did all the work for the ceremony. Atin called Professor Ghosh and said that he will meet after the ceremony was over.

There was no dearth of food thanks to Sohini and the family members actually put on weight from vegetarian food and it was good for mother. Sohini's mother came one day with supplies and though it was embarrassing, it could not be refused both as courtesy and ancient social mores that the bereaved should live on alms and cannot refuse anything given out of charity. That exercise on humility is a feature in many Hindu rituals. Sohini's mother reminded them of that and Amit was overjoyed being an atheist and reveled at what he called the better side of religion. Sohini could not stop laughing the day this happened, and told Tanima that she pitied her for having two sons like this. What she whispered in reply made her blush, and she left the place to hide until she regained composure and none seemingly noticed that.

Thus there was a relaxed holiday atmosphere in the house and plenty of time to talk and discuss their ideas and experiences, a gem of a time. Amit was the centre piece of the discourses and swore everyone to secrecy, including Sohini, who was a frequent participant. Without any official attachment she became a member of the family and everybody loved it.

Interrogation of Amit started from a question of Sohini, 'Dada why did you join the Naxalites so late in the day when the peak had passed and the party was in disarray, how, where and whom did you join?' Amit looked at her with affection and said, 'I knew the first salvo of questions would come from you. If there is one thing you must realize, is that nothing dies in this world. Anything that holds a little grain of truth lives forever in human mind and consciousness. Yes the madness of the initial years died down but not the reasons of its origin. You have seen the breakers on the seashore. A large breaker starts rolling in the distance and rushes towards the shore and breaks and then peters out, but the momentum continues, and a second wave rises nearer the shore and starts rolling towards the shore. Naxalite revolt started as a spontaneous agrarian revolt of the landless against landowners in the small village of Naxalbari in North Bengal. It lasted on the peasant base for a while and spontaneously rolled over to the cities, especially Calcutta, teeming with unemployed educated youth, an urban guerilla revolt originated and we had the horrible days of murders and clashes with the police, between political parties and what not. These events did not happen according to any plan and in spite of the absence of a properly organized structured leadership. There were of course visionaries, who were aware of the deprivation and discontent among people, but that is not the same as organized leadership. These discontents come from social disparity in many levels, from starvation to inequality of opportunity.'

He continued, 'I think the days of organized revolution by one or more political parties are a thing of the past, though I may be wrong. It may still happen in some special situations. But in general it is gone because people no longer believe in political parties, because of their hegemony of power and greed and bitter inner struggle for leadership that forgets what people need. Those who do not like us loosely call us Maoists but Mao belongs to a different time and place. The 'Urban Guerrilla' movement is a product of Bengal and afterwards it has surfaced in many countries, in many different forms and ideologies, and is still doing so even in affluent countries, but this is where it all started. It will continue in future in our country and others. With progressive urbanization of the world, the cities are the new jungles and we have real jungles in our country and wherever people's lives, liberties and wherewithal are marginalized revolts will occur. Such revolts may be minority movements in many places, at least to start with. Except in old established democracies political parties will find it difficult to hold the confidence of people and new orders will emerge that are difficult to foresee. Among poorer countries democracy is more firmly grounded in our country and may survive after many trials and tribulations that may alter its form but not the content and I hope that will be the case and we shall be lucky. But large pockets of anarchy and exploitation in such a large heterogeneous country are unavoidable and those will not be cured unless the exploited go up in revolt. Otherwise being minority events they will not be noticed. Our infant democracy needs to develop mechanisms to bring the deprived within view. In that sense these revolts are ultimately beneficial to democracy.'

Sohini asked, 'But could they not be nonviolent?' Amit answered, 'Violent or nonviolent is determined by the degree of oppression used. That turns nonviolent struggle into violent or vice versa.' Atin asked, 'Did you work out all these when you joined?' Amit laughed, 'Have I claimed to be an astrologer? No, I did not foresee all that I have described but was generally aware and gradually these thoughts came and strengthened my conviction. History has always been my passion apart from my subject of computers and software. I am probably one of the earliest batches of Indians to study that subject. History has made me aware of the rolling of the seas, and waves succeeding waves in the socioeconomic and political history of the world. And as a discerning Indian that is not as difficult as you think. You hear that roaring in Vivekananda's writings and lectures, if you read between the lines. The educated British were aware of that, and had he lived longer the British colonialists would have probably arrested him. Just remember him saying "Christs and Buddhas are but waves on the boundless ocean which *I am*. Bow down to nothing but your higher inner Self" and you shall hear the roar of the seven seas calling for men in India to rise, "out of potters' wheel, washer man's tub and thatched mud huts of the poor" and you shall understand revolution. Vivekananda is the sanest and greatest revolutionary in the history of mankind. He did not speak of armed revolution, but arms become unavoidable when no one cares to listen and people wake up after lives are lost. But he did foresee people's revolution in India after Russia and China, events that were still in future in his time. He wrote to Hem Chandra Ghosh "travel and study and the future of the world will be revealed to you". I have traveled in nooks and corners of our country.'

There was total silence in the room that was finally broken by Atin's remark, 'I did not know you were a follower of Vivekananda.' Amit laughed and said, 'Say that to him and he would hit you on the head for he never meant to contest an election for which you need followers. He wanted us to evolve. Follower is a recent term used profusely by his followers.' Atin would not let go and said, 'So though you are an atheist you trust Sri Ramakrishna.' Amit looked thoughtfully at his brother and asked 'Do you?' and not finding an answer said, 'I cannot say I understand Sri Ramakrishna, nobody does including the monks who swear by His name, but if he can produce one Vivekananda not to speak of one hundred thousand, which Vivekananda said he could, I have no problem with him. I do not think I can be a Ramakrishna but may be a tiny version of Vivekananda, if I honestly try hard and for me that would be enough.'

Sohini intervened impatiently, 'Talk about yourself Dada, I want to hear what you think of the present.' Amit answered slowly, 'For me the man of the moment is Mikhail Gorbachev of Russia. Read his books Glasnost and Perestroika that are available. See how he is trying to transfer power from the entrenched hardcore Communist organizations to the people. He became a party secretary of agriculture in 1978 at the age of 47 and a full Politburo member two years later. He had seen the devastation of agriculture under Stalinist policies and the chronic famine situation in the countryside. He is trying to democratize governance and reduce the centralized power held in a few hands. I do not know whether the centralized power will stand that strain. That will mean collapse of Communism in Russia. In any case their economy has been drained by decade old Afghan war. These are momentous times in world history. Too much centralization of power can also happen in a democracy, people have to guard against that. It can be done in a democratic country, without breaking up the system that is the value of democracy. But the struggles are necessary.'

Sohini interjected, 'It will mean America will win, isn't that so?' Amit smiled at her and got up, 'I don't know. But it is not America that will win, capitalism will win with checks and balances installed, but by its very nature money will flow wherever there is profit. It has been flowing for a long time but was restricted by the global situation and technology of the time. The flow of capital created wars and colonialism. With communication technology, computing and others that are just round the corner, we shall face a different not yet known world. In affairs of mankind there are very few absolute wins, you win some and you lose some. But I doubt that exploitation of man by man will ever cease and so also the struggle against that.'

Atin blurted out, 'What are you going to do, now that there are no revolutions?' Amit laughed at the twinge of jealousy in his voice that must be from the amount of attention he was getting from Sohini and said, 'Revolutions never stop. Do you think we are alone in this world? In every country, including the rich countries, there are people who think like us. Social exploitation does not stop with riches. In many countries there are people and press and publishing houses that publish such material that will be called Naxalite here. We are in touch with some. With growth in computers and information technology, which is round the corner, the world will be more connected and it will only grow. Politicians are blocking computer use in our country, and curiously the left parties are in the vanguard. They follow Stalin, they do not know Gorbachev. This is the tragedy, we are always copycats, cannot think for ourselves. When shall we learn to think? But they cannot hold back for long and I am an expert in that subject. I am already needed. I do not have a university degree but I have got a degree from a private institution that is considered just as good. You and Sohini decide what you are going to do. Medicine is a vast world of many variations and you have already got some taste of that. So decide what you people are going to do. I am tired from so much talking and if you allow, going to rest awhile.'

Sohini also got up to go home. Atin rushed out to bid her goodbye and they waved at each other. But she was thinking. The little twinge of jealousy did not escape her and she was in deep thought as the car started toward home.

Flow of Life

Shortly after the last rites were over Amit left and as usual nobody knew where he was going. Atin asked once and was told the truth that Amit was not sure where he was going. He was going in search of a career and promised to keep in touch. Father's death meant that Atin could not leave mother alone. So his base was the house while preparing for the examination and join Professor Ghosh in practice to earn for the family of two. It also meant that even if he was nurturing a faint desire to go abroad with Sohini, it was no longer possible. Their meetings became fewer, as the circuits were different. Sohini kept contact through Atin's mobile phone, asking how he was doing and how mother was, but the conversations were short. He rarely called to avoid increasing his mobile bill.

They met once after more than two months, when Atin went to the college on some errand and looked her up. As they stood talking, they looked around and to Atin and possibly also to Sohini the place looked drab and dull. Atin commented on that, and Sohini smiled and said, 'The place is just the same as it always has been but what have changed is us. The place looked romantic once and now it is not.' Atin asked whether she had some free time to go for a cup of coffee and she agreed.

They went and sat down in the coffee house and ordered. Atin was silent and Sohini pushed the desultory conversation asking how mother was and how was the household, whether she had some domestic help, how was his work and study with polite answers from

Atin. Sohini asked about Amit and Atin replied, 'I do not know where he is, he has not contacted since he left. I was expecting to get some news from you.' Sohini replied, 'How would I know, he does not know my phone number, not to speak of my home addresses and sat silent looking at her nails. After an awkward silence she looked up and said, 'Look how bad my nails are now. I cannot keep them long nor keep them polished and painted. I was so proud of them once and now they look so ugly.' Atin looked at her hand but did not reply. Sohini remembered that there was a time when it would be an invite for him to hold her hand.

She sighed and withdrew her hands and looked straight at him, 'what is the matter Atin what is wrong? Why should I know your brother's whereabouts? I went to your house because I loved you. You are not responsible for me, nor am I your property to guard. Can't we be at least friends as two free individuals?'

Atin smiled a bitter smile, 'Yes, you are free. You have already put a past tense to love and I do not blame you. I am a loser and I do not know where I am going. My mind is in turmoil and I see only darkness all around.'

Sohini's eyes were burning and she felt tears coming that she checked with effort. Instead she said with affection, 'You are suffering from depression after father's death and you have not recovered. I do not blame you; it is only to be expected. But please do not think that you are alone in the world and do not bite the hand that is offered. Then you will sink to a greater depression.'

Atin said, 'And that hand is slipping away'. Sohini's rejoinder was quick 'Then as a man you should not allow it to slip.' Atin asked, 'How?'

Sohini said, 'Grab, grab by your self belief. I am not leaving tomorrow and even if there comes a distance between us do not allow it. Now the coffee has gone cold and I have to get back to the hospital. We cannot see very far in the future but belief we can hold on to, that is in us. I have a mobile number now and note it down. Give a missed call and I shall call back. Now get up. Enough of this self pity; tomorrow is a new day, remember that always.' And they got up and went their different ways.

That night Atin lay in bed awake ruminating the day. Amit said Sohini was his energy. She was really a bundle of energy and she radiated that. He was not feeling that hopeless and lost now. Instead he felt a new surge of optimism. It is funny how the world changed by the way you look at it! Tomorrow is a different day, and he peacefully slipped in to deep sleep after many a tormented night.

His confidence in study and work increased. His teacher was impressed and increasingly dependant on him and left some parts of operations to him. He was not yet in a residency program in a teaching institution and private cases could not be solely left to him but he taught him all the intricacies and risks of each diagnosis and operation and encouraged him, that when he starts in the program he would be able to do a lot by himself. Time went fast and almost at the same time, Sohini finished her internship and got full registration and he passed his examination with high grade and got admission to a two year residency program in the postgraduate institute in preparation for appearing for the Master of Surgery degree and also got a scholarship. With the scholarship and money he earned with Professor Ghosh his finances became comfortable.

They celebrated by a dinner date hosted by Atin followed by a long kiss as he dropped her home and Sohini pushing him away as he got more amorous by saying, 'No, No, No, not now, not today, or else you will sink in depression and guilt again from tomorrow. I am not ready for that. And for your information, I applied for a House Job in surgery and I am in, starting tomorrow.'

Atin gaped and asked, 'What, you are not going to England?'

She gave him a pat on the cheek and said, 'Dummy, don't you know that if I go after doing six months of house job in surgery and six months in medicine I become eligible for British Registration and can get a Senior House Officer's job? I want to do Pediatrics.'

Atin said, 'You cannot do both not by our rules.'

She replied, 'I can manage six months of medicine anywhere, it is the surgical job that is difficult. Or else I go after six months and do the medicine half there or else go after one and half years. It will be my choice, none of your business. You are not responsible.'

Atin was silent and kept looking at her, would he ever understand this woman? Aloud he blurted out, 'Why don't we get married in the meantime?'

She almost choked and laughed loudly, 'Oh my Romeo, suddenly full of confidence! No, I do not want to marry a greenhorn surgical resident and keep awake through nights. You may be an old man but I am a young woman, I can wait and don't want to spoil your residency and our friendship. Marriage should be a bond not bondage.'

Rolling Waves

Time flows in gentle ripples, peaceful and pleasant, undulating life and we enjoy the calm, and float on that. Atin and Sohini floated on life, content with a life of work, study and friendship absorbed in each other. They would have long talks on phone; meet occasionally to have coffee, a rare film show or dinner. Past the first flush of love the intimacy grew deeper with a confidence in each other. Physical intimacy could not be entirely avoided, as they both desired each other but were discreet, and few as Sohini being a resident house officer lived in hospital quarters of her college and Atin alternated between home and his hospital. So the opportunities were few and far between, but it did not bother them. They discussed marriage at times and kept postponing because of difficult logistics. They rarely visited each other's house as it was difficult to face the mothers. But the sea of life is never the same over time and space, calm changes to rough, like the sea from whence we came. When there is calm at one place, there is a storm at another, that the two young people absorbed in each other did not notice.

The storm was in mother. Atin officially stayed at home but the demands of work kept him in the hospital for long hours day and night. A part of his free time was devoted to Sohini. On many nights he could not return home. He had a room to himself in the hospital. On call and on duty he would spend the night there and on nights he was late, he could not return home. The old woman who gave her life bringing up the children, and looking after the family, spent many lonely days and nights only with the memory of the past. Atin hired a full time maid to

150

stay with mother, to do the household work and look after the house generally, and a night nurse to guard her. The maid was conscientious and faithful and looked after household well. But Tanima, the mother, who spent her whole life known as mother, remembered her name now, as she lived alone with no one to talk, to share her mind and nothing to do except silently ruminate on the past. In the family ethics of Bengal of her days, the husband never called the wife by her name and the children called her mother. Friends and relatives were few and distant and after her parents' death, which she could only vaguely remember, nobody called her by name. In her loneliness she would now stand in front of mirror, look at herself and call herself in whispers 'Tanima Tanima' and stare at her image wondering whether she heard her. The nurse reported it to Atin, but he could not fathom what was wrong. He asked mother but she only smiled. Only once she asked about Sohini, whether she could come to her and whether she was married, but Atin gave only vague replies.

The young can never understand the loneliness and depression of old age. They do not understand that doing one's duty was not enough. It was not a problem in large joint families of yesteryear. There were many people of similar age groups and there were younger people, children grandchildren nephews and nieces, even unemployed brothers who had no earning and would be called parasites today, had very important roles in the stability of the family. The joint family system collapsed as years passed, still existing in parts of rural India that escaped the vagaries of history. But they are also changing, as money has become the most important identity and scarce for most. The old crave for the company of the young, and that was not a problem in old family life but the change has occurred rather fast. The economic dependence of parents has become an irritant to the young, working hard to make ends meet, and there is no end to that end point in the modern world. Even the mother son relationship degrades to casual and desultory contact. Conversations are scratchy and empty of emotion. Nobody has time for that. Many a night when Atin returned home he would look in to mother's room and find her asleep. He did not have the sensitivity to realize that she was not asleep, but wide awake and waiting, hoping against hope that the son would come in and embrace her and say a few words of love and affection. But the young are oblivious that the old need love and comfort as much as or even more than the young, and old age depression is mainly because of the lack of that. Love resides in the mind more than in the body and is not the sole right of the young, but they think that only they have the need for that. The old would be jeered for their desire for love if ever expressed.

In affluent countries the old shift themselves to old age homes, even if they have the wherewithal to live at own home, sometimes only for companionship that can mature to love and even marriage between the very old. But that sort of affluence of the old has not come generally to Indian society, and where there is, the old rules as the patriarch and it happens mainly in the business communities. In a poor or middle class family the old lose on all counts. Their only use is as babysitter, when new babies arrive. Financing a parent to live in a well appointed old peoples' home, which are very few, and visiting them with small gifts and genuine affection would be scandalous in our society, but their lonely isolation and incarceration would not.

Tanima was withering and withering slowly while life for Atin and Sohini was blossoming with excitement of life and work, dreaming and planning for future and love. Sohini visited her once with Atin and she asked, 'When are you getting married?' Sohini blushed and was silent. Atin replied, 'How would that help you Ma? She will be out of the house as much as me. And how shall I feed both of you with my little earning. So it would all be the same.' Tanima mumbled, 'In our days nobody used to think about earning, everybody married at the right age. Your father earned very little when we got married yet we led such a happy life together suffering and enjoying what little we had. Gradually his earning increased and we rejoiced together having children and when we could take a trip somewhere and build a house. I do not understand what is it with you nowadays, that you have to earn a lot when you marry.' Atin had no answer, there is no answer except that is how it is today, for better or for worse. In life probably there is no absolute win, we win some and lose some in equal measure and are happy when we do not miss what we lose.

Amit suddenly appeared months later. He informed Atin before coming that he would be in for about a couple of days and looked forward to meeting everybody. Atin was home when he came. Sohini did not want to be present at the family reunion and said she would try to meet later. Amit's coming was never a quiet episode. He shouted from outside calling mother and almost jumped in, threw his bag to one side and embraced mother rocking her to and fro. Mother shouted in delight, 'Mad boy careful now, let me go; you shall break my bones.' He picked her up and pirouetting once deposited her on the bed and said, 'You are so light Ma, I can pick you up in one arm and jump out of the house.' Tanima said, 'Yes you can you were always the big Hanuman. So what is all this joy about, are you going to get married?'

Amit said, 'Better than that Ma, I have got a fixed job now after moving around like a vagabond so long. I shall have a fixed address and you can write to me or call me whenever you want.'

Tanima eagerly asked, 'So you would be staying home?'

Amit said, 'I am sorry Ma the job is not here it is in Bangalore. An IT firm that is going to be very big has recruited me. As one of the first appointee I have been given a rather senior position after a lot of tests and interviews and I passed all of them by just remembering you and taking your name, do you believe that? There are not many people in this field yet and I was the only one without a university degree but an official degree of some sort. But I beat them all by my ideas and innovations that I had worked out in my days in jail and afterwards. They did not care for university degree. They are not a government organization, but they are the people of the future.'

Tanima did not understand all but asked eagerly, 'How far is Bangalore from here?' Amit said, 'It is far, takes more than one day to go by train and you have to change in the middle. There is no direct train yet but soon there will be. I can of course travel by plane while on duty. It is there that all these new things are coming up.' She was silent.

Atin was silently watching this reunion and listening to Amit. He now interjected, 'By IT you mean information technology dada?'

Amit said, 'Yes Bacchu, it is the thing of the present. It is changing the world very fast, it is a revolution that has been late in coming to our country but it has come after all through private initiative. It will change our country and the world. It is a revolution and being a revolutionary I am in it' and he broke out in loud laughter.

Atin was quizzical. He had heard of computers and software and cybernetics and thought of them as intellectual curiosity. He did not see how that will change the world and least of all India and expressed his doubt. Amit then explained in greater detail what it would do what man has dreamt for decades or even a century.

Tanima was silent through all that discourse not understanding a thing but only watched her elder son with pride and affection. She knew he was a good boy and one day will be great as astrologers had predicted. People only said he was gone, fallen in bad company but she knew what he was and can never do anything wrong. As the brothers stopped talking she asked Amit meekly, 'Will you take me there?'

Amit asked in surprise, 'Where Ma?'

She answered, 'To Bangalore where you will be.'

With more surprise Amit asked, 'Why would you want to leave this house, your house where you have always been? This is your place' and he looked at Atin.

Tanima said, 'May be for that reason. I have been always here never been out of it. Can I not also want to see the world outside, see new places?'

Amit was puzzled. She never wanted to leave the house not even for a day or even half a day so long as father was alive. Now that father was no more her younger son was here and his fiancée whom mother liked. So why was she wanting to leave? From all accounts they should be on the verge of marriage. He looked once at Atin and mumbled, 'Yes of course you can come and stay with me for some time once I get an apartment. At present I am staying in a hostel for new entrants where I have a room. I have not thought of taking a flat yet and that would be far from my working place. But I sure can have one.'

Tanima's response was quick, 'And who would cook for you and look after your home? Are you thinking of getting married?'

More puzzle and Amit smiled, 'I have not so far met a woman I want to marry or who wants to marry me. If you want to arrange a marriage no father will be foolish enough to give his daughter to a vagabond like me with my past records.'

Tanima flashed, 'Don't say that. I know my son better than anybody else. Now wash up and be ready to eat. I have cooked things you used to like' and she moved to kitchen.

Two brothers sat staring at each other. Amit asked, 'you are not getting married Bacchu?'

Atin replied, 'Not immediately. We are not ready yet, working most of the time and with all that study. You know what medical examinations are.'

Amit said haltingly, 'If it is a question of money I can help.'

Atin looked at the ceiling and said, 'No it is not that it is a problem of logistics.'

Tanima called from the kitchen and as they got up Amit said almost in a soliloquy 'Mother has become very thin and weak.'

Atin replied, 'She does not eat well, I have told her many times. I don't know what to do.'

Deep in thought Amit did not reply.

The brothers sat down to eat and mother served. None of them seemed to have any appetite. Tanima complained, asking whether the cooking was not good. She lamented that with age her cooking is not what it was. Atin said he had a late lunch and was not hungry. Amit said that the food was nice but he ate less nowadays having to eat all that unfamiliar spicy food.

The dinner was over somehow. Mother ate very little. Amit cajoled her to eat more but she said she had taken her quota and is unable to eat much. She coughed too much. Amit asked Atin why was she coughing so much and was told that she had a recent attack of flu and the cough was lingering. It was made worse by the fumes as she insisted on cooking that day. Amit did not comment. Atin left after dinner saying he was on call that night. He would try to come home late next afternoon to see him off. Amit said he would stay the next night too and leave the morning after. He requested Atin to come even if late and come with Sohini if possible. Atin said he would try but could not be sure of Sohini. As it happened Sohini could not come.

Amit slept with mother that night embracing her and kept her warm by rearranging her cover as it slipped off with coughing. She kept on coughing but not as much as during the day. Next morning he went to a local doctor and requested him to come and look at her. He came and examined her and said an immediate chest X-ray and a few simple blood tests were necessary before he could say anything. With the help of local boys he took her to a local diagnostic clinic and implored them to give a rapid report. Knowing him they agreed and gave the reports by afternoon, which he took to the doctor. The doctor said that she had chest infection with patchy bronchopneumonia but he could say nothing more. She had to be seen by a chest specialist.

When they returned an old man, a friend of his father waiting by the door took him aside and said, 'You have come after a long time. We were worried about your mother but what could we do? This is the predicament of the old. We can survive only by the love and care at home. But most young people are leaving home because there are no job opportunities in this city and we are left to our fate. What can medicines alone do?' He went away shaking his head.

That night when Atin came he showed him the reports. Atin said he would take mother to the hospital and consult the most well known chest physician. Amit told him, 'Brother, I am in no position to pontificate and blame you for I am equally to be blamed. But please take care of mother, show some love and concern because her love can never be replaced and will haunt us till our dying days. You are busy and I am busy too. It will take some time for me to find an apartment in an unknown city but then I am alone too. If necessary admit her to a nursing home in the meantime. I shall find the money somehow.' Atin had never argued with his elder brother so Amit did not know his thoughts but got the reply, 'I shall do the best I can, but do not know beyond that.'

Amit left next day promising mother that he would look for an apartment and would take her as soon as he could but meanwhile she must make herself fit for the journey.

Next day Atin took Tanima to hospital and consulted the senior most chest specialist, in fact the Professor who was his teacher in the undergraduate course. He looked at the reports and said more investigations were needed to decide what sort of infection she had. He also said that she might be aspirating stomach contents at night or aspirating food while eating due to weakness. Atin requested that she be admitted in the hospital or in a nursing home to go through the tests and treatment. He said the hospital was overcrowded as it is, with serious patients and she needed personal care that will be difficult to provide. Atin requested to admit her in a nursing home under his care but he did not encourage that either. It would be unnecessarily expensive and what she needed was home care. He suggested that Atin could employ private nurses at home and he could send two trained nurses for day and night. Atin could supervise and report to him as often as necessary. Atin wondered how far his advice was influenced by his reluctance to take the burden without much financial return from a student. But that could not be questioned.

He followed the advice of his teacher and informed Sohini. He had no idea how the household would run with mother, the housekeeper and two nurses. Sohini said she would help out and visit as often as possible as she had more free time than Atin. He in turn informed Amit of the whole arrangement. Amit approved and asked him to thank Sohini on his behalf.

Thus the care of the mother continued. Amit was sending money and Sohini must have been spending off and on but refused to divulge the amount. Atin spent a major part of his earning keeping only the essential for himself. Tanima showed some improvement. It was probably as much from more frequent visits from Sohini as from medicines that gave her nausea. Medicines were changed several times. She just talked her heart out to Sohini. She was a patient listener. Once or twice she would regret that they were not married then Sohini would hold her close and talk to her in a voice as if to calm a child that her stay could not be any longer than now as she had to work and Tanima would be pacified for some time. A fondness grew between them beyond relationship allowing Sohini to become firm sometime as one would need to control a parent and as in all such situations Tanima would protest but feel happy within. But Sohini never stayed the night as her parents would not have liked that. In any case they were not very happy with the situation but did not oppose knowing their daughter well.

This happy interlude continued for nearly two months until one night while in an emergency operation Atin got a phone from home that mother's condition had suddenly deteriorated and she was having severe breathing problem and he rushed home asking someone else to scrub to assist the resident surgeon. By the time he reached home mother was dead. The attendants had fallen asleep, one of them in mother's room, and she vomited and choked drowning in her own vomit before they could do anything. They could not have done much in any case. Atin collapsed on the bed in the other room, his mind blank unable to react and decide what he would have to do now, what the priorities were. Nothing mattered now. The house was eerily silent. Mother's dreams seemed to pass through him as if she was transmitting them. What could have been but did not.

Amit could have been an established senior engineer by now, probably would have married with children, grandchildren of father and mother. The family would have been affluent and the house probably larger with the top floor built as father dreamt. There would have been a car in the garage. He would have been a more confident doctor sure of his future as a surgeon with a sweet sister-in-law as a friend to him and Sohini. There would have been no constraint in marrying her and studying together to become specialists and look forward to a happy life. There would have been laughter, merriment and music in the house, traveling together and enjoying the holidays. The whole picture was playing like a cinemascope in front of his eyes. He was woken up as someone was shaking his shoulder. He opened his eyes and as he focused he saw Sohini shaking him by the shoulder. The picture stopped and he was really sorry for that. It was already morning and someone had called Sohini.

She asked him, 'What are you dreaming?'

He actually smiled, 'It was a beautiful dream of what could have been but have not become. It is nobody's fault.'

Sohini stared at him, 'Are you all right?'

Atin laughed this time, 'You bet, absolutely. I have seen God, he that gives and takes away, without any rationality, like a little boy, like the seas and the mountains, quite oblivious of us. Why the hell we live here' and he laughed again.

Sohini pulled him up by the hand, 'Enough of that. There are things to be done here and who will do those? Get up and get going. You do not have the luxury of dreaming.'

Atin got up with an effort, 'Yes, you are right, I know no luxury, not even luxury of tears, no embraces, no playing of the bugles, 'not with a bang but a whimper' remember?' He noticed the curious neighbours and checked himself.

Then the usual paraphernalia started. Amit was informed and he was shocked and said he could not come for the last rites. Atin could perform them. He will obey his side of the rituals over there. He could not say when he would be able to come. Atin went to the crematorium, could not touch fire to mother's body and when everything was finished came to the empty home and broke down all by himself, none to disturb. He shifted to his hospital room with a few memorabilia. A shortened version of the rites were performed in the house after cleaning it, helped by Sohini and at the end of it he closed and locked up and went back to his duty at the hospital. He only once looked back at the house, the end of a dream, the end of a dolls house erected in dream that is nobody's fault, nothing special, just another one of those. A wave has finished its journey.

Waves collide

Atin's life outwardly remained the same but inside there was a sea change. It had lost its moorings. Perceptions develop slowly in people who are not imaginative in their approach to life. Only after mother's death he realized the void. Imagination is like oil on a turbulent sea. People without imagination lead a life that they call practical but in its essence it is animal life that cannot see farther than the immediate concerns. A human life cannot be totally devoid of imagination as there is always some projection of the future, some assessment of what is around and what needs to be done. When it is restricted only to material things the mind dies. Like everything in life imagination and thinking has to be exercised, and then it reveals its gems like love, faith, trust and deeper sensations that enrich life, bring equanimity, tolerance and acceptance. If Atin was sensitive to mother's suffering he could have foreseen things easily. It was not that he did not love mother but she was a fixed entity in his life and did not need to be concerned about as long as the material adjustments were in place. He did not imagine the scenario of her absence or how much he would miss her until she was no longer there. Such closed minds poorly appreciate love or the environment they live in or the world they live in. Therefore every twist and turn of fate brings trauma and series of reactions that lead to maladjustment of life. Our imagination makes the world we live in. The world looks different to different people as perceptions are different and we perceive only those things that we are accustomed to perceive. This world of ours in its essence is neither reality nor illusion as we understand them, but beyond them both and more we grasp in our mind the more it reveals itself and provides peace, knowledge and endurance.

For the same reasons his relationship with Sohini was also going stale. Their relationship continued mechanically through the usual habitual course. They met when they could, that slowly grew less frequent. The conversations grew stereotyped. They would have coffee and sometimes dinner together, there would be furtive kisses but the passion was slowly draining out. If someone asked whether they were still in love the answer would be, yes they were. But love means different to different people; love was more from Sohini's side. She knew how much he needed her support and her heart would cry but she could not bring Atin out of his shell of despair, he just did not know how to break out of his self imposed mental prison to think of new roads to happiness, alternate pathways, to discuss them energetically together. In other words he had no imagination to recreate their lives.

After a long gap a letter came from Amit. It came to the home address. Atin rarely went home. When he saw the letter it was lying in the box for weeks.

My dear brother,

I am writing this letter since we have no other communication except short telephone calls just to say, 'Hello, how are you?' I do not know what you think but I love you very much. Who else is there for me? You would notice I am not addressing you as 'Bacchu' for you are no longer a child but a grown up man and a doctor. We should talk man to man but the opportunities are few and far between. I am very busy in my work as the company is growing fast and there are a lot of things to do. It is impossible to get a long enough leave to make a trip to Calcutta and sit down with you. And to tell you honestly I am feeling this loss. That is why I am writing. So please do not think I am advising or pontificating and do not take offence. Brothers should be able to talk freely even if a distance separates them, we can cross distances through love.

You may ask why suddenly now after a long time. I have no excuse or apology. We live through life mechanically and then something happens out of the routine and we wake up and look around and I remembered you and felt guilty. So that is my apology.

I unexpectedly met a young couple at Bangalore I knew a long time back. I knew Saroj and Meena in my jungle days, which was a long time back. They were members of our outfit. Saroj was a city boy from Calcutta and Meena was a local tribal girl. Saroj was a graduate from a middle class family and he had no wherewithal to go any further, as was very common with young men in those days. Meena grew up in the jungle and got free education in a Christian school till the school leaving examination and that was the end. She too had no means to go further. She was a sturdy tribal girl, pretty in her own way and fluent in English. She also knew typing and that was all. The agony and anger of such people are more than those that have never seen the light of education and they are increasing in number. The jungles are a rather risky area for a pretty girl, and she suffered and as an escape joined our group, more for security than any ideological belief to start with. In fact most of our workers were people like that, people who could not get a decent foothold in society. When the so called civil society calls us insurgents, revolutionaries, Maoists and killers they do not realize that most of our people were creations of that society. I do not know how much they understand those epithets they hurl to condemn the less fortunate ones or for that matter know about weapons and combat, if at all, but what my people really got in the camp was dignity. When you hold a rifle in your hand, even if you do not know how to use it, gives you a mental strength against all the ignominies you have suffered. That makes you feel worthy as a human being and not worthless that the society makes you feel. I used to be surprised to see the human development in these sad people and thought even this prize is enough for me. Revolution is not a child's toy, but the growth of human dignity and human interests, they never had, was so glorious to see. In their leisure hours many of them studied and I would joke that if they had studied this hard they would have been officers and they would smile shyly. Some loved to draw and paint and we provided them the materials as much we could. Meena was one such. I loved them and they formed the main bulk of our so called force. There were of course action squads, they had to be there, at least to save these children from the marauding police and soldiers and village tyrants, like those who made Meena's life hell. You people living in civilized societies cannot even imagine the torture that may be unleashed by these people. Your news media do not report it for fear of losing government payout. That is what used to make our outnumbered action squads so valiant, so cunning. And the non-fighters used to provide background support.

Saroj opted to join the action squad; he had to take revenge on the society that neglected him. Blind anger no doubt, cannon fodder to the revolution that will probably never happen, but man making, not only for him but others too. We were not blind lunatics. We knew Che Guevara said that armed revolution is not possible in a country with a legally constituted democratic government. So why did I join? I for one and many of us gave up the theory and saw the practical plight of these people, who were invisible to the democratic society until they fired a gun or attacked the police.

I used to hear from elders that in the post-independence era their was National Cadet Corps and Scout organizations that the school and college children were encouraged to join and these instilled discipline and group feelings and many activities that increased their self belief. These have vanished and do you know why? Because rulers were afraid that such mass training would produce rebels like us. In affluent developed countries military training at some stage of education is either compulsory or encouraged to build character and national feeling. Today the youth are encouraged to participate in a traders' culture spending time in shopping malls, food courts and bars. The desire for making money is instilled in youth, not national feelings and disciplines. The parents get hard pressed and they in turn concentrate on earning more money and that has made our society corrupt, selfish and self centered. Those that cannot or do not want to cope become antisocial. Do you think that creating a soft bellied corrupt society is nationalism, or is really a terrorist act for there were such epochs in our history when we went down under pressure. Why are the scams created by government, if not to siphon the state wealth into private coffers for political reasons? That money will not be available to the state in urgent situations when calamity strikes. I can give two well known examples from the beginning and end of the Islamic period of Indian history but there are many. Prithviraj Chauhan did not have enough money to raise an army to go on hot chase against the defeated Muhammad Ghori and Siraj-ud-daullah begged Jagat Sheth's help to no avail against Lord Clive.

To come back to my main story, Saroj and Meena fell in love. It was literally love at first sight but calf love of innocents. I do not know whether you know, this was not allowed in our organization. They were watched but they never broke the rules and never neglected their duties. It was mainly of eye contacts and at most sharing the community tiffin eating together. Some of their friends noticed and used to joke but they took it sportingly without even blushing. Because of their different routines, their meeting was few and far between. So it was mainly a case of friendship not interfered with. Then one day there was a sudden police attack on our camp. We had no prior warning as our lookouts were nabbed. They had become callous because of long period of silence from the police. The noncombatants had to be quickly removed from the danger zone through secret jungle paths. The action squads had to go forward and defend till the camp was cleared. Saroj was on the forefront as a platoon leader. Meena was being evacuated with others. It just so happened that Saroj got the first hit. He was not hit on the torso but in thigh and he fell down and could not get up. Probably the bone was broken. Meena had almost cleared the danger zone when she noticed Saroj falling. Before anybody could stop her she raced back and fell by his side. He was bleeding profusely and she desperately tried to stop the bleeding with her first aid training. Thus they were both arrested and the rest of the group cleared out. Saroj was taken to hospital and the police captured his country made gun before it had fired any shot. Meena was taken to the police lock up. I was worried about Meena in police lock up. Saroj, I knew would be taken care of as we knew that the hospital had good doctors and we had contact with some. I had personal contact with a wily lawyer in the locality not known to our organization. I sent some money to him with a note giving Meena's details, her parents' name and home address requesting him to get her release as soon as possible. I do not know how he did it but she was released from the police lock up without registering a case and sent back home. Saroj got better in the hospital and in time was discharged with a plastered leg, produced in court accused of violating the Arms Act and sent to jail. He did not have the time to fire a single shot.

The jungle camp was gradually closed down. The organization was breaking up anyway. I left last with a disguise and became a wanderer moving from safe house to safe house. It must have been more than a year later I had to go back to that area in nearby sub-divisional town on some errand. I suddenly spotted Meena on the road. After walking unobtrusively close to her for some time and watching the surroundings I got closer and called her name softly. She turned too sharply in surprise, and I had to leave her and enter a shop. I thought, 'Holy ghost, she has forgotten the training.' But she remembered and stopping on the road, opened her small tiffin box and frowned. Then she looked up at the sweet shop I had entered and came inside. She came straight to my table and placed the box and asked, 'Would you please look after this box while I buy some sweet for my husband?' I smiled, 'Newly wed?' She smiled in return and whispered, 'Only legally'. She came back with a cardboard box and brought out two sweets putting one inside the box and leaving the other where it was in front of me and saying, 'Marriage feast' she vanished. I kept looking at her, what a girl! My wily lawyer must have procured a marriage certificate for her, complete with a forged signature and, probably also a joint photograph and she used that to visit Saroj in nearby prison. The vermilion mark on her forehead and other paraphernalia were too prominent to be real, but obviously satisfied the jail authorities. I was arrested soon after and hoped it was not because of our meeting and it was not.

In a Bangalore shopping mall a few days back, as I was standing at a counter, my two hands were gripped firmly from two sides and in a fit of dejavue I jerked my hands free only to be embraced with loud laughter. I started laughing too and they mocked, 'Will this never leave you Amitda?' They pulled me by hand and said, 'We will not leave you, you have to come to our house. It is close by.' I had no option. I went to their small neat flat in a good locality and met their sweet little daughter. I was so happy I cannot tell you, as if I met my long lost children after years as in a Hindi movie. Gradually I heard their story mostly from Saroj, as Meena kept running in and out of kitchen. I had to have dinner with them. Saroj got permission to study while in jail. He enrolled in Indira Gandhi National Open University and studied law qualifying with distinction. After coming out of jail they got properly married at Calcutta with their families around. In the meantime Meena had become a qualified beautician. Saroj is now working in a corporate law firm and dreaming of opening one of his own. Meena has opened a beauty parlor and a small boutique where the tribal artifacts from the junglemahal sell like hot cakes. As I was coming back from their house I was dreaming and feeling very happy.

Driving my car back to my bachelor's pad, I was thinking what made them go so resolutely to build their lives when so many just could not recover. And I came to the conclusion it was their love that they held supreme and the rest just grew around that center point of their lives. It is so important to judge life's priority! I am established as an individual but I am not established in life. My position does not give me the satisfaction I should have, not like them. Achievement is not enough, it has to be shared with somebody or else it is a life without satisfaction. In my case I have never met a woman I could love. But I had my parents, my father and my mother whom I loved so much. Instead of running around as an angry young man I should have settled at home looking around for a career and looking after father and mother. There could have been frustrations, but their satisfaction of having their son close to them would have gradually spilled over to me and made me quiet and satisfied instead of keeping me a rebel forever. After all life is all about adjustments, other things would have adjusted around that. We could have become a happy family. My ego did not allow it, the ego of a rebel, never to bend. Life is not like that, it is of adjustment with situations as they come and to make it as best as it can get. You must be laughing at the death of the rebel in me thinking like the ordinary middle class man but the latter is not to be laughed at. His honesty and integrity is the backbone of the society. There is a time to be rebel and a time for adjusting to peaceful life. And now I cannot go back in time, there is never a return journey in life.

When I was thinking of myself I was also thinking about you. After all we are brothers and there are similarities in attitude. I thought you were lucky. God has given you a center point of life in Sohini. You do not know how lucky you are. Sohini loves you deeply, with all her heart. Do not ask how I know that. I know in the same way I knew about Saroj and Meena from those camp days. When someone is eager to give you something for your sake without any demand for his or her own there is real love. Just imagine if you had married her when mother was alive how much satisfaction she would have had. How long you people could stay at home would not have mattered to her. She would have been absorbed in her happiness. That satisfaction would have come down on your head as blessing and solved all other problems. That was the center point. You missed that and now immersed in remorse and depression. That depression is paralyzing you again. Wake up now, it is not yet too late and not difficult. Both of you together earn enough. All other things would smooth out gradually. Do not miss this center point of your life. There is a special joy in growing up together sharing things that life offers. Do not discuss too much, just ask Sohini to marry you. Women love demand, they want the man to be proactive. That settles the question of love for them. Like everything in life, love gets stale if kept on the shelf for long, the passion diminishes. Ride a wave on the high tide and go to your destination. Do not let it die in a trough.

Events keep happening in life and if you are not tied, it can pull you apart. And then you will be lost. You will probably ask how I know so much. Do I now believe in God? Solitude has one good thing, it makes you think deeply. I of course have resources to know what you are doing and how you are. But about God I do not think I know Him. But I know about life. I know much of what happens in our lives do not go according to plan, however much we think that we are masters of our life and fate. Chance plays a big role. And I have seen what a non-believer calls chance a believer calls God. The latter has an additional advantage of having a feeling of support and is more at peace. This is what Spinoza advised—to see oneself on the background of an eternity. And he reached that conclusion through mathematics! His most well known book is *Ethics Geometrically Demonstrated*. And by placing himself against the background of eternity he could ignore and take in his stride the trauma he would have otherwise suffered when he was excommunicated and his wife, family and society in general, deserted him. Einstein said that he could not believe in a personal God dispensing reward or punishment but he could believe in Spinoza's God. Spinoza's God is the Brahman of Vedanta.

Leaving all this philosophy aside your absolution lies in marrying Sohini as soon as you can. Do not forget this advice from your elder brother and I shall surely go to arrange your wedding. Move fast or else I may miss it. My company is thinking of sending me abroad and I do not know when. I am the only eligible bachelor and it is cheaper to send a man without family. I do not want to miss your wedding, to be the guardian of the groom.

Your anxious and loving brother
Amit

Atin went through the letter twice and then kept it in his pocket. He thought of calling Amit but put it off for later. He had to think. Next day at the hospital when he finished work he read it again. He thought of showing it to Sohini but put it off. In any case he was not meeting her till next week. The letter languished in his table drawer. Next week when he was to meet Sohini he brought out the letter, opened and looked at it once, but instead of pocketing it put it back in the drawer after pondering for sometime. He had always been a hesitant doubter, not a decisive man of action and it had become worse after mother's death. Professionally he was decisive as a surgeon but in ordinary aspects of life he could not decide when faced with a choice. Sohini took all the decisions; even his wardrobe was her creation. She mothered him and he was becoming dependant on her for every little decision but could not bring himself to mention the letter or propose marriage. He kept thinking and Sohini noticed it. She asked one day, 'Why do you look so thoughtful nowadays, what are you thinking about all the time?' His short reply was 'About us.'

'What is it about us that you are thinking so deeply about? You should have been a philosopher instead of being a budding and a good surgeon. Everybody thinks you are brilliant, all except you.'

Atin protests, 'No, No it is not about that.'

'Then what is it about? Is it that you no longer like me as you used to?' Atin shook his head. The words were on his lips 'Marry me' but he swallowed it. They were not able to meet as often as before and not as intimately. After every meeting as they parted Atin would regret for not uttering the all important words and became more depressed. Atin thought Sohini's parents were watching with concern as the courtship was prolonging, and people were talking, but could not decide whether it was real or he was only imagining. Instead of coming out he was sinking further within himself. 'Devil may care' attitude was Amit's nature, not his. He thought what if the answer became a big no? Will he lose Sohini? Sohini did not care what others thought but he could not decide and could not open himself to the only person in his world he loved and trusted and kept postponing.

The Storm

It was a Thursday, a light working day for Atin. He had come back to his room, bathed and after picking at a cold lunch lay down on bed with a book waiting for Sohini's call. She had exchanged her duty of the day with a colleague and they were going to have a date as she jokingly said on phone. Her parents were out on a short trip and she was alone. Atin was steeling himself throughout the day to pop the all important question. He would not waver today. The call has not come yet, may be Sohini is stuck at something. He dozed off a bit when the phone rang. He jumped up and almost dropped the mobile and in a hoarse voice asked, 'Why so late?'

A male voice answered 'Atinda Sohini has burnt herself badly and has been admitted in the emergency ward. She dropped her mobile and I saw your number and calling you. Please come quickly. There was no answer from her home.'

Atin could hardly respond, 'How did it happen where and who are you' as he hurriedly pushed his toes in the slipper lying in front of bed and rushed out. The male voice said, 'Her sari caught fire in the ward. It was a thin silk type sari, the girls here say it was partly synthetic and so the fire spread rapidly before we could put it off. Please come quickly,' and he was sobbing.

Atin was already out of the building and jumped into a cruising taxi and shouted at the driver, 'Medical College, drive fast, serious emergency' and was weeping.

The Calcutta taxi drivers have developed the custom of waving a red cloth as a warning flag when they have to drive fast in an emergency and are obeyed like an ambulance, a typical Calcutta innovation in a city ordinarily ruled by chaos. Atin could not check his tears but not making any sound. 'Sari, why sari?' he thought and then he remembered that it was his order for the day, not salwar nor pants, as the right dress to hear him propose. Not able to guess the real reason she replied, 'It would be diaphanous and transparent, do you think you can handle that mister?' Saris are notorious for catching fire but why hers? Oh God and he tried hard to control his sobs and covered his face with hands. Why did she go to the ward wearing a sari, must be to see a sick child once again before leaving the hospital and her sari must have caught fire from one of the stupid open heaters on the floor that were still being used against all laws. She was so sincere and loved her tiny patients so much!

It seemed an eternity by the time the taxi reached the hospital. He threw some money at the driver and rushed up to the ward. She was lying on a bed on a sterile linen sheet and covered by a thin fresh cotton sheet. That is the best the emergency ward could do. Two young doctors were standing at bedside and moved on seeing him. He asked them, 'What is the burn area' and they stammered, 'about thirty percent' and one of them added 'Mostly deep'. The sob he was trying to control burst forth as he knelt down at her bedside and held her hand. She was asleep with a sedative. Her pulse was feeble and running fast. He looked at the two young faces and they said, 'We are giving fluids and have requisitioned blood and informed sir' meaning the consultant.

He got up and ran to the blood bank. He and Sohini had the same blood group and once out of frolic cross matched their blood and it matched. He cried to the blood bank officer, 'Take my blood'. The officer said, 'We have enough blood of the same group, you need not donate. It will take a few minutes to cross match.' Atin shouted, 'No, take mine, fresh blood, not bank blood. No need to cross match. And take full five hundred cc.'

This was one of the many curious Bengal phenomena. When the first Blood Bank in the country was opened at Calcutta under the British

Raj it was decided that since the Indians were frail bodied they were not fit to donate one full unit of blood as in other countries and would donate half unit of blood. Since then the legacy has continued though the Bengalis were no longer frail. In other states the practice has been changed but in Bengal donation of half unit continued. Atin, a robust young man, was fit to donate one full unit and the blood bank officer demurely obliged. But he did the cross matching as he could not release the blood without certification. Atin was impatiently stamping and ran with the blood as soon as it was released.

Blood transfusion along with other fluids brought back some colour in Sohini's face and blood pressure stabilized. But the doctors knew it would not last because the burnt area was more than thirty percent of body surface and a considerable part of it was deep burn, the burning synthetic sari having clung to the body. There was no burns unit in this college. She had to be shifted to a burns unit and as soon as possible. Her parents were not in town and were not reachable with mobile phone.

Atin decided to take the legal risk as he had signed the papers as local guardian and arranged to transfer her to the Burns Unit of his Institute. He booked a bed and paid the admission money and transferred her at a time of day when traffic was light. It went smoothly. The real treatment then began. More fluids of different types and another unit of blood stabilized her blood pressure and made her fit next morning for first dressing under light anesthesia. The extent of the burns was revealed and it was alarming, particularly the extent of deep burns. Sohini would be losing large quantities of body proteins and fluid from these areas and it would be difficult to replace them adequately. Her parents returned and were aghast at the plight of their daughter. She was conscious enough to greet them with a wan smile.

The Professor said that only a skin homograft from a donor will be able to save her oozing, if possible alternating with some grafts from areas of her healthy skin but it may be too much for her at this stage. Atin asked whether he could donate the skin as they had the same blood group. The Professor demurely looked at him and said a substantial amount of skin would be needed to cover the deep burn areas, preferably from hairless areas. Would he put that trauma on himself and there is no certainty that it would be accepted in her body and for how long. Atin did not hesitate for a moment and gravely said that it was worth taking the chance. The Professor asked who would give the consent and Atin said, 'I shall sign the consent, I have no guardian. You can take as much skin as necessary.' When he told Sohini's mother of this plan she started crying and silently embraced him.

So it was that on the appointed date Atin and Sohini were laid side by side on two operating tables and under general anesthesia strips of skin were lifted from Atin and put on Sohini's burns. When Atin woke up in pain the first thing he asked the nurse was how Sohini was. On being assured that she was all right he asked for a sedative and went to sleep. He was released after a week with two bandaged thighs still having difficulty in walking as the thighs rubbed. He went back to his hospital room since he had nowhere else to go. Sohini's mother wanted to take him home but he declined since he wanted to be near Sohini and the nurses were taking good care of him. Sohini's father never came to see him. He was never happy with their relationship, but did not interfere knowing how stubborn his daughter was. After another fortnight his bandages were taken off as the skin cover had grown back. It was still tender but manageable.

Sohini made rapid recovery, her general condition stabilized, the skin graft held and dressings became less painful. He visited her everyday spending his free time with her. After another fortnight portions of his grafted skin on Sohini was peeling off but not all of it. The areas had to be covered by small grafts of Sohini's own skin but large areas held. She needed several such grafting sessions but gradually became stable. Doctors were surprised that Sohini's body had actually accepted much of Atin's skin. They wondered how similar they must be even in their tissue antigen structure but there was no means to check that. This is the plight of doctors in underdeveloped countries, where they have the knowledge but few facilities for their application. It was a frustration the doctors suffered that others did not understand.

Atin spent most of his day sitting by Sohini's bedside. Although he did not tell her he felt guilty. He blamed himself for his indecision and remembered his brother's letter. He once told her that as soon as she was better they must get married, to which Sohini's answer was to hold his hand and smile. He used to say, 'We have passed many adversities together and this one we shall also cross together' and she would say 'Yes, of course.'

Then a time came when she needed only ordinary dressings on alternate days and could walk a little supported by walking sticks. Her parents wanted to take her home and arrange for dressings at home. They appointed two nurses to look after her and one doctor from the hospital agreed to do the dressings. Their home was a few minutes' walking distance from the hospital. The Professor agreed but advised, 'She will need some plastic surgery in near future to prevent contractures and restore normal gait. In the mean time she can go home.' Atin's contact with her became less. He was a frequent visitor in the early days, but home was a different thing and he sometimes felt as an intruder. Her mother always welcomed him but now there were relations and her father to account for. His final postgraduate examination was coming near and he had to study seriously as the price of failure will be unemployment. He had lost major part of his savings in her initial treatment and to ask it back from her parents was below dignity. He felt responsible for her and regretted his indecision. Professor Ghosh, his mentor was sympathetic but advised him not to neglect his studies, which was his first priority and duty to himself. He studied hard as to him it was not just duty to himself but Sohini too.

He used to call her on mobile and sometimes had long chats and at other times just, 'How are you' and a few more words. She kept encouraging him to study seriously. She reminded him, 'Once you had suffered not studying seriously for my sake and not clearing the entrance exams. Please please study seriously, this time for my sake, for our sake. I know nothing can pull you down except your own self. You are a brilliant surgeon and going to be one. Do not neglect yourself.' Such conversations were becoming fewer but Atin stuck to his task of studying and working seriously. He had submitted his thesis and was given extension of appointment for one year in view of his merit and sincerity.

He had not called for a few days being busy in work and called at the weekend on her mobile but there was no response. May be she was asleep. He thought of calling the landline number but Sohini would not be able to come to the phone and he gave up. Next day he called and again there was no answer. A couple of days passed and he tried again with no luck. That weekend he was on call and could not go out and her mobile was switched off. Next week on a light day he went to her house. The door was opened and to his surprise he was asked to sit in the living room. Sohini's mother came to the room and on seeing him she started crying. He asked anxiously, 'How is Sohini?' In response she gave him an envelope she was holding in her hand. He was amazed and asked, 'What is this?' Still crying she said, 'Sohini's father has taken her to England for further treatment. He said enough liberty had been given to her, actually both of you. He would not allow her life to be spoiled and this nonsense has to end. I tried hard but could not change his decision nor was I allowed to inform you. Sohini has left this letter for you,' and pressing her sari on her face she retreated. Atin's head was reeling and he dropped down on a sofa. Everything was in turmoil, the room was spinning. He heard her mother was saying something but did not comprehend. He heard a male voice close by that was saying, 'I shall drop you home, please come' and looking up saw Sohini's driver, the witness of much of their courtship and he was wiping his tears. Helped by him Atin slowly got up and was led outside to the car. Entering his room he threw himself on the bed and pushing his face in the pillow he let himself go, crying loudly with abandon. Eventually in sheer exhaustion he fell asleep fully dressed.

When he woke up the sun was up. He was still in a daze as if he was hit on the head. He looked around the room taking in the objects as if not seen for a long time. His gaze fell on the clock. It was quite late. He remembered it was his operating day and he had been given a major case to operate all by himself for the first time and his professor had said, 'We shall see how you do it and I am sure you will be as good if not better than me.' He steeled himself, washed and went to the hospital operation theatre. Everybody around him was smiling and the nurses greeted him with admiring smiles. He scrubbed and entered the operation theatre and the surgeon in him forgot the outside world. The operation was beautifully done, there was a clapping all around and the professor came forward and hugged him saying, 'You have passed the acid test' and Atin wondered if he only knew how much of an acid test it was.

He finished his working day and came back to the room. Everything was scattered all over as if a storm had passed. He picked up the clothes piled on the bed. Something crackled inside. He brought out Sohini's letter. Was it only yesterday or eons have passed? He gingerly tore open the envelope and extracted the letter. Sohini has written in her clear handwriting. Tears welled up in his eyes and a drop fell on the letter. He controlled himself and started reading.

Atin my darling

I am crying as I write and I can see you are crying too. (Atin checked his tears and noticed her tear marks on the paper—in the tears we unite he thought and grimaced)

I am going away not by my own volition. Father had been shouting for days, 'Enough is enough, I am not going to stand this nonsense any more.' There was more but you need not know that. Know only this much that I love you just as much as ever. I know you shall believe that, I have never met nor will ever meet a kinder or sweeter man. But our destiny has separated us or else why should the accident happen on the day I was determined to give myself to you and force you to propose marriage breaking all your doubts and hesitations. I know it was your consideration for me that was holding you back. When I think how much you have sacrificed for me I wonder whether I was worth all that. I am not fit for the high pedestal where you have put me. Whenever you used to say whether you were worthy of me I used to flare up, but now I realize this was not your estimate of yourself but concern for me. You would allow nobody to touch a single hair on my head nor would you bring me down from the pedestal where you put me.

Darling I was not worthy of so much love or else why this accident should happen. I have nothing left to give you, no surprises, no magic and you gave me everything. You have taught me what love can be and I have lost it. The failure is mine not yours. I am carrying you in my mind and body till I die. I have your blood, I have your skin that I touch and shiver in the thrill of touching you. But I have given you nothing except pain. I have nothing left to give you, nothing of the mystery a woman should be, no wonder, no thrill of discovering every day the unknown unexpected, no surprises, no romance. I am finished, pervaded through and through by you. I wish and pray that you find love, love that is worthy of you, will fill you and fulfill you. Forget me please but I shall never forget you.

Your poor sad crying
Sohini

Calm after the storm

Atin woke up with a start. Someone was calling him faintly from afar and then the touch of a soft hand on his forehead. He had finished a difficult emergency at night, a case of stab injury with multiple injuries in abdomen and chest. Leaving his assistants to close up the wounds, he lay down on a couch in the surgeons' room. He had a hectic busy day followed by this emergency. He was tired and fell asleep. He opened his eyes to look at the face of Madhuri. In his sleep he was seeing the video replay of his life and realized he was actually crying as he felt his wet face. With a shy smile he looked at Madhuri. Madhuri asked quietly, 'Sorry Sir, I was just checking whether you are sleeping. Would you like to have a cup of coffee and something to eat Sir?' Madhuri was the nurse in charge of the operation theatre and a very efficient one at that with a high degree in nursing, specializing in operation theatre work. She was a calm sedate person and an asset to the operation theatre, never losing her calm and efficiency and nobody ever saw her lose her temper and poise even in the tensest and trying situation. She was an excellent assistant when she scrubbed and joined the surgical team in operation. She assisted Atin in this operation as the resident was busy elsewhere and he had left the wound closure to her. He knew her stitching would be finer than his.

Atin sat up and wiped his face with hand. Madhuri turned around and brought out a fresh towel from a cupboard and handed it to him. She said with a soft compassionate voice, 'you have had a tough day Sir and then this emergency. I have brought some food and made a cup of coffee. Please have it and rest for some time before you drive home.'

Only then Atin noticed the trolley table beside him with a steaming cup of coffee. He thanked her gratefully and turned towards the food. It was quite wholesome for a late supper. Madhuri left the room without a comment as he started eating. He looked at her departing figure and wondered. This was not exactly her duty.

She mentioned 'home' but did she know what that home was? It was an empty apartment with a servant cum cook who took care of his household. There were two bedrooms in the apartment and the servant occupied one. He after all needed to live somewhere and being the only relation, he had the right to live in the spare bedroom. He was uneducated but could answer the phone and had picked up some quaint words that amused him. As a cook he was nothing to write home about and he smiled at himself, but he was honest and if he ever pilfered anything Atin would hardly notice. Apart from the two bedrooms and one kitchen there was a living and dining space whose disorder would make anybody shiver. There were four desultory chairs with a measly center table and an office table, all of them piled with books, journals and all sorts of papers lying in total disarray. Those things also covered most parts of his bed and he slipped himself in whatever empty space he could find to sleep. His housemate had no right to touch them as he would not know what was what.

His mind turned to Madhuri as he continued to eat. The food was delicious. It could not be hospital food by any stretch of imagination. It was home cooked food. Madhuri must have brought it for her own consumption. He knew nurses often brought that instead of taking hospital food. He rang the bell and asked for Madhuri. When she came he said, 'This is not hospital food.'

Madhuri replied, 'No Sir I cooked it at home. Did you like it?' Her voice was matter of fact.

Atin said, 'Yes, immensely. But what are you going to eat?'

Madhuri replied in the same manner, 'There is hospital food in the refrigerator. I shall heat it and eat. That is what most girls do.' Again there was no emotion in her demeanor.

Atin kept looking at her. She was pretty in a homely way. Age wise she must be in her mid twenties or a bit more definitely has not crossed thirty. He had seen her off and on from her student days but never took any notice. She was there during Sohini's accident. Everybody knew about the incident but there was never any personal comment from her, though they discussed a lot of things related to the operations and the operation theatre. She often had a literary work on her table. Once he saw a copy of Dostoyevsky's Crime and Punishment and wondered what sort of person would have such a book as a light reading in between duties to perform.

Madhuri felt uncomfortable under the stare and asked, 'If you have finished eating shall I remove the plates?'

Atin asked, 'Why, are there no bearers?'

She replied, 'No Sir they have gone for their food. They were hungry so I let them go.'

Atin was surprised at his own feeling not wanting her to go. He asked, 'Do you live with your family?'

She replied with the same nonchalance, 'No Sir I share a small apartment with another girl. My family that is my parents, two sisters and one brother do not stay here.'

Atin asked, 'And you get the time to cook.'

This time there was a small flicker of smile on her lips. 'Sir I am a village girl. We learn cooking at an early age. It is not a big deal.'

Atin asked, 'Is that so? Where is your village?'

Madhuri said, 'You would not know Sir. It is a village in Midnapur district not far from the Digha sea resort.'

Atin said, 'Really? Well I have gone to Digha more than once. I must have crossed your village.'

This time there was a definite smile. 'I don't think so Sir. My village is not on any main road. It is a bit far.'

'What is the name of your village' he asked.

'Mahadebpur Sir' was her answer.

'Do you often go home?'

'Yes Sir, whenever I have leave I go home, not anywhere else.'

'Is it such a nice place' he asked.

'Yes Sir. Have you ever lived in a village? Life there is quite different from city life.'

'No I have not though my parents at one time lived in village before the Partition.'

Atin thought he has done enough beating around the bush. He asked directly, 'You were around during Sohini's accident, were you not?'

She visibly stiffened 'Yes Sir.'

'What did you think about it?'

She was grave and cautious. After a pause she replied, 'It was terrible Sir and many of us cried that fate would inflict such a terrible blow at two such nice people.'

Atin looked away from her not knowing what to say but kept staring at his hands.

Madhuri picked up the dishes and made a motion to go. Then she stopped and said, 'If you do not mind Sir and with apologies may I say one thing' and as Atin looked up she said, 'Life never stops as long as we are alive. One has to hope and trust in God' and she left.

Atin looked pensively at her retreating figure. What did she mean? Was she suggesting something or was she only feeling sorry seeing his tears after years of Sohini's departure? He decided it must be the latter. The pain of her departure had become tolerable by now but it must have been his tiredness that brought back the memories. He was living the life of a recluse all these years. Professionally he has been successful beyond his expectation and in a comparatively short time. Not interested in an academic career or government service full of politics and intrigue, he chose to join a new modern private hospital. He joined as a resident surgeon to start with, but soon was offered a staff position because of his abilities and has built up a busy practice and his reputation is growing bringing money and fame. But he has remained a recluse avoiding human contact and least of all with the opposite sex. He had no one to share his success with. He is invited to deliver lectures in many forum that he does expertly and is known as a good speaker. But he avoids all personal contacts. Many stories circulate about him and he is aware of those, some of them ludicrous to say the least. He realizes that it is foolish to live under the shadow of tragic experiences of his life but finds it difficult to break out. His loneliness is only aggravating his distress. Madhuri was probably aware of that. She joined this hospital soon after he did and at there first meeting she looked at him strangely, but controlled immediately saying, 'It would be a pleasure to work with you Sir, I have heard so much about you.' Until today she never tried to be personal. He had given her that opportunity, she did not create it. She is also a damn good cook and he smiled as he got dressed and left, not finding Madhuri anywhere to thank her.

From that day he became conscious of her presence and his eyes repeatedly drifted towards her without any conscious effort. In the beginning he used to be embarrassed and looked away but gradually it became a habit and he watched her and loved to do it. She had a shapely figure neither skinny nor plump. She administered the staff in a friendly reserved manner making them obey her without ever raising her voice or faulting them. The operation theatre staff including the doctors loved her easy inoffensive manner. His anesthetist was good in his profession, but had the added quality of keeping the operating room and the surgeon relaxed by easy conversation and jokes now and then and assuring everybody that the patient was doing fine, a quality so desirable. Atin was a silent worker serious in his job. But gradually he looked more relaxed and seemed to enjoy telling short anecdotes and participate in jokes, which made the operation team more relaxed without losing concentration. Now and then his eyes would stray at Madhuri after telling a funny anecdote to see whether she was smiling behind her mask and she did now and then and strangely that made him happy. Actually her eyes had more laughter than her face, she was reserved there. It became a fascinating game with Atin in relaxed moments and that surprised him. Needless to say others noticed this attention before long, and muted smiles went around with whispers when the coast was clear.

Madhuri and Malati were good friends since their nursing school days and shared their tiny rented apartment. They could ill afford it but loved the privacy and somehow managed. Malati worked in radiology and had regular hours. She was a good housekeeper and Madhuri was a good cook. Cooking one day was good for a few days, and being intimate friends ran their house well. The whispers reached Malati. She was a happy jovial girl.

One weekend both of them were free and Malati was making the house tidy and throwing the washing things in a basket and Madhuri was cooking the Sunday lunch. Being the beginning of the month they had decided on a feast hosted by Madhuri.

Malati shouted from her place, 'Listen Mad what is this I hear that a certain surgeon is giving more attention to the non-anesthetized patient under his scalpel than the anesthetized one in the operation theatre?'

Madhuri shouted back, 'that is no wonder for a third rate scandalmonger like you. I have heard no such story.'

Malati entered the kitchen and said, 'How would you hear darling as your ears have become like Radha, only tuned to the flute of your Shyam' and she stood in the cross-legged pose of Krishna with the flute.

Madhuri in sham rage turned around with the hot ladle and said, 'One more word of scandal and this one would blacken your face like Krishna for ever.'

Malati danced two steps away and said, 'tut tut chhi, our Krishna is not black, he is so fair and tall and such a bearing' and she mimed the words with gestures.

Madhuri chased her, 'Get out of the kitchen this is my space. You will spoil the chicken roast and no Krishna in the world will bring another for you.'

Malati caught her by the waist, 'Tell me tell me please, my beautiful sweetheart, should I be the last one to hear, I am your Chandrabali?'

Madhuri extricated herself and went back to kitchen laughing, 'OK OK I shall send him to your kunj garden Chandrabali.'

Malati made a face and started laying the table. Madhuri brought the steaming roast to the table followed by other accessories like garlic toast, green veggies, sauce, slices of plum cake and whipped cream, and making a face asked, 'Would this be enough for you glutton?' Malati sighed, 'I have lost all appetite for food, want only the food for thought' and laughing they sat for their meal.

Malati inhaled deeply the aroma. She wanted a western style lunch and Madhuri cooked. Cooking was her hobby and tried out many types of cooking. After the first few mouthfuls Madhuri asked, 'How is it, do you like it?'

Malati said, 'Simply delicious. It is amazing that a village belle like you can cook so many things so well! Are you equally expert in making love darling' and startled Madhuri jumped up and banged her lightly on the head with her fist, 'I shall kill you if you make one more comment' and the friends burst out laughing.

Malati became busy with the dishes and Madhuri cleaned the table and the kitchen. They were relaxing in Madhuri's room. Malati was an occasional smoker and she said, 'Oh dear, such a meal for Sunday lunch. I must have a fag' and she went to her room and came back with a lighted cigarette and made herself comfortable. Taking a deep drag she blew the smoke and said, 'Now I am ready to hear your affair.'

Madhuri retorted, 'There is no affair.'

Malati sighed, 'You innocent girl two things are essential to enjoy a love affair—there has to be a man of course, but you have to have a confidante to pour the sauce. Come on let us have it how you managed to get to that glum faced handsome surgeon.'

Madhuri blushed and regretted that she did, 'I did not get on to him and he did not either.'

Malati smiled at her blush and said, 'Ok Ok, the two innocents were standing under the apple tree and Cupid threw his arrow. Come on don't be shy.'

Madhuri described what happened that night in the operation theatre. Malati listened absorbed and fascinated, watching the spreading blush on Madhuri.

When she finished she blew another ring of the smoke and said, 'Phew, the crying weak surgeon and you shot him through the heart? What a rogue!'

Madhuri protested, 'Nothing was done by design. I just felt sad for him and saw he was tired and hungry. That was all. You also know about his burning fiancée but I was closer and saw the whole tragedy. Seeing him crying in his sleep moved me. I did what any human being would have done.'

Malati looked at the ceiling and said, 'Oh God why have you never placed me before a crying dumb headed rich surgeon' and before Madhuri could react she asked, 'And what are you going to do about it now?'

Madhuri said, 'Nothing, it was only an accidental event.'

Malati winked, 'But he liked your cooking, a lethal weapon. Have you never heard that the best way to a man's heart is through his stomach? You have even conquered a woman, me, with that weapon, what to speak of a man. You have to chase him now. It is absolutely unethical to leave an injured animal and not go for a kill.'

Madhuri was angry and got up to go. Malati was quick to get up and embracing her said, 'Calm down darling and forgive me for teasing. You have to chase him for his own good.'

Madhuri was still angry, 'Why should I do that, I am not responsible for him.'

Malati calmed her down by saying, 'I am sorry girl for being frivolous. But don't you see that he has given that responsibility to you? There are two types of men in this world, those who love to chase and those who love to be chased. The second type is by far the better. If he were a chaser he would have been married to Sohini by now with a few kids to the bargain. I did not know Sohini well but he was obviously too shy or too reticent or too something else—a very good man hesitating to assume too much responsibility, a big man with a teenager's mind. Even if apparently in love, sometimes they are too terrified by an aggressive woman. Knowing you so well by now, I know you would love him and you two will make a good match.'

Madhuri was silently fiddling with her fingers and looking down at them whispered, 'I also do not know how to chase. I am not a flirt by nature and what am I compared to Sohini, nothing!'

Malati affectionately put arms around her shoulder and sweetly said, 'You may be better in many scores. Do not have a low self-esteem. Look at yourself through a friends' eye, mine. You don't have to flirt, not in your nature. You just return his smile when he smiles at you and encourage him, watch the effect. Your smile is far sweeter than Sohini's, trust me.'

Change of Seasons

Madhuri tried to follow her friend's teaching to smile whenever the opportunity presented but she did not succeed much, being too self conscious. But this cupid's weapon became even more effective as Atin unconsciously used to try even more than before to make her smile. She was amused by it and so did others. Atin needed her more as his workload increased and he increasingly depended on her for everything in the operation theatre. It was not all smiles but serious work and discussions. But it was obvious to others, as much as to them, that they liked each other without any exaggerated show of friendship. Others noticed their mutual liking but there was nothing more to create a gossip.

Malati demanded an almost daily briefing but there was nothing more that Madhuri could relate and she became exasperated as the days and weeks went by. She would ask, 'There is no more talks than instruments and operations, what sort of people are you two? He never asks you to go for a cup of coffee even, not to speak of going to see a movie or something? What does he do with his leisure time?'

Madhuri replies, 'People say he studies a lot and is writing some papers for publication.'

Malati throws up her hands and exclaims, 'I have never seen two such extremely cold-blooded animals. You become a bit more proactive then. Ask him out somewhere, to an art exhibition or musical festival or anything. You are interested in those things. Does he know how accomplished you are?'

Madhuri smiles, 'I don't have a clue but rumours say he does and he is also interested.'

'Then pull him out of his box. People who know him well say that he is no virgin. The affair with Sohini was a pretty torrid affair. So what is wrong with you? Just tell me when I have to stay clear off the flat and I promise I won't peep.'

Madhuri's grave reply was, 'I like it this way and I presume so does he.'

Months passed, the rainy season was over and in came the autumn, the best season in Bengal with Puja festival and long holidays. There was a buzz around the operation theatre, people discussing what they plan to do during the holidays. Women discussed shopping, what dresses they plan to buy for whom, especially the married ones.

One day during an ordinary operation Atin looked up at the anesthetist and asked, 'Salil what do you plan to do during the holidays, plan to go somewhere?'

Salil also looked up and said, 'Me? I love to stay at home, eat as much as I can and sleep through most of the day keeping my cell phone in silent mode.' Then he asks, 'How about you, what is your plan?'

Atin replied, 'I think I shall drive down to Digha. I have booked a bungalow there and will spend a quiet holiday with books and drive around the countryside looking at the beauty of Bengal villages during the festival.' There ensued an excited exchange of glances around the room with most of them landing at least once on Madhuri and she turned purple under her facemask.

Salil asked in a neutral voice, 'Why should a man like you go to Digha, why not Switzerland or at least Kashmir or Goa if you do not want to go abroad?'

Atin replied, 'Why waste days in traveling when there is so much unseen beauty close at hand? Don't you know those beautiful lines of Rabindranath Thakur after he traveled far and wide, 'I have not seen opening my eyes two steps from my doors, that one dewdrop on one corn of rice paddy' you remember that?'

Salil in a puzzled voice replied, 'Yes I remember. But I did not know you were interested in poetry.'

Atin said, 'Is there anybody who is not moved by poetry or music? It is an essential part of our life in whatever we do including and especially in a surgeon's life. Look at this human body I am cutting, is there not a rhythm or poetry in it. It is created in a cosmic rhythm, the heart the nerve cells translate that rhythm, the blood flows in that rhythm, in its deepest depths the cells and molecules dance doing their allotted tasks in a rhythm of harmony that we do not even understand. When I cut it with knife, I feel like intruding a temple, a house of God, am I worthy of it? Am I disturbing that rhythm, do I understand it enough to perform my task without violating that rhythm? If I do violate beyond tolerance I am not worthy of doing my job. When I lose a patient I spend sleepless nights thinking where I went wrong, where did I violate the rhythm and music of life? Is that not a poet's frustration if he cannot catch the rhythm of life and creation in his work that would give him satisfaction and mark of greatness?'

There was hushed silence around the room. Something has been uttered that is so stupendously greater than what everybody thinks. A surgeon operates on a patient to cut out or join parts and goes away with his fees and that is the universally accepted picture. Can there be anything so great hidden in that mundane daily work? Does anybody look inside the mind of a surgeon when he prescribes operation to a patient and then goes on to do that? Is that a reality or is the commercial exploit of collecting fees and then splitting it and sending commissions to get more referrals the only reality? In the constantly opposing forces in our material world probably both are realities. That depth was surprisingly revealed in the normally silent self evasive nature of Atin.

The operation ended in that grave silence. Normally voluble Salil was also silent. Atin left the room, washed hands, and changed clothes in silence. Even he was overwhelmed by what he uttered, his innermost thoughts and feelings so openly. He looked for Madhuri without asking anybody but did not find her. A junior nurse volunteered gravely, without being asked, that she has left. After a second look in the recovery room at the patient just operated and a few other postoperative patients Atin walked to his car in the parking lot. There he found Madhuri seated on a bench partly hidden by his car.

He went towards her asking, 'What are you doing here?'

'Waiting for you Sir' was her reply.

'Why?' He asked in surprise.

She took a moment and then replied, 'I came in anger but now I am confused.' He looked at her quizzically without saying anything.

After a few poignant moments she said, 'The anger is because you are making me cheap. You do not need to announce to the world that you are going near my home and actually want to go to the villages around that may include my village, though I am not sure of that, increasing the merriment all around.'

Atin was a bit puzzled, 'Why should there be merriment in that? Actually I do want to go to your village if you do not mind but why should there be merriment in that? Of course I should have asked you before announcing it but I did not mention your village. In fact it occurred to me only as I was speaking. Can I go to your village?'

Madhuri kept looking at him, what a man or is it a little boy in a man's body full of simplicity who cannot think of anything surreptitious or dirty or is he just naïve or even worse, a scheming man? But can a naïve or scheming man say the things he said spontaneously that must have come from deep within him?

In her confusion she burst out laughing, puzzling Atin even more. He asked, 'Now what is it? There are tears in your eyes and you are laughing, what a picture! Wish I had a camera with me but I wonder what would be the title of the picture.'

She said, 'That is easy, title it 'a stupid little girl' because I now want to touch your feet' and as she bent low Atin jumped out of her reach in surprise. Then he said, 'Ok I concede that I do not understand a bit of what you are talking about but I think we should remove ourselves from this parking lot and if you allow, I can drop you at your home.'

Madhuri said, 'Only on one condition that I can serve you tea at my home.'

Atin said, 'I agree only because I have already eaten your salt on that day I fell asleep and it was delicious, no harm in a repeat' and laughing together they entered the car, Madhuri imagining Malati's face and praying that she had not yet reached home.

They reached her apartment and she was relieved to see that the door was locked from outside. She opened it with her keys and letting him in closed the door and asked him to sit. Fortunately Malati had done the room before leaving and it was spick and span. She ran to the kitchen saying, 'I am giving you a cup of coffee or tea first and then making a snack, what would you have coffee or tea?'

Atin burst out in laughter and said 'You could have asked coffee tea or me.' She got rooted to the spot in confusion and blushed and hated herself for that. Embarrassed Atin was full of apologies and coming forward held her hand, an automatic reaction. Her hands trembled like a shivering bird. Both of them were shocked at the sudden turn of events and stood transfixed looking at each other Atin still holding her hand. Madhuri recovered first and slowly disengaged her hand and walked slowly to the kitchen. Atin stood for sometime and went back to his seat.

Madhuri called from kitchen and said in normal voice, 'I am making a small snack and would bring with the tea. Is that ok with you or will you rather have coffee?'

Atin had recovered and said with a smile, 'Tea would be fine.'

Madhuri found some bread and eggs and fried them to make four slices of French toast also called Bombay toast in local parlance and topped them with cheese. She made two large cups of tea and placing them all on a tray brought them to the sitting room and placed before Atin and smiling at Atin said, 'You have to make do with these for today. That is all I have. Next time I shall arrange better food.'

Atin relaxed and returning the smile said, 'So there is the possibility of a next time? I thought I had burnt my boat.'

Madhuri laughed and said, 'Would you mind starting, you are hungry. I shall take two minutes to freshen up' and went to her room while Atin kept staring at her.

She came back faster than Atin expected surprising him with her change of appearance in a fresh silk sari that clung to the body, a quick face work, whiff of perfume and untying the hair and combing and brushing to let it fall in a cloud on her shoulders. She was looking much younger and beautiful. Atin looked fascinated and remarked, 'You have done all that in exactly five minutes!'

Madhuri said, 'I am a working girl, cannot spend a long time at dressing. Am I looking ugly?'

Atin said staring at her, 'On the contrary you are looking beautiful.' His face confirmed his opinion and she blushed.

Avoiding his gaze she pushed the plate at him and said, 'I am only an ordinary village girl, can't do better than this. You would do better to concentrate on this meager food instead. Finish it; it is all yours. I had a snack just before leaving the hospital.'

Atin picked up a slice and said, 'This is the second time I am hearing about the village belle. I shall need a long time and a lot of scrutiny to accept that definition.'

Madhuri picked up a cup of tea and sipping looked at him over the edge and said, 'You will get tired very soon. How is the toast, is it edible? Sorry I could not do any better at such short notice.'

Atin chewing a mouthful said, 'I have a lot of time and I do not get tired easily. Speaking of edible things I see a number of them around.'

Madhuri averted his gaze taking time to place her cup carefully on the table, and asked shyly, 'Are you really planning to come to our village during the holiday? What about your relatives, don't you wish to visit them?'

Atin was regretting his last word and felt ashamed. It just came out. He did not want to be that close. What would she think? But to apologize would be even more ridiculous. Madhuri understood his silence and a little smile flickered at the corner of her lips. At last he said recovering his composure and with extra gravity, 'I have no relations. Both my parents are dead and I have one elder brother who works at Bangalore that is if he is still there. At our last communication he said he may go abroad' and in utter confusion added 'it was some time back' and stopped.

Madhuri caught the hesitation and asked in mild surprise, 'He is your only relation and you don't even know whether he is there?'

Atin replied, 'It is a bit complicated and will take a long time to explain. We love each other but we have grown up differently and that is the shortest reply I can give. Why are you asking, don't you want me to go to your village, would your elders mind?'

For the second time that evening their hands met as Madhuri with alacrity touched his hand and said 'NO NO, I shall be very happy if you visit our village and stay in our house' and then stammered and withdrawing her hand and blushing said, 'I mean my parents will be very happy to have you as a guest in our house, a famous surgeon like you' and then in confusion sat looking at her hand.

Atin pointing at her hand said, 'This time it is not my fault surely' and leaning back on the sofa said 'so I get a holiday with free board and lodge' and added more deliberately than the last faux pas 'is there anything else thrown in?'

Madhuri jumped up collecting the dishes dropping a spoon on the floor and bent down to pick them. Atin held her face between two hands that had come close to him in the process and looked intently. Madhuri was shaking all over and only managed to say, 'Please, no' and Atin let go.

As she disappeared in the kitchen Atin got up and looked around to see the paintings on the wall. She came back to the room poised and Atin asked who painted those. 'I see no name but they are pretty good.' She replied shyly, 'I love painting but now do not find the time. It is nice of you to say they are pretty but they are ordinary. I paint only for my own pleasure.' Their eyes were locked and he said gravely with a thick voice 'I shall look forward to seeing a lot of ordinary things and love them.' She stood silent.

He turned towards the door and she came round to open. As they were going out Malati came panting up the stairs and talking at the same time to Madhuri whom she saw first 'what is this I hear darling . . . . ' and froze gulping strangely. Atin bade Madhuri goodbye and said, 'You don't have to come down, I shall find my way' and went down past the two silent friends standing like statues.

Atin drove slowly through the late evening traffic and the omnipresent crowd that thronged the footpath and spilled over on the road. In Calcutta it is the driver's onus not to hit them but the pedestrians are confidently careless. He has heard from friends that in rich developed countries there are strict rules about the right of the pedestrians and the motorist and they are strictly obeyed. Even here there are a few laws but the pedestrians violate them more and have the right of way more than in developed countries, in other words chaos. Accidents do happen but what surprises him is that they should have been many times more. He could only ascribe that to an instinctive organization within chaos and woe betide the motorist who hits somebody. Depending on the area, often his only option is to run away or be lynched. But it is the general picture in almost every aspect of Indian society that one has to get accustomed to. Is that the primary definition of underdevelopment? The reverse of that would of course be overdevelopment. How is that defined? He had no idea but historically highly organized societies have collapsed faster than less organized ones. Biodiversity is after all the order of the nature and every animal seeks its comfort zone. The problem with human beings is that they or some of them want to create their own social environment. That responsibility has been given to man in the evolutionary process but are they trained enough for that? Atin smiled at himself and thought that if one day he is labeled as a philosopher the credit would have to go to traffic jams of Calcutta for patience and acute mental and physical concentration needed to zigzag out of them without hitting the chaotic pedestrians of Calcutta.

As he neared home the traffic and other obstacles thinned and his thought turned to the events of the day. They were also chaotic, happening without any preparation and premonition, a day of unexpected events. Can he or should he judge the significance of those events or is there nothing in them to philosophize? He parked the car and went up the elevator to his room. As he slowly undressed the face of Madhuri lightly held in his hand floated in his mind. Why did he do it? He had never thought of her in that way. He liked her as an efficient nurse and a comrade in arms but nothing more. A plaintiff in one corner of his mind interjected, 'Are you not cheating yourself?' The reply from his thinking mind was, 'Well, may be a little. I did look at her eyes and face and surreptitiously at her body may be once or twice. But that is nothing unusual. A man does it all the time out of habit.' The plaintiff replied, 'Are you sure? Why did you bring up the subject of holiday travel in the operation theatre among all your juniors and assistants?' His reply was, 'That is also nothing unusual. Most surgeons do light chat in operation theatre when the situation is not tense and holiday plan is a common subject.' His accuser replied, 'But you have never talked much in operation theatre and actually been known as grumpy but you are doing quite a bit of talking recently.' His advocate replied, 'Yes may be, I wanted the atmosphere to be a bit relaxed and happy.' The antagonist replied with a chuckle 'Happy for whom?' Atin replied 'Go to hell' and went for wash.

Afterwards he sat down at the dining table, his favourite haunt, with the half read newspaper and a cup of tea and a few biscuits provided by his manservant. The biscuit tasted a bit mouldy and he grimaced. He remembered the tasty snack at Madhuri's house. What was it; a cheese and egg toast? It was delicious that he had never tasted before. Was this the sort of snack that they had in starving Bengal villages? He smiled and thought it was becoming difficult to take Madhuri off his mind. He gave up the effort and dropping the newspaper stared at the wall remembering the face of Madhuri in between his two hands. Why did he do that? It was almost a reflex action but he loved the touch, it was so soft! Her lips were trembling and she shook slightly as she said 'Please, no.' He was relishing the picture and thought her body language was opposite 'Please yes.' If he was serious he should have kissed her but he did not. Why not, it was not a big deal. In fact he quickly withdrew his hands. Why? He was immersed in deep thought traveling his mental space he has not touched for a long time. He was actually afraid, afraid of the passion in her voice. But with passion there was restraint, a desire to give in but a hesitation to commit and lose her self, signature of a sensitive tender mind. Atin felt pleasant warmth inside that he could not remember having felt with Sohini. May be he was too young then and is more mature now. He frowned and thought only that could not explain it.

The revelation surprised him and he got up from the dining table to recline on the sofa and think. Since the departure of Sohini from his life he had no female contact. Not that there was any dearth of opportunity or approach. To the known circle he was a romantic recluse and to the less known a handsome and eligible well established bachelor in the prime of youth. He was in love with Sohini but it was calf love of adolescence, inexperienced and tinged with the romance of the unknown, the first love painted with many colours of unknown passions. May be there was also a tinge of fear impinged by the overwhelming personality of Sohini. The pain of that love made him afraid of passion and he started detesting female company. He had to grow out of that or else he would continue to suffer loneliness. Psychologically he was still in those teen-age fears and a sense of guilt. Passion is an important component of love but by no means the only one and may be even not the most important one. And nor was it a guilt. Real love is more broad based and encompass many things primarily of mutual respect and joy of togetherness. Physical passion by itself may die but real love endures and overcomes every obstacle. That does not mean passion is a crime or ought to be shunned but it has to have other elements for fulfillment. Passion by itself can also fulfill in creativity and life till its memory lingers but not in a life like his. It would have been grand if the passionate relationship with

Sohini, the first love, had matured to the lasting love of togetherness but unfortunately that did not happen. That is not a total loss because it has matured him to a richness he might not have attained otherwise. And that also does not mean that either Sohini or he should block out life and commit mental suicide. Sohini wished him fulfillment in love and he should wish her the same sincerely and wholeheartedly. There is no guilt and after a long time he felt himself free.

Atin's revelry was interrupted as the mobile rang. He picked it up to hear a sweet voice say, 'You have left your handkerchief here. I do not know how to return it to you.'

Atin smiled and replied, 'You don't have to. Keep it with you, I have others. Is this your mobile you are calling from? I did not know you had one.'

Madhuri said, 'Yes this is my mobile. I always called you from hospital exchange.'

Atin asked, 'If you do not mind can I preserve this number? I may need it sometime.' There was no reply.

Atin asked again, 'Is your friend with you?'

Madhuri replied, 'No she is in her room.'

Atin said, 'I am relieved. I thought you had disconnected. Women used to leave their handkerchiefs behind in romantic days of Europe. I was afraid you may think I left handkerchief on purpose.'

There was a sweet giggle from the other side, 'I did not know you were a coward. I have to go now because my friend is pounding on the door to hear stories but I have no story to tell. Bye' and she called off much to Atin's chagrin. He thought about the gentle tease, and he felt warm at this innocent cultured expression of something deeper.

Atin got up and went to bedroom to lie down to rest his aching back and lay with arms crossed behind the head and eyes staring at the ceiling and whispered, 'Is this woman the reason and result of my self analysis God? Please see that she does not get to know it at least not till it is time. I am not sure yet and I do not want to hurt her nor do I want to give her false hope. She is just too good,' and he fell asleep. His servant woke him up informing that dinner was ready. Half asleep he tottered to the dining table and sat in front of the food with no appetite. The food was the same that he ate days in and days out, wholesome but just the same diet. He desultorily picked at it here and there and got up. The servant anxiously asked whether food was not good. He answered it was ok but he had eaten earlier in the evening and was not hungry. Actually he was feeling his loneliness acutely as never before. He took refuge in bed to try to sleep and eventually fell asleep.

The shore breeze

Thus it happened that Atin had to cancel the bungalow booking. He could not go back on his word. That would insult and embarrass Madhuri. He would have to spend the holiday in Madhuri's house. Her father insisted when he heard from his daughter and even offered to come to Calcutta to escort him. He was desisted from doing so with some difficulty. Atin loved to drive alone. As a matter of fact he never had a passenger since he bought his own car except the day he took Madhuri home. He hoped there would be no more episodes with her and his behaviour would have to be proper, as it was not only she now but with the family and the entire village looking on. He would be driving around most of the time and that would seem natural to them. It is only a matter of a few days and he did want to look at life in a village intimately.

Madhuri left before Atin to make the house ready for him. Atin drove down just before the worship of Mother Goddess Durga started. He had a leisurely drive stopping at places to take in the scenery and the people and taste the local delicacies and cuisine. Digha was a beautiful seaside town at one time with pine and cocoanut trees swaying in the breeze on the seashore. But it had been somewhat destroyed by the large crowds descending from the cities on holidays and the erosion of the sea destroying most of the pine forest on the shore. But driving away from the town on offshore road one could catch a glimpse of the old beauty. He drove around the small town and drove on the offshore road till he reached the interstate boundary and then drove back. He took in with great delight the rural scenes. The dried mud road with brick reinforcement billowed dust behind him and he slowed down instinctively when there were people on the road moving, to the side both to let him pass and to avoid the dust cloud, which they did not seem to mind. It was totally different scene from the city. There were women with bundles of rice paddy on their head, men and boys driving cattle and giving him the pass, bullock carts loaded with goods or empty, who had to be given time to move to the side without sounding horn so that the bullocks were not startled. On both sides there were empty fields after harvest interrupted by cluster of huts, some were mud huts with thatch roof and some were brick houses with a roof of painted asbestos sheets or tin roof. The richer ones had concrete roofs. Some mud huts had two floors and Atin learnt later that they were cool in high heat of summer. The people and particularly the women smiled at him as almost the entire locality seemed to know his coming. He was overwhelmed by this show of affection that is hard to find in a big city. His mind was at peace.

Guided by Madhuri's mobile phone he slowly drove inshore to reach her village. He was overwhelmed by the welcome. Almost everybody on the roadside knew who he was and where he was going and he did not really need Madhuri's guidance. But her anxious voice on the phone sounded so sweet. She still addressed him as *daktarbabu,* which sounded funny. It was sweet to hear and essential in the presence of her folks. In fact she has not called him by name yet and in a village it was out of the question where even husbands and wives do not call each other by name. Actually this sort of indirect address had a peculiar sweetness about it that Atin had heard between his parents. Calling somebody as, 'Hey are you listening' or 'Where are you' made that person special 'You,' instead of calling as John or Mike. He regained and enjoyed that sweetness along with everything else. In the hospital he was 'Sir' or at most 'Dr. Roy' to Madhuri, both out of place here. In this place *daktarbabu* is most appropriate though nobody would mind his calling her by name since she is younger but calling her as Sister would be totally out of place. If she had an elder sister many years her senior he would be expected to call her Didi but fortunately she had none, being the eldest of the siblings. Addressing a person is rather complicated in India and the address itself signifies old or young or denotes respect.

Madhuri's father whom Atin addressed as *sailenbabu,* his name being Sailen, was a rich farmer, not very rich but tolerably so, with a well spread out two-story brick and concrete house. The whole house was admirably decorated that was natural in this festive season, with a little bit extra thrown in for the honoured guest in the form of flower buntings, curtains and festoons. The only problem was to talk to Madhuri. She was scarcely visible and there was no lonely moment. That was helpful to Atin, as he did not have to be self conscious in talking to her or make a loose talk. There was no problem in following her with eyes and he did that a lot to see how she behaves with others or jokes and laughs in the middle of all the work of arranging the worship and household chores, but little did he imagine that his watching was being watched to the delight of specially the womenfolk. Madhuri was dressed a bit specially from her sisters. This was an educated family, almost all members being literate and Madhuri's brother, an engineer and one sister, a school teacher, having gone to college. In the holidays everybody has gathered at home. For most of the time his companion was Madhuri's youngest sister Tapati, addressed as Tapu, the youngest of the four children in her early teens. She was a lively jolly girl always waiting on him for his slightest need and looking at him with adoring eyes. But she had her innocent pranks and Atin, never having a sister, enjoyed that.

The day Atin arrived Tapu forced everybody to sit down to a musical evening that apparently was a regular family affair where all members had to sing. Some hesitation was there with the newly arrived guest but Tapu broke through all barriers. As things were being arranged, putting instruments in position, and matting on the floor, Tapu whispered to Atin, 'You shall hear my eldest Didi sing and you will be amazed' and ran away before she was caught. The rule was everybody must sing something and so they did to the best of their abilities. Tapu started the evening and sang several songs consulting her sister and they were good. Atin patted her on the back and she whispered, 'Wait till you hear Didi sing but you won't be able to pat her, sorry' and she made a funny face. Atin was spared in spite of Tapu's insistence. But actually it was Madhuri's concert. She was very shy in his presence but was prevailed on. She had very sweet and melodious voice of almost professional standard. The brother and one of his friends alternately accompanied on tabla. She first sang a few devotional songs followed by modern and then going to film music by popular demand. It was magical as the whole house reverberated with the sweet sound of music. When she stopped there was total silence as everybody was immersed. Only her father regretted to Atin, 'This daughter of mine is so talented, and taught by real masters, she is in great demand in all surrounding villages but she joined nursing to be independent and went away to the city.' Atin could only say, 'She is very good in that too' out of politeness but he was also moved. Atin asked his father, 'Why has she not gone for audition on radio and now television has come?' Father sighed, 'We live in back of beyond, more so until very recent times, and such opportunities were difficult.'

Worship of the goddess started the day after Atin's arrival. The image of the goddess was small but beautifully made by local artisans. The first day is spent in preparatory rituals and welcoming the goddess as the image is brought to life by the devotion of the worshippers through chanting of the priest and established in her place of honour in the household as a divine guest for four days, actually a daughter of the house arriving with her children to her father's home on earth from the icy heights of the Himalayas, her husband's abode. All Hindu image worship is about bringing the idol to life and where does one find life apart from the worshiper? And they through worship fill the image with the best qualities that man can attain in courage, strength, love, compassion, tolerance and forgiveness. This worship is primarily family worship. But only about a century back, in the city of Calcutta, the public worship through public donation started and it has become a carnival where much of the close devotion has vanished. Here in a village farmer's house Atin realized the true significance of the worship and its beauty. It is expensive to perform the worship for four days, procure everything that is necessary and feed the guests with *bhogprasad,* that is the blessing through the Holy Mother's blessed meals and almost the whole village turns up. The entire expense is born by the family, which in Madhuri's family is contributed by the earning members. The rice, grains, lentils and the vegetables come from the fields. Madhuri's father was saying, 'We do not know how long we can continue this with rising prices and diminishing income. Land holdings and the yield are reducing with new laws amid political unrest. It is Mother's wish how long she will accept our worship. Already much of the pomp is gone and community worship has come to the villages too.' Atin made a hefty contribution by local standard amid strong protest, defending himself by asking whether he was an outsider. If family members who earn their livelihood elsewhere can contribute why can't he? *Sailenbabu* wiped his moist eyes and said, 'I cannot refuse you because you may have come by Mother's grace that is beyond the understanding of an ordinary man like me. Please forgive me.' The gentle humility of the man was so touching that Atin was without words. He just had a glimpse of Madhuri beyond the door wiping her eyes with the end of her sari. After that merriment of the family increased and everyone was so happy that they included him in all the tasks of carrying this and that and doing chores and he doing mistakes with redoubled laughter and fellowship, making him one of them. Atin hardly had any experience of family life and loved all of it to the core of his heart. He was pampered and overfed with luxuries much to his embarrassment, in spite of his loud protest. The four days of worship passed as if in a dream. After immersion of the Goddess on the last day of worship in a nearby stream with much pomp and boisterousness of the men and sorrow of the women, calm descended on the house.

Atin thought of leaving. But the family would not let him go till the worship of Goddess Lakshmi, the deity of wealth and family happiness. The holiday actually extended to that day and he had no excuse. But Atin was feeling uncomfortable to be close with Madhuri's family in her presence and feeling as usurper without commitment. As long as the festivities were on it was different but now it was close family life, and he was feeling awkward. Even family members were planning their departure. Madhuri understood his predicament and pleaded with her mother to let him go for he was a busy surgeon and many patients were waiting for him. Mother understood her daughter's concern and spoke to her husband.

Sailenbabu spoke to Atin with great affection and said, 'my wife is asking me to tell you that you are free to return to Calcutta if you so desire. Tell me how do I say this to you? Who am I? You have come to us to our great delight and you will leave just as Mother Durga has come and gone. We neither come to this world by our own decision nor go out of it. In the middle we think we decide what we do but chance takes us another way. You can use Chance or God as you wish.

I am saying this because I do not know whether you are a believer or nonbeliever but it does not matter what you are, the truth is the same. But we are free another way because in ultimate analysis we are not liable for anything, we are free. When I die shall I come back to see who is doing what? Therefore go where your *manas,* your mind, takes you and we shall be happy that we had you for four days among us and we should not be greedy to have you longer. I have not had much education but this village and these fields has taught me that trees grow and give fruit not by my wish, paddy is plentiful some year and near zero in another irrespective of what I do. Only thing I can do is accept in good grace. We live by the sea. People say the sea gives back what it takes, but it may not give back the same thing or what you want in return. Or may be it returns nothing, so what would you do, sue the sea?' And he breaks out in loud laughter. Atin stares at him. What a loving man, and that love is not just for him but for all he comes in contact with, yet unfettered by that love. And he says he is uneducated which he probably is in a formal way. Atin planned to leave the next day.

But like the unpredictable sea, that did not happen. In the afternoon three men came carrying a very sick boy complaining of abdominal pain. They had come hearing that a big doctor had come from Calcutta in this house. Atin examined the boy and found that he had a fulminating appendicitis with peritoneal inflammation that was still localized but the appendix was on the point of rupture. He needed immediate operation to remove the appendix. The boy was toxic and had received no real medication. Atin looked up at Madhuri helplessly, and described his findings. Automatically their professionalism came to the fore.

Madhuri asked, 'How quickly he needs to be operated'.

Atin replied, 'As soon as possible, may be within the next couple of hours. In the meantime he needs intravenous fluids and antibiotics. He had been vomiting and his pulse is too rapid.'

Madhuri shook her head, 'The nearest hospital with operation facility is several hours away and it is doubtful whether they have such emergency facility especially in this holiday season.'

Exasperated Atin asked, 'Is there no hospital close by that can be reached quickly?'

Madhuri replied, 'There is a primary health center in the next village with a few indoor beds and probably a small primitive operation theatre for minor operations. But there is only one doctor unless he has gone on leave. I do not know what he can do.'

The villagers confirmed that the doctor was at home as his family now lives here. It will take ten minutes to go there by car.

Atin took the decision to go there and start the treatment and find out.

All of them climbed into Atin's car. The three men sat in the rear seat laying the boy on their lap and Madhuri sat in front beside Atin. They reached the hospital in ten minutes. One man brought the doctor from his quarters nearby. Fortunately intravenous infusion set and a few bottles of fluid were found and also some cheaper antibiotics and Atin said they would suffice. Madhuri started the infusion and Atin went to inspect the small operation theatre.

By the time he came back, Madhuri had got the drip started and given the antibiotic and a mild sedative to make the boy quiet. She looked up askance as Atin entered. Atin spread his arms and said, 'There are a few instruments in the cabinet that would need to be boiled to sterilize. For this operation we do not need many instruments but we need an anesthetist. Where do we find one?'

The resident doctor Arun came forward and said, 'I worked as house officer in anesthesia after graduation but not being able to get in to the postgraduate course I took this job and came here. There is no anesthesia machine here yet and I give open ether anesthesia through a mask for small cases like setting a fracture or stitching a wound. I do both things myself, while an orderly keeps on pouring ether. It is very primitive but that is all I can do alone.'

Atin slapped the young man on the back and said, 'I can see you will do fine. You are a sincere doctor and tell you what, in your position I would not have dared what you do and the villagers love you, I have already heard that. You have to keep the boy asleep for about twenty minutes and we would finish our job with the help of this expert nurse' and he pointed at Madhuri.

Arun smiled shyly and said, 'I know Didi though never met her and I have heard about you. It is a great honour for me.' Atin laughed and called, 'Let us see who gets the highest honour but I am more or less sure that your Didi will run away with that.' His enthusiasm caught the others and all three of them including the orderly, who had come in the meantime started their assigned task without fear.

Madhuri found a small autoclave and got it started to sterilize a few sheets and some fine instruments that will not stand boiling. Others she put to boil. Fortunately there was electricity because of the holiday times, as offices and factories in the region were closed. The hospital being built and supplied recently, most things were fresh.

Arun found and organized his instruments, the facemask to pour ether, the ambu bag to ventilate if need be, even endotracheal tube and a laryngoscope that worked. There was a small suction machine in the theatre that he commandeered for his use and nobody grudged that.

Atin was alternately seeing theatre arrangements, and looking up the patient. After about an hour he reported that the patient was better, his pulse was not running as fast, temperature was falling and he was quieter with a normal breathing and blood pressure.

After about two hours from their entry the operation theatre was ready, the patient was put under anesthesia and the shaved belly of the patient was painted and surrounded by the sterile sheets. The operation started and to Arun it seemed that it was finished in no time. He had never seen an appendectomy done so fast and that precisely. After closing the wound by meticulous suturing so that it does not get infected Atin held up the excised appendix for everybody to see. It was large and swollen and angry red with a perforation in one part initiating peritoneal inflammation. He exhaled deeply and said, 'We were just in time. The boy is lucky' and looked up at Madhuri to receive that special smile.

The boy woke up from anesthesia breathing normally and opened eyes and Atin was so happy that he slapped Arun on the back and said 'bravo, shorter the time gap between the end of operation and opening of patient's eyes the greater is the anesthetist. If you really want to be anesthetist you just call me. I shall fix you in a position and you can take your examinations as you earn. I was a junior doctor once and I know how it feels.'

They shifted the patient to a bed with clean sheets and Madhuri tucked him in nicely. He was fully conscious and wanted water. Madhuri gently caressed his face and said, 'You cannot drink water now brother, but I shall moisten your tongue with a few drops' which she did and looking up, addressed the others and said, 'I shall be with him for the night and all of you can go and rest' and looking at Atin 'You Sir can go home and sleep.' Atin protested, 'No I shall sleep in the next room and you can all rest.' Then looking at Madhuri he said, 'It will be enough if Arun here and I stay. If you could drive' and before he could finish Madhuri smiled, 'Which I cannot do because I am' and with alacrity Atin concluded, 'A village belle? Sorry I am only recently learning about village belles. Please take the car and go home.' Madhuri said in a huff, 'It is the nurses' duty to keep awake with a patient. You can go home doctor.'

Arun, unable to fathom their conversation meekly said 'Didi can sleep in my house. We have a spare bedroom and I can keep guarding the patient Sir. I have not yet forgotten that and I shall be so happy to do it. I get so bored here.' His pathetic plea from a position where he thought his career was getting finished silenced the elders. In the end all of them stayed in their chosen places. Arun was awake with the patient, Madhuri slept in Arun's house and Atin in the other room in the hospital, occasionally waking up and checking until he fell asleep.

It was early dawn with the sky turning from deep gray to light gray when Atin got up. He was an early riser by habit. It was his philosophical hour for thinking and reminiscing about his own life. Very few people are able to analyze their own actions with complete honesty. Many of us, if confronted, will cheat our own selves on our failures, on our mistakes and our mental and material corruption. Even with complete honesty we sometimes cannot reach a conclusion on the motivation behind our many actions. Sitting alone and analyzing our own mind is a form of meditation where one can go deeper and deeper into its essence. This morning there was no scope for that. He went in the patient's room. The patient was wide-awake and alert but the doctor had dozed off leaning against the cot. As he was examining the patient he woke up with a start and apologized.

Atin smiled and said, 'No need to apologize we have done that umpteen times in our young days. Personally I have done that for nights together with serious cases. That is the only way to prepare for hard work. Now you go and freshen up, I am sitting by him. He is fine and does not need much looking after. I shall wait till your return.' He turned to the patient and asked, 'How are you feeling?' He pointed at his tummy, and said, 'I am feeling pain there and feeling thirsty.' He checked the tummy and saw it was not distended, the pulse rate and blood pressure were normal and sounds in abdomen were normal. He assured the boy, 'You are doing fine. You will get water by mouth in small amounts and gradually have more. By tomorrow you shall be up and about and in a few days you shall be able to go home.'

He walked out of the building and looked around at the still dark cluster of trees, the birds calling and flying busily around. Their call announced the dawn, waking up the living. Theirs was the call of joy announcing the imminent sunrise brushing off the fears of darkness. The primitive caveman would look at his family and note whether any predator has taken away any member and cautiously crawl out of the cave. The dawn and sunrise is a time of rejoicing and still is and sun is the earliest god worshipped. Later this sun worship has been rationalized by many philosophies, but the joy of looking at the rising sun is felt equally both by the learned and the ignorant.

He heard footsteps and turned around to see Madhuri looking fresh and pretty and Arun carrying a tray with three cups of steaming tea. As they were drinking tea he said, 'my wife has said you must have lunch today at our house and please do not say no. It will be such a great honour for us. You can go and take rest and bath and then come back please. The patient is doing well and I shall look after him and inform you if there is anything to ask.' It was impossible to say no. A gentle breeze was blowing from the sea playing with Madhuri's hair. They got in the car and drove off promising to come.

As they drove off Atin said, 'I want to go to the sea and see the sunrise and get this breeze on my face. Can I?'

Madhuri smiled and said, 'You have a poet inside. Yes let us go. The sunrise is not very great here, sunset is better. The sun comes out of a headland and sets on the sea.'

'I like sunrise more than sunset. One leads to light the other to darkness, one is gorgeous and the other is melancholic' said Atin.

'One is the call to action and the other is for rest and peace' commented Madhuri. Then she added 'Let me take you to a place you will like, it is not far off.'

They turned on the offshore road towards the interstate border and went for some more. They came to a place where the foliage was denser and darkness of night still lingered. There they stopped at a clearing. Beyond was a small temple half in ruin but the goddess statue was intact and a lamp was burning. They went to the door and looked inside. It was a Kali Temple and Madhuri said, 'People say the goddess is alive and she will give you whatever you wish. Wish silently what you want.' They went inside to bend and honour the goddess.

Atin looked at her and said, 'I cannot wish anything without knowing what you wish.' Even in the darkness her blush was clearly visible.

Madhuri got up and turned around, 'Clearly you have no wish. So there is no point standing here. Let us go towards the sea.'

On the other side of the road there was a dense jungle of tall pine trees swaying in the breeze and making a continuous swishing sound, now muted now louder. The ground below was still in darkness. Madhuri said, 'It is dark here, not safe. Let us walk back a little distance where the jungle has thinned and there would be more light and you can see the sea and the rising sun as it clears that headland and the swaying pine forest from the beach—the traditional beauty of this place.'

As they were walking side by side on the paved road she said, 'You were brilliant today. I mean I have seen your many operations, most of them more difficult, but not in such operating conditions. The anesthesia was not proper, no relaxants to relax the abdominal muscles, poor instruments, poor light and yet you operated so fast effortlessly. Someone has said genius shows up in adversity and I shall never forget this operation.'

Atin was silent for sometime and slowly said, 'My thought was somewhat different. I was thinking here I was operating under such conditions and the poor boy will probably get well in next couple of days. I have two more days to spare and if I leave, you can delay your departure to look after him for a few days, till stitches are removed. But if we were not here and he became real sick by the time he was taken to a hospital miles away, where who knows what care would have been available? In the city there are hundreds like me and we fight to get a patient to earn money. But the satisfaction of saving this boy in this village is many times more. Why don't I leave the city and come to a village like this and build a small nursing home and give service and earn whatever they can give? I do not need much and I shall be out of the rat race and be a contented man among simple folks.'

Madhuri stopped in her tracks and turned around. 'What are you saying? It is a romantic madness. You are where you are suited best. You come here and they revere you because you are great there. You become one of them and gradually they may not see you as anything special. You want to play God but can you guarantee cure to everybody? You get mingled in village life and village politics and that is no better than the city. There is jealousy and meanness of another order and you will lose yourself because there will be nowhere to go, when you are tired with that. In a city you can be choosy, in a village you cannot. On the contrary you will do injustice to your abilities and your growth. Never even think of it in your wildest dream.'

Atin walked on silently and after some time he started narrating his experience in the nursing home in the earliest part of his life. When he finished Madhuri said, 'You were at the scum level of city at that time and you have risen far from there. Would you like to go back? It is the same thing here. Something happens, a patient dies or you upset a political leader and they break your hospital. There is nothing you can do. We snigger at ivory tower but it is much better to live there if one has a choice. You want to serve, you can come here or any other village as many times as you like. With growth, facilities will come closer to the villages and your effort will have no special virtue.'

Atin realized that Madhuri was right. But then she would not know what a rising surgeon has to go through in our society, and to maintain his position in profession. It hurt him more, because being alone his needs were less and on the negative side he had nothing or nobody to lean back to for emotional support. He has been overwhelmed by the affection and beauty in the family life of Madhuri's house for the last few days. But does that continue beyond the festival—probably not. His hankering for the family life he lost or never had, made him so sensitive. The guilt of his mother's death never leaves him, though it could not be his fault alone. Yet he continues to run and hide from life. That must end. It is much better to plan a family life he could have and he glanced at Madhuri. Would she change from what she is now? Is there anything that is changeless? If there is change so what? Has his life experience made him too soft? He should have had some of Amit's devil may care attitude.

Madhuri turned towards the sea and said, 'Look here we have come to the right spot. The pine forest has thinned to only three or four rows and the light is filtering through them. You can see the sea through the gaps; the sound of breakers and the cool shore breeze are coming through the swishing pines. Let us get down to the beach. The beach here is firm because of mixed clay and you can drive on the beach though that is prohibited now. I have heard that at one time a small plane of an English family used to land here.' She went down ahead of Atin and at the last line of pines ran down to the beach and looked back.

Suddenly she shouted a desperate cry, 'Atin careful' and jumping towards him caught his hand and gave a mighty tug. Unprepared Atin tumbled over her and together they rolled down the beach before Atin could take a breath and ask, 'What's the matter?' Still in embrace she pointed to the nearest tree and in the lowest branch a long green snake was hanging with its body partly camouflaged by the green leaves. Its head was hanging less than a foot from where Atin's head was. She was shivering and shaking all over and started crying pushing her face in Atin's chest. Atin saw that the snake made no move and was hanging still. He tenderly disengaged her face and wiping her tears kept saying, 'It is all right, all right it is not coming and probably not a poisonous snake' and to stop her shaking kissed her on the forehead and the cheeks and finally her lips in a kiss that she responded to and calmed down. Then as if in sudden realization she disengaged herself and sat up covering her face with hands, and her moist eyes looked at Atin through the fingers. What a sight Atin thought! She then got up and started walking towards the sea over the wide beach. Atin jumped up and followed her and caught her by the shoulder and turned her around. Now quietly she came close and hid her face in his chest while he caressed her head.

She looked up with tearful eyes and said, 'I did not want this to happen. What you must be thinking, that there was a scheme behind inviting you?' And she kept on sniffing.

Atin laughed out loud and said, 'Not to speak of my scheme for accepting your invitation?'

She looked up and asked childishly, 'You had a scheme?'

Atin said, 'Oh yes. I schemed that I would want to leave after Durga Puja and then there will be a boy with appendicitis and we would operate on him and then come to the seaside and meet Mr. Snake. And this sea and the sky and the pine grove all of them including the peeping sun were my accomplices.'

Madhuri was coming out of the shock 'You are a romantic philosopher but I am sorry, it was so sudden that I thought you were going to die right in front of my eyes. What has happened is an accident. You have no liability.'

Atin said, 'Is that so? Then let us complete the accident and sign the deed of liability' and turning her face he kissed her long and hot, Madhuri sighed and the sea blushed scarlet as the first rays of sun touched her.

Madhuri detached and pushed him back and holding his hand said, 'Please do not misunderstand me, I am so ordinary that I am not suitable for you. You will not be able to respect me and without respect love does not last. You need someone gorgeous to adore and love as your companion. I shall cherish this day till the end of my life but do not try to prolong it just because this has happened, and keep misery in store for future. You are a very good man and I do not want that to happen to you.'

Atin sighed and said, 'You do not know how miserable my life has been and how ordinary I am. Just because a man can expertly cut other men does not make him extraordinary.'

Hand in hand they started walking towards the breakers and Madhuri quietly said, 'I know your misery and feel sorry but I do not want to take advantage of that.'

Atin walked silently thinking what gossips must be circulating about him that has made him a recluse. But he must not be afraid to face them and not go back to his hole. He wants to lay himself bare to this woman but can he do that or should he retreat. Atin let go of Madhuri's hand, a signal enough for Madhuri. In a grave voice he said, 'I know you have heard about events and gossips about me that everybody has and why shouldn't you, may be I am the subject of much research. But has anybody told you about the man behind the events and gossips, has anybody ever been interested? Or should the man be eternally condemned to dungeon suffocated by rumours?'

Towards the end his voice broke and he kicked at the sand. Madhuri herself close to crying grasped his hand with both hands and said 'No I did not want to hurt you, I can see your hurt though do not understand, as I do not know enough about you. You are admired as an upright doctor and the gossips do not bother me. I want to hear everything you want to say, but let us do that as good friends without hurting each other. I shall be patient and understanding.'

Atin looked at her and smiled wanly, 'You are so innocent that you do not understand that even sharing my life theoretically will smear you. This conversation we are having here will not be possible anywhere without tainting you. I have destroyed my life, I do not want to destroy yours unless you accept whatever happens. It was not just my fantasy that I wanted to build a small hospital in this village, I need a home that I never had, but not by circumstantial pressure on you.'

Madhuri held his hand more tightly and said, 'And what risk is there for an ordinary nurse? I am not important enough and people will say it happens all the time with doctors and nurses. Open your hurt to me if it soothes your heart. I shall not spread any more gossip I promise.'

Atin turned to her with great affection and said, 'Scandal is already brewing with our absence for so long and it is time to take another look at the boy. Let us go back to the hospital with some flowers from the temple for him and have the lunch as we are and then return home' and they turned back to the car.

Thus in the next two days Atin unburdened himself of all his woes and self doubt in the privacy of the hospital when Arun was not around. Madhuri was a patient listener only occasionally asking a question. Atin warned sometimes, 'This is only my view of me, may not be right all the time' to a returning smile from Madhuri. The last question she asked, 'Is your house still there or have you sold it?' Atin replied, 'No it is locked up. My brother is least concerned but I cannot sell it without his consent. He has his right. But why do you ask' to which Madhuri's nonchalant reply was 'No particular reason.'

Across the Seas

The British Airways Boeing was airborne like a big vulture running a distance with wings spread and then taking off and after short climb swaying on its wings side-to-side and gaining altitude. The aircraft was half empty and Amit got a comfortable seat on the aisle in economy class. The seat beside him was empty and he could put his working things on it. The flight was non-stop to London. He would then have to spend a few hours in the transit lounge to catch another British Airways flight to Newark in USA and then hopping to Philadelphia where his office was located. It was a small office to start with and was growing fast covering the East Coast. The colleague there was junior to him and needed some support. He is expected to stay for some months that may run to a year and then relocate to the West Coast where workload was larger and growing fast. The plane broke through cloud cover to the dark sky and continued to climb gently. Eventually it settled in or near its cruise altitude and seat belt and smoking signs were put off. Smoking was allowed in some rear row of seats that he had no problem with, as he was not a smoker. He made himself comfortable as much as possible and waited for captain's clearance to work with his laptop. It was a brand new one given to him before the trip and he needed to familiarize with this rather new contraption. In the meantime he made a trip to the conveniences and got a long drink of cool water from the stewardess, paying her a compliment that was returned with a smile. He would need to spend some time under her care and it pays to make a bit of friendship. Coming back to his seat he opened the overhead locker and brought down the laptop bag and couple of books and kept them on the empty

seat beside him. He took out the laptop and placed it on the unfolded
table in front. It had enough charge to last a few hours and then if he
needed further, he would have to recharge somewhere with the help
of the stewardess. He had a lot of work to catch up with, as he had
no time for many days before departing. He remembered that he could
drop only a postcard to Atin and could not talk. He regretted that but
thought he would make up after settling down. There was none else to
inform.

He spent an hour familiarizing the contraption and looking at the
massive data that had been loaded into it by his office. After about an
hour he felt tired in the eyes with the small screen and small keyboard.
He has to get used to that. Meanwhile the pedestrian traffic on the aisle
had increased and he noticed the young boy who was standing beside
him a little to the back and watching his computer. He said, 'Hello'
and the boy smiled. The laptop was still a rather new thing and he was
keenly watching it. He was a westerner with sandy blond hair and fair
complexion and would be about five or six years old. His face had a
sweet softness, almost babyish, but intelligent eyes. Amit asked him,
'Are you familiar with this thing?' He replied, 'I know computers but
have not seen a laptop.' His accent was not pure but a sort of mixed
one. He asked, 'where are you going' and he replied Philadelphia. 'By
the way my name is Amit what is yours; and the boy replied 'Ravi'.
The stewardess announced to clear the aisles as breakfast would be
served. Amit asked, 'You are not traveling alone, are you' and the boy
replied 'I am traveling with mother. She is in the next cabin. I saw
your computer and stopped to look. I must go now' and left. 'Come
again' Amit called and waived and he waived back. Smart boy Amit
thought, but mother and not mum and the accent? His name is Ravi
and the R rolled a bit, could be from anywhere. The names are getting
internationalized earlier than the people.

After the meal dishes were cleared and Amit dozed off to sleep
almost immediately, not having had much in the last few days. He
slept deeply for long until the stewardess asked 'Would you have
something to drink Sir' awakened him. He looked around with bleary
eyes 'Drinks!' She said, 'We are serving lunch, would you like to have
something to drink before?' He was still not fully awake and looking at
the lighted sky outside asked 'Lunch?' Stewardess smiled sweetly 'We

are flying east to west, the days go faster.' He regained his faculties and returning the smile said, 'I would like to have a light beer if you have one' and then looking at the bottle said 'Make it two please'. The effect of the beer with a sumptuous meal pushed him to sleep again. When he woke up next the cabin was dark with curtains drawn and lights dimmed. He picked up the book he was reading but found the effort tiring, then looked at the film being projected but it was not interesting and he did not have the energy to get the headphone working and dozed off again. Next time he was awake the pilot announced 'we are commencing our descent to Heathrow.'

After nearly an hour the plane touched down and reached the parking bay. Amit collected his handbags and went out with the stream of passengers. He moved towards the transit area and through the glass looked at the gloomy foggy sky of London. He had a good few hours' wait as the Newark Philadelphia flight leaves late. The New York flight to JFK airport was a fast connection. The transit lounge was large but crowded, scattered with pieces of small double sofa for two, very practical Amit thought, typically British. He occupied one and looked around at the crowd. It was fascinating to look at people with different dresses and different languages coming in streams and emptying like waves of sea. He used to see the same during his trips to Singapore but the crowds were more colourful and varied. Here there were more occidentals. Flights were being announced at regular intervals and a wave of humanity disappeared only to be replaced by another. During one such emptying he saw Ravi sitting not far away and he waived and it was returned. He was sitting with a lady who was decidedly Indian but dressed in loose comfortable pants and top. She was pretty with a head of brownish black hair and very fair in the golden white Indian complexion.

Ravi said something to his mother and came running to him. He complained, 'I went twice to you but you were sleeping. Did you sleep all the way?'

Amit smiled and said, 'Almost, I was very tired.'

Ravi said, 'Come to our seat, mother told me to ask you.'

Amit looked up and the lady smiled. Amit told Ravi, 'Won't we be crowded?'

Ravi replied, 'I shall pull another sofa close' and tugged at his hand, another Indian identity Amit thought.

He carried his things and Ravi pushed an empty sofa opposite to come close face-to-face while he was shaking hand with the mother and she said, 'You are obviously a Bengali and so am I, my name is Rupa.'

Amit said, 'I am Amit and I know I look a stupid Bengali even from afar.'

She laughed looking at his tall muscular stature and said, 'Why, Bengalis are not stupid at all and the world knows that. Ravi was disturbing you throughout the flight and I wanted to apologize. He seems to have taken an instant liking.'

Amit said, 'You do not have to do that, I enjoyed his company thoroughly. He is intelligent and inquisitive and not shy at all like the usual Indian child of his age.'

Rupa said, 'His father is Dutch American.'

Amit said, 'Beg your pardon, I was not being inquisitive. You are going to join him I suppose.'

Rupa said 'Y-e-s.' Amit did not miss the slight hesitation in her voice but ignored, it was none of his business. Long distance unknown travelers, especially Indian women often exchange information that they would not normally do with people they knew.

Instead he turned to Ravi and asked, 'You want to see the laptop, don't you' and he nodded. 'Do you play computer games' and he nodded again. 'There must be a few games loaded but you have to be careful not to touch anything else, for if I lose any data I shall be in trouble.'

Rupa was alarmed, 'Don't let him. You come to me Ravi we shall do something else.'

Amit said, 'Don't worry; I shall secure everything else. Let him play' and the two of them got busy with the computer and Ravi was knowledgeable and they became good friends while Rupa looked on bemused. 'Be careful Ravi' she called once.

Rupa moved and made space for him on the sofa as the other one was occupied entirely by Ravi and the computer. She asked him, 'Are you a resident of USA?' to which he replied 'No, this is my first trip to America. My IT Company has sent me to USA to look after our two branches, one on the east coast and the other in the west. I shall spend a few months in Philadelphia, may be a year and then go to the west for how long I do not know. In the end I may or may not be permanently located. I have no family so it does not matter to me and convenient for them.'

Rupa smiled, 'Really it does not matter to you? You are changing country of residence and it is a different society, it might matter in some way.'

Amit said, 'Women have never chased me and I am too old to be chased now. As for me I am OK as I am.'

Rupa asked 'Where would you stay?'

Amit said, 'I have no idea. My colleague will come with his car. He lives in a small apartment with his wife. They have no kids. He has rented another for me in the same building for as long as I am here. I think he should have purchased it as we are expanding. Do you know this town well?'

Rupa said, 'I should for I have lived here. But it is a big city, can't say I know every nook and corner. I know the university area well.'

Amit asked, 'Is that where your house is?'

Rupa said a curt 'No' and shut up.

Then the conversation became desultory talking of this and that avoiding any personal angle but he need not have worried as he found

Rupa was a very polished individual. Eventually their flight was called after a fair amount of delay and they went for boarding. Rupa chose two window side seats while Amit as always chose an aisle seat across. The transatlantic flight was full but Indians were few. They mostly chose to land at JFK. They were scheduled to touch down at Newark in the early evening. Now that would be delayed and if there was further delay at Newark, they will arrive real late at Philadelphia. Newark is a busy airport especially at that time with commuter traffic.

Amit's apprehension was proved right by the time they landed at Newark, the disembarking passengers left and the captain announced that there may be a slight delay but the plane will reach Philadelphia in good time.

Amit asked Rupa after the plane took off and they were settled, 'I hope someone is coming to pick you up at the airport because we may be uncomfortably delayed. You of course know the city, I don't.'

Rupa did not immediately reply and looked a bit worried. Amit did not press with the question. After a period of silence Rupa spoke with hesitation, 'Since we are both Bengalis can we speak in that language?'

Surprised Amit looked around and said, 'Yes of course', there was nobody around who was likely to understand their conversation. Then he looked at Rupa, 'You do not need to tell me anything if you do not want to.'

She was flushed with embarrassment. Hesitatingly she said in a low voice, 'I think I better, for Ravi's sake. May be I am feeling nervous because it has been few years since I have lived here, probably grown soft' and she smiled shyly.

Amit said, 'Say what you have to say, I am not of the suspicious kind and I even may not be able to help you. To tell you frankly your distress was quite apparent when I first saw you and you did call me.'

Rupa swallowed and said, 'Nobody is coming to receive us. I lived here as a student, did my Masters and PhD and fell in love and got married and got Ravi' she said in one single breath as if she had to unburden herself and will not be able to complete if she stopped. Amit remained silent.

Rupa was also silent for sometime looking at her fingers and drawing a deep breath as if for a desperate dive said, 'I had to go back home for my mother's illness as she was living alone and my stay was prolonged as she was crippled by a heart attack. She died a few months back.' She looked up at Amit with tearful eyes unable to talk.

Amit handed her his handkerchief and asked, 'and your husband?'

Through the handkerchief she said, 'We got separated.'

'Divorced?' Amit asked.

'I do not know. I signed everything I had to sign but never got the notice.'

'So you have come to find your husband?'

'No, I have come for residency and visa regulations and for Ravi; he should not suffer for me, though I do not know what I can do.'

'So where are you going to stay, have you booked an accommodation?'

'As a student I used to live in a student accommodation in a sort of hostel where bed sitters were let out at low rent. I sent them an Email to book a room but I got no reply. The net connection with India is not yet very good or they would not allow the child, I don't know what.'

'May I ask how you maintained yourself?'

For the first time she smiled, 'I have a good job as a physics teacher in a school' and she mentioned the name of the school that was famous and expensive and Amit nodded. She said, 'You can ring and verify I have the phone number of the Principal and it is daytime there.' Amit nodded.

She continued, 'my salary is good and Ravi got maintenance from his father through bank transfer, there was no other communication and the bank is located near our home that was' and she pressed the handkerchief to her eyes. 'He loved his son. So if I can go to that bank and find his address and communicate to ask whether he would take his custody, I shall be free to return.'

Amit was silent for a few moments and then laughed, 'So you jumped into the unknown like me. I have done that several times in my life.'

She removed the handkerchief, 'Have you, how come?'

Amit said, 'We are not exchanging biographies just tell me how can I help you?'

She said, 'I could have managed if the flight was not delayed. After landing I could ring the address where I wrote and if I do not get there, ring other accommodations and find something and would ask them to send a car to the airport. But it will be late when we reach and I am a bit scared now, probably grown old.'

Amit winked at her and said, 'The last assumption is quite obvious' and she smiled, 'But I have an alternate plan that we can pursue if you want. We can go to my place and find the facilities whether we can sleep off our jet lag. You can sleep in my friend's apartment. He has his family and the apartment must be better appointed and from tomorrow morning you start your search. How does it sound to you?'

Rupa could not suppress a sigh of relief, 'What can I say, I am ashamed and at the same time with great relief. But why do you want to pass me to your friend and his family?'

Amit said, 'For the safety of both of us, this is America remember?'

Rupa said, 'Oh shit.'

Clearing immigration, collecting luggage and clearing customs took more than an hour and they met Amit's friend Sasank who was junior to him. After greetings and 'How are you doing' Amit introduced Rupa and asked whether they could be accommodated.

Sasank said 'No problem, your apartment has two bedrooms.'

Amit said, 'Why two?' He was not keen to share apartment with an unknown female.

Sasank did not catch it and replied, 'We want to keep it as a guesthouse. People are continually passing through and it is a necessity. We would buy it and decorate if you approve, that is the instruction.'

Amit turned to Rupa, 'See how kind God is to you? You get an assignment on landing to decorate our guesthouse with Sasank's wife as partner.'

The men laughed but Rupa was grave. She turned and held Ravi's hand. She did not want to impose more than what she had to. It may not turn out convenient.

They drove in silence each absorbed in thought. Amit and Sasank had some discussion about the company and work. Rupa was silent.

They reached the apartment. It was not large but not small either and well appointed. Sasank's wife Sumita came in to meet them. She said, 'I have cooked a light dinner for you that may help you sleep better.' Rupa said she had no appetite and took Ravi to bedroom to put him to bed. Amit said, 'It is the same with me but I would come with you and have something and talk. There is a lot to talk about.' Rupa came out of bedroom and said, 'Ravi was tired and fell asleep as soon as he hit the bed.' Amit had noticed her discomfiture and said, 'You would probably want to stay with your son' and Rupa nodded. 'I am going with Sasank and taking the door key, you can go to bed' and they went out.

Next morning Amit got out of bed late. After he shaved, washed and came out of his room he found Rupa was sitting near the phone with a guidebook. Rupa got up on seeing him and said, 'Breakfast is ready. I shall make you tea or coffee?'

Amit asked, 'Don't bother I can do that, what about you?'

She said, 'I am sorry, we have already had our breakfast we were so hungry. Ravi is in bedroom probably fallen asleep again.'

Amit went to kitchen and found that a double omelet was waiting for him in the hot case. He dropped two pieces of bread in the toaster and made a cup of coffee. The kitchen was well stocked, enough for at least a week. He placed the things on the dinner table in the living room and saw Rupa busy with the phone and asked 'Who are you calling in the morning? It is a working day.'

Rupa said, 'I am looking for an accommodation and trying to look up people I knew.'

'Any luck yet?'

'None so far' and she came forward and asked, 'Do you need any help to unpack.'

Amit almost choked on his food and laughed, 'That is one thing I am hearing for the first time in my life; no thanks. I have to go to office. Will you be ok here?' Rupa nodded.

When Amit returned he was quite late as he had a lot of things to catch up with. As he turned the key in the door lock it was opened by Rupa from inside. She must have been awake and sitting close to the door. Amit was a bit surprised but said nothing.

'I was waiting for you and could not sleep in any case. The sleep rhythm would take some time to normalize, I suppose,' replied Rupa.

Amit asked, 'How is Ravi doing?' while unfastening his tie and thinking this is a habit he would be happy to get rid off.

'He is doing fine. Children take it in their stride better than the adult.'

Amit asked again as he sat down, 'So have you been able to find an accommodation?'

Rupa said, 'That is something that is bothering me. I found accommodations all around but none of them would take a child. Those that agreed asked for high rent beyond my means. I have never faced this before. It seems I have to look at suburban areas away from these central areas.'

Amit asked, 'Would that be convenient for whatever you want to do?'

Rupa mused, 'No, not really.'

Amit asked seriously this time, 'If you do not mind can you tell me what exactly your plan is, what you want to do?'

Rupa looked down to avoid his gaze, 'I wanted to do two things, one to find Ravi's father and two to go to my old university and find out whether they could offer even a part time or temporary job.'

Amit was still staring at her, 'And with that aim you jumped in to the unknown with your son? Was life that bad at Calcutta?'

Tears started welling in Rupa's eyes and she was failing to hide that from Amit. She said almost in whisper 'Life was so aimlessly dull. We had no relations and no close friends.' Then she looked up at Amit not even trying to wipe her tears 'Do you have any idea about the life of a lone single mother in our country? My visa was ending and what do I do with my son and his future?'

Amit kept looking at her both in concern and in fascination. She was really beautiful and looked more so in her defiant posture. He stood up and looking away said, 'Well, one problem can be solved. You can live here as long as you wish or as long as I am here unless of course someone else comes. That chance is remote so long I am here. Nobody would mind your occupying the extra bedroom. Food is not a problem in USA not for home cooked food. That is quite cheap. Ravi would not be alone here. Sasank's wife is fond of him and she is not working. That sort of thing is no problem in an Indian family and she will be happy to look after him.'

Then he turned to look at her, 'that leaves only your tasks' and she smiled, smiling through her tears, what a sight Amit thought and looked away. Only Bengali women can look like that with their large dark brown eyes and long lashes. Amit turned towards his room saying 'I am going to bed. We shall discuss the rest at breakfast.'

Amit got up early and came to the living room to find Ravi up and fiddling with the laptop without putting it on. He has slept off jet lag. He called out, 'Hey young man how about giving me a hand in the kitchen to make the breakfast and surprise your mother?'

Ravi jumped up in delight and said 'That will be awesome' and surprised Amit looked at him but made no comment as such exclamations cross continents faster than the jets. Ravi looked at him quizzically 'But what do I call you?' Amit said 'You can call me uncle if you like.' Ravi looked serious 'How can I call you uncle, you are not my dad's brother and not my mom's?' Amit said 'Oh, so now it is mom and not mother?' Gravely Ravi replied 'I sort of alternate between the two and also Ma' and Amit laughed. Ravi insisted 'but you have not answered my question, how do you become my uncle?' Amit said 'I do not know your dad so as your mom's brother.' Ravi seriously looked at him and swung his head side to side 'No you are not my mom's brother.' Amit was alarmed, kids perceive things faster than the grown ups and have the disturbing habit of blurting them out in wrong places. He said, 'Ok old man. I am almost through with the eggs, would you please throw some bread in the toaster' and Ravi with a whoop got to the task.

Rupa came to the living room freshly washed and bathed and filled the room with the sweet aroma of soap and shampoo and perfume. The lush growth of partly dried dark brown hair fell in thick curls on her back and shoulders and framed the pretty smiling face that had not been touched with make up—a complete family picture that made Amit uneasy. She asked 'What is all the merriment about? Is it somebody's birthday' and promptly Ravi said 'Yes, uncle's' and pointed at Amit. Startled Amit unaccustomed to family life never having any female member apart from mother and no children, chased Ravi with a shout 'Now old man I shall show you', and Ravi quickly slipped behind mother grabbing her with both hands. Rupa laughed loudly and said 'Ravi shouldn't we kiss the birthday boy' and Ravi quickly placed a kiss on Amit's hand near him and Rupa blew a kiss. Embarrassed Amit threw up his hands and said 'You mother and child go on having fun, I am famished' and sat down at the table.

Days passed as usual with Amit attending office and coming home with a book or toy for Ravi and he was delighted with the new toys and strange but absorbing books. Rupa would go out to buy groceries and refuse reimbursement from Amit. Rest of the time she would be at the phone or with Ravi in whatever he was doing. The first weekend arrived. On Saturday after breakfast each had some chores to do. Amit spent most of the day busy sending messages or writing letters on the computer, reading the newspapers thoroughly to familiarize himself with everything that is happening in this new country and washing a few of his things refusing Rupa's help. After that he had to go to office as his Company could not afford two full holidays with their nature of business. At night they went out for dinner in an Indian restaurant that was delicious but with somewhat new taste as it had superimposed American flavour on Indian cuisine. The mixture seemed to have gelled. Amit and Rupa discussed and debated the spices used and called the chef twice as referee. Ravi took to the food lustily.

While returning from dinner Rupa said, 'I did not imagine you would know cooking so well. What are your other abilities?'

Amit said, 'You would not want to know that. As for cooking I have spent almost a quarter of my life cooking, as I have mostly lived alone.'

Rupa said shaking her head like an obstinate child, 'I want to know what I would not want to now.' Amit cast a sideways glance at her bobbing curls and said, 'All in good time if good times come,' and Rupa replied, 'The best time is now.'

Amit said, 'My, my, you are not only an optimist but an aggressive American optimist.'

Returning home and after Rupa put Ravi to bed they sat down with coffee and a bottle of liquor that Rupa liked and purchased. Amit looked at the bottle and asked, 'So you drink?' Rupa said, 'Only liquor and this one my favourite; and you, don't you drink?'

Amit said, 'I have no prejudice and no attachment. But I have not had such fashionable things, only country liquor available in the jungles.'

Rupa asked in surprise, 'Jungles! Ok now you have to be American so pick up American habits and tell me about the jungles.'

Amit did not like that the word slipped out of his mouth but feminine curiosity would not allow him to swallow it back and he said 'not as in picnic or camping trip.' 'What then?'

He described his life in patches, leaving out the difficult areas and the death of his parents and personal and family life.'

Rupa's eyes widened as he went on. When he stopped she asked part in wonder and part in reverence, 'You became a Naxalite revolutionary? You did not go to jail? What about your parents?'

Amit's curt reply was, 'They are dead.'

Rupa was bursting with questions but only managed to say, 'Why?'

With a wry smile Amit said, 'To do good to the country I suppose.'

Rupa asked in rapid succession, 'How did you get a passport? I mean how did you complete your studies and got such a big job and American work visa?'

Amit laughed, 'One by one please. I became a good boy. I was studying computers and information technology in college and left college in my final year. After release I enrolled in a private institution whose certification was recognized and I was good in my work. I am good you know, in fact very good' and he burst out laughing.

Rupa was wide eyed and whispered, 'Have you killed anybody?'

Amit smiled and after a pause said, 'Nope, I would have liked to though, some of those lecherous scoundrels who tortured innocent tribal people. Don't you know that generals do not shoot?' and his face hardened that fascinated and alarmed Rupa.

She still continued, 'Planners are not punished?'

'Jailed may be nothing more. Two bullets for the computer would do if things get real bad. Killing a computer is no crime, stray bullets. There will be a back up somewhere.'

She was now afraid and quickly said, 'Let bygone be bygone. Don't you have any close family?'

Still stiff Amit said, 'I have a brother.'

With a forced smile and light voice she asked, 'Really? Where is he? What is he? Do you love him?'

That voice made Amit laugh, 'Do you always ask questions in a bunch? You must be a dreaded interrogator. To answer in a row he is a good boy, a doctor and a budding surgeon of repute at Calcutta and yes I love him. Now it is your turn to say your story.'

Rupa relaxed and asked, 'What is his name?' and Amit replied, 'Atin.'

In the same light vein Rupa said, 'Amit and Atin, two precious bright boys! Your parents must have been a very happy couple?'

Amit gravely replied, 'They did not have the time to be proud.'

Sensing that she had touched a sensitive chord Rupa let it pass and said, 'My life is not also a happy one though it could have been very happy.'

Amit now looked at her and asked, 'How come' and Rupa gave a short summary of her life skirting the painful ones or with short laughter as if they were not that painful.

Amit was silent for sometime and then said, 'We are so alike in hiding the really severe painful memories even from our own minds as if we are afraid that just by uttering them the pain will be renewed. But they do not go away, do they?'

Rupa nodded and abruptly got up and said in a choked voice, 'I think I am getting tipsy, must go to sleep' and went away to her room.

The next day was Sunday. The mood was heavily weighted by the revelations of each other's life and the sumptuous dinner and late drinks and they were not communicative. A snack brunch was all they could take. In the afternoon when Rupa was thinking what to serve for dinner a call came from Sumita inviting them to dinner. It was an early dinner and the conversations were desultory. They mostly centered around India as there was something on the television. The dinner ended they came back and went to bed early.

Flotsam on the Sea

The following week Amit was very busy. A lot of instructions had come from India on new customer contracts with new tasks. Almost every day he had to work till late evenings and came home exhausted. There were days when he was not present at dinner and went straight to bed. At others also he barely exchanged a few words with Rupa and Ravi. He realized the real purpose of sending him to USA is happening now.

Rupa followed her routine, not much in house hunting, but she visited her old university and college looking for people she knew. She visited the professor who showed her mother's article to her in the Nature. He had aged but recognized her with glee. She asked him about job opportunity, part time or temporary. He could not promise anything but asked her to leave an application. On other days she roamed around the campus visiting familiar favourite spots.

One day she walked in to the cafeteria and bought a doughnut and came to the tree where she used to sit with Bob and sat down on the grass. Tears streamed down her cheeks at the first bite which she wiped with a tissue and quietly finished the doughnut. Then she sat thinking the actual reason for her trip to the USA and rummaged and dissected her mind. Has she come to get back to the life she has left behind? But that is impossible. He thought of Amit and his joke about jumping to the unknown. He was right. But it is not always easy to know the reason for an action even in our own mind. She just caught at the last straw to get out of great abyss. The thought of Amit made her feel warm inside and she smiled. He is a nice man and such a gentleman! She could see he liked her and she liked him too. He is a bachelor may be somewhat older than her but a strong body. Thinking of his body made her blush and she shook her head. That made her aware that a man passing by had stopped and was looking at her intently and she looked up.

The man said, 'Are you Bob's wife, I mean separated wife?' She kept looking at him without answering. 'I am Michael remember?' She was still speechless and could vaguely remember a much thinner man than this fat one with round face. She nodded. He said, 'If you are looking for Bob he isn't here, has moved on.' She got her voice back to ask, 'Where to?' The man said, 'dun no. Ok so long, have a nice day' and he was gone.

Her mind in turmoil she stopped thinking and closed her eyes. Image of Bob has become blurred she could not see the details. Then there was Amit with his strong muscular body and gentle smile and she shivered and shook her head. She slowly got up and started walking towards home. It was a long walk but that would cool her down and clear her mind. On the way she found a roadside automat and stopped and then hesitating bought something. Back home she called for Ravi and he came running from auntie and rattled the door to produce a racket. She opened the door in alarm and said, 'You would have broken down the door and uncle would have been angry.' Ravi said, 'Sorry' and then showing a packet said, 'Look what auntie has given me' and opening it brought out an air pistol with plastic bullets and loading one fired at Amit's closed door shouting boom. Rupa was alarmed as Amit had said he would never buy toy guns for Ravi, the bane of American civilization. Rupa said, 'Don't do that, uncle would be angry,' Ravi asked, 'Why? He told me one day he knew about guns and they were bad.' 'How could he know about guns without having one?' Rupa sighed and said, 'Ok desperado, now you change your dress and wash and sit for dinner. Uncle will be late today.'

She did not lie; he did come late and opening the door saw her sitting waiting for him and smiled with a glint in his eyes. She tiredly said, 'It was not a long wait. Change and come for dinner. I have cooked something special today.' He was all smiles, 'Have you? I won't be a minute. But you look tired.' Rupa said, 'I have walked a lot today to the university and back. I am getting fat sitting at home.' His grin widened, 'Is that so? Well it is not gentlemanly to comment. Have you met someone you knew?' and Rupa said, 'No.'

He went to his room to change. She started to lay the table. The door was a crack open and Rupa could see him undress and got rooted to the spot for a minute. When he moved she moved too and came to a corner of the table resuming her task. He came out buttoning his shirt the process not yet complete. She cast a glance at the bare chest and looked away. They sat down to eat. She had cooked legs of chicken in a special way and Amit relished it taking lion's share and exclaiming, 'Why do you bother so much about your university? Let us open a restaurant and you cook like this and we would be millionaires like that lady who introduced Chili con Carney. This is a hundred times better.' Rupa smiled saying nothing and watched him eat only picking at her own food. Amit finished eating and got up saying, 'I shall do the dishes' and Rupa rose quickly and said, 'No you will not' and they collided at the sink. Amit said sorry and Rupa smiled, 'I beat you to it' and Amit bowed and said, 'You would do that every time. In some situations I actually like to lose.'

Next Saturday week Amit came home early. Rupa was going through a magazine. She looked up and said, 'Work is getting light?' Amit dropped on a sofa and said, 'No, getting organized' and reclined in relaxation. Rupa got up and made tea and brought a steaming cup with a slice of cake. After a bite of the cake and two cautious seeps of hot tea he exclaimed, 'Ah that was good. You know you arc spoiling me I am beginning to like this domesticity.'

Rupa said with nonchalance, 'Would not last long though.'

Amit wanted to say something and then checked himself and continued munching. And then aiming at Rupa's face behind the magazine he asked, 'How is your project going?'

Rupa's grave face emerged from behind the magazine, 'What project?'

Amit asked, 'Project hubby search?'

Rupa made a graver face and said, 'Please do not joke. I have renewed our social security cards and residence visa just in time. I looked at my name in the computer and found it. The name is Rupa Lind and it does not say divorced.'

Amit said, 'Good for you. What do you plan to do now?'

Rupa said, 'I went to the bank and asked. They do not have Bob's address. They are only a forwarding bank for sending overseas. They just have a number account.'

Amit was thoughtful, 'Your Bob is hiding himself well I wonder why? Did you bite him?'

Angry Rupa got up and moved towards her room. Amit jumped up and caught her by shoulder from behind and as Rupa looked back in anger he removed his hands and said, 'Sorry. That was stupid of me. But please sit down we must think of something.'

Rupa came back to sit and said, 'I was thinking of going to my old house. I do not expect to find Bob there but somebody in the neighborhood may know something. The house is a bit far off and I do not know whether I can find it. There have been new constructions everywhere.'

Amit said, 'Don't worry. We shall go tomorrow. I shall borrow Sasank's car. I have an international driving license that is valid here.'

Rupa said, 'You are not accustomed to driving in USA.'

Amit said, 'Do not worry. Driving with your left hand or right hand makes no difference. I have done tougher things in life. I need a map and Sasank must have one in his car. I shall mark the route with him and then it is just a piece of cake' and he pointed at the empty plate.

Rupa laughed, 'Nothing bothers you? What are you a demon or a human' and got up to bring another slice of cake and more tea.

Amit chuckled, 'I often wonder.'

The three of them went out on the expedition next day. Rupa was impressed by the ease with which Amit drove on the right side never faltering or missing the road signs and signaling. The map was open on her lap but he hardly ever looked at it or needed direction. The map seemed to have been imprinted in his brain. Instead of directing she went on with a running commentary 'I remember that shop; that is a Laundromat I used to come to if our washing machine did not work. Actually I could not often work it in the beginning.' Amit paid no heed and concentrated on driving slowly looking at the house numbers when they were near. At last they found the house and Rupa shouted 'That's it' when Amit had already parked at the verge. They got out of the car and stared at it. It was a sleepy neighborhood on Sunday morning.

Amit said, 'We cannot park in front of a house and just stare at it. People would wonder.'

He had hardly finished the sentence when Ravi with a shout, 'That is my house' ran towards it across the front lawn and as if on a signal a medium size dog ran out of the house barking madly towards him. Rupa froze with fear and before she could make a sound Amit had shot like an arrow and picked up Ravi before the dog could reach him. Instead of Ravi the dog caught Amit's leg in his jaws and growled. Rupa started shouting. A man emerged from the house and whistled and the dog ran back home. But the damage had been done. There were tears in his jeans and he pulled up the torn legging and found there were superficial bite marks. He put Ravi down and walked firmly towards the house and his face was as hard as Rupa had seen.

The man came out of the house again and Amit faced him putting up a clenched fist and hissed, 'I have a mind to put this feast on your face and you may die.' The man cringed at his size and blood shot eyes.

Amit continued, 'But I am not going to do that because you will tell police that you were assaulted and let out the dog. You have kept an untrained dog unchained and that will be reported and what could have happened if this boy got the bite.'

The man got back his voice and stammered, 'Where are you from?'

Amit hissed again, 'That does not matter what matters is that I am
black and the few people who walk this road are black and you keep
this dog in front to chase them because in your view they are thieves.
That is what you are and you shall pay.'

The man implored, 'Please come to the house and we will settle
things.' Amit looked at Rupa and she shook her head to decline.

Amit returned to the man, 'This lady owned this house when it was
new and you have made it dirty like chicken shit. We do not enter such
houses.' He pointed at a name plate on the front door and asked 'Is that
your name?' The man nodded and Amit said, 'That is all we want to
know. We shall have to go to hospital and police now.'

The man had recovered and said, 'I shall come with you with the dog's
registration and vaccination certificates. The doctor will need them.
We have a good hospital nearby.' Amit relented as that would make
things easier. He was cooling down.

They went to the hospital and he was wheeled in to the emergency
room with Rupa following and Ravi was kept quiet by the nurses.
Rupa came out and sat with Ravi as Amit's trousers were being
removed. The doctor and the police came at almost the same time, the
doctor first. With tearful eyes she helped them to fill the papers. On
their relationship she said 'Friends.' The shock was affecting her now.
The doctor came out of the emergency room and said, 'The wounds
are only skin deep because of the thick jeans. Just simple dressing was
enough. Remove it after five days and apply some antiseptic lotion
written here along with a few pain killer tablets.' He looked at the
dog's vaccination details and found them up to date. He said, 'We will
give just two shots and that will be enough and get other medicines
from the pharmacy.'

The police were doing their job. Bit by bit they got the whole story
out. At the end they asked, 'Do you want to press charges' and Rupa
said 'No.'

They asked, 'So you have not found Mr. Robert Lind' and Rupa shook
her head.

'We can try to find him for you if you want.' Rupa said, 'Please don't bother.'

'But you are not to leave this town without informing us' and handed her a slip.

When it came to payment the dog owner put forward his insurance card 'Let it stand on mine and for the medicines too. I owe you that.' When formalities were over he told Rupa, 'I apologize I am really sorry. Please come some other day' giving his visiting card.

Amit came out hobbling slightly. Rupa asked, 'Can you drive?' Amit said 'I am ok.'

They drove back in silence. Rupa asked several times whether it was hurting and Amit replied he could bear it. It was late afternoon and Ravi was hungry. They stopped at a roadside café and had lunch. Dusk was falling by the time they reached home. Rupa and Ravi supported him from two sides and Amit laughed for the first time, 'I wish I had such support when I needed it most.' The proximity of Rupa sent a sensation up his spine.

Amit was tired and excused himself to rest a while. Rupa changed and went to kitchen. After cooking dinner he got Ravi, changed his clothes, gave him dinner and put him to bed. She then cautiously opened Amit's door not to wake him up. He had changed to pajamas and was lying flat with an arm across the eyes. The bandage around his leg was visible. She knelt beside the bed and lightly touched the bandage. Amit opened his eyes.

She was sniffing and said, 'I am so sorry for troubling you so much. Is it hurting?' He said 'Not much.' She kissed the bandage. Amit asked 'Why are you wasting it?'

'Wasting what' she asked.

Amit said, 'You have wasted one in the air and another on the bandage, now put it in its proper place' and getting up on his elbow drew her beside him and held and kissed her with all the pent up passion and she responded. He held her tight against him and touched her breast. She whispered in his ears 'No not now darling' that pricked up the hairs at the nape of his neck and he released her. She stood there with an indescribable smile on her lips and glowing eyes and then bent down kissing him on the forehead saying 'That is the prize for being such a nice boy.' Amit sighed and kissed her hand and said 'You are so soft I could die.' She smiled and said 'Dinner is ready. Come and eat and then I shall give the pain killer and you can go to sleep.'

Whole of next week Amit worked from home using computer, video conference and phone. Actually he worked longer hours continuing at night and doing more. When Ravi was not there she would stand behind him with her hands on her shoulder feeling the strong muscles or bite his ear and he would shout 'Do you know what you are doing to me' and she would innocently ask 'What?' He would try to get up in sham rage and she would say 'No you would hurt yourself' and he would gnash his teeth and say 'I want to hurt you.' She would laugh her heart out.

It was another weekend by the time the dressing had to be opened. Rupa was nervous but Amit asked not to worry as he was trained in first aid and wound dressing. The dressing was waterproof that allowed him to bathe. The pharmacy had given a dressing pack and she opened the cover carefully without touching the contents and there was one similar inside. She took off the old one carefully afraid all the time of hurting him. He assured her there was very little pain.

When the wound was open both of them watched it minutely with interest and Rupa said, 'It is not as shallow as doctor said.'

Amit said, 'Yes it is shallow it is the surrounding swelling that makes it look deep. You go wash your hand and dry it with some antiseptic.'

Rupa asked, 'Can I use the hand cleaner antiseptic that we normally use?'

Amit said, 'Yes but don't touch anything. I shall teach you non-touch dressing technique, always very useful whether it is an emergency or in hospital.'

She turned the room lights to high and Amit shifted his leg under the brightest beam. She came back after cleaning hands. Amit said, 'Now pick up that small packet and open it without touching the content. Now pull out that swab by holding one corner and hold the four corners together without touching the center. Well done, it is already wetted with spirit and I shall pour a little bit of this brown antiseptic liquid on that center, done. Now you swab the center of the two bite wounds to remove whatever is inside. The trick is to go from center to the periphery. Well done now repeat the procedure with the other swab' that Rupa did expertly and they both looked closely at the two bite wounds.

Amit said, 'Look the floor of the hollow is pinkish white. That means the wounds are mostly healed. I shall squeeze some ointment from this tube on those shallow holes; done. Now you pick up that waterproof dressing and peel off that pink thread and take it out holding only the two sides in your hands and press it down on the wounds and wrap around the leg; well done. Now lower your head' and Rupa did so and asked 'What' and he kissed her on the cheek and in false anger she said 'That was uncalled for' and Amit laughed 'As if you didn't know you naughty girl' and both laughed.

When Rupa returned Amit was feeling over the dressing and said, 'I really did not need another dressing, it is healed.' She said, 'This is waterproof dear, may come in handy' and he chased her out. She came back after sometime with a cup of tea and handed that to him. As he was sipping she stood by the bed and asked innocently 'that was great, the teaching of non-touch dressing. Do you also know non-touch undressing dear' and then shouted 'No getting up you will spill the tea all over' and jumped back. Amit said, 'Just you wait, you will get all that back with interest, you teaser,' and she blew him a kiss.

It happened a few nights later. Amit was lying in bed unable to sleep thinking of Rupa in the other room. There was a light sound of the latch from the door and turning his head Amit saw the crack of light with a silhouetted figure beyond. He lay still and the door opened a little more and then wider. He jumped from the bed and grabbed her and pulled her inside while she pushed the door shut and kept saying, 'I was looking for something' but could not finish as their mouths fused. He almost tore her top off and she kept on saying, 'No No'. Something dropped from her dress and Amit picked it up and in semi darkness saw the sachet of condom and opened it saying 'What a gorgeous woman you are and I am going to eat you' and he put his face in between her well shaped ample breasts and lifting her rolled on to the bed. They made love lustily and at the end she lay on his strong pectorals nibbling at the nipples. He caressed her gently on her head and face, she lay still on his chest and he passed his hands down to her buttocks and grabbed them in his large hands and squeezed hard. She moaned and he asked, 'Tell me when you bought the condom, before or after seeing me naked through the crack in the door?' She turned her head in surprise, 'You knew? Believe me I did not want to.' 'In jungle training we develop eyes at the back of head and slightest sound alerts us and we know what to believe.' She said 'You really are a wild beast' and enjoyed his moving hands. He gave a jerk 'Tell me' and she replied 'Before' and with a hard squeeze he said, 'And you kept torturing me?'

She raised her head and looking at him said, 'You must understand I am a married woman and an Indian. We have to cross many hesitations and risks. Ravi was oops baby but it was different, I was unmarried. I was not sure how you would take it.'

She sat up and he looked in fascination at her figure. She said, 'May I ask you something? You are a bachelor but not a virgin. You must have had many women?'

He said, 'Not many, only occasional but they were not like this.'

'In what way am I different?'

He said, 'Stop it and do not spoil this night like which I have never had in my life.'

She insisted, 'What is the difference?'

He said, 'There was no love, no responsibility of love but just animal passion not meant to last. It happens in the jungle when you are facing death. But love happens in the jungle too and I have seen that, love deep enough to sacrifice one's life. So I cannot insult them but it never happened to me. I am not very imaginative may not be able to express well. I feel deeply protective towards you, want to protect you from any harm any bad reputation. Do you think I had no hesitation? Put it this way, you are a woman in deep distress and I take advantage of that wearing a mask of benevolence. How does it sound? How would I face myself? I am not that much of an animal if you can believe me. If you cannot believe I shall not look at you again I shall forget you as I forgot others.'

She put her hand on his mouth, 'Please stop. I have insulted you I am in confusion not in full control of my own mind. My instinct was also passion to start with. I did not have strong arms around me for a long time, fought alone for many years. There was no look of love only lecherous smiles. And when you came with strong body and gentle manners and I saw your love for Ravi I saw dreams that had no chance of fulfillment. I became desperate and out of my mind. Please forgive me' and she started crying.

Amit kept caressing her and said, 'Stop crying. We are not always masters of our fate; a lot of things happen that we never anticipate, beyond our control. Some of that may be bad and some good. But have faith that if we have been honest to ourselves and others, there will be good. We are little parts or specks of a big picture and the big picture finally decides we do not. Must have that faith whatever the suffering is.'

Rupa asked, 'What would you do if I find Bob and go away with him?'

'That would also depend on the big picture. But I shall not be unhappy as much as you had been because our life situations are different. I shall be happy if you become happy. As for me I have been floating on the sea of life for a long time. The flotsam on the sea has no agenda, no responsibility it just dances on the waves and dips in the trough. And floating like this goes away to oblivion. There is some type of joy in that too, of freedom, of unconcern. No responsibility, the rolling of the sea determines the fate.'

Rupa was silent for some time and then said, 'It is strange. My mother used to say something like that. The rolling of the sea produced life and evolution on earth and the rolling seas originated from cosmic accidents of mind boggling dimensions and who knows they were accidents or not. And that wave pattern whether in cosmos or in our world is the rhythmic reality of our lives, now up and now down. We are the sons and daughters of the cosmos.'

Amit sat up and tenderly covering Rupa with a sheet said, 'You will catch cold; your mother was extraordinary, wish I had met her and grown up with you.'

Rupa laughed and pushed Amit hard, 'Dummy then we would be brother and sister. No this is better, take life as it comes like the flotsam on the sea and be honest to yourself and others. I like that. I have learnt something new from you.'

Rupa was thoughtful and asked, 'I want to know a bit more. Be honest with me. If I leave you after all this you would not be resentful you would not hate me and not be angry? I know you would have every reason to be but would you be? I want to know that straight.'

Amit laughed, 'It is almost impossible for anybody to predict what would be his reaction in a given situation at a distant or not too distant future. Our mind is a complex matter. What we think may not be what we really think or what we think today is not what we would think tomorrow. The famous Bengali novelist Sarat Chandra Chattopadhyay wrote something in one of his books that has stuck in my mind since childhood. He wrote that when somebody criticizes someone else's action and thinks he could have never done something so bad or so low it makes me laugh as I know that a man or woman can never foresee that given the circumstances and situations they would not do the same thing.'

He was silent and Rupa pushed him anxiously, 'That is not the answer to my question.'

Amit answered, 'Yes I know that. What I meant I cannot tell you what my reaction would be at that moment or five minutes or five days or five years later. In general I love freedom, individual freedom and I think the success of a society can be judged by the degree of individual freedom citizens enjoy keeping the society's integrity, happiness and prosperity. If I love freedom I must love it for both men and women equally. If I want complete freedom for women as much as men then I must want freedom for female sexuality too. Throughout history men have been afraid of that and made many social and philosophical means to control that. If I am honest I should accept your right of your own sexuality, which is what it is right now, your loneliness and deprivation of sex to have the feeling of strong arms around your naked body. My reaction at the actual moment I cannot fathom now, despair, desolation, anger everything is possible or may be nothing.' Rupa said in exasperation, 'You are impossible. You have to philosophize even the most intimate moments' and tried to get up. Amit restrained her, pulled off the sheet and embraced her tight that winded her, put her under and said 'enjoy the moment darling, do not imagine the future, that is also female sexuality, reckoning the future even when relishing the moment' and they made love again lustily.

Being properly tired now they reversed their position and Rupa said brushing off the hairs fallen on her face and kissing his chest, 'You are a demon; now let us get some sleep. You have to work tomorrow.' Amit murmured, 'There is one problem still unresolved, I really love you' and they slept in each others' arms.

On the Seashore

Part 3

She walks in beauty, like the night
Of cloudless climes and starry skies;
And all that's best of dark and bright
Meet in her aspect and her eyes:
Thus mellowed to that tender light
Which heaven to gaudy day denies.

One shade the more, one ray the less,
Had half impaired the nameless grace
Which waves in every raven tress
Or softly lightens o'er her face;
Where thoughts serenely sweet express
How pure, how dear their dwelling place.

And on that cheek, and o'er that brow
So soft, so calm, yet eloquent,
The smiles that win, the tints that glow,
But tells of days in goodness spent,
A mind at peace with all below,
A heart whose love is innocent!

Lord Byron

CONTENTS

The Quiet Silent Sea

The Sea covers two thirds of the earth's surface but does it care what happens on the one third land surface? Why should it? It has seen continents appear and disappear, majestic mountains proudly touching the sky disappears in its fathomless depths. Life forms undergo evolution and devolution, proud and powerful civilizations vanish, some of them going to oblivion, some leave relics and others faintly present in human memory. All those constitute our proud human heritage that is but a blink of the eye, even in terrestrial time not to speak of the cosmos, perishable by a tsunami, a giant meteor strike or an apocalyptic flood. And that pride divided and subdivided to miniscule fragments reside in us and we strut around the earth proudly calling it ours, like strutting pelicans and birds and dinosaurs on the shores, dropping the poops and when that becomes too much the earth turns with a sigh. But that pride is also a part of the cosmic drama, played for whose pleasure? Might be for something or somebody, but who or what? Does that thing care? There is no answer.

Atin was sitting on the beach, and looking at the setting sun, coloring the clouds and the sea with a magnificent kaleidoscope of hues that people round the world stare at, with varied emotions, a play of colours on a grand stage beyond the capability of man to duplicate. This was his second visit to Madhuri's house, but he was not staying there much to their disappointment, instead he was staying in the bungalow he was supposed to stay on his last visit. It is winter now but at this latitude and closeness to the sea, it is mild. The full moon is visible in angle of the sky waiting for the sun to hand over the colouring brush. The deep blue sky is cloudless. Soon it will turn azure and a new drama would start with strong silver beams from a cloudless pollution free sky dancing on the waves and rushing to the beach to bathe in liquid silver the sandy floor. The deep blue of the sea is the colour of Lord Krishna, with the silvery crown on his head rushing to the land calling for love. The folklore says that Sri Chaitanya in the ecstasy of love for the Lord, jumped in to the sea never to return. Nobody knows whether it is true but the previous night he could feel that ecstasy, and jumped in to the cold waves and was out shivering in cold. He smiled that this stupid story can never be told to anybody.

He was enjoying his solitude but next day he has to go to Madhuri's house and pop the question to her father. He had already asked Madhuri and she looked at him in a peculiar way and burst out laughing.

'I can see you have seen many foreign films of holding hands and proposing marriage or kneeling down and asking for her hand or even dismounting from horse removing your crown or sword or whatever and proposing. But I am a stupid poor Bengali village girl. All those theatricals is making me laugh, I am not laughing at you. You have to go and ask my father for my hand and if he says yes I shall walk to the end of the world with you. You go and ask him. Next weekend is a long holiday and there is the full moon night, an auspicious day. Go, go, I am already feeling impatient.'

Atin asked, 'Will you not come with me?'

Madhuri said, 'No, I am feeling so shy that I shall not be able to face them, father, mother and specially Tapu.'

Atin said, 'I am feeling very scared too.' 'Why' Madhuri asked.

Atin hesitated and then said, 'I am scared because I am alone, a single individual without father mother brother sister or any relation worth mentioning. Would your father agree to give you in marriage to such a loner? That is unusual in Bengali household. Moreover I have some sort of a history, what if they have heard it? What if he says no?'

Madhuri understood him and coming forward embraced him and said, 'I shall fill up your loneliness. I shall be your wife and your friend, sister, mother everything and so will you be mine. My father is also not an ordinary man. Do not be afraid' and she kissed him and they stayed in embrace and she felt his passion rising and pushed him off saying with a smile, 'Be patient darling, we shall discover ourselves through our lives, it will never end. But as for myself, I promise you that I have no pigmentation or ugly wart or fatty tumour in my body,' and burst out laughing. Atin made a face and laughed.

Madhuri added seriously, 'Jokes apart, if my parents give consent, which I know they will, I shall not come to your flat to meet you because we will be betrothed and it would not be proper. Marriage is a solemn sacred vow, is it not?'

Atin nodded and asked, 'How shall we meet or communicate? It will be difficult for me to live without seeing you.'

Madhuri said, 'We shall meet outside, go to see movies, meet in the hospital, talk on phone and go for walks, will that not be enough?'

Atin said with a sigh, 'It has to be and I understand and agree' but looked a bit downcast.

Madhuri smiled, 'Now you are not looking like a big surgeon, but a little boy in front of a candy shop. I shall make it worth your while dear, I promise. We have a whole long life to share, let us not start with a blemish,' and held his hand.

Tomorrow is that dreaded day. He has been invited to lunch and the lunch would probably extend through the day. He was still scared. He has rehearsed many times how to broach the subject. He has called Madhuri many times and repeated his speech only to hear her laugh, which was not a bad compensation. He described in detail how he passed his days, omitting only his night dip in the sea.

So it was that next day he went on his expedition. While driving he thought it would have been better if he rode a horse and smiling he immediately transmitted it to Madhuri and she laughed and said, 'Why is the road not bumpy enough?' He said, 'Yes that is there, but riding a horse gives some amount of courage.' Madhuri asked, 'Do you know riding?' Atin answered, 'Just a little bit.' She asked, 'Is there anything that you do not know?' and he replied 'Yes you.' He disconnected as he saw Tapu at the last turn of road to the house.

He picked her up in the car and asked, 'You have come so far from the house to welcome me?'

Gravely Tapu replied, 'No, to inspect you.'

'To inspect what?' Atin asked.

'Your dress, you are not properly dressed.'

'Why? What is wrong?'

'Bridegrooms are supposed to come wearing Dhoti and Kurta. You obviously do not know how to wear a Dhoti. I can teach you.'

He held her ear with a light pinch and asked, 'Who told you I am a bridegroom you are too young for me.'

She moved her head and sticking out her tongue said, 'I shall have a much better one.'

The car stopped and Madhuri's mother, all smiles hurried to the car and as Atin was alighting asked, 'That little scorpion was irritating you again?' Atin smiled and said, 'Not at all. I have never had a sister Ma, she is so sweet.' She was overwhelmed hearing Ma and touching his chin she kissed her fingers as Atin's mother used to do and his eyes became moist.

Madhuri's father had gone out on some errand. Mother asked whether he would like to have bath and change. He said he had bathed in the morning and has not brought any change. Mother said he could have a fresh Dhoti and Atin said that would be fine. Tapu was always hovering near and he winked at her. Mother noticed that and asked 'is this little one teasing you again?' Atin said, 'No Tapu wants to see whether I can wear a Dhoti and I have to show her or else she will teach me.' Mother laughed and said, 'Naughty girl.' *Sailenbabu* came back and changed and the three of them sat down for lunch and mother insisted on serving. The lunch went on with ordinary conversation.

After lunch Atin sat with Sailenbabu and said, 'You of course know the purpose of my visit.' Sailen smiled and said, 'Your coming is the big event the purpose is a small thing.'

Atin said, 'Still I have to request your permission and blessing to marry Madhuri. In normal circumstances my father or mother or some elder would have come to do this. But I have nobody. My elder brother is in the USA and I do not know where precisely at this moment. I shall inform him of course, but I do not think he will be able to come. So I have to ask you myself, which is not usual. Moreover not having any close relative is not the ideal situation to give your daughter in marriage, it is not auspicious. So I shall understand if you refuse. As for myself I can say' he could not finish the sentence before Sailen raised his hand and stopped him.

With a smile on his face and a wink at his wife he said, 'Do you know how many systems of marriage exist in our Hindu tradition? There is Rakshasa system where you snatch your wife against even her will and marry her by force. Then there is Gandharva system when you steal your willing wife by force against the wish of her kith and kin and carry her off and marry. There are many others I do not even know. You have come to us begging her hand in marriage and you say you have no elder relative. I think this is not even a special category. You say you are alone but then she is going to marry only you and not your entire family, not even like Draupadi who married all the five brothers. We know our daughter and have full faith in her judgment. By and by you shall also agree with me. Apart from that what is so special about it? We are all alone in this world, who else carries our baggage? But yes there are some rituals where an elder is needed. I shall fulfill that role. It is so easy.'

At this point mother intervened, 'No not you, I shall be on his side.' Everyone was startled and looked at her, all except the father who was smiling at his wife. She continued, 'This is what happens to men in old age. You do not even remember that you have to present your daughter to the groom, in fact even tie their hands together. How can you be on the groom's side? I shall be on the groom's side; I shall be Atin's mother. I shall welcome the bride to her new home.' Everyone applauded with laughter all around and Sailen said to his wife, 'You must thank me for giving you the chance.'

Tapu suddenly blurted, 'But wherefrom the bridegroom's procession will start, which house?' The room was silent and then a shy voice said, 'My house'. All eyes turned and it was Arun the young doctor from the small hospital. Embarrassed he said shyly, 'Me and my wife will look after the groom's entourage. There will be enough space for them and we shall look after them. We shall decorate one room for the bridal night before they return to Calcutta. I owe this much Sir.' There was again hurray all around. Thus in barely half an hour all nitty-gritty of marriage were solved and in stunned silence Atin sat in the middle of all this. Sailen whispered in his ear, 'Don't worry we are all your relatives.' Even an auspicious wedding day was fixed about a month later in early spring.

Atin was on cloud seven when he returned to Calcutta and excitedly described everything that happened to Madhuri. She listened quietly and said with a smile, 'All that is very good but the main thing has not been decided; where shall I live after marriage?' Atin looked dumb. Madhuri suppressed her smile, 'Definitely not in your flat with a manservant. Give me the keys to your house.'

Atin was bemused, 'Keys to our house? I have to search.' Madhuri ordered, 'Well then, let us go to your place. I shall sit in the car while you get the keys. We don't have a lot of time to waste dear.'

Keys were found and Madhuri tied it to the end of her sari. 'Now let us go,' she ordered 'tomorrow is a working day let us start today.'

They reached the house, unlocked the door and went in. The dingy smell of an unlived house with old things scattered all around overpowered them. Madhuri moved around the rooms, the bathroom and kitchen. She opened a tap and water flowed. She went to the kitchen garden and looked at the small flowering tress that still stood and tenderly touched them as if caressing.

Atin caught up with her and asked, 'What are you doing?'

Madhuri looked up with tearful eyes, 'You said a dream had died in this house. Dreams are precious things, we cannot let them die. You heard from mother's nurse that she used to stand in front of mirror and call her own name and I cried in silence when I heard that. You men cannot understand the pain of a woman. I can feel her presence and her blessing around me. I shall renovate this house and my first step as a newly wed wife will be in this house. I shall enter no other house. If necessary our marriage will have to be postponed by a few days,' and tears now rolled down in full stream. Atin pushed her chin up, to look at her face and said in a thick voice, 'Do what you have set out to do. It will be my redemption too. There will be no dearth of money,' and wiped her tears.

An old gentleman was peeping through the front door. Atin came out and recognized the old neighbour and paid his respect calling him inside. Entering he said, 'You are Atin are you not? We hear about you that you are a famous surgeon now. What are you doing here do you want to live here?'

Atin said, 'Yes uncle we are thinking of renovating the house and live here. This is Madhuri and we are going to be married soon and then move in here.' Madhuri touched his feet.

The old man shook his head and said, 'That is very good. There was a lot of madhuri (sweetness) in this house once, joy and laughter and your learned father and now Madhuri will reenter.'

Atin asked, 'Uncle, are masons and contractors available nearby to renovate this house?'

The old man said, 'Plenty of them. There is a building boom. In fact there is a young contractor who lives close by and is very good and honest and has made quite a name. Today is Sunday, he may be available. I can call him if you want.' As Atin nodded and asked where was his house the old man started off in a hurry without even replying.

The young architect and builder's name is Somen and he recognized Atin immediately. 'You are Atinda are you not? Are you coming back here? We hear so much about you.'

Atin said, 'Yes, I am getting married and this is your boudi (elder brother's wife) Madhuri. We want to live here.' Somen touched Madhuri's feet and she jumped back. He continued, 'We are ordinary middle class people boudi and we love the traditions we learnt from our parents. You do not worry we shall do it just as you want and at minimum rates. You just tell me what you want. People are moving away from this locality to multistory apartment houses but we love to stay here among people we have grown up with.'

Madhuri said, 'Brother, I shall call you brother. I come from a village and I find it difficult to live in an apartment. Can you make another floor on top of our house?'

Somen laughed, 'Yes of course. When Atinda's father built this house I was a boy and he used to tell the masons to make the foundation strong so that one or even two floors can be built on top. And the masons used to laugh that the old man was spending so much on foundation that he will have nothing left for the superstructure. He used to say that he has two sons and would have many grandchildren. Is Amitda coming back?'

Almost simultaneously Atin said, 'Don't know' and Madhuri said 'Yes' and Atin looked at her in surprise.

Somen without noticing that went on, 'Atinda I shall give you another advice. Your house is a corner house. The house behind you is up for sale the owners are leaving. If you can buy that house and break the boundary wall in between you shall have a lot of space for a back garden. That house is in better shape and can be remodeled. If two brothers like you live together, this place will be famous. People will love and adore you. We are proud of you.'

Again Madhuri was first to react, 'How much are they expecting?'
Somen quoted a figure and said, 'But they will come down.'

Now Atin recognized the young man; he was in the truck during
father's last journey. He said, 'It is nice to see that you have done
well.'

He smiled, 'Yes much better than expected. I was doing graduation
in architecture that was interrupted, but I somehow cleared the course
later. Business is increasing. There is another thing Atinda. During the
last land alignment and fixation of boundaries a small slice of land was
added to the front of your house. I can build a front porch and a grill
fence with a small lawn and gardening area, with car parking between
the houses.'

Atin laughed loudly, 'Somen please finish this house first. Negotiate
with the other house for sale but please finish this house within a
month or else your boudi will not marry me, because she will not set
foot anywhere else.'

Somen smiled and said, 'I can see that Atinda, boudi is like aunt, your
mother personified. We used to torture her so much coming at odd
times demanding food and she never said no and never got irritated.
Whatever you ask for will be done. One month is enough.'

Madhuri said, 'I shall come frequently to see and discuss with you as
your Dada will not have much time.'

Somen said, 'As frequently as you want boudi and you must eat at my
house. Leave the keys at my house and your phone numbers when you
leave and rest assured' and he left.

They looked at him as he walked away and Madhuri said, 'What a
man! He backs out at nothing. I really wait eagerly to meet Amitda.
What a man he must be to be revered by such young men.'

Atin smiled, 'Again you are making me jealous.'

Madhuri pinched him and said, 'I shall eat you piece by piece, I love sweets, just you wait mister' and Atin sighed deeply, 'What a long wait' and got another pinch.

Then they rummaged through the house amid the debris from another life. They took down old framed photographs covered with cobwebs. Madhuri discovered an old moth eaten album in a trunk with other knickknacks from bygone days. She collected every little thing like Atin's books and notebooks from school days, old letters, a scrapbook with mother's handwriting even small poems she wrote without anybody's knowledge.

Atin said, 'How much junk are you collecting and where will you keep them?'

Madhuri said, 'They may be junk to you but I am collecting dreams, a woman's dream. The continuity of life in this house must be maintained for future peace. There is no end, no interruption, the love with which this house was built will be continued and the link cannot be broken. We want a home, not just a house. I shall come again and ask Somen not to disturb the rooms till then.'

Atin followed her through the small house with a new respect and love and remembered her father's words. What a woman!

Spring Flowers by Seaside

It took a bit more than a month to complete rebuilding of the house. The marriage date was postponed by about a fortnight when the spring would be in full bloom. She went back home a few days before marriage. By that time the house was looking beautiful with two floors and a floating porch. The number of rooms increased by one more on each floor as Somen discovered an unutilized part of the foundation. He strengthened the old brick foundation with concrete. An extra bathroom was added. The bathrooms and the kitchen were modernized. When Madhuri left, painting was in progress and she chose the colours. Her energy was phenomenal and surprising. She would get up very early and go to the house on way to the hospital and then send the car for Atin. She will again go there from hospital and go out on shopping with Atin in the evening. He would warn her to take care of her health but she would only laugh. Paperwork progressed for purchase of the adjoining house and the deal would be completed after marriage.

Malati took leave with Madhuri and accompanied her to the village. She was a few years younger to Madhuri and Tapu was delighted to have a senior bridesmaid. They hit off nicely. The house was decorated nicely with new coat of paint, again of Madhuri's choice. The ground in front over a large area was flattened and hardened with soil powdered through a sieve mixed with cow dung and straw in the traditional village manner. When settled and hard it would form the floor of a large hall with a canopy and carpets on the floor. It was partitioned to sitting and dining areas. The ground floor rooms of the

257

house were emptied. The large room in the centre facing in the right direction would be used for the marriage ceremonies. Another fairly large room by the side was the groom's sitting room with his entourage and changing room before the actual marriage. The groom enters the marriage seat first and completes his worship, before the bride descends from the floor above, down the stairs marked with all sorts of holy symbols and faces the groom. By any standards it was a grand ceremony. Apart from Atin and Malati all other people were locals divided in to groom's and bride's parties, and there was a lot of fun as the groom's party usually takes the upper hand.

Atin arrived the day before marriage with his anesthetist Salil. He was the sole true groom's party. Arun was delighted to have them in his house and spent the rest of the day and half the night chatting with Salil about anesthesiology and career prospects. Atin asked Salil to encourage the young man, and find an opening for him. They were offered a sumptuous dinner and when they protested, Arun's wife told Atin that he would have to fast most of next day till the marriage ceremony was over. Therefore he should gorge himself at night and Atin protested that he could not eat two meals in one go. He went to bed early because he had to perform some worship and rituals the next morning that mainly consisted of worshipping the gods and his forefathers asking their blessings for his married life. He was supposed to fast through the day, till completion of marriage ceremony, but a bit of cheating was allowed consuming fruit juices, cold drinks and sweets, as long as there was no cooked food.

The groom's procession started in late afternoon. The bride's party insisted that the groom must come on horseback like a king, surrounded by his entourage as foot soldiers, especially since he knew riding. A saddled horse and a band party were arranged along with portable lights. Thus with sounds of kettle drums, flutes and shehnai playing ahead of the procession and foot soldiers dressed in their best, with the groom in the middle on horseback, the procession started. After a little more than half hour they reached bride's house where they were welcome with rose petals and flowers thrown on their path and sprinkling of perfumed water. After Atin alighted he was greeted with honour by bride's mother, who performed as the groom's mother in the morning, with a large brass plate piled with holy symbols and flowers and was brought in to the house to his sitting room. After resting for sometime, chatting with people, parrying naughty mischief of Tapu and exchanging jokes with Malati, though she was still overwhelmed by him, the notice of the holy hour was declared by the priest.

The room was cleared and he changed to white silken dhoti with bare body and washed himself. He was then taken to the marriage arena. *Sailenbabu* was already sitting there on a small carpet and got up to welcome him and requested him to sit. Then Sanskrit mantras were uttered by the priest and repeated by both sides. The mantras were really simple, the bride's father expressing joy and honour for being able to welcome the groom to his house and look after his every comfort and the groom responding. At the end of this part the groom stands up and is covered by a silk cloth. The bride is then carried to the arena sitting atop a wooden seat born by four sturdy brothers of which one was real in this particular case and others cousins. The bride covers her face with a pan leaf and goes around the covered groom seven times carried by the brothers and then faces him. The silk curtain on the groom is then lifted and pulled over the bride's head as a canopy to conceal them from onlookers, though that never happens as women gather around in glee to see how they have their first look at each other under public gaze. The bride removes the pan leaf from her face and they look at each other amid sound of conch shells and ululation. In this case Atin was dazzled by Madhuri's beauty in the brilliant coiffure. He had never seen her like this. She hardly cared for her appearance but she is so beautiful!

The bride is lowered to the floor on her seat and the groom sits down. The bride's father offers her daughter's hand to the man since he has seen and liked her and wishing they remain in a happy alliance ties their hands together. The marriage vows uttered are so similar in every language, in this case priest utters the vows one by one and the groom holding the bride's hand says the equivalent of 'I do' to every one of them. Then fire is lighted and Agni or Fire and Narayana or Vishnu are made witnesses to all that happened and are given the offerings first by the priest and then by the couple jointly, Atin holding Madhuri's hands from behind encircling her in the process to give offerings to the fire.

All the rituals being over they retire to the room and guests and relations come one by one to give their blessings and good wishes. This goes on for a long time and the guests are fed. When most have gone, Atin and Madhuri had little bites of food with the elders and other family members and retired to the bedroom specially made for them with a new bed and flowers all around. This is the bridal night and being very tired they sat on the bed facing each other and devoured with their eyes, with a shy smile hovering on Madhuri's lips. Atin made a gesture to move but Madhuri in alarm bade him not to, pointing at the windows where young ladies peep to see how they make their first communications. There were bellows of laughter from outside at Madhuri's gesture. A resigned Atin gave up and stretched out on bed and fell asleep. Madhuri sat looking at him sleeping like a child and happily smiled. She has done the right thing. Next morning she could not remember when she fell asleep.

Next morning there was a small ritual of applying vermilion on the bride's forehead, the sign of a married woman that Hindu women carry in different manner, obvious or not. This is equivalent to wearing the ring. After a family lunch they started for the groom's house, in this case Arun's house. A cable in Atin's name was delivered at midday by the peon from village post and telegraph office. He had sent an email to Amit giving his date of marriage and the village address. The cable was from Amit.

> Dear brother so happy spring flowers by seaside bloomed in
> your life. Wish you happiness. Second chance is the best. I
> am in Philadelphia. Remote chance of flowers too, nothing
> sure in my life. Her name is Rupa.

Atin read the cable twice and then looked vacantly at Madhuri. She asked what the matter was and he silently gave her the cable. Madhuri looked up and saw his moist eyes and he said, 'My apology for a family.' Madhuri looked around and came by his side and held his hand, 'I am there. Be gracious and happy for him.' That night they went back to Arun's house, which was the groom's house and was to be welcomed by groom's mother. In this case the role was played by Madhuri's mother as she had demanded. The couple had to sleep in different rooms as it was called 'kalaratri' or black night following an ancient legend and were not meant to cohabit as that would bring bad luck. Next day's lunch was bride's lunch for both families. Arun organized that and Atin paid. There was no more routine. That night was the conjugal night in groom's house and they had to sleep on a bed strewn with flowers, must be uncomfortable Atin thought. Next day they will leave for Calcutta.

In the afternoon Atin told Madhuri, 'So long all were public functions when do we do our own function?' Madhuri looked askance.

He said, 'Let us drive down to our place that nobody knows.'

They drove to the temple by the pine grove. They went inside and paid obeisance to the goddess who brought them together. Then they drove to their familiar spot and Atin said, 'I hope I find the snake to thank him,' as they got down from the car and walked down to the beach.

Madhuri laughed, 'Today you do not need the snake for that. Just look at the vista. The sun is setting, painting the sea and the sky with shades of red to yellow to violet as far as you can see with a pale full moon in one corner. Not a soul to be seen not even a stray dog. There is no village and no town nearby. We are the two lovers in the primordial world standing by the sea with wonder, and deeply in love. Can you make love to me here,' and jumped on him smothering him with kisses.

Her hunger surprised Atin, 'Tigress where did you hide your fangs so long?'

'Waiting for opportunity to kill,' she whispered breathless in between kisses.

With a whoop he picked her up in his arms. She moaned hiding her face in his chest and said, 'No, No that is not what I meant. How could I say what I just told! What came over me? I am not that sort of a woman you know?'

Atin breathless replied, 'We shall soon find out what sort of a woman you are' and carried her to a clean area on the beach cloistered by the trees.

Later as they lay side by side with the setting sun spreading a golden light on the sky that lighted the earth Madhuri said, 'Who said the first one is not so good? Would all of them be just as good darling?' Atin pinched her nose, 'You need an expert for that.'

Madhuri gave him a push, 'I know that, don't rub it in. But Dada has written second chance is the best. Do you agree?'

Atin said in mock anger, 'I am going to hit you.'

Madhuri said, 'Really I feel so happy and relaxed in body and mind, is that real?'

Atin replied gravely, 'It is more in the mind. It mainly comes from there.'

'Have you felt it before,' Madhuri asked.

'Honestly speaking not as much,' Atin replied, 'It was marred by a sense of guilt.' After a pause he added, 'I am not sexually that active, I was activated. You may be disappointed.'

Madhuri sighed and said, 'Not at all so long as you love me.' Then she added, 'I did the right thing then restraining you so long. I do not mind the past I look only at the future. It is better that one of us is not a greenhorn,' and quickly added, 'Please do not mind, I am not trying to hurt you. You were so tender and understanding that I almost went through a dream. I am surprised that I could enjoy so much. That is not what I heard from friends.'

Atin laughed and said, 'Look at that vast sea spreading to the horizon and that sky the gateway to the unfathomable mystery of the universe, they have challenged man since antiquity to voyages of discovery to cross the oceans and exploring space. The entire experience and development of humanity is from this adventure of discovery, not only in the outer world but also in his inner world, this curiosity defines man from other animals though some animals do possess some of that but not to the extent of man. It comes from what we have in our brain. Our mind drives us to this and develops from it. It is a continuous autonomous process, never seen to this degree on earth. Newer species may come in future with more efficient systems, but man's development is not yet complete. There would always be mistakes, dangers and sorrows but they are equal drivers of the mind. Success and new discovery brings unparalleled joy. Look at that sea dancing in joy in small wavelets that can be taken over at any time by huge waves. That is how our mind and life goes, up again and down again, developing in adversity and happy and dancing in achievement. In our tiny life we have achieved that together after suffering, like dying sailors in a boat lost on high seas shouting, 'Land ahoy'. The memory of this sensation imprinted in our brain will carry us through our lives. That is the joy of discovery. Those lengthy rituals of marriage are probably meant to build up the tension.'

Madhuri said, 'You are an amateur philosopher, how much you have thought!'

Atin said, 'That is one of the plus points of loneliness as you play with your mind and discover things you never knew existed there. Lonely living, at least in patches, is after all essential for meditation, whether on philosophy, science, arts or God.'

They got up and rearranged their dresses brushing off sand as much as possible. Atin said, 'we would be caught with all that sand.'

Madhuri laughed loud and said, 'Caught at what darling? You will be caught, not I darling. The folds of my sari will hide the sand. You could be with anybody, may be your past love or a new one,' and she ran to the car chased by Atin.

World Oceans Connect

One of the great geological features of the Earth is that watery oceans are interconnected. This connectivity makes her a balanced place in atmosphere, ecology, flora and fauna without enforcing a rigid uniformity. This balanced diversity has produced many different life forms spread over the globe that are independent yet interdependent. The oceans also produce a unique communication system not only in sound, as in whales who can hear each other's calls almost from the North Pole to South Pole, but also in many other matters and were the main communication system for man till the days of flying machines. In a world with landlocked puddles of oceans this would not have been possible. The human beings also evolved because of this connectivity. The white men who first set foot in Africa did not even consider them as human beings but more as biped animals who could be taught to understand command and were hardy workers ready to be deported wherever necessary. Slave trade was not invented in Europe, it was extensive in Asia with no less barbarism, but its origins were because of the sea and over centuries led to the birth of humanism and the sensation of one earth. The earth was not born yesterday but the length of man's history on earth is but a few seconds of cosmic time. And in that short period the connectivity has increased to a grand spectacle not yet discovered anywhere else in the cosmos. If we do not succeed in destroying our Mother Earth, who can imagine what it holds for the future. Water exists in scattered or frozen state in many places in the universe but not yet found in the way it is on our Earth. Amit was pondering all this sitting on the sands of Laguna Beach as he stared at the Pacific Ocean.

His days in Philadelphia came to an end as he had to move to the West Coast. In this one year of stay, his life with Rupa gelled to a happy family life. They had a small circle of friends. People were not curious as in India, about other people's personal lives. In any case their surnames were the same as Rupa used her maiden name Rupa Roy. Ravi had a different name and different appearance but people are busy and do not enjoy gossip. At most they were a live together couple, nothing great to discuss about. If anybody ever asked the obvious answer was that Ravi's parents were separated, not an unusual event. The Americans did not care and not even members of the resident Indian community. They were a charming couple and that was all. So they lived a pleasant life. Ravi had been admitted to a prep school and he adjusted nicely.

The only thorn was that Rupa could get no substantive employment. Her dreams of entering the university did not materialize and she could not have school teaching job as in India, because she did not have the requisite training. As a result, she remained financially dependent on Amit and did not like it. Amit tried to explain, it did not matter. His salary was more than adequate to support a family and it did not matter whether they were legally married or not. She was free to move out whenever she liked and that could happen even if they were legally married. People should learn to accept different situations in life without becoming depressed or reactive to it. Take life as it comes without attaching a lot of baggage. But it was not in Rupa's nature. They were deeply in love and discussed everything openly but that did not assuage her despair.

Therefore when his transfer to the offices in the Los Angeles County became final, he asked what she wanted to do. She could go back to India if she wanted and await his return or else go West with him and he would arrange accommodation accordingly. He said that he loved her and did not want to lose her and Ravi. Chances of finding Bob were becoming more and more remote. She could not decide and Amit could not blame her.

She said, 'I love you but cannot live as a parasite on you. I cannot marry you because I am not divorced. Ravi is growing up and going to school. If he asks me one day what shall I answer? There is very slender chance that I shall find Bob to ask for divorce. It probably would not have mattered so much if we could marry in India, but you cannot return to India in near future and I cannot destroy your career. So what should I say?'

Amit said, 'I have asked before and I ask again do you have any relatives in USA?'

Rupa was choking and said, 'I could not answer last time and it is even more difficult now. After my mother's death there is no one closer to me than you, no relation I can depend on or like to be with. Yes theoretically I have a close relation, my brother Asim and his wife Rati. They are supposed to be living somewhere on the West Coast, but I do not know where. There has been little communication for a long time, none after mother's death. I hear rumours that they have separated but do not know for sure. Even if they were not, I would much rather ride on your shoulder than theirs. If God does not give me the means to stay with you, I shall have to go back to India and accept defeat. I do not like defeat and what shall I tell Ravi? He thinks I am searching for his father with your help and he loves you. But for how long,' and tears started rolling down and she covered her face.

Amit embraced from behind, 'The decision then is made. You are coming with me to Los Angeles and we look for your brother and Bob. How does that sound?'

Rupa turned around and said with tearful eyes, 'You heard me mentioning God and I am a physicist.'

Amit smiled, 'I see no contradiction there and your mother would have said so,' the mention of her mother brought forth another burst of tears as he kept consoling her.

So they moved West and Amit rented a two bedroom apartment paying the extra over and above what the company paid him for residence. He told Ravi that they were moving to West Coast, for his father may be there and all of them would search for him.

After settling in their new home he asked her, 'What is your brother's profession and that of his wife?' and she replied, 'Both were computer and software specialists and would be in IT companies, but different ones.' Amit asked, 'Why so?' and she answered that Rati did not like to work in the same company. She was good in her job and had contacts with American clients from India. Amit said it would not be difficult to locate them.

It did not take long to locate Rati and she was doing well. There was no information on Asim but rumours said that she was separated from her husband and enjoying a jolly good life. He called her company and tried to locate her but it was difficult. Nobody wants to give personal information of their employees to an unknown voice. After a lot of effort giving details of his position in his company, his name and personal details he said he knew her in India and could make them agree to note down his office phone number. After a few days he heard from his senior colleague that a company from the Silicon Valley enquired about him. 'What is the matter?' he asked. Amit was frank and said, 'The lady living with me is her relation and wants to contact her. Her name is Rupa.' A few days later his phone rang but did not show the caller number.

A female voice spoke, 'I cannot place your name but I know Rupa, my ex-husband's sister, if she is the same woman. What does she want?'

Amit answered, 'Yes she is your ex-husband's sister if his name is Asim. She wants to know his whereabouts and how he is and how to contact him.'

She asked, 'And you? Are you a family? I do not remember but I may not know all.'

He lied, 'Yes I am. Can you help me?'

She said, 'Don't know much about him or where he is at present.' Then with a cruel snigger she added, 'Could be in a correctional home for alcoholics or somewhere worse. Sorry not to be of much help,' and she hung up.

Amit hung up and sat silent. He knew the call has been recorded somewhere in his company. That does not matter but he cannot give the information to Rupa and increase her misery. He felt deep sorrow but he had to lie to her and did not know how. He kept up his cheerful demeanor but might have overdone a bit. Rupa was suspicious and asked when they were alone, 'What is it you are hiding from me? Is it about Asim?'

He told half truth, 'Could not locate him and yes he is separated from his wife.'

Rupa mused, 'Could be in a correctional center for alcoholics or worse. I saved him once and he has gone back. His wife was always a careerist and did not love him, used him as a carrier to reach USA. Only thing he needed was love that he never got,' and this time she did not even cry and looking up at him said, 'My fate is closing all paths around me.'

Amit said, 'Don't say that, I shall always be there with you as long as you want me. Difficult path sometimes lead to better end, be optimistic.'

Life became gloomy. It became very difficult to take her out anywhere. She would ask how much it would cost. She was sinking to depressive psychosis, not really gone but on the way. He tried utmost but it was difficult. She was not always gloomy as she saw it was affecting him and forced herself to be her normal self that was even more pathetic. Then one day he sat her down when Ravi was coming late from school and said, 'Rupa Roy, will you please marry me? To hell with divorce and all that, we shall get married in Hindu way and when my term ends we shall go back to India. It may not be very far.'

She patted him on the cheek and said, 'That will be your suicide for my sake. I cannot allow that. God will not forgive me.' Amit did not comment that she was speaking of God more frequently nowadays.

Then came a long weekend and he asked Ravi, 'How about a weekend out Ravi? We shall go to the seaside somewhere and swim, have barbeque and check in a motel and visit Disneyland next day to spend a whole day and then come back. How would it be; would you like it?'

Ravi was jumping in joy, 'Swell, awesome uncle, Ma let us go please don't say no.'

The little boy was growing up and knew mother may reject and the poor boy was not having as much fun as his mates. Amit looked at Rupa and said, 'She would not say no when you want it so much. We have to pack and do not forget to take your swimming things Ravi.' Rupa also smiled and said, 'Of course we shall go. I shall make everything ready.'

Amit shouted at Ravi who had already rushed to his room. 'Ravi, tell Ma to take her swimsuit or else we would not go.' Ravi shouted back, 'Okay uncle.' Rupa looked at him and said, 'You know I do not like the sea much, makes me even darker.' Amit laughed, 'Not much, not as much as me and it is for Ravi's sake.' Rupa winked, 'And not for you?' Amit had a hearty laugh not only for what she said but more that she said it at all after a long time.

Amit looked at maps and made the necessary bookings and they drove out after breakfast. There was a lot of fun. The bathing area was protected and Amit and Ravi swam together with snorkels and flippers. Rupa sat under an umbrella with a book after just one dip. She looked ravishing in a swim suit and Amit winked. She responded with a stern look pointing her chin at Ravi. Amit stuck his tongue out like a kid and she laughed.

After shower they sat under a canopy and had excellent assorted barbecued lunch. Amit gulped two beers and ordered Rupa's choice of red wine. She was lively and her colour returned. There was an amusement park nearby. They went there and Ravi was ecstatic going from one game to another. They had seafood supper. Rupa ordered her favourite liquor with coffee and Ravi went to bed early. Amit and Rupa went for a walk on the beach in moonlight and after a long time Rupa was lively and embraced and kissed him tenderly.

Amit said, 'Should have booked two rooms instead of a family room.' Rupa laughed, 'You must be joking. The way I have made you suffer you would have wanted nothing of the sort.'

Amit said, 'You bet. Give me the chance and see. But jokes apart please come out of your stupor and take life as it comes. Do not worry, everything will be all right.'

Rupa sighed, 'Mother said the same thing and I trust her.'

Amit said, 'Do be honest, tell me what would you like most happening to you.'

Rupa's answer was prompt, 'To get out of my cursed marriage.'

Amit said, 'But you are already out. How many years have you been separated?'

Rupa said, 'Yes I know but I would like to be properly out of it and give all of me to you without hesitation, if you still take me, yours by all counts with head held high.'

Amit said with conviction, 'Then it will be so' and he wished a fairy flying by has smiled.

Next morning they woke early by the strident call of Ravi. 'Get up ma get up uncle it is getting late. We have to go to the Disney.'

They got up in a hurry, washed had breakfast and drove out.

Disney was very crowded. In front of popular attractions one had to push through the crowd and stand in queue. It was difficult to keep Ravi in check and they did not want to. But it meant running after him disappearing among the legs. Amit did all the running and kept one eye on Rupa that was not so difficult. She stood out and eyes followed her. She was dressed in tight jeans and a close fitting top and her figure was gorgeous. After finishing all the rides, where Amit accompanied Ravi as Rupa was not fond of them, Ravi slowed down a bit. Amit suggested lunch and they sat down in the open in front of a cafeteria finding a rare empty table. Amit asked them their choice and went to collect food. When he returned Ravi was not there. Rupa said he has gone to look at a magic stall facing them. Amit went to call him but did not find him. He came back worried to Rupa. She said, 'Don't worry. Kids do not get lost that easy if they know where the parents are sitting and Ravi is fairly grown up.' Amit was still worried and looked here and there.

Rupa laughed, 'You will be a bad pampering father.'

Amit said, 'I am not the father that is the problem,' and Rupa said, 'Cool down he will come.'

A little later Ravi turned up with a little girl hanging from his hand. She would be barely three years old and sweet looking with a cascade of blond hair. Rupa asked, 'Who is she Ravi?' 'My friend' Ravi triumphantly declared.

An elderly gentleman was following them and stopped a little distance from the table. Amit asked the little girl, 'What is your name?' and before she could reply he saw Rupa stand up slowly. Following her gaze he saw the man with sparse straw coloured hair. He did not look very healthy. His eyes were locked on Rupa. A faint sound emitted from Rupa's lips, 'Bob!' He did not respond, looked at Amit and stayed where he was.

Amit recovered first and getting up extended his hand, 'I am Amit. Good day to you Mister Lind. Please come and have a seat.' He kept standing swaying a little.

Amit went forward and shook his hand and brought him to the table and offered a chair and he sat down with his eyes still on Rupa. Amit said again, 'I am Amit, friend of Rupa. Can I get you something?' He shook his head and said, 'I have to go.'

Rupa had recovered by now and leaned forward to ask, 'How are you Bob? You do not look so well.'

He looked at her and hesitated and with an effort said, 'I have leukemia.'

Rupa asked with concern, 'Oh God, since when? And who is she?'

He gulped and looked distressed. Amit handed him a glass of water and he emptied it. Then looking at the girl he said, 'She is Linda. Catherine left after she was born. I developed leukemia.' There was a stunned silence nobody talked.

He made a move to get up and told the girl, 'Please come Linda, we have to go home.' The girl still holding Ravi's hand shook her pretty head and said, 'He coming along Dad?'

Amit understood the situation and seeing that Bob was suffering under the sun, got up and said, 'Let us go and sit in some cool shady place. Come with me Ravi and Linda' and holding their hand started walking. Rupa and Bob slowly followed. He heard Rupa's voice, 'You never informed me of your illness,' there was no answer from Bob.

Luckily they found a shaded place soon and sat down, Linda still holding Ravi's hand and he rather amused carried her along.

Rupa asked, 'Are you still working?' With a flicker of smile Bob replied, 'Yes a bit.'

'But you are still sending money in Ravi's account!' Bob said, 'Managing somehow.'

'Did you recognize Ravi?' and he nodded.

Amit realized he would have to control the situation and getting up asked Bob, 'Do you want to go home Mister Lind, do you have a transport or can we drop you and see your house? You people need to talk a lot,' and looked at Rupa. Bob nodded, 'Yes thanks if you can give a lift,' and Amit started at a slow pace, Ravi and Linda holding his hands.

He looked back only once and his eyes met Rupa's for a second and they told something he never saw before, love or gratitude or something he could not fathom?

They reached Bob's house not far from theirs, but in a poorer section. The houses with small apartments having small windows badly needed a coat of paint. Amit alighted and held open the door for Rupa and Bob to get out, but Linda shook her head. She would not leave the car. Rupa said, 'That is ok. She can be with us a couple of days, can't she Bob? I can bring her back. Let me reach you upstairs' and they entered the house. Amit kept strolling on the footpath whistling and keeping an eye on the kids in the car. In a sudden throwback to the jungle days, he remembered he did this when the going was tough.

Rupa came out with a tissue in her hand, wiping eyes and quietly sat down in the passenger seat beside Amit. He started the car and drove off. Only once she put her hand on Amit's and he looked at her but could not read her eyes.

They reached home and Rupa took the kids to her room. Amit changed, had a wash and got in bed. He pulled the covers, but sat on the bed in deep thought. One weekend has changed everything. Rupa came in after sometime and said, 'Children fell asleep as soon as they hit the bed,' and sat on a chair.

She was silent and busy inspecting her fingers not looking at Amit. After sometime Amit broke the silence, 'If you have something to say you can say it and if you want to sit silent that is also ok with me and I shall sit with you through the night.'

She looked up at him and said, 'I cannot ask him for divorce now.'

Amit said, 'No you cannot.' There was silence again.

To prod her he asked, 'How is his apartment?'

'In size it is not very small but filthy, very filthy,' she said followed by silence. Amit waited. She looked up and asked, 'Can I go back tomorrow morning and clean the place a bit? I have brought the spare key.'

Amit said, 'Yes I shall drop you on my way to office and bring you back when I return.'

She said, 'You don't have to. I do not want to stay that long. I can come back on my own, it is not far.' She was silent again.

After a long pause she asked with the same grave face, 'Can I share your bed if you do not mind? The two children have taken up my bed.'

Without a word Amit moved to one side making space for her. She came in silence and got under the sheets and holding his hand said, 'Thank you' with shy imploring eyes. Amit said, 'You are welcome' and brushed hairs off her face tenderly. She smiled and fell asleep like a child holding his hand. We are all children Amit thought, God's own children.

Next morning Amit dropped her with two kids on his way to office and brought them back too as they were busy through the day and Rupa called asking to be picked up. He said he would ring when he was close by and they could come down. He did not want to go up or meet Bob. He was also puzzled by the events and turmoil of emotions and had a bad day in office. As Rupa sat in passenger seat he asked, 'Would you like to come back tomorrow?' to which Rupa's reply was a short 'No'.

Rupa was in shock most of the week and hardly spoke. Next Friday evening they went out to dine in a children's place that the kids enjoyed thoroughly. Returning home the children went straight to bed and Amit asked Rupa, 'Can I make some coffee and would you like some liquor?' Rupa nodded. He placed the coffee and liquor and some cognac on the table and they sat face to face.

Amit realized that he would have to start the conversation. He asked, 'Have you been to Bob's house or talk to him?' Rupa replied that he called and asked for Linda, he is missing her. Amit nodded and there was silence again.

Amit asked, 'What are you going to do?'

Rupa replied, 'I am so confused I do not know what to do. I can send Linda back by somehow making her agree and promise to visit her with Ravi though I am not sure that I shall succeed. What else can I do, Bob cannot come and fetch her as he has no transport.'

Amit was silent for there was nothing to say. Rupa as if suddenly waking up shook her head and said, 'The situation is so hopelessly tangled. If he was not sick I could have asked for divorce. It would have been easier if his second love had not deserted him. She left at the first sign of the disease without taking her daughter. He could have forced her but he did not or probably could not, being himself paralysed with fear. It is all on my shoulder now, Bob's mother is dead. If I leave him now, I shall be doing the same thing he did to me. How can I do that? And what happens to Linda, what happens if he dies? I am left alone with two kids and I have no right of custody of Linda and no money of my own' and she started crying 'and there is you.'

Amit stared at her and then said slowly, 'Rupa Roy I love you and I am amazed. You are taking responsibility of all on your shoulder though none of it is your creation. I admire you for that. But do not add me as the proverbial straw on camel's back.'

Before he could finish Rupa cried, 'You shall not be there?'

Amit quietly said, 'I shall always be with you. To me that is what love is all about. You first decide what you want to do. Any or most American women would have walked out of the scene without looking back but not you. That is a greatness I admire, you are like your mother. But there should be a practical approach that is feasible or else you will not be able to untangle it. First of all Linda must be sent back, you cannot hold her, you have no right. Secondly you have to live here with me and not reunite with your husband that will complicate matters. Ravi, I am sure would love to be here once he understands. You two can go as many times as you wish to visit him and take care as much as you can but Ravi, I think would not like to go often. Rest I do not know, we have to consult a lawyer for that. We do not know anything about laws or institutions in this country. Do you know how far Bob is gone and in what condition he is? What is his income?'

Rupa answered, 'He said he had a course of chemotherapy but that did not do much good and he is going on some new course of treatment. The cost of treatment is paid by insurance but apart from that I do not know how much he earns or gets from insurance.'

Amit said, 'Ok, you look after his home comfort as much as you can but do not spend nights there or go to the hospital with him. There must be arrangement in place for taking him to hospital and returning. I shall discuss with people in my company and consult lawyer.'

Rupa said, 'Lawyers are expensive here.'

Amit replied, 'You do not worry about that. You just think of the possibilities of Bob recovering and Bob dying, after suffering for how long nobody knows and your options in either case. You decide what you want to do in both situations without worrying about me, promise that.'

Rupa said, 'No I shall not promise that. I shall keep worrying about you, how much I am hurting you and wonder about what you are.'

Amit smiled, 'Do not place so much faith on me. I may run away or fly away as has been my habit so long. But I am here now.'

Rupa smiled for the first time, 'I shall still keep that faith.'

Thus went their life on a new trajectory. Rupa managed both ends well, keeping Bob in as much comfort as possible without spending nights there and looked after Amit, cooking his and Ravi's meals in time as they liked them and washing things. She renewed her American driving license after going through a few tests and Amit bought a small used car for her. She also managed to get a part time job by virtue of her American Ph.D. taking special science classes in a junior school as an intern. Ravi became less interested in Bob and preferred Amit's company. They drove out often on weekends but Rupa was too tired to move out. Amit's lawyer succeeded in locating Catherine and after some legal processes induced her to come and take Linda away under her care and forego her legacy in Bob's estate, if there be any. They arranged the timing so that she never met Rupa.

Bob was not responding well to treatment and his condition was worsening.

One weekend driving aimlessly alone, Amit came to Laguna Beach area. He knew this was a playboys' haven at one time. But those days have gone as situations have changed and there was the fear of skin cancer caused by too much exposure to sun. The seaside cottages still stood, some of them big enough as luxury residence at one time. Amit left the main roads and entered beachside roads with cottages. Driving slowly he saw a cottage with Hindu religious insignia in the front gate. He was curious, stopped in front and entered, tinkling the small hanging temple bell. Through the small garden he came to a covered veranda with a hall beyond. The hall was a Hindu temple. Finding no one around he entered and was stunned by seeing an image of Goddess Kali standing on alter with another image further up. A serene looking white lady entered and joined her hands at him in namaste.

Utterly surprised he asked, 'Is this a Kali temple?'

The lady nodded and asked, 'Where are you from?'

Amit said 'I am Indian' and smiled because he remembered that at one time Indians had to introduce themselves as Indian from India or Indian from the East or else they were mistaken to be native Indians or Mexicans, especially in the south depending on their skin colour. The days have changed.

The lady asked, 'Are you a Bengali?' and Amit said, 'Yes'.

She said, 'Then you should recognize the upper image. She is a replica of Kali Bhabatarini from Dakshineswar Temple near Calcutta.' Completely taken aback Amit prostrated in front of the image. The lady gave him something to eat as Prasad.

He stammered, 'How come she is here and who are you?'

She said, 'She has come from Dakshineswar and I am her daughter. Priests come from there to worship her on auspicious days three or four times a year.'

'How did you become her daughter?' Amit asked.

'I was blessed,' and she smiled.

'Does that mean you have become a Hindu?' he asked again.

The lady's smile broadened, 'I did not know one has to become a Hindu to worship her. How does one become a Hindu? There is no conversion in your religion. She is the mother of the universe and there are mothers in most religions. She blessed me and I have her mantra given by a great ascetic.'

He moved around the place guided by her. There was a small residential cottage and a small garden, full of flowering small trees, creepers and shrubs, neatly kept. The flowers were familiar to him and were used in the worship of the deity. He asked, 'You have planted them?' She said, 'Yes. They grow nicely here.'

Amit came out bidding her farewell but still wondering, Laguna Beach transferred and transformed from playboys to Goddess Kali! How the human history changes! She is conquering America. He must bring Rupa once to tell her she has nothing to fear.

He walked over the sand dunes down to the beach and sat a little distance away from the water's edge. There were masses of black storm clouds over the Pacific Ocean covering the entire horizon and rising high on the sky above his head turning the sky and the sea like black ink on canvas, in different shades. He stared in fascination. Black is mystery, black is the unknown infinity, beyond which mind cannot go, as if the black Goddess Kali is standing covering the world in love with her fathomless infinity. The grandeur of that darkness was unimaginable. He dug his hands in sand in awe. He picked up two handfuls and stared and looked around. He had a vision that the sand is also infinity spreading as far as eyes went around the world and beyond into planets and the stars and galaxies as the constituent of the material world. He looked back at his hands in awe and thought I am holding in my small hands a part of the infinity. A part of infinity is infinity! Then he raised hands at the pitch black sky and said aloud, 'I am able to hold infinity in my two small hands and releasing it in honour of the great unknown unknowable infinity, the microcosm from my hand with my prayers to the macrocosm, both are same.' He touched his forehead on the ground and released the sand as offering and prayed for safety and happiness of Rupa. He drove back in profound peace.

He returned home and found Rupa in sitting room looking relaxed and rested. He smiled and Rupa asked, 'You are looking so serene and happy without that frown in between eyebrows that was almost a constant feature for last few days, what happened?'

Amit laughed, 'That is an overstatement. It was not a constant feature,' and told her what happened through the day. Her expression changed and she said, 'I want to go one day.' Amit said, 'Sure you will.'

Months passed and the routine of their lives continued. Only Ravi underwent some change growing up and developing new interests. He was becoming computer savvy rather fast. Amit bought him a nice laptop with internet connection and assorted accessories. His knowledge base increased very fast and he was doing well in school. He was good in physical activities too, his passion being baseball and he was a good pitcher. A new single bed was purchased for him and it was placed in mother's room. After some days he asked Amit in presence of Rupa, 'Mother's room has a lot of things. Can I place my bed in your room?' Amit looked at Rupa and said, 'Of course you can if your mother does not mind,' and Rupa said with a smile, 'It is ok with me.'

Ravi looked up Bob's disease on computer one day and asked Amit, 'He is not getting well, is he?' Amit replied, 'Does not seem to be but then doctors are not giving up hope' and Ravi looked at him in a peculiar way. Amit asked him one day, 'How do you compare your life in Calcutta with your life here? Of course you were much smaller then.' With a lot of gravity he replied, 'Not much different but mother had less work and you were not there.' Amit hugged him and said, 'Everything will be ok' and he said, 'Yeah I know.' Amit looked at him with deep affection and smiled, the boy was growing up faster in adversity. He was also becoming darker, a handsome boy with brownish tint in his hair.

Bob was not getting better. He was developing secondary symptoms. One day he bled from the nose and fortunately it was during the day and Rupa became alarmed. She called the hospital without disturbing Amit. They asked her to give a nose pack with lint and cotton and told her how to do it. They assured it would stop and in any case he was due at the clinic the next day and to call again if bleeding did not stop. The lint and cotton had been supplied from the clinic anticipating the event and Rupa did it expertly. Bob could no longer continue the part time job and that money stopped, but Rupa was earning enough by now to manage Bob's household.

The day came when Amit was called back to India. He had completed his assignment and the company had grown, drawing higher profit. He had made a number of new software to serve different areas of business in the western world not only USA and they were patented and gave a steady profit. The market was expanding in India and new innovations were necessary. Without informing Rupa he asked for an extension of his term and a three month extension was granted. Being a born leader he was popular wherever he worked. In addition to being talented and innovative he had no mean streak and being jovial and accommodative he was liked by all. His unusual life, achievements and happy go lucky attitude with serious sense of responsibility was making him almost an icon. The story of his life with Rupa circulated among people close to him and he was admired for his honesty, courage and humanism by those who knew it. He slowly planned his departure avoiding any difficulty for Rupa and Ravi. He knew that if he needed and asked for, another extension for three months could be granted. But he did not want to ask unless it was absolutely essential. The company felt responsible for him and he was also responsible for his company. He thought out the plan and made arrangements slowly.

He had to first know Bob's prognosis and what the doctors felt, how long he might live. This was the most difficult task. An ethical and legal bond of privacy strongly existed in the medical world that was impossible to break. He suggested to Rupa casually one day that she might visit the hospital occasionally with Bob, now that the legal situation was not that difficult and people knew her. It will be encouraging to Bob and doctors may need to talk to the next of kin.

She was obviously the only one, his legally wedded wife. Rupa stared at him and did not comment. She was so intelligent and impossible to fool. She nodded and said, 'Yes it may help him' but her eyes asked, 'Why now?' but she did not utter.

A few weeks later she told Amit, 'The doctors said there was nothing new to try. Symptomatic treatment will continue to give him relief. They did not mention any time frame.'

Amit nodded nonchalantly, 'There may be time.' Rupa challenged, 'How do you know?'

Amit became alert, 'He is looking better nowadays, you said so.'

Rupa said, 'You are forgetting that my father died of cancer. I have seen that in the last days he became jovial and energetic so that when he actually died we as kids were surprised. I was too young to serve him. I am compensating for that now.'

Amit said, 'I am sorry I did not know that.'

Rupa flashed, 'What, did you not know that my father died of cancer?'

Amit alarmed sat up, 'No, I did not know that they sometimes feel better in the last days. I have never seen a cancer patient.'

Rupa said, 'They do sometimes. It is like a convict who learns after prolonged trial that a death sentence has been passed. They sometimes actually gain weight.' After a pause she added, 'But there is something else in your mind you do not want to tell me.'

Amit asked in surprise, 'What can that be? I have never kept anything from you, have I?'

Rupa said, 'No you have not but you are doing it now.'

Amit realized hedging was impossible, so he got up leaving whatever he was doing, came near her and sat down. 'I wanted to keep it from you as long as I could to postpone my agony as much as yours. I have been asked to return to India and the order came almost two months back; I am on extension. I can ask for further extension but I do not know whether it would be granted. I am supposed to leave after one month and I do not want to apply for a further extension. They may or may not refuse, but what do I say?'

Tears welled up in Rupa's eyes, 'So you plan to leave us?'

He came close to hold her hand, 'No I am not leaving you. I just wanted to know how long shall I wait for you. I can wait a lifetime. Your love and being able to love you over last two years has transformed me and will last a lifetime. Seeing your sense of responsibility and commitment even in adversity has taken away my high ego. But about you and Ravi, you are now adjusted to life here and so is Ravi. I shall make all provisions for you that may last for months or even longer. After that you can choose your life freely and I shall wait for you my whole life if need be. But I do not want to tie you down. You make your free choice. You will be self-earning, as you have become a very coveted teacher. Ravi may like to settle here. You remember you hated to be dependent on me? I want to keep your alternatives open so that you come to me out of your own free will and not under compulsion of circumstances as you did last time.'

Rupa started crying freely, 'Oh my God, have I not gone through enough tests in my life? Why do I have to suffer more?'

Amit embraced her and wiped her tears, 'You are not suffering alone, I am suffering with you. This short separation would not have mattered if we were married, happens all the time. It is happening because you are married to someone else. You finish that and the situation has offered us a choice, I did nothing. I just saw it as such, did not like, but accepted as God's will if you like or an opportunity to rethink our relationship if you like that. But let us not make a bad start through bitterness that I hope I can ask from you.'

Rupa stopped crying but raised her red eyes to Amit and said, 'I shall miss you so much' and could not finish as she choked and tears flowed again.

He said soothing words and made her quiet and said, 'Let us discuss practicalities Rupa there is not much time left' and she shook her head like a little girl and said, 'No I shall not listen, you kiss me first,' and they were locked for a time and taking a long breath he said, 'I shall sleep with you tonight,' and she laughed. Inwardly she knew he was right.

He continued, 'I have paid six months' advance rent for this apartment you can recover the balance if you leave earlier,' she kept making noises and kissing, 'Listen to me, I shall make you nominee and make my bank account joint taking half the money with me,' amid interruptions, and he gave a big squeeze to her breast and she said, 'Uh do that again darling make love to me' and he looked back at his room and finding Ravi deep in sleep carried her to her room. Before falling asleep she mumbled, 'I know dear that your arrangements will be as perfect as your software but where shall I get the hardware' and fell asleep in his arms.

Amit woke up early and kissed and cuddled her tenderly. She moaned, sighed and gradually came out of sleep. He kissed her and said, 'Darling I am leaving you with full confidence knowing that you shall manage everything perfectly. You may even like that life of freedom and want to settle down here. You are free to decide your life.'

Rupa was now fully awake and wide eyed, 'You will not miss me?'

Amit hastened to reply, 'Of course I will. I shall be devastated but I am a vagabond and will probably adjust, I do not know how. But I want you to become yourself, settled in your own life and then if you still want this vagabond and no one else then come to me.'

Rupa sat up, 'You want to test me?'

Amit said, 'No I want you to test yourself and decide with your free will. We often do not know our own self, our own mind until we are in a different environment. You came here prepared to settle if you found Bob and he still wanted you. You were curious because he was sending Ravi's maintenance but not signing divorce. You thought something was amiss, something you did not know. You have found out what you did not know and are doing what as a wife you would have done. Now follow that course and settled in that life if you still want to come back to me and not under duress, I shall be overwhelmed and I can wait for that. If we continue as we are then at some point there may be regret. That is the worst thing. Life will become bitter. I play for high stake. And I must say I admire Bob for continuing to pay Ravi's maintenance through difficulty. The two of you were made for each other, but fate intervened. I shall wait for a woman like you for my entire life if you decide to come to me.'

Rupa asked, 'And what if you find someone else?'

Amit laughed, 'The chances are very very remote. You are my first love and at my age it will be difficult to adjust to a second love. That happens in calf love or young love not in middle age love.'

Rupa made a face, 'Oh you are middle aged? I didn't even know. How old you actually are, ok you don't have to tell me. If middle age love is this good it is much much better than young love. Amit Roy will you tell me what stuff are you made of?'

Amit laughed again, 'May be the same as you. You have revealed yourself I have not.'

Rupa kept looking at him and said, 'You must take me to Laguna Beach before you leave.'

Next day he sat with Ravi and explained all the arrangements and the reasons for it. He listened gravely. 'Do you think you can handle all that Ravi and look after your mother now that you are a big boy' and he replied 'yep can do.' 'And when Bob dies and everything is clear will you come back with your mother to me' and again he said seriously 'yep will do.' At his age he could not accept Bob in sickness not having any earlier memory and never referred to him as father. He tousled his hair and said 'good boy' and kissed him that was still possible he thought, and sighed, 'For how long? Is this the last chance?'

Ripples on the Shore

Atin and Madhuri started their new life in the house that Atin's parents left behind. It has been converted to a modern house with a lawn intervening between the two buildings, the residence and the outhouse. Madhuri started decorating with zeal but keeping within the bounds of what she thought the old couple, now dead would have liked. She mixed old age comfort with style as rich people used to live in days gone by. She did not complete with haste like in the books, but in a leisurely way as a lived in house does and not out of a catalogue, done and finished.

Atin's surgical practice flourished increasing his income. His practice was mainly in the hospital he was attached to but he was called from other places for consultation in serious cases. In the outhouse he opened a free consulting chamber on Sundays for local people or any other day if the situation demanded. He knew and abided by the exhortation of Susruta, the father of surgery not only in India but the world over, who lived four thousand years back. Susruta wrote in Susruta Samhita "Only the union of medicine and surgery constitutes the complete doctor. The doctor who lacks the knowledge of one of these branches is like a bird with only one wing."

This has been paralleled in surgical sciences with the advice that a surgeon is a doctor first and then a surgeon, an operating physician. Unfortunately in modern surgical practices in India the surgeon is mainly known as a 'cutter' not knowing anything beyond and a distressingly large number of surgeons even take pride in that sort of practice. This intellectual bankruptcy bedevils the profession. A part of this psychology is driven by financial concerns of sharing profits with fellow specialists. This increases the cost of treatment unnecessarily, in many cases draining the patient. Reading Susruta early in his career he had studied assiduously all branches of medical science seriously in his undergraduate career. He saw all types of patients in his free chamber, advising treatment when he could, and referring others to the appropriate doctor who he knew were honest and competent. He had felt that the main distress the patient and his relatives suffer from is helplessness, unable to decide the course of action from differing choices put before them by different doctors. So his treatment in many cases is to guide them and he neither charges for that nor takes commissions from the referred places. He sends them to people and places where he knows they will get sympathetic treatment. This alone was a service in a heterogeneous largely poor country like India where an organized system had not yet developed and some doctors and hospitals milked that deficit.

Although Atin earned a lot of money, Madhuri did not allow that to influence their lifestyle, living in conformity with the middle class neighbourhood where they lived. She knew that money in large excess of necessity for a professional could become a curse in capitulating to greed and her family had to be protected from that. So she had a helping hand for anybody in distress saving only for future security that cannot be foreseen. Growing up in village she had the mentality of collective social security. Atin handed over his earnings to her to disburse in any way she liked.

A substantial portion of Atin's earning was spent by him in researching problems he faced and had no answer. When he could not find answers from books he tried to find them by himself. There was no fund and no mentality for research in Bengal where it had flourished for a short time in colonial times. There were many disease conditions in a poor tropical country for which no answers were provided from western texts and no interest existed. He spent money and effort to investigate problems he faced by sending patients and samples to sister institutions where such special facilities existed. Naturally for some of them he had to pay.

Thus their life went until after two years of marriage Madhuri conceived. Some changes are inevitable in family life when a child is expected. Madhuri carried her pregnancy without any fuss and both mother and baby were normal. Atin tried to spend more time at home as there were no other elder at home and cut down on some of his activities. Madhuri's mother was unaccustomed to city life and could not leave her father for any length of time. Madhuri told Atin not to fuss about her pregnancy. She was a village girl and pregnancy was an event that was commonplace in the village and went the nature's course. Atin insisted on appointing a cook to look after her diet so that the mother and the baby were properly nourished without giving the burden of cooking on Madhuri. She agreed to that but supervised the lady so appointed. She was good in ordinary cooking and Madhuri taught her special dishes to her taste. With these minor alterations the ship of life was steadied in the family.

Madhuri entered the third trimester of pregnancy and her abdominal bulge became significantly visible but not abnormally so. Sonogram showed the baby to be normal in every respect. Identifying the baby to be a male or female child was banned by law and no exception was made even for Atin. There was a bit of surplus amniotic fluid around the child, more than normal but not alarmingly so. Atin asked Madhuri to be careful and not do any strenuous work, rest for major part of the day and avoid infection at all costs. Her toilet was made exclusive for her and Atin took personal care in keeping it disinfected. Madhuri laughed at Atin's concern and joked about it as father's anxiety in first pregnancy.

'Will you be as careful if we have a second pregnancy dear,' she asked him 'I shall be an old wife then? Will you be as much nervous for an old wife?'

Atin became so upset by this simple joke that he did not talk to her for one whole day. The tension was telling on him and Madhuri was surprised, but understood. She realized that mother's death and Sohini's accident when he least expected was playing on his mind probably not even consciously and he was worried about Madhuri's safety. The memory of bad luck long forgotten comes back haunting in another tense situation in life. Madhuri understood but did not like it.

The relaxed household became a little bit tense and Madhuri could not stand the gaunt face of Atin. She complained and implored him to be relaxed, that nothing will go wrong and doctor has said everything was right and she would have a normal delivery. He would smile at that but the smile would look more ghastly on that tense face. Madhuri gave up and prayed to God that everything goes well. Atin was not sleeping in the same bed with her for the fear of inadvertent trauma to her. Instead a night nurse was appointed. That made her more upset.

Two weeks before the expected day of delivery Madhuri had leakage of amniotic fluid. It happened at night and the nurse woke up Atin. Awakened from deep sleep he was confused at first and then alarmed, he rushed to Madhuri's bedside. At first he was at a loss what to do. He called up the gynecologist, his colleague. His description of his wife's condition was so garbled that the gynecologist, woken from sleep could not make head or tail of what he was saying. He asked Atin to calm down and talk slowly. He understood what was wrong and advised to remove Madhuri to the hospital. He reached hospital almost at the same time as Atin and Madhuri and asked both to calm down as it was not such a catastrophe. He examined and assured both that the leakage was not severe and the baby was fine. Madhuri would have to lie flat in bed with foot end of bed raised and antibiotics were given. Sonogram and fetal monitoring were necessary. It was difficult to arrange that at the dead of night but they were arranged. While all those were being arranged Atin restlessly paced up and down the corridor. Nobody dared to ask him to sit down and relax.

All examinations completed, the gynecologist took Atin to his office and sat him down offering a cup of coffee that Atin declined. He asked Atin not to be tense as this was not a serious situation. Madhuri was near term and the baby had not grown to full body weight but was not small either. The worst thing that could happen was a Cesarean section if she drained more fluid or the baby was in distress and both baby and mother would be safe. It will not be a case of premature child, may need close care for a few days but nothing more. Madhuri has to be in hospital because she may need the operation at short notice. But there is no need to panic. He asked Atin, 'I learnt that you have been in nervous tension for last few weeks. You know that is bad for the mother; then why? Not that this rupture has been caused by that but

the pregnant mother near term need to be kept relaxed and happy.' Atin
said, 'I am sorry but you would not understand why.' He said, 'May be
I can guess knowing you almost since our childhood but get rid of the
ghosts and get some sleep. You can sleep in the hospital if you like or
better go home, I shall be here.'

Atin went home but could hardly sleep. He got up early, got ready
and turned up at the hospital at unearthly hour and asked the nurse
how Madhuri was. She said she was fine, the leakage has reduced
but there is still small treacle, and baby was doing fine. He went to
the gynecologist's office and woke him up. Bleary eyed he rose
and asked, 'Why have you come back at this unearthly hour?' Atin
said, 'To wake you up so that you can go home and freshen up and
have some rest.' He smiled, 'You got more marks than me even in
Obstetrics and Gynecology but you have forgotten that gynecologists
and obstetricians hardly sleep. I shall have a look at Madhuri and cool
you down if that is ever possible and then go.' Atin hung around in
the hospital though he had no work having cancelled his schedule. He
went to Madhuri's room a few times but did not disturb her if she was
sleeping or had her eyes closed. Once Madhuri caught him and asked
him to come in and tenderly held his hand and asked, 'Have you slept
last night? Did they cook your food well and have you eaten?' She
smiled and said, 'Take it easy darling I am fine and this brat inside is
kicking me hard. So there is nothing to worry and I cannot bear to see
you so upset.' Atin said, 'No I am all right, do not worry for me, stay
relaxed' and kissing her forehead went out. Madhuri kept looking at
him and the nurse wiped her tear.

On the third night Madhuri started having labour pain. The fetal
monitor showed unacceptable rise in the child's heart rate. The
gynecologist was informed and he ordered the operation theatre to be
ready and rushed to the hospital. Atin was also informed and he also
rushed but took longer as his house was a bit further. By the time he
reached Madhuri had already been wheeled to the theatre. He entered
the operation suite but did not enter the theatre sitting in the surgeons'
room. After waiting for what he thought were ages he heard the
lusty cry of a newborn child and relaxed slightly. After another three
quarters of an hour the gynecologist came out and informed that both

mother and child were all right, it was a boy. At long last after how many days he could not count, Atin was relaxed.

The gynecologist laughed at his condition and said, 'This is what happens when I operate on a surgeon's wife. They are the worst case because they think of all the rare complications that can happen during operation that will fill a few pages of answer paper and get so afraid while they themselves do much more serious surgery. But to tell you frankly it is a good thing that we operated because the baby had the chord around the neck, which was not detected in the sonogram although suspected because the baby's head was not going down, but not told to you. It is a good thing that she had that leakage or she would not have been in the hospital and operated so quickly. There is a silver lining to everything and obstetricians believe in God more than general surgeons of your eminence Sir.'

After they were wheeled to the recovery room Atin peeped and saw that both mother and baby were sleeping peacefully and their breathing was normal. He heaved a sigh of relief and after loitering a little went back home to sleep. He returned in the evening and saw that Madhuri was awake, though a bit drowsy. He held her hand and she squeezed and looking up at him said, 'Now I hope you are relaxed as I have not left you like Sohini.' He asked in surprise, 'How did you know?' Madhuri smiled, 'We women are the mother race and men are all children, sometimes difficult to manage like that brat in the neonatal ward, but we always know. So never try to cheat me,' and smiled again with another squeeze of his hand.

A few nights later Atin was awakened in the early hours of the morning by the shrill ringing of the phone and jumped out of bed seeing the hospital number and almost shouted, 'What has happened' only to hear the voice of the emergency medical officer, 'Sir a boy in early teens has been brought with a fulminating appendicitis and he is very toxic.' Atin was irritated and angrily said, 'It is not my admission day and I have said that no patient be admitted under me till I say so.' The flustered EMO said shakily, 'I know Sir, but this is a foreigner and has come specifically for you. He will not admit his son under anybody else. What do I do?' With resignation Atin said, 'Ok you admit and inform my resident to have a look and call me.' There was no point to try and get more sleep so he left the bed. The resident called after sometime and confirmed the diagnosis saying, 'He is quite toxic having suffered since the afternoon. I have started intravenous and given antibiotics but he needs to be operated.' Atin sighed and said, 'Get the operation theatre ready. I want to operate before the day's schedule starts or else it will be much delayed. I do not want to hang around.' He reached the hospital and went straight for the operation theatre meeting the boy's father on the way, a tall gentleman with an English accent who said he was so grateful that he could come so early. Atin nodded and went inside and examined the boy and asked him to be wheeled in. Salil had already arrived. It was an obstructed appendicitis swollen with pus and inflammation. He completed the operation taking extra care not to spill the infection and cleaning the area and abdominal wall with antiseptics. After coming out he met the father again and told him that the boy should be Ok in a few days and asked why he looked for him. He replied, 'We are here on holiday. The boy got sick before lunch and vomited. We asked our friends and they gave your name and the hospital but we could not contact you because you were on leave. At last in desperation we came to the emergency and asked for you. It is so good of you to come when you are on leave and we shall remain ever grateful' and shook his hand. Atin nodded and said, 'He should be able to go home within a week' and went to the rooms to have a look at Madhuri.

Madhuri was surprised to see him, 'What are you doing here so early?'

He said, 'It was an emergency. A foreigner was asking for me so I thought it was better to come. I would have come in any case to see you.'

Madhuri said, 'But you are on leave.'

Atin shrugged, 'He insisted on seeing me. I could not refuse.'

Madhuri asked, 'What was the case?'

Atin said, 'A simple one of acute appendicitis.'

Madhuri mused, 'Appendicitis and a foreigner asking specially for you,' smiled and added 'I told you shall have international fame some day. Did the nurses take good care of you dear' and winked at him. Atin laughed and said, 'Stop the nonsense' and kissed her.

Madhuri went home after a few more days. She had recovered and so had the child who was called Raju by the nurses for some unknown reason. He was a lovely child with a great appetite and Madhuri whispered in Atin's ear, 'Like you' and he blushed and looked around admonishing Madhuri, 'Stop it' and laughed.

He rejoined his work and was overwhelmed with waiting patients. The days were busy. The foreigner boy recovered fast and was discharged. The father met him as he was entering hospital and thanked. After usual politeness Atin asked whether he had a transport and he said that he had and pointed.

His operating schedule was light that day and he returned home early. Madhuri was delighted to see him and remarked, 'What is the matter; you have become a petticoat man?'

Atin laughed, 'The schedule was light and I am becoming home addict but do not have any misconception, it is not for you but that little man.' Both laughed in happiness and looked at the child happily asleep.

Madhuri said, 'The weather is so nice that I want to go down and sit in the back lawn. I can negotiate the stairs now, I have no pain.'

Atin said 'I can carry you down.'

Madhuri said, 'Don't even try. I am so fat and heavy now. My doctor has allowed me to take the stairs one at a time. Just support me.'

Atin was alarmed, 'Be careful now' and they slowly went down the stairs and sat on the chairs placed in the lawn.

After settling Madhuri said, 'Now tell me how your day went. You are looking happy and relaxed after a long time.'

Atin said, 'Yes I am. I discharged Sohini's son today.'

Madhuri sat forward, 'What, Sohini's son?'

Atin said in matter of fact manner, 'Yes, that boy with appendectomy.'

Madhuri's eyes dilated, 'He is Sohini's son? And I thought my husband is internationally famous? Oh God! Did she talk to you?'

Atin said, 'No. I saw her sitting in the car looking away.'

Madhuri said, 'She did not even thank you? She must have sent her son to you without mentioning your name to husband. She must have told through her mother. I would have loved to meet her, she is a fine woman and still in love with you.'

Atin laughed, 'Feminine imagination at play again?'

Madhuri eagerly said, 'She still loves you darling or else she would have met you to thank you. Did she look as beautiful as before?'

Atin said, 'I did not see any detail but she seemed to look the same. She had a younger son with her.'

Madhuri sighed, 'Not fat and rounded like me. Were you happy to see her, must be?'

Atin frowned, 'You are talking nonsense now.'

Madhuri hurriedly added, 'Nothing wrong in that. I feel so proud when I see other women admiring you. But tell me darling this connection between love and appendix in your life is it not curious?'

Atin laughed loudly, 'Your new discovery. If I had as many loves as appendectomies I have done I would have been dead by now.'

Madhuri held his hand, 'I am not jealous darling. I have not heard your hearty laughter for so long, I love to hear that. I love you so much and trust you. We are starting a new life and we shall be happy in that won't we?'

Atin looked seriously at her, 'I love you more than I ever loved Sohini, I did not know then what love was.'

Madhuri held his hand and emotionally said, 'I know that darling but it is nice of you to say it. It is nice to hear once in a while specially after pregnancy. But I was just teasing you for fun not seriously' and she laughed.

The sun went down and Madhuri shivered. Atin was alarmed and holding her carefully took her up the stairs.

Denizens of the Sea

Bob died within two months of Amit's departure. He died in sleep and Rupa was by his side. She was staying the nights for the last few days. Ravi allowed her that when she explained that the day was near. He had matured fast and did not mind staying alone in house at night. Rupa called him on phone to give the news and asked him whether he could miss school for a day. Rupa called up his school and gave them the news and got permission. She then went and picked him up after giving him a sumptuous breakfast. She was feeling lonely and needed someone by her side. She did not send any message to Amit, need not bother him.

She called the hospital to give them the news and asked for necessary papers. They were kind enough to send a doctor to confirm death, and sent all necessary certificates. She got busy with arrangements for funeral and connected to the nearest funeral parlor. They sent all papers for signature and after those were completed they removed the body for embalming and the date for funeral was fixed as soon as possible. There was no one else to inform but she contacted their lawyer to send a message to Catherine so that Linda would know, even if she could not come because of the distance. Bob had very little money in his bank account and no other savings. Rupa had become a co-signatory to that account and withdrew whatever cash was there and closed the account. She made necessary purchases that included one black dress and veil for her and the first black suite for Ravi. On the funeral day a black car was sent for them and that was the only one that followed the cortege to the cemetery.

After the priest's chanting the mother and son together did the first earth on the coffin and stood until it was covered. Rupa could not check her tears remembering their early days and felt sorry for Bob that a life that was good and noble was finished without reaching its potential. She was happy that she had given him company in his last days and did her duty as wife. Bob used to tell her often in these last days that he did no mistake in choosing his wife and it was just bad luck that they could not enjoy their life together apart from the first couple of years. He apologized many times for his affair with Catherine and every time he tried to talk about the circumstances, Rupa would stop him by saying, 'There is no point to discuss the past and blame.' Only once Bob talked about Amit and said he was a great man and he is dying peacefully in the knowledge that he is not leaving Rupa and Ravi lonely. Otherwise there was not much conversation between them apart from food and drug. Rupa remembered all that standing by his bier. She felt happy that she could do what she did. She had arranged a headstone and wrote the inscription mentioning his parents.

The black car dropped them to Bob's house and after collecting her personal items, she drove her car with Ravi back to her apartment. Bob had completed deal with a property dealer to sell his apartment after his death and give the money to Rupa. Rupa did not want to remove a single article of furniture or gadget from the house and it was sold wholesale by the dealer. They lived a few gloomy days together and then the days continued on the usual routine. She talked to Ravi about his father, and what sort of man he was and their student days and that he sent money regularly for his schooling at Calcutta, so that he developed some respect for his father that she thought was essential for normal development.

Only once he asked about Amit and Rupa said, 'He is waiting at Calcutta for us to return if we wanted.'

She asked him, 'Would you like to go back to him and study there?'

Ravi answered like an adult, 'What do you think, would it not be better? It is kind of lonely here,' and she tousled his hair and said, 'May be we would do that but we have to settle a few things here and finish your semester so that you do not lose a year. Would you like to go back to your old school or would you like to change?'

Ravi said gravely, 'Nothing wrong with that school Ma.'

She did not tell Ravi that among a few things to settle she was thinking for the last few months about Asim, her brother. He was still lost. She did not want to leave without clearing that unknown. She felt responsible in the same way she thought for Bob. It was a duty not only to him but their parents too and she could not be happy without knowing what has happened to him and how or where he is. She thought of the lawyer Amit employed to trace Catherine. She did not know how much he charged for that. She thought of contacting Amit but did not want to disturb him for her personal problem. Actually they had not communicated much in these months being busy in their own life. She called up Mr. Anderson the lawyer and introduced herself but he already knew her. She fixed an appointment and met him. He listened through the whole story calmly without interrupting and then confirmed a few details. Rupa liked his style. He asked, 'Do you know whether he was involved in any crime?'

Rupa said, 'I have no idea. But his ex-wife made a remark that he could be in correctional centre for alcoholics.'

Mr. Anderson said, 'But you have seen some homosexual tendencies in the past.'

Rupa hesitated, 'I do not know if I can say that with surety. He came out of it.'

Mr. Anderson said, 'It is possible to slide back to that under the circumstances. Have you any idea of his last employment,' and Rupa said 'No.'

He said, 'It will probably be correct to search first from the crime angle though I hate to say that to you.'

Rupa asked about the charges and he brushed it off saying he did not know whether he will succeed so there is no question of charges now.

Then he asked, 'Mr. Roy has left his organization, has he left USA?' Rupa confirmed and he asked what her situation was at present. She said, 'I shall join him after I am through with this' and added, 'Most likely.'

The lawyer looked at her for some time and asked, 'And how are you doing now?' took some personal details and said, 'It is not common in this country to look for a lost brother whose whereabouts you have not known for years and he has not gone to war or something, but from the last case I have known that you are somewhat unusual, if you do not mind. I shall try my best but cannot promise success. It will take time. Do not worry about charges now.'

After almost a month he called on phone and asked her to meet him in office fixing a date and time. She remembered that last time the business was concluded on phone.

At the appointed time he made her sit comfortably and asked whether she would like to have tea or coffee or something and already nervous Rupa asked for a glass of water.

Then he said rather abruptly, 'Your brother is in jail.' Rupa sat forward and leaned back again after she absorbed the shock and stared blankly at the lawyer.

He continued, 'He was convicted for murder of his gay companion. The record says his name was Fish, no other name of the victim recorded.'

Rupa stared vacantly. After some pause the lawyer cleared his throat and said, 'That was first conviction. During his first internment he murdered a fellow prisoner and he was declared mentally challenged and convicted as a dangerous psychopathic criminal and imprisoned in High Risk category. He avoided death sentence by being mentally sick.'

Rupa was stunned and speechless. The lawyer was sympathetic but little he could do. After some time Rupa almost whispered, 'Can I see him?'

Mr. Anderson said, 'I shall advise you against it. Prison visit is very traumatic. Permission for visiting a high risk convict is difficult to get. He is kept locked up and when he comes out for obligatory exercise hours he is kept in handcuff and chain. If you get permission he will be brought out wearing those and sit in front of you for a 'No Touch' visit beyond a thick glass partition guarded by prison guards. The whole environment and people are such that it is no place for a person like you from a different country.'

Rupa was deathly pale and silent. After a while she whispered again, 'Can I see him just once and come away?'

Mr. Anderson sighed and said, 'Misses hmm' and then he stopped in confusion and continued, 'It is difficult to get permission to visit a high risk category patient. You have to give all your personal details and identifications, relationship with the convict and purpose of visit that you have not done so far. Your application if approved will be sent to the convict for his acceptance that he wants to meet you and then you will be given a date and time to go to that out of the way place obeying all sorts of regulation regarding dress and what you carry and may be even undergo body search. The permission if granted will take a long time to come. And then how shall you reach the prison? Your son will not be allowed because he is not next of kin. Where will you keep him? Your brother no longer remembers you, let him live rest of his life like that.'

Rupa asked again, 'Where is he?'

Mr. Anderson said, 'In a prison and correctional facility not far from here, a few hours' drive. For a time he was in San Quentin prison and then transferred here. But for you to drive that distance alone and come back after reaching in time and passing through God knows how many protocols is in my opinion an unnecessary exercise.'

Rupa openly in tears said, 'Please make the application and I shall ask Amit for his opinion. I owe this to my late father and mother. You will not understand that. I shall do this somehow. Just one visit' she implored.

Mr. Anderson stared with a mixed feeling of awe and admiration and said, 'I shall do it for you, something I have never done before.'

A few weeks later he called, 'Your permission has come to visit Sunday after next at 11-30 AM to 12 noon. Here is the plan I have drawn. I am free that day, my wife taking the kids to a swimming day out. I shall drive you and your son early in the morning and wait with him in the visitor centre while you take your trip in a bus to the prison visiting facilities with a crowd the like of which you have never seen and hopefully never see again. This service is free because I have never seen a determined lady like you and the reasons for that. I shall mail you the dress regulations and what you can carry and what checks will be done and at what point. Memorize it and carry a copy in case someone violates it that sometimes happens. Please do not wear your Indian dress, though theoretically it would pass nicely not having metals and without body exposure only if you do not wear any jewelry, which is forbidden; people will stare at you more than at the convicts,' and he laughed that was also a first time.

Rupa thanked him but was surprised by his offer. Then she brushed it off her mind. He looked a fine enough gentleman and a lawyer and known over quite some time. She shrugged off the apprehension. She thought of writing and informing Amit but decided not to. He would unnecessarily worry. She thought of mother and what she might have said, probably would have said that she could not protect herself with fear but only with courage and strength of mind. In any case this was the best possible solution, carrying her lawyer and her son. She was feeling scared of driving alone on unknown roads.

When the email came she looked at the dress requirements. It has to be loose fitting non-transparent without metal buttons, belts and bra support, well below the knees more or less round neck and no bare midriff, covered shoulder and arms and in proper colours avoiding orange, blue or green. The last one was not mentioned but shades could be confusing. She must wear flat shoes without metals. Only handbag allowed was a small six inch by eight inch plastic bag and nothing else, no food or drink. No headgears allowed. Any deviation will lead to body check by the same sex, how ghastly, Rupa thought of those Amazons seen on television. Any paper, letter or photograph carried has to be submitted for checking. Sunglasses have to be left in the car. If it is raining waterproof has to be taken off and probably subjected to body check. It was better to get wet as long as the dress was not remotely transparent. She now realized why Anderson mentioned Indian dress because a salwar and full arm kamiz would have been most suitable. The admonitions were more stringent than her mother's when visiting temples.

The drive in the early morning was pleasant with a cool breeze and clear sky. They reached the prison complex by 10-30 AM as per instruction and were surprised by the large crowd. The car could enter through the outer gate and driven to the car park near the visitor centre. Anderson guided Rupa near the buses to the one for the 'no touch' visit. The venue and entrance for different categories were different. After passing through metal detectors and checking of ID and other papers she entered the hall beyond which were the glass panes of visiting area. She had to wait till her name and number were called. There were not many people in this area. The paper said that the prisoner would be brought in handcuff and chain and seated, the handcuffs would be removed and then the visitor would be called. In Rupa's case due to some confusion in timing she saw Asim with the handcuffs and was shocked to see him. It was difficult to recognize him in prison attire. They sat facing each other across the glass. The visiting would last fifteen minutes but none of them could talk for first three or four minutes. The guards were standing fairly close. Asim spoke first, 'Hi sis how are you?' through the microphone.

Rupa recovered and said, 'Not too bad and how are you?'

Asim smiled and said, 'You can see for yourself, not too bad really,' and waived around. Then he asked, 'How did mother die? What happened in the end?'

Rupa said, 'She had this massive heart attack you know. She recovered from it and was weak not recovering properly. So the doctors did a coronary bypass and that made her somewhat better.'

Asim sniggered at the mention of doctors and said, 'Butchers not doctors. They should be in this place not me. You know how they butchered father and he also betrayed us never telling us how bad he was. Do you remember that,' and his face distorted with anger.

Rupa mildly said, 'He used to love you very much, used to say that you will do very well in life.'

Before she could finish Asim shouted in anger, 'All false all false,' in excitement he was almost getting up from chair and was restrained and he calmed down.

Rupa was afraid to say anything. Asim was grumbling, 'Everybody betrays.'

He looked at Rupa and said, 'Do you know that Rati betrayed me? She was fornicating with her boss just to get a promotion,' and he started crying that was ghastly to see.

He was silent for sometime morosely looking at her and she felt so sorry.

At last he asked, 'How is Bob, your hubby doing?'

Rupa said, 'He is dead, died last month from leukemia.'

Asim said, 'Good for you. He was no good son of . . . . . . '

Rupa was at a loss. She timidly said, 'Is there nobody you love and who loves you?'

Asim smiled, 'Yes you, I love you and you love me that is enough.'

Rupa said, 'But you are in jail and I have nobody to love me,' and she wiped her tears with her bare hands.

Asim was genuinely disturbed and said, 'Don't cry just let me get out of this place. These jokers are holding me here because I killed some no good mother . . . .who were destined to die. Do you remember Fish?' That son of . . . . . . .tried to betray me because another bastard promised to feed him better. So I killed him. Is that wrong?'

Rupa tried again, 'Mother used to love you very much. She was so happy when you went to Calcutta to see her.'

Asim was more sober, 'Yes she really used to love me. But unfortunately she married the wrong guy.'

Rupa had enough and the bell also sounded ending the visit. She came out morosely got in the bus and reached the visitor centre. Ravi saw her first and came running hugged her. 'Ma Ma this place is awesome, look so many games to play. Uncle here said he will bring me here again.' Rupa unmindfully replied, 'No Ravi we shall never come here.'

Anderson had a look at Rupa and understood everything. Without a word to her, he called Ravi, 'Come Ravi this is lunchtime and I am awfully hungry are you not' and Ravi said, 'You bet I am' and he said, 'Let us go, there is this awesome place where you can eat as much as you like and don't have to pay' and Ravi jumped, 'That is awesome' and Rupa laughed. She looked around and saw the world was as it was, just the same and not so bad. Where was she so long, a dark gloomy place; poor Asim! An intense father hatred arising out of his resentment at his death has vitiated his entire world. Mother was afraid of this and tried very hard to prevent. If only Rati was really in love with him!

She remembered Amit and warmth spread through her. That was her place. Never lose what God offers. She will go back as soon as she can. Never play with fate she told herself, it may turn before you know it.

That night she wrote a long message to Amit, her first, describing her life as well as she could paint and Ravi's progress in studies and extracurricular activity. How happy he was. She also wrote sweet words for him how she missed him but did not mention anything about her return. Do not capitulate too soon she told herself. Let him simmer a little. She wrote everything except her visit to Asim and any hope about her imminent return. Instead she cooked up a story about a visit to the ocean park to see the sharks, the denizens of the sea. Who did she go with? Could he guess? She had to leave now, would write the rest later. She waited for him to beg her return. There was little risk to play with this denizen at least for now.

The game was difficult to play with a man like Amit. He sounded very glad that she enjoyed her stay in USA so much, but warned her about the denizens not only of the seas but land too. He advised her that they were not all bad; some of them were interesting to play with if she could handle them. If she thought she could handle them well that would be cool. He actually got a message from Anderson giving him details of the expedition and asking him how he should charge, not the trip but the service.

After some weeks close to a month or little more, she got a call from Anderson requesting her to see him in his office. She thought it must be about his bills that he could have sent. But he had been nice to drive them to the prison. So she agreed and an appointment was fixed. He rose from his chair as she entered and offered her a seat. He offered some drink or a snack as she might be coming from work that she refused politely. Then after some polite talk he became serious and arranging some papers on his desk he said, 'We have to talk about some things.'

With a polite cough he started, 'You probably know or may not that the visits to high risk criminals are recorded by the prison authorities. This helps them to evaluate the prisoners and kept in their files. I as a lawyer asked them whether a copy could be sent to me and they did. So I know how your visit went. They have also sent a psychological profile of your brother. I am not allowed to give them to you but I thought I should discuss them with you to give you an idea of what is wrong with him at least as criminal psychologists see them. You may or may not agree.'

He paused and took a sip of water from a glass near him. 'They say that your brother had a traumatized adolescence because of your father's disease and death. But that is not where it started, it had a base. He was attached to her mother more and there was nascent father resentment. This aggravated with his father's disease and death because it affected his future as he saw it. He did not like to be sent to hostel though he was not conscious of that at the time but it came to him later as he ruminated. Going to hostel led to his partial separation from his family and mother, that he did not like and blamed it on father.'

Rupa interrupted, 'Our Indian family life is different from yours. I know of this mother attachment and father resentment in your society but in ours this is the routine and taken as natural and not traumatic.'

Anderson allowed her time and then said, 'It is not about ours and yours. Human society and psychology are not that different from one country to another. In your ancestral social order or even not so ancestral, boys entering adolescence were sent to their teachers' home to live and study there, being later identified as much with the Gurukul to which they belonged as their family. This was the routine in many or most ancient civilizations. In your society the system changed in the past centuries due to many changes in social order caused by historical events. Modern science has discovered genetic predispositions to these tendencies. I do not know whether such predispositions existed in your parents' ancestry. In any case these are not verifiable predispositions like heart disease or diabetes but more statistical.'

He again allowed time for her to respond but she did not. 'This psychological beginning developing from father resentment to actual hatred may have many ramifications in later life. Most men in their youth through intelligent analysis rationalize and get over that. The only answer seems to be education and constant analysis of our own selves from the behavioral point of view. Are we under reacting or are we over reacting or wrongly reacting? It is very delicate. With profuse apologies I would mention that your brother told you that you are the only person he loves. There is nothing wrong in a brother loving his sister but it is bad for him if he transposes mother on sister and bad for you too. I am mentioning it because the video shows you were at the point of tears. They were recording not for you, but because they had never seen a close relation visit your brother and wanted to study. But I thought I should let you know so that you are conscious about your real loves and not so real ones. I beg your apology but I am saying this because I have known you for sometime and admire your courage and commitment and honesty that must have had its base in your family and grown with you.'

Rupa stared at him and asked for a glass of water and continued staring at him while she drank. Wiping her mouth with a tissue offered by Anderson from a pack she asked, 'Are females also prone to suffer from these dangers of adolescence as males?' He smiled and said 'I was expecting that question. The answer is yes they do but their reactions are different. Women are after all creators of this world. But much of their emotional world is internalized and altered by their basic tolerance. A female will never accept a male unless she feels protected. That natural instinct comes from her instinct to protect her children that governs many of her reactions. What it will be in future nobody knows.'

Rupa asked him, 'Are you a criminal lawyer?'

Anderson said, 'I studied criminal law and criminal psychology is a part of the course. But I did not want to practice it. I thought I would serve better by working at the origin of criminal behavior and would rather try to prevent instead of defending or convicting after it has happened. So I became a family lawyer. It is more satisfying.'

Rupa was immersed in thought as she drove home. What Anderson said makes sense. She changed and cooked and heated some. At dinner Ravi was very excited. They were given puzzles to solve at school and he did all of them before anyone else. He was rambling about the puzzles. Rupa listened unmindfully. As she did the dishes and he went to his room it suddenly struck her. She went to her room and opened the laptop to read Amit's last message. 'Denizens of the land my foot' she said aloud and smiled. He is asking her to return through Anderson. She felt very happy and warm but thought it will be fun to continue the puzzle game. She sent a message to Anderson 'Forgot to ask your fees for the service. Please let me know unless you have been paid already.' Next day Mr. Anderson read the message and smiled. His job was done. What a woman he thought.

Deep Undercurrents

The calm surface of the sea near the shore with regular rolling of the breakers can sometimes conceal a deep under current especially at times of low tide. The fishermen use this to move out to sea without much effort to place their nets and come back with the tide with their catch. Those that bathe or swim near the shore can be unwittingly pulled to a greater distance and depth.

Life of Atin and Madhuri settled down to a routine. Atin's practice increased and he gradually became very busy spending much less time at home. His hours for charity work in the neighborhood were getting less. He would get up early and after some free hand exercise and breakfast he would leave home and return late at night very tired. On the days he could return earlier he would sit down with his computer to write papers on his research work and clinical notes on difficult operative procedures for publication in medical journals and work past midnight. Writing scientific papers for publication took a lot of effort as published references have to be looked up. The best papers put forward an unknown angle to a disease or its treatment and identify the areas where the current knowledge was not complete and then describes experiments and or procedures to clarify at least a part of that deficiency. So every scientific paper must contain a small portion of original discovery or opinion. Just the description of a hundred or thousand appendectomies would not be published anywhere. Major part of medical faculty had no knowledge how such papers should be worked out and presented for publication. They were busy in practice in earning money and enjoying life. Since every human being wants to go up the ladder whatever that ladder might be, for majority it was for earning more money by any means at some point of time of their career. For Atin it was intellectual growth he craved for and therefore in practice he was not drawn to unethical temptations. But he worked more and very hard.

There was severe dearth of good medical libraries in the city, a few only in medical colleges and institutes. So he had to move around and give a major part of his time in these libraries searching for references. It was a most thankless task otherwise, because it brought no direct remuneration except his satisfaction as a professional. Name and fame were more easily obtained in a poor society by amassing wealth. Although Atin had a more than decent income, Madhuri did not understand this part of his labour that reduced their time together. She was housebound having left her nursing job as Atin wanted and now she began to regret it. The first two years were not too bad as Raju needed looking after, but he has started attending nursery school and when he goes to prep school his absence will become longer. Madhuri had to go to his school alone most of the time as Atin had no time for that. She tried to take up music once again and some painting but they were not satisfying. Occasionally she would force Atin to sit down with her and even sing with her or appreciate what she had painted but his mind was elsewhere. Quarrels started for the first time in their life with very minor issues and Atin did not understand why.

One day Madhuri told him, 'I can understand a little bit how your mother felt staying alone in the house.'

Atin was irritated 'Do not compare your situation with hers. You have enough money, a houseful of maids and servants and Raju to look after. She had nothing.'

Madhuri said, 'That was at the end but before that she had her husband. I hardly see you and when I do you are dog tired. You will not understand. You were so sensitive and kind and now I hardly see you. Even at home you are wedded more to your computer. The only time I see you happy is when one of your papers get published and I feel happy too.'

Atin dryly said, 'I try to do my best, I am sorry I cannot do better.'

Madhuri said, 'I want another child, I want a daughter.'

Atin laughed, 'That cannot be ordered. You had a Caesarean last time and next time that is almost obligatory and then you cannot have another child. Why don't we wait a bit longer?'

Madhuri said, 'I want to go home to village. I have not seen my parents for so long.'

Atin asked, 'Would that be safe for Raju at his age?'

Madhuri flashed, 'If it was Ok for me and Ok for you to marry why would it be unsafe for Raju? My parents do not want to come here because they have to look after so many things and they do not like it here. Does that mean I have to be a prisoner for life?'

Atin cooled down, 'Yes of course you can go when it is a bit cool during Raju's holiday.'

Madhuri stubbornly said, 'Little bit of absence from school will not matter at this stage.'

Atin capitulated, 'Ok you go when it is a bit cooler.'

Madhuri went home with Raju during the Durgapuja holiday. They had two cars now and a driver for Madhuri. She drove home and the driver was kept with an extra bonus. Her parents were extremely happy and so was Raju. Everything was new for him, from the farm lands to the cattle. Milking of cow was a new experience for him. Madhuri beseeched Atin to join them for at least a few days. He did go and was happy and relaxed for the period. Madhuri whispered one day, 'Shall we go to the beach?'

Atin laughed and said, 'I would rather sleep and eat and fight with you.'

Madhuri said, 'Do not blame me, only if you worked a bit less.'

Since then Madhuri started going often and even on long weekends. It was only about two and half hours' drive and it helped her parents' finances as she went with provisions and equipments. Atin left all financial management to her and never questioned. But he felt lonely when she was not home. For the first time he realized the value of having a loved one at home.

One day entering the Institute's library he saw Sohini near a book shelf looking for some book. He had some notes to take and sat at a table with a pile of journals. Sohini saw him as she was about to leave and came to his table.

'How are you Atin' she asked.

'Can't complain' he replied.

She smiled and said, 'That is not enough reason why you should ignore me.'

Atin said, 'I did not want to disturb you and we are not supposed to talk in the library.'

She raised her eyebrows, 'Really so? Even whispering has been banned?'

Atin smiled, 'Our whispering age is long behind. And this is postgraduate institute.'

She asked, 'Tomorrow is Sunday; are you busy through the day?'

He said, 'I have to work with these notes I am taking.'

'You are still your studious self. What about in the evening, would you need a coffee break or your wife will mind?'

Before he could think words came out, 'She is not here, gone to her parents' and regretted.

Sohini smiled, 'You are still the same never able to tell a lie. You live in your old house beautifully renovated by your wife and there is a new coffee house nearby. The area has become posh. Can you please invite me for a cup of coffee?'

Atin could never refuse her and not even now though he wanted to and nodded '8 PM' and asked, 'How do you know so much about us? Are you tracking us and have employed detectives?'

She said, 'It is not difficult to know about prominent people in society. In this country rumour carries it all and you hear even if you do not enquire. Shall meet you tomorrow, there is a lot to talk about among old friends.'

Next evening they met and after coffee was served he smiled, 'Now it is my payment' and Sohini laughed. He noticed the lines in her face.

He asked, 'Where is your husband?'

She said, 'We are separated.'

In surprise Atin asked, 'Why?'

Sohini was casual, 'Happens all the time. I am Senior Registrar in Pediatric Medicine and will soon become a Consultant. He is Professor in University. Our hours never coincide. He is somewhat older than me. The boy you operated is from his first marriage. The younger was mine and he is here with me. My father is dead and mother is alone. So I come whenever I can. And how about you; I know you have a son. But how are you otherwise?'

Atin said, 'I already told you nothing to complain about, including your disappearance. But tell me why you avoided my eyes when I saw you last time? Does that also happen all the time when husbands are around and you cannot even tell him that you knew his son's surgeon?'

Sohini asked, 'Are you in a fighting mood or are you upset?'

Atin smiled, 'None. I am only curious about cultural differences.'

Sohini said, 'I do not know about cultural difference but person to person difference is there. As for my disappearance I told you that it was not my decision. I had grown weak physically and mentally and had no strength to fight. Are you still upset about it?'

Atin laughed, 'No, not at all. It was bound to happen in one way or another. I think it was obvious to both of us. It was really a question of who blinks first. We were too young. At least that is how I look at it and don't blame you for anything. No regrets.'

The coffee was finished and Atin made a move to go, 'I have work left, Madhuri will come back tomorrow.'

Sohini said, 'I got to go too. It was nice to meet you.'

Atin asked, 'Do you have a car' and Sohini said, 'don't bother, there are plenty of taxis.'

As they separated Atin thought, 'I was correct and did not give her any extra welcome' and Sohini thought 'methinks the man was a bit too sour.'

When Madhuri reached home Atin was already out, leaving the message that he would be home early. He reached home early evening and ran upstairs. Entering bedroom he found her standing facing the mirror doing her hair. Face was already perfect. He jumped in and grabbed from behind almost taking her off her feet and rocking her.

Madhuri shouted, 'Wow if two days absence ignites the flame of love to this degree I am going to live on moon and come occasionally,' and Atin stopped her with a firm kiss on mouth and said 'Never say that, you are going nowhere. Instead we are going out for dinner to the most posh place in town. May I have a date darling,' and Madhuri laughed 'Yes but I have to redo my make up since you have spoiled it.'

They had a lovely evening. A band was playing and at Atin's insistence they went on the floor and Madhuri whispered, 'Can you dance picking me up from the floor because I am in seventh heaven and I can never step correctly?'

Atin laughed, 'Don't feign because you dance very well. I just wonder who taught you.'

They returned home and found Raju in deep sleep in his cot in the adjoining room. He was on training to sleep alone. They undressed and got in bed and Madhuri snuggled close. Atin said, 'I don't think I ate much for I am hungry.' Madhuri put a finger on his lips and said, 'Just one morsel and no more big boy.'

As they lay relaxed and content Madhuri hid her face in his chest and asked, 'How was last evening with Sohini darling?'

Atin turned her to face him and asked, 'How do you know?'

Madhuri smiled and said, 'I am not upset or anything. Somen came on some errand and told me. I told him it must be some patient's relation. But somehow I thought it must be Sohini. A man like you would go to the local coffee house with a pretty lady, that is how Somen described, and the locality would not know? I love you for that.'

Atin was baffled, 'Why would you love me for that?'

Madhuri said, 'Because it shows your mind that you did not think it was something to be concealed. But tell me how the conversation went and then I shall judge you.'

Atin described in detail the conversation and asked, 'Was my response right?'

Madhuri considered for sometime and said, 'Well almost right and I like it knowing how you are and your manner of speaking. You say what you think, no camouflage. But thinking from Sohini's point of view I think she might have detected an itch.'

Atin was surprised, 'An itch? What do you mean?'

Madhuri laughed, 'You have married a plain village girl. How would you know how a female mind works? She must have detected a mild resentment that was natural for you. But if she thinks there is an itch she will come again because such sophisticated females especially in her condition as you described would love to scratch that itch to find if there is some deeper wound and think about enlarging it, may not be out of malice but just curiosity.' She laughed again, 'You have no idea of this surgery darling. Do not worry I am there to assist you. But promise me that if I assist well you shall allow me to go back to real surgery. Please darling I want to go back to work, please.'

Atin said, 'I was also thinking about that. You are getting bored at home.'

Madhuri quickly added, 'And I shall see you through the day the whole day.'

Atin asked, 'And what about Raju?'

Madhuri said, 'Do not worry about him, I shall arrange. First let us see where I am placed.'

'Night duty will be best, don't you think,' she made a face and Atin pinched her nose.

The little cloud between them was cleared surprisingly by the advent of Sohini. Three days later the front door bell rang in the evening. The maid opened the door and the visitor asked for Atin. The maid said he was not home but Ma was there and politely requested her to sit. Madhuri came down from upstairs and stood puzzled in front of her for half a minute, and then with sudden remembrance said, 'You are Dr. Sohini Singh, are you not?'

Sohini asked, 'Do you know me?'

Madhuri said, 'Yes of course though it took a minute. I worked at the hospital when you had your accident. We were so upset and we cried for you. You have come for Atin? He will be back soon. Please stay for dinner. We seldom have guests. Atin will be happy to see you.'

Sohini gravely said, 'I have had dinner in this house, it will not be a new thing for me. It was a small house then.'

Madhuri said, 'Have you? Then it will be nothing new for you. Please stay. Atin will be upset if you leave. The house has been enlarged and renovated. Would you like to see? Come upstairs and let me show you. There is nothing special of course. I have decorated the house to the best of my ability. But I am after all a village girl.'

Sohini asked, 'You are a nurse did you say?' There was a veiled insult, a slight emphasis on the word nurse.

Madhuri laughed, 'Yes I am. I was operation theatre in-charge, we, I mean Atin and I, met there. I am not working now Atin will not let me work. I want to go back to work; our son has grown enough to allow that. You tell me isn't it boring to be a full time wife? Please come upstairs and have a cup of coffee. Atin will come anytime and then you can decide on dinner or we can go out for that, the three of us. Atin will love to see you.'

Sohini made no effort to move and asked, 'You are a village girl and were at the hospital as what, in what capacity!'

Madhuri sat down and said, 'You do not seem to like the idea of going upstairs. I wanted to show you our bedroom and ask your opinion. I know you are living in England and wanted your opinion about the décor. You people have great taste. As to my education I did B.Sc in nursing from Delhi and came to your hospital with a scholarship to do postgraduate diploma in operation theatre nursing and assisting. I actually wanted to do anesthesia but it is not yet in vogue in our country. I planned to go abroad; there is a great demand especially in America. But then I got caught by Atin. Just see my fate! I am of course very happy, Atin being such a nice man and I can go to my village to see my parents whenever I like. It is just two hours drive and I have my own car and driver.'

Sohini had stood up by now. She said, 'Thank you very much for your hospitality but I have to go now.'

Madhuri almost cried out, 'Why so soon? Atin will be upset. He talks often about you. You have not taken anything in our house. By Hindu belief that is bad omen for the family.'

Sohini was already out and said, 'I do not believe in such things and tell Atin that I came and will call him on phone before I leave.'

Madhuri asked, 'Do you have his number? Just a second I shall give you.'

Sohini was already off waiving her hand and walking towards the main road for taxi.

Madhuri closed the door and went upstairs and catching her tummy kept laughing. When Atin came she described everything and he said, 'Your hunch was right. She came when I would not be home. Why did she do that?'

Madhuri said, 'I knew she would come to see me, to see how dowdy and rustic I am. And then she would probably have told you that. I have offered her full hospitality and she refused everything. I have done one sin. I have told some lies that I shall have to beg forgiveness from God. But I have given two correct informations one that you are a very nice man and two I love you very much. I did not say that you love me very much because then the lies would be too many' and she ran down the stairs to the kitchen chased by Atin.

Sitting down for dinner Madhuri said, 'You know I was thinking about her visit and feeling sorry for her. I should not have been so catty. After all she really loved you and you also loved her. But your circumstances were so different that both of you hesitated. None of you can be blamed for what happened. The accident that happened was not her fault nor afterwards. Chance determines our life so much!'

Atin said, 'Chance or God you can say. I learnt that from your father. He is such a wise man that I had no hesitation to touch his feet when I had to.'

Madhuri said, 'I am father's undeserved offspring. I shall call Sohini for dinner one day or better you shall.'

Atin said, 'About the first one, no you are not and you have proved it right now. But about your proposal to invite Sohini I would say no. Let bygone be bygone, do not wake up the sleeping dog do not play God. Excessive emotional response to both good and bad, to both happiness and sorrow is unwise. You are not the determinant you had no role in Sohini's sorrow you do not even know that there is real sorrow. Take life as it comes with equanimity without emotion. I love you very much and adore you those are the reality now and stay there.'

Madhuri laughed and said, 'Mr. Philosopher the last thing you said I want to hear more often and again and again. Will God be angry?'

Atin laughed 'You are getting spoiled and too greedy.'

Madhuri ultimately got the job of nursing tutor for teaching the student nurses in the newly opened School of Nursing. It fitted with her academic records which were after all not lies, well might be a little bit but not much. That meant that she got higher salary and a routine that fitted well with Raju's. On the debit side, she was seeing Atin seldom at work and in the long run that was good because they had different tales to tell about their own experiences and their life went in even keel.

Ships Anchor

One Sunday morning Amit suddenly landed unannounced. He had timed it well both Atin and Madhuri were home. The first reaction was a stunned disbelief. Then the house exploded in raucous laughter and hugs. Amit held Madhuri at arms length and stared at her and said, 'So this is the wildflower by the seaside? What an apt name, the sweet somber fragrance of the wild personified! The quiet beauty of mother blended with that of a heart teaser. I shall call you sister because I have never had one but you are truly our mother and I am not joking.'

Madhuri blushing deeply touched his feet and said, 'You are my Dada, I have never had an elder brother to protect me.'

Amit let out another bellow of laughter, 'Protect you from whom, that rascal' and he pointed at Atin, 'I am sorry sister I cannot; look how cool he is. He went through so many difficulties and yet he plucked a flower like you! Shabbash Bacchu, oh sorry I cannot take that name for the most talked about doctor in town,' and he embraced Atin.

Madhuri looked around and asked, 'Where is your luggage Dada and Rupa?'

Amit said, 'The two are a bit different, luggage is in left luggage at the airport but they could not keep Rupa so she vanished,' and another bellow of laughter.

Shocked Madhuri asked, 'Do you laugh at everything Dada?' and gravely added 'she will come, I know it in my heart.'

Amit calmed, 'All in good time sister. What a beautiful house you have built!'

'Not my house Dada it is the house of father and mother and their dream that both of you would reside here. They died with that dream and unworthy I tried to fulfill their dream. You will live here, won't you Dada?' and she was close to tears.

Amit said, 'I have no better place to live and I could see our mother in you the moment I saw you. It is amazing.'

Atin could find his voice and said, 'Give me the locker key Dada I shall bring your luggage from the airport.'

Amit said, 'All in good time brother, I am not going anywhere. Let me savour this moment in full, rest of life is there anyway.' Then he saw Raju slowly climbing down the stairs woken by the racket downstairs. Amit gave a shout, 'Now the real owner comes' and galloped up the stairs to pick him up. Raju perplexed just out of sleep was between crying and laughing with distorted face. Mother had told him that big boys do not cry and he was not able to decide.

Madhuri said, 'This is your big uncle Raju, your Jethu, you call him that,' and took him from Amit. 'Come let us show Jethu around the house.'

Amit was on a guided tour and more he saw he was surprised. He asked Madhuri, 'Tell me sister, our house was not this big as I remember. Décor is nice in your hand but how could it grow in size?'

Madhuri smiled, 'The house was large in foundation but much of the planned area father could not afford to build; dreamed that one day his sons will build. Your brother has fulfilled that dream.'

Amit said, 'My brother may have given the money but you have built. Did he know that there was a large foundation, I don't think.'

Madhuri said, 'Nobody knew. It was found by one of your ardent admirers and he has rebuilt to his hearts content without specific instructions. He found the extra land from settlement maps and built the porch. I do not even know whether he charged his normal fees. He would not answer when asked, only smiles. You do not know what you are Dada. The young generation here simply adores you.'

Thoughtfully he asked, 'What is his name?'

Madhuri said, 'His name is Somen.'

Amit thought with furrowed brow, 'Can't place him.'

Madhuri said, 'He was very young when the house was built and used to play on these grounds and he remembered that the masons used to laugh that father is spending so much money on the foundation, he will not have enough to make the superstructure. He dug up the foundation and reinforced with concrete and then built over it.'

Amit said, 'Now I vaguely remember that a young boy used to hover here extremely interested with what masons were doing and father used to shoo him out. I was in junior college then, before entering engineering. He has become a builder?'

Madhuri said, 'A qualified graduate in architecture and builder.'

Amit said, 'How time flies! You must have been a tiny girl then.'

Madhuri said, 'I was not that tiny then, I must be older to Somen and I knew your name.'

Amit stared in disbelief, 'How come you knew me?'

Madhuri laughed, 'I am a Midnapur girl Dada and who has not heard your name there, either in fear or admiration? We must hurry through the house and then I shall serve you breakfast before the crowd of local people engulf the house.'

After going through the house they stood on the upper floor balcony and Amit pointed to the other house, 'What is that house within the compound wall?'

Madhuri said, 'Your brother has purchased that house too. It was up for sale. As a result we have a lawn between the two houses.'

Amit asked, 'What is that house for?'

'There Atin holds Sunday chamber for people in the neighborhood,' Madhuri said, 'We can build another floor above if the need be.'

Amit said, 'That is superb. I can open an IT business there if I want to. And from that little house I shall control the world you shall see.'

Madhuri said, 'Please do Dada. All of us can live in this house including Rupa. I hope she agrees.'

Amit looked at her quizzically, 'You seem to be rather sure she would come. Why are you so sure? And you also hope she would want to live here not knowing anything about her!'

Madhuri smiled, 'By looking at the trend of events Dada. A wave of the ocean does not go on back gear. The strong desire of your father and mother is pulling all of us together that is what I feel, I felt it the first day I landed here.'

Amit stared at her, 'Are you that clairvoyant?'

Madhuri said, 'Not clairvoyant, just the progress of events and my desire must also have been added to theirs.'

They sat down for breakfast and had scarcely finished when the first doorbell rang and then there was a barrage of people who came to see Amit and wish the family good luck. Atin slipped out with the locker key and papers to bring Amit's luggage and to see the patients who needed to be seen on the way back. He told Madhuri, 'I may be late. Do not wait for me for lunch and give Dada a change from my wardrobe, we are same size.'

But they did not need to wait, the procession continued well past lunchtime. Only Raju was fed and sent to rest. Amit was overwhelmed by the show of love and respect. Atin came back with luggage and all of them had bath and changed and sat down for a sumptuous lunch. Amit protested that he would grow fat with all that food like Atin and everybody laughed and on Madhuri's order went for rest or sleep as per choice.

In the evening the family was left alone. The few people who came were requested by Madhuri to come next day as Amit was tired after the long journey. It was not a lie, he was really tired by the same questions over and over. As the shadows fell they sat on the lawn with tea and snacks.

Amit came down and said, 'I think I should print my short biography, leaving out the unspeakable things, and distribute through the neighbourhood. Even then perhaps curiosity would not be satisfied. You please do not start asking questions.'

Atin said, 'I for one would never ask from past experience I know that they will not be answered.'

Madhuri said, 'And I am never curious about other people's lives and least of all you. You shall say what you want to say and when you want to say, I just want you to stay.'

Amit said, 'Then digest my first bombshell, I have resigned from my job at Bangalore, I am unemployed now.'

Atin and Madhuri simultaneously said, 'Good,' followed by Madhuri saying, 'You can teach Raju' and Atin said, 'You can do the lawn since you have been in the jungle, Madhuri is making me mad saying I am good for nothing.'

Amit said, 'Bah what reception from the near and dear ones, one gives me the job of private tutor and the other gardener. What unexpected love!'

The evening was spent in light conversations and laughter. They reminisced their young days and their parents. They had much to exchange. Madhuri said, 'Mother's name is Tanima. What a beautiful name! Can we commemorate that in some way?'

Amit said, 'The house is their memorial and commemoration in our mind.'

Madhuri said, 'I have arranged your room Dada but I have not unpacked your bags. That is your private area unless you want me to.'

Amit said, 'Nothing very private in there. But I want to take it slow. I have never moved with baggage at least not until last few years. I want to do it slowly.'

Madhuri said, 'At least show us a photograph of Rupa. She must be very beautiful.'

Amit said, 'Why are you assuming that?'

'Because of her name; Rupa is from Rup, Beauty. Her parents kept that name for her and that means she is a great beauty. You are concealing her from us.'

Amit said, 'I do not even know whether I have her photograph. There was no occasion to take formal photographs unless some were taken on some trip of which there were not many. She was passing through her tragic phase of life for quite a long time and tragedy reveals the personality and character of a person. That way she was beautiful and that impressed me more than her appearance, which is not bad by any measure. She is as stubborn as me in feminine way and therefore unpredictable.'

Normally silent and patient listener Atin interjected, 'Then you are made for each other?'

Amit and Madhuri were startled and burst out laughing and Madhuri said, 'Did you know that your brother is a philosopher? He will suddenly come up with a deep observation.'

Atin said, 'There lies the difference of two brothers, he is an action man and I am a thinking man. I have become more thoughtful after meeting Madhuri's father. I did not expect such deep wisdom in a man with no special education but what he says goes straight to your heart. That is probably because it is no theoretical wisdom it is event based and comes out in response to a situation and makes the issues clear.'

Amit said ponderously, 'I have met such men. They seem to carry practical wisdom on a deep philosophical base that is not in keeping with their position in life. Such people are seen everywhere, but most commonly in India. Go to remote villages and jungles and mountains and you shall find them. A few thousand years of culture seem to have given a granite base to their character and culture. To tell you frankly, I have become interested in this foundation and with apologies to you, I have also become a thinking man.'

Madhuri laughed, 'Oh God! Two philosophers in one house! I do not know what is happening in this house.'

Amit smiled and said, 'What is happening in this house is that this house has now got a mother that is you and the dryness of philosophy is going to dissolve in laughter and fine food.'

Madhuri said, 'I cannot handle that all alone, Rupa Didi has to come.'

Amit said, 'Suddenly she has become your Didi? If we get married, the chances for which seem remote, she will be your Boudi.'

Madhuri clapped in glee, 'What great fun, you two are not married and living together for God knows how long. You have at last found your match Dada. But she would be on my side, my elder sister. Or else how do I control the two of you?'

Amit looked at Atin and said, 'See how she is constructing a whole story out of nothing? We men would never be able to do that. She is practically pulling the story out of me as she wants it to be.' Then looking at Madhuri he laughed and said, 'Just one like you is enough you do not need a partner. You never even think of disappointment?'

Madhuri firmly said, 'No I do not think negative, I am always positive. If negative happens I ride it but always think positive and I know it will happen.'

Amit again looked at Atin and said, 'What have you picked at the seaside? She is infectious.'

Atin gravely added, 'Who picked who has not yet been settled. Let us go for dinner or else we shall spend the whole night on the lawn.'

Sunset and evening star and one clear call for me

Next day was the beginning of the week and Atin and Madhuri got busy on their jobs. Atin left first thing in the morning. Madhuri left a little later dropping Raju at school. At midday she returned with Raju and sat down for lunch with Raju and Amit. She left again and returned in the afternoon. Atin returned late around dinner time. That sort of routine continued with some variations and adjustments from Madhuri. She apologized to Amit for leaving him alone. Amit assured her, 'Don't worry I love loneliness. It is better that I take time to adjust to family life bit by bit.'

Madhuri could not always return for lunch. Instead she sent the driver to pick up Raju and drop him at home. Even when she was home for lunch Amit did not always join her. Gradually they developed a lifestyle where no one impinged on the other's routine. At dinner time all of them were together except Atin who was irregular. Amit had a lot of time with Raju and he loved to talk to the little one like an adult just as he used to do with Ravi. Many adults do not know that children like adult talks rather than baby talk from adults. He sometimes wondered whom he missed more Rupa or Ravi. Being a private man since his youngest days, he could not discuss it with anybody. But Madhuri with her intelligence and sensitivity got his story out bit by bit through the long evenings before Atin returned. For Amit too it was a new experience to talk to a woman like her, who was not inquisitive or probing but loving and sympathetic. His frequent expression was, 'You are really a mother personified both for Raju and me.'

Major portion of Amit's luggage were filled with books and his computer and accessories, many of which were unknown to Madhuri. Madhuri organized his room which was the largest one on the upper floor. Seeing that he lagged in dresses and attires she shopped for him, occasionally succeeded in taking him to shop.

Amit's days were well spent. On some days he spent the whole time on his gadgets and computers connected to the cyber world. He watched how his company was doing and how the software he created was doing. He started to think why not develop software for himself. So long he was doing for his company and they held the patent. Why not try to invent and patent and see how they did? That research needed greater concentration and time and he gradually got absorbed in that. On other days he remained absorbed in books. Madhuri will occasionally peep in and seeing him absorbed went away. One day she found he was not there, probably gone for walk and books were lying open and papers scribbled with texts and mathematical calculations strewn all around. She looked at the books with open pages and the scribbles and she wondered.

When he came back she accosted him. 'What are you working on Dada? All sorts of books were lying open and I could not help looking. They were so diverse. Books on religion, Upanishads, higher Physics and mathematics are all jostling with each other. What are you working on actually?'

Amit laughed, 'Nothing in particular and I am not working but playing. I have not had time to play since childhood. So I am doing it now. Mixing things together in random and see what comes out, if anything.'

Madhuri said, 'It seems to be a very odd mixture. You are searching for something.'

Amit said, 'Searching for myself I suppose. Actually enjoying random thoughts to see where they lead. This is a very relaxing mental exercise. The origin of knowledge in humanity is from man's sense of wonder at what he could see, touch, smell, taste or hear? The earliest thinkers of humanity were called philosophers in almost every culture, irrespective of what they introspected on, nature or health and human body or how to make weapon or how to calculate. There were some mind boggling conclusions in many branches of human knowledge that sound amazing today. Take for example Kanad and his atomic theory, combination of atoms to form molecules and from there the Vaisheshiki philosophy of structure of the universe. A few centuries later Democritus in Greece propounded his atomic theory. Take for example the origin of Zero in mathematics in our country. Confucius is called a philosopher but today he will be called a social and political scientist. He has influenced Chinese history till today. Legitimacy of changing an ineffective government by any means has extended through history from Confucius to Mao, as that of an efficient secular bureaucracy selected on merit alone, irrespective of regime change. This practical philosophy coexisted with the spiritual philosophy of Lao-tzu, the slightly senior contemporary of Confucius and the father of Taoism, whose book Tao-te Ching has been valued by Prof. Suniti Kumar Chattopadhaya as an Upanisad formed outside India, proving the perennial presence of that philosophy in human mind. Confucius made a compromise with God by saying the King rules by divine order, but when he is seen to lose that divine order by his actions, the people have the right to change that king. His encounter with Lao-tzu, if true, is an interesting episode.'

Madhuri said, 'This is in the domain of philosophy. But what would you say about the sciences? The objectivity of science surely is a modern phenomenon that no amount of introspection would have succeeded to deliver?'

Amit said, 'The total objectivity of science has been questioned in modern physics but I am not going into that. Science appears to man in two different ways. One is utilitarian that influences our daily life that is really technology born out of science. The invention is not always from the need of the society and it gives rise to discord. For example you have a standard television and science then brings a large high definition television and says you will be a happier person but you do not become and others who cannot afford go one step lower in social scale. This is the critical problem of our age. It affects your profession, the medical sciences. The inventors of computerized tomography (CT) got Nobel Prize, then inventors of MRI got Nobel Prize and now we have Micro MRI that has also got Nobel Prize. The last one is still in research domain. But some commercial use no doubt would be found or generated. If it is in health care it may produce greater despair among poor patients who cannot afford or it affects Health Insurance system in rich countries.'

Madhuri said, 'What about mathematics? That cannot be coloured by ideas or emotions and even by material benefit.'

Amit smiled, 'Yes it can be and I am most concerned about that. Mathematics appeared in philosophy from Plato and has continued till modern times. Plato said that there was something unchangeable in the changeable world. If all things change then there must be something unchangeable or else world would not have existed. . He categorized human experience into the world of senses and world of ideas putting the latter in a higher order and Mathematical logic is its highest level. A study of Plato's dialogue and those of Neoplatonists shows close theoretical and historical correlation to Vedanta. I shall show you in details one day. '

'Then in seventeenth century a great philosopher Baruch Spinoza wrote a book titled "Ethics geometrically demonstrated". He demonstrated through geometrical terminology that God controls the world through Laws of Nature and advised humans to view themselves on this large background. The goal is to comprehend everything that exists in an all embracing perception as none of us is full master of our life. Einstein said that he did not believe in a personal god but believed in Spinoza's God and he called this a cosmic religious experience. This ideal Spinoza followed in life through great deprivation.'

A modern day physicist and mathematician Sir Roger Penrose says, "The arguments from Gödel's Theorem serve to illustrate the deeply mysterious nature of our mathematical perceptions. We do not 'calculate', in order to form these perceptions, but something else is profoundly involved—something that would be impossible without the very conscious awareness, that is, after all, what the world of perception is all about."

Madhuri smiled, 'With great difficulty I can follow the gist in a crude way may be.'

Amit laughed, 'Everybody understands in a crude way, including the masters. My problem is about now. You can see that mathematics and science developed worldwide to find greater happiness for man and was close to philosophy and life's inescapable spirituality. Today it is opening the frontiers of space and knowledge of the universe. But this is also the first time we are using mathematics as a marketable tool for money and power. The entire cyber world is driven by mathematics and producing huge amounts of wealth for those who can manipulate it. It is such a boom market that along with other benefits there will soon be a world where there will be no privacy; there will be such congestion of microwave radiation that people may be affected, specially children.'

'Life developed on Earth in a cocoon, protected from the lethal radiations of outer space. Now we are producing that radiation environment inside, both by microwave and use of nuclear energy for peace and war. That is why I am studying how and why this rupture took place in human brain that the goal of mathematics and science was changed from knowledge and happiness to money and power. Why? In all this the main thing involved is the human brain. I may not find a solution but I want to understand and I am going to the source from antiquity that great men and their followers went to. I am searching the entire Vedanta. It came from our ancestors proved by reason, examples and experiences who made development parallel to man, not against. I have to understand that.'

Madhuri was absolutely silent. She could not speak for several minutes by the force of his speech and passion. She could only say, 'Would this quest take you away from us?'

He smiled, 'Not necessarily: actually the fight is in the mind. I do not know how to explain it because much of it is not clear to me or anyone else. For computer, software and all else in the cyber world we work on algorithms. The earliest algorithm was that of Euclid and the term itself has come from the name of a Persian mathematician Al-Khwarizmi in the ninth century AD. We create the problems, pathways, machines that are mechanical or mathematical to arrive at a function or conclusion. Basically these may be deterministic or randomized. But with advancement in the later part of the twentieth century a huge variety of methods and systems have come into existence. All these inventions in science, whether in computing science or other applications and discoveries, where also computing is involved, have come out of human brain. The human brain is the only source which feels happy or sad, creates revolutions or wars, thinks of philosophy or science, create societies of one type or another. How the human brain can function in such different domains is beyond all answers so far. Penrose compared the human brain with the 'Turing machine' and concluded that the human brain is not a computer and cannot be explained by computational process. Something else is deeply involved.'

'I am an ordinary man nowhere near these giants of science. But I understand a little bit of that. I want to understand why at the end of twentieth century the same human brain that thought of peace and happiness of society and employed science to achieve that ideal is now glued to the general trend of suicide through ideas of greed, power and money and other peculiarities of human desire. Spinoza did mathematics for happiness of the individual. The present mathematics is working for greed of all. Would Plato born today place mathematical logic in its lofted place?'

Madhuri wiped her eyes, 'Dada why do you always choose the impossible fights? You shall go mad fighting only with yourself. The world is so simple and beautiful! It is the Garden of Eden, made by God. Just look around at the universe as far as you can see. There is not one single planet like our Mother Earth. It is God's Garden of Eden protected from the burning fires or frozen emptiness of outer space. It is decorated beautifully with mountains and seas, the burning desert and frozen ice, the lush tropical jungles and barren rocks, so many different animals in His aquarium and zoos where rain falls, volcanoes spit fire and He has built this garden only for us and other life forms, which is beyond the capacity of the richest man ever born on Earth to build. Why can't you live happily in this without worry? Do you have any explanation for this phenomenon? Why there is an Earth?'

Amit said, 'If He or the Cosmic Intelligence has really done this for us then he has also given us this quest to understand a little bit through our very inadequate reasoning and sensations and ask the question 'Why are we destroying it in spite of all our knowledge?'

Madhuri said, 'But for that quest you need happiness in your own heart and not bitterness, to share it with somebody and be cooled. This is not a desperate fight but quest.'

Both were silent for sometime immersed in their own thoughts. Then Madhuri asked quietly, 'When is Rupa coming Dada?'

Amit laughed loudly, 'Does all that boil down to Rupa? You have no other solution?'

Madhuri said, 'No I am not asking this as a solution but as a means. I cannot believe that running around in jungles rejecting all desires is the only means. If there is a God then I cannot believe that He lives only in the jungle. You are saying this urban civilization we live in is the jungle of today. We can find Him here in peace and quiet as Spinoza did. Have you asked her to come?'

Amit said, 'No not directly but I have asked her to come when she is sure and want to come and I shall wait for her.'

Madhuri asked, 'Why did you say that?'

Amit said, 'Because she came to me in utter distress as she had nowhere to go. I wanted her to come on her own free will and not under duress as she did the first time.'

Madhuri asked, 'And you have never asked her to come since then?'

Amit said, 'No, why should I, is it not enough to ask once?'

Madhuri asked, 'And she has not written once since you returned?'

Amit said, 'Oh yes, she has written often about how she is, what she is doing and sounded happy but not about coming. I think she likes it there.'

Madhuri sighed, 'Oh, you men! I feel sorry for her. If you decide to go to the real jungle and lonely mountain, would you inform her before going?'

Amit smiled, 'I have not yet thought about that.'

Madhuri said slowly, 'I have not heard everything about you two,' and Amit added with a smile, 'you better not;' not listening to him she sighed and said 'your love is also like a computer program Dada?'

Both were silent for some time. Then Madhuri slowly said 'The Vedanta that you are studying in your quest were created by two types of people, one group who were celibate and were called monks or *Sadhu* and another who pursued the path of knowledge and were called Rishi. There were men and women in both groups. The Rishi were not necessarily celibate. One great example is Rishi Yagnavalkya. He is a prolific writer of Vedic and Vedanta literature that had spread throughout contemporary world. The most poignant and popular among them is Brhadaranyak Upanishad. In this Upanishad through a chapter, which is great in literary value as also knowledge, he shows, through the conversation between him and his beloved wife Maitreyi, the presence of Brahman or God in the universe and within us in our familiar life of emotions and desires. His lesson to his beloved wife was "As a lump of salt dropped into water dissolves with (its component) water, and no one is able to pick it up, but from wheresoever one takes it, it tastes salt, even so, my dear, this great, endless, infinite Reality is but Pure Intelligence. (The self) comes out (as a separate entity) from these elements, and (this separateness) is destroyed with them. After attaining (this oneness) it has no more consciousness. This is what I say, my dear." I cry every time I read this; God is so easy and near yet we make Him so difficult! He is in everything around us. One just has to realize Him within one's own self. There is a parallel in another Upanishad, the Isa Upanishad, which in simple translation says 'He is infinite and we are infinite and this infinite is realized from that infinite and through knowledge

becomes that infinite and remains in infinity alone'. Yagnavalkya
had a large ashram that was almost a university, where students used
to come from the entire known world, not only to know spirituality
but learn material sciences too, and Maitreyi was not only his wife
but also a co-teacher and coordinator. Rishi were equal partner of the
Monk in propagating the Veda and Vedanta. It was also the same in
the renaissance of modern Europe and Western civilization. There
were and are celibate holy Archbishops, Bishops and Padre but society
did not develop until enormous numbers of Rishi were born since
the sixteenth century, who created a revolution of knowledge and
discovery that made the modern material life of mankind and also
consolidated religious belief, relieved of its bigotry and superstitions.
To achieve that people have jumped into the unknown, both physically
and intellectually, ignoring fear, shame, death, wealth, loss of family
and not caring for fame. Is not that what Upanishads teach us to do?
They did not reject the world.'

'Dada, a man is not complete unless he knows both the worldly life
of the householder and the spiritual life of sublime knowledge. Both
are needed for peace and development. Sri Ramakrishna was both a
householder, knowing all the nitty-gritty, joy and sorrow of family life,
and was a great Sannyasin, the greatest. He is incomparable and He
is contemporary. In His time, after He attained the highest spiritual
state, He was surrounded by Rishis like Keshab Chandra Sen, Iswar
Chandra Vidyasagar, Bankim Chandra Chatterjee, Ram Chandra
Dutta and a number of others. Ramakrishna's interaction with them
spread his message in early days. One amongst many men who was
touched by this was Professor William Hastie of Scottish Church
College at Calcutta, who sent young Narendra to Ramakrishna and
he became Vivekananda. Ramakrishna entrusted a family man to
record his life, spiritual quests and teachings for his disciples and
civil society and he was a Rishi who identified himself only as M,
the writer of the Kathamrita, the Gospel. Ramakrishna came to this
world at the precise time and place where the East and the West were
meeting and Professor Max Mueller, a Rishi, spread his teachings to
the West. Otherwise it would have been difficult for the civil society
to comprehend His message. He forbade his monastic disciples to
write His biography. Vivekananda was the first and greatest among
the disciples; he refrained from discussing Master's life, apart from

recording his own obeisance as he saw Him. You are a Rishi Dada, you should not think of becoming a monk now.'

'Great monks have since continued to arise in the Rama Krishna Mission who realized the highest spiritual level and spread education among people. But the importance of the Rishi has been lost in our times, creating ignorant ritualistic idolatry in the civil society, who are eager to score brownie points for their desires. This trend in the past had affected even the monkshoods and religions had withered. An overarching monasticism can paralyze a largely selfish, unconscious and uneducated civil society to disorientation and disintegration, which has been seen in historical phases not only in our country but others as well. A society needs to be balanced in its esoteric scholarship and knowledge base, material structure and spiritual ideal, without rejecting or dominating one with the other, which usually comes out of greed. The destruction of this balance increases envy and hostility, in a vicious cycle and destroy societies in all aspects. There are examples in history. So both sides are needed.'

'In Vedanta, Brahman is enveloped by Shakti, the active principle for the cycle of creation, destruction and back to creation that the present day science and cosmology can no longer deride as mysticism. This vast energy has been imagined as a feminine entity by the ancients. It was not the product of random imagination or fancy, but a product of keen observation and contemplation of the characteristics, by innumerable ascetics of different religions over millennia of contemplation. The feminine aspect of the divinity promotes the complimentary powers of love, tolerance and acceptance in societies parallel to the qualities usually attributed by us to manhood. This is not imagination but real. The Undivided Universe, the title of the famous book by Bohm, is as much a reality in science as it was in our philosophy. That reality operates not only on a balance in the cosmos but also in life forms. Non-acceptance of this Mother in many religions at some periods in time has made societies cruel and unforgiving. You shall see that easily in history of religions. You are a Rishi Dada and remain that. A wife is not always a handicap but may be a co-worker. And from what I know, Rupa is a great physicist but unassuming, and so was her mother, who did not care for name, fame and money. I am an ordinary woman, a village girl trained to be a nurse, but Rupa will be a great companion for you, because you really love her, but deny out of your male vanity, which is not desirable even in a monk. Forgive me and get rid of that, for it is not easy to know one's own self; sometimes an ignorant can open your eyes.'

Amit was spellbound and only uttered, 'You an ordinary woman? You are the mother!'

'Haminastu Haminastu Haminastu'

Madhuri was as much affected by what she said as Amit was. She wondered whether she ever thought, what she uttered for Amit. She could not remember. Then how come she said those things? From where did they come? She remembered the last three words from the Persian inscription in the Red Fort in Delhi that she had seen umpteen times and never thought of them. The words mean 'it is here, it is here, it is here' and before them were words that meant 'if there is a heaven' obviously referring to the power and wealth of the mighty Emperor. But it was only those three words that had stuck in her mind, not in relation to power and wealth, but something else. What was that?

At night in bed she asked Atin, 'Can I ask you something? I spend time with Dada when I am home and talk and discuss so many things. The poor man has nobody to talk to. I may be saying things that I do not know much about. Is that wrong?'

Atin looked at her in surprise, 'Why such an unusual question?'

Madhuri said, 'You had told me once that when Sohini showed her admiration for Dada and was talking to him you felt jealous.'

Atin laughed and embracing her said, 'That was passion and this is love. Love loves to give and passion is selfish. I had solved that in my mind when I met you.'

Madhuri pushed her face in his chest, 'Sorry darling for asking. But I get to see you so little and talk even less. I know what you are but want to know more often.'

Atin caressed her head, 'I am what you have made me.'

Madhuri disengaged her face and asked him; 'I want to do something else for Dada if you think it is right' and Atin asked 'What?'

Madhuri said, 'I want to write to Rupa if you think it is right' and Atin looked in surprise. Madhuri insisted, 'I want to write to Rupa.'

Atin raised himself on elbow and asked with further surprise, 'What you want to write and why? I presume you want to write without telling him and that is why you are asking me as witness. Would that be right?'

Madhuri sat up and said, 'Because some men have great difficulty in uttering three simple words 'I love you'. I have known one such man' and she poked a finger at his chest 'and now I know another. Does this thing also run in families?'

Atin protested, 'Didn't I express my love?'

She said, 'Yes ultimately you did after a lot of time spent at looking, staring, telling tales to others to make me laugh, withdrawing hand as if by electric shock after accidentally touching my hand and not until the snake appeared from the tree—the proverbial snake' and laughed at him.

Atin said, 'You are insulting my manhood and need to be punished by making amends.'

After some time Madhuri asked, 'You have not answered my question. Should I write to Rupa?'

Atin replied, 'Do what you think is best. I am not an expert in these things. You are the expert; you are the mother of the house after all.'

Some weeks passed. Amit was getting restless. It was not very obvious but Madhuri with the sensibility of a woman could feel that. She would express her anxiety to Atin and he would console saying, 'Leave it to God, you are not responsible for everything' but he too worried because it would break Madhuri's dream and a broken dream may have unpredictable consequences?'

Then one day at dinner table Amit said in the middle of ordinary conversation, 'I am getting bored sitting at home. I think I shall go out for a break, may be for a few weeks.'

Atin asked, 'Where you would go, have you decided yet?'

Amit said, 'Not particularly, but I think I shall roam a little, going to some places in the Himalayas. The weather is excellent there in this season.'

Atin asked, 'What about the computer and IT centre you said you would open in the other house?'

Amit simply said, 'I am not ready for it yet.'

Atin asked, 'When do you intend to leave, have you fixed a date? We would miss you very much especially Raju. He was thinking of learning computers from you.'

Amit smiled, 'He has a whole life left. I am not going for good. A vagabond like me feels restless sitting at home that you and Madhuri must have felt' looking at Madhuri sniffing and wiping her eyes. She said nothing.

Then the weekend arrived and on Saturday everybody was home. Atin had returned early and Madhuri was arranging evening tea. Chairs had not been placed on the lawn, they would have tea wherever they liked probably in the dining room. There was a pall of gloom on the house. Amit had announced that he would leave after the weekend. He was in his room arranging things.

Suddenly Amit's loud laughter reverberated through the house. Startled Atin and Madhuri ran upstairs and Raju, suddenly awake from his midday sleep, started crying. Atin and Madhuri entered Amit's room together and Amit said, 'I am leaving' and laughed more looking at their bewildered faces. Atin asked, 'What, right now?' Madhuri looked at Amit's face and said almost simultaneously, 'No Rupa has come' and snatched the tablet from Amit's hand. She looked at the email message. There was just one line 'I am back' then scrolled down further and there was another line, 'Could not forget the squeeze' and she burst out laughing and crying at the same time and accosted Amit 'Dada what is this, I have to change my ideas about you,' and kept running around the room as Amit tried to recover the gadget.

Atin perplexed asked, 'What is it, can I have a look?'

This time Amit and Madhuri said simultaneously, 'No you can't.'

Amit sobered faster and told Atin 'The message is from Rupa saying that she is back but no mention of where she is.'

Madhuri still unable to control her laughter said, 'I know, but I will not tell you' and she kept dancing like a little girl.

The brothers looked at each other and at her, with Amit smiling and an irritated Atin asked, 'Come on Madhuri tell us.'

Madhuri jumping less, but letting the tablet go, said, 'Remember? I am the mother of this house. So I will say one by one. She is in this town and Stop' putting a finger on her lips.

Atin said, 'Come on Madhuri where she is in this town?'

Madhuri said, 'In her mother's house.'

Impatient Atin asked, 'Where is her mother's house,' and Madhuri said 'I only know.'

Amit getting the whole picture by now took Atin aside and said, 'Bacchu give up,' suddenly remembering his boyhood nickname;

'There is a deep conspiracy against us. These women are dangerous. We have to solve it by ourselves.'

Atin smiling said, 'You keep solving it Dada, I know a little bit but not all. They were conspiring behind our back. I am going down to fetch the car and if you and your sister or mother or whatever you wish, you can join me or else I shall roam the town asking everybody have you seen my Boudi and spread a scandal.'

Everybody piled in to the car including Raju and Atin asked, 'Where should I go?'

Madhuri gravely said, 'Driver you just drive the car to the main road and turn right. You shall get further direction as you proceed.'

Raising his hands in despair Atin started to drive but Madhuri gave him the locality and the name of the street smiling at Amit 'Dada that is your in-law's house, though none of them is alive, where your darling lives locked in a castle. Keep the address in your memory bank.'

Atin asked, 'But how do you know all that,' and Amit stopped him, 'Ask no questions and hear no lies, haven't you heard that before? My computer has been burgled for her email address and who knows what more.'

The door of the house opened as soon as the car stopped and nobody came out. Amit asked Madhuri, 'How was this done' and Madhuri lifted her cell phone and said 'One ring and stop; that is how.'

Amit alighted first and as he took a few steps forward Ravi rushed out of the open door as if preprogrammed and shouting 'Uncle' jumped on Amit and embraced him and a deeply emotional Amit with tears in his eyes lifted him and kissed him on the head.

Perplexed Atin asked, 'Who is that boy' and Madhuri whispered 'Dada's son and your nephew. See Dada is so clever he did not have to work hard like poor you to get a son.' They had not left the car yet and Atin said 'But he looks' and before he could finish Madhuri whispered

'In America they do everything artificially, the hair, the looks in fact everything.' Then out came Rupa, a mature ravishing beauty in the golden light of the setting sun and even Madhuri gasped. Madhuri whispered again 'That is Rupa, the boy is from her first marriage and the husband is dead. Do not ask any awkward question, all in good time' and they alighted from the car.

And to their utter surprise Ravi rushed forward and touched their feet one by one and in clear Bengali said 'Uncle and auntie I am Ravi.' Atin almost lost balance as if he had hit something. Ravi then held Raju by the shoulder and said 'Brother Raju come let us go inside.'

All of them went inside and Madhuri said to Rupa 'Now I can take dust of your feet Didi' and Rupa saying 'Dust from my foot!' embraced her and rocked her in embrace. To Atin she said 'Brother Atin please no taking of dust from my feet, I do not trust famous doctors like you' and everybody laughed.

Madhuri asked Rupa 'Is the house Ok Didi?' and Rupa said 'Absolutely, with all those new draping and curtains. How could you do it in such short time? I do not know how to thank you. This house holds such memories' and she sighed.

Amit told Atin, 'Just listen how long and deep the conspiracy was. Your wife looks so honest and simple but I tell you she is no better.'

Madhuri said, 'What could I do when you cannot write the simple thing, I love you Rupa, please come quickly, I am missing you and could not even hide your despair? I being the Mamma I had to write for you. And then I found we like each other but I had no idea that she is such a stunning beauty.'

Rupa said, 'And what about you Madhuri, you are Wordsworth's daffodil, both in beauty and nature' and Madhuri blushed and Atin enjoyed that thoroughly not having seen that since, he could not remember when.

Amit said, 'That is not enough, she is our mother in new incarnation, the mother whom we brothers could not save. And as all of you can see, to protect her family she can go to any length. That is her in a nutshell,' and looked at Madhuri with affection.

Rupa said 'All of you are having dinner here tonight. I have made all arrangements.' Then pointing at a bag in the corner she told Amit, 'That is your favourit beer, you can share with brother.'

Madhuri objected, 'Beer yes, dinner no Didi please. The two of you have a lot to share. I hope we can leave Dada safely to your care. He has this habit of running away,' and everybody laughed.

Rupa said, 'You must stand guard then, so that he does not try to run away and we do not have a fight.'

Madhuri said, 'So you see, I have to arrange your marriage Didi to bind him down. I was married to a lonely man and my parents played their role on both sides. This time will also be the same. You will see what great fun that is.'

Rupa feebly said 'Marriage' and she shivered slightly.

Madhuri said, 'Why are you afraid of marriage? Look at me, I am surviving and I shall have you on my lifeboat. Mother would have been so happy, your mother too. The micro family system of today is not good for the children. Just look in the next room how Ravi and Raju are talking and playing!'

Amit sensing a mild tension intervened, 'All in good time. Those things would be taken care of in due course. Let us have dinner, enjoy together and then we shall take Rupa and Ravi to our house to look around either today or tomorrow, if it is too late and have another round of merrymaking. There are no formalities, let us take it easy and break in slowly. Tomorrow is Sunday. So let us take it easy tonight, open the bottles.' Then looking affectionately at Atin he said, 'We would just have to take care that my brother does not fall asleep at wrong places as he used to do as a child' and everybody laughed.

Atin smiled and said, 'Yes you can pile it all on me, I am easy.'

Madhuri said, 'Now we have three houses instead of two and we can live near with comfortable closeness keeping our individuality intact. There will be plenty of places for you to hide Dada. If necessary we can also create some jungle' and there was another round of laughter. And thus went the first day.

Epilogue

This story ends here. It does not really end nor is its progress predictable beyond chance. Stories never end in the world. It is our existentialist finite that apparently ends. Humanity across the world is an infinite. As long as it maintains connectivity like the oceans, it will never end. The story may continue in another country or another planet, it will never end. Waves may rise and waves may fall, sometimes calamitously but the story of man continues. Colour of skin may change, food may change, stature, habits may change, man continues. There have been prophets galore in human history on earth but none have foreseen the story of man unfolding. But till the dying day of universe, if it ever happens, man will still look at it with the same wonder and think of immortality, which they actually are for they will leave their seeds over the firmament of creation.